CODE NAME
SAPPHIRE

PAM JENOFF

PENGUIN BOOKS

PENGUIN BOOKS

UK | USA | Canada | Ireland | Australia
India | New Zealand | South Africa

Penguin Books is part of the Penguin Random House group of companies
whose addresses can be found at global.penguinrandomhouse.com

First published in Canada by Park Row Books 2023
First published in Great Britain by Penguin Books 2023
001

Copyright © Pam Jenoff, 2023

The moral right of the author has been asserted

Printed and bound in Great Britain by Clays Ltd, Elcograf S.p.A.

The authorized representative in the EEA is Penguin Random House Ireland,
Morrison Chambers, 32 Nassau Street, Dublin D02 YH68

A CIP catalogue record for this book is available from the British Library

ISBN: 978-1-405-95657-4

PENGUIN BOOKS

CODE NAME SAPPHIRE

Pam Jenoff is the author of several books of historical fiction, including the *New York Times* bestsellers *The Lost Girls of Paris* and *The Woman with the Blue Star*. She holds a bachelor's degree in international affairs from George Washington University and a master's degree in history from Cambridge, and she received her Juris Doctor from the University of Pennsylvania. She lives with her husband and three children near Philadelphia, where, in addition to writing, she teaches law school.

Also by Pam Jenoff

For my family. For always.

1

Micheline

February 1942

Micheline threw the still-smoldering Gauloises cigarette to the ground and crushed it with the high heel of her black leather boot. Then she marched across the darkened Paris street and grabbed the man she'd never seen before by the lapels, throwing him back against the stained brick wall of the station.

"Kiss me!" she ordered in English, whispering tersely.

The airman, his crew cut a dead giveaway despite his French civilian clothing and chapeau, stood motionless, too surprised to move as Micheline reached up and pulled him toward her, pressing her open mouth against his. His musty scent was mixed with a hint of tobacco. The streetlight cast a yellow pool on the pavement around them, illuminating their embrace. Micheline felt the man's body responding against her own. The navy beret which covered her red curls tilted off-center, threatening to fall to the ground.

A second later, Micheline broke away and brought her mouth

close to his ear. "If you hope to live, follow me." Without another word, she started away down the Rue des Récollets. She sensed the one-two beat as he hesitated, followed by the rapid pattern of his footsteps against the icy pavement. She strained hard to make sure she did not hear anyone else following them but did not dare to look back.

Micheline slowed, allowing the airman to catch up. When he reached her, she moved closer, linking her arm in his and tilting her head toward his shoulder. Anyone watching would have thought them just a smitten couple.

Micheline had spotted the airman a few minutes earlier, standing on the pavement outside the Gare de l'Est, a half kilometer from the intended rendezvous spot, looking out of place. It was always that way with the Brits, scared and barely out of school. The *passeur*, a girl from Brittany called Renee, was supposed to escort the airman. Her instructions had been simple: deliver the soldier to the Hotel Oud-Antwerpen, where a local contact would take him and hide him for the night. But Renee had never shown. Something must have gone wrong and she'd panicked and fled, leaving the airman alone.

Another ten minutes outside the station and the police would have picked him up. There was already a gendarme at the corner, watching the solider too steadily. That might have been what spooked Renee. Micheline, who was in Paris on an unrelated errand but was aware of the planned pickup, had seen the stranded airman by the station and knew she had to intervene. But Micheline had no way to lead him away on the open street without attracting attention. So she had resorted to The Embrace.

It was not the first time she had feigned passion in the service of the network. The Sapphire Line, as it was now called, had formed almost immediately after the war started. They had a singular purpose: ferrying downed British airmen from the Dutch or German borders across Belgium and occupied France to freedom. This was the hardest part of the journey, getting the airmen across Paris from Gare de l'Est where they arrived to Gare d'Austerlitz where they would set out for points south. It was a few days across France to the Pyrenees, with only a brief stop or two for rest. When the line worked, it was brilliant. But when it failed, catastrophe. There were no second chances.

When they were several blocks from the station and out of sight of the policeman, Micheline pulled the airman into a doorway. He looked as though he expected her to kiss him again. Instead, she adjusted his chapeau in the classic French style so as not to give him away as a foreigner. The disguise, consisting of secondhand, outdated trousers and a too-large shirt, would not fool anyone. And if the clothes did not give him away, his tattered army boots certainly would. He would be forced to take those off farther south anyway. The evacuees tied their shoes around their necks and replaced them with *alpargates*, the strong laced sandals necessary for crossing the Bidasoa River into Spain.

"Where are you from?" Micheline demanded. She hated to speak aloud out here, but she had to verify that he was actually an airman and not a German spy before taking him to one of their safe houses. If the line was infiltrated even once, it would spread like a cancer, and the entire network would be gone.

The airman paused, his trained instinct not to answer. "Ely in Cambridgeshire."

"What is the most popular movie in Britain right now?"

He thought for a second. *"49th Parallel."*

"Good. What type of plane were you flying? How many men?"

"Halifax. Six. I don't know if the others made it." There was a choke in his voice.

"I'm sorry." There were a half-dozen other questions she wanted to ask to verify his identity, if only there was time. But they had to keep moving. "Come."

She started walking again more briskly now, savoring the familiar surge of adrenaline that rushed through her as she led the airman to safety. Though just twenty-three years old, Micheline had risen quickly to the top of the network, and she seldom got to undertake rescues herself anymore, instead overseeing operations from her headquarters in Brussels. But the job was fluid and changing. Sometimes, like now, when the mission called for it and there was no one else, she had to jump in. She had nearly forgotten how much she liked being in the field.

As the bell of the church of Saint-Chappelle tolled eleven, Micheline calculated mentally, judging the best way to protect the airman for the night. They had already missed the rendezvous with the contact at the hotel who would have hidden him. Paris was the most dangerous segment of the escape line, but it was often necessary because so many of the trains ran through the French capital. An airman could not simply be dropped at Gare de l'Est and be expected to make his way across the city to the southern stations where the trains left for Lyon or Marseilles. No, he had to be individually ferried through the back streets and alleys by someone who knew the city and how to avoid the security checkpoints, and who spoke impeccable French in case they were stopped and questioned.

When they reached the banks of the Seine, Micheline led the airman across the Pont au Change and into the shadowy alleyways of the Left Bank, clinging to the shadows. The cafés were already closed, barkeepers turning chairs onto tables, snuffing out the candles that burned low. She forced herself to walk at a normal pace and not to run. Her close-fitted trench swished smartly below her knees. She looked to the passersby like she belonged in the throngs of students who frequented the Latin Quarter.

Thirty minutes later they reached the safe-house apartment on Rue de Babylone. Micheline took the airman's hand and led him up the stairs to the apartment, a room which was bare except for a mattress and a weathered armoire and a sink in the corner. He would stay no longer than twelve hours in the city, just enough time to rest and carry on.

Inside, the airman looked weakened and confused. "We went down quickly after we were shot," he offered, saying too much, as they all did. "They hit the fuel tank."

"Are you wounded?"

"No. There were others, though. Someone will look for them, right?" She nodded, but it was a lie. The network could not spare the resources to go back and search for those who were wounded and presumed dead. He opened his mouth to ask something else, but she put her finger to her lips and shook her head. It was not safe to say too much anywhere, even here. The airman's eyes widened. She had seen more than once how very afraid the young soldiers were, the ones who panicked or cried out in their sleep. They were eighteen and nineteen, not more than boys, and thousands of kilometers from home. Micheline herself was just a few years older and sometimes wondered why she could be strong when they could not.

"Empty your pockets," she instructed firmly. There were too many times when a well-intentioned Brit carried something sentimental from home which would be a dead giveaway if he was stopped and questioned.

The airman glanced around the apartment. Then he turned back toward her hopefully, as if the kiss had been real and matters might continue here. "Did you want to...?"

Micheline stifled a laugh. She might have been offended at the overture, but he seemed so naive she almost pitied him. "Here." She rummaged in the armoire for new clothes. Then she threw the clothes at him and gestured toward a screen that offered a bit of privacy at the far end of the room. "Get dressed." He moved slowly, clumsily toward the divider. A tram clacked by on the street below, rattling the cloudy window panes.

A few minutes later, he reemerged in the simple shoes and buttoned shirt of a peasant farmer, an outfit that would help to get him through the south of France to the Pyrenees. She took his old clothes from him. "There's bread in the cupboard," she said. "Stay away from the windows, and don't make a sound. Someone will come for you before dawn. That person will have a key. Don't open the door for anyone."

"Merci," he ventured, and it seemed likely that it was all the French that he knew or understood.

"Bonne chance," she replied, wishing him luck.

Without waiting for a response, she walked briskly from the apartment. She wondered uneasily whether he would still be safely there when the new *passeur* arrived to claim him for the next leg of his long journey home or whether another calamity would befall the already-struggling network.

2

Hannah

Hannah peered through the tiny window of her second-class cabin, the lights along the shoreline twinkling in the distance like a mirage.

It had been more than two days since the *MS Brittany* had pulled into Havana Harbor. When the ship had first docked, the passengers had gathered too eagerly at the gangplank. But as the hours passed in the Cuban air, muggy even in February, and they were not let off, their bodies grew sweaty under many layers of clothing and the stench that had been with them all along became insufferable. People dropped their heavy suitcases and sat on them. Confusion bubbled around Hannah in multiple languages, replaced eventually by quieting fatigue. "Paper-work delay," the steward claimed, though she suspected it was a lie. They were urged back to their rooms with promises of a nice meal. No one wanted to eat; they all just wanted to leave.

Hannah had spoken little to the other passengers during the long journey. But after they were not permitted to disembark, she found herself moving closer to groups of people, trying to overhear snippets of conversation that might have some bit of information. They were not to be let off in Cuba, she gleaned with alarm from the rumors. The landing documents they had purchased were, in fact, fraudulent. There was talk that they might disembark in Miami instead. "The United States will take us," an Austrian woman with several small children had proclaimed confidently. Hearing this, Hannah had been less than certain. Freedom and equality, she knew from experience, were a promise made only to some.

Hannah lay on her narrow berth now. Her memories reeled back, as they always did in the darkness, to that final night months earlier in Berlin as she lay on the cold floor of Isaac's long-shuttered kosher butcher shop, certain each breath would be her last. She could still feel the sharp pain of broken glass shards as they pressed against her belly. There had been Nazis, violent S.S., rampaging in the streets of Scheunenviertel, the city's ravaged Jewish quarter, with knives, terrorizing any remaining Jews they caught. What would stop them from doing the same to her and the child she carried? She had dived behind the meat counter in a panic.

As she hid in the darkness, Hannah's heart pounded. The truth was she and Isaac were not just any Jews. They were part of the resistance, Hannah drawing anti-Fascist political cartoons under a pseudonym and Isaac printing them in the underground newspaper he distributed across the city and beyond. If the Germans found the printing press hidden in the back of the butcher shop, it would mean death not just for her and Isaac but everyone who worked with them.

The men drew closer to the door of the shop, undeniably marked as Jewish with a swath of yellow paint. Their shadows loomed large and menacing across the floor. She slid awkwardly behind the counter, hindered by her rounded stomach. She held her breath, trying not to move. "Stop!" she heard Isaac's voice commanding, with only a trace of a waver in it. He sounded so firm that for a minute she thought they actually might listen. He had stepped out from hiding in the cutting room purposefully in order to direct them toward the opposite end of the shop, away from her and the materials hidden in the back room.

Of course, the men did not stop. They crashed through the door and knocked him to the ground. Isaac let out a wail as he fell to the floor. The men beat and kicked him with dull, sickening thuds. For a moment, her eyes locked with his beneath the counter. She wanted desperately to leap out to his defense the way he had to hers. He averted his gaze, willing her not to move, to stay hidden and save their child and herself. But his cries were unbearable. Blood flowed from his head, mixing with stains left by slaughtered animals on the floor.

Soon Isaac grew silent. The men stormed through the store, running past her without seeing. She covered her head with her hands and burrowed deeper beneath the counter, praying. She heard tables and shelves crash to the ground and a shout of glee as they discovered the printing press. Her papers were there, and now they would know that Maxim, the pseudonym she used for her comics, had originated here. As they smashed the press to bits, she held her breath, waiting for the men to discover her and kill her as well.

But the men left the shop, satisfied that they had finished the job. As they ran back onto the street in search of new prey, Hannah started crawling toward Isaac, then froze. A lone Nazi brute, who she had not noticed remained in the store, was looking through the counter for bits of meat. As she crouched lower, a floorboard creaked. The Nazi's head swung in her direction and she waited, holding her breath for certain detection. But he turned back to his attempted looting. The store had been closed for many months, though, and so he found nothing.

When at last the would-be thief had gone, Hannah scurried to Isaac, praying he might be alive. She knew he could not survive the beating, but she wished he might linger for a few minutes so that she could touch his face and whisper words of comfort. She leaned her head close as he whispered his very last instructions, the one thing he needed her to do. "Go. The newspaper is finished, and it isn't safe for you to remain here anymore. Save yourself and our child." He could not protect her any longer.

"I will. I swear it." She hoped desperately for a bit more time. But his eyes were already open to the sky. She kissed him again. "You saved us. We are saved." He needed to know that his sacrifice had meant something. Her words hung in the air above them, unanswered.

She looked around the shop, wondering what to do next. Something burned in her stomach. For a second, she thought it was a labor cramp. But it was too early: the baby could never survive. Though she had felt fluttering kicks, she was only five months along and nowhere near a life that could sustain itself separate from her. Then she felt something warm between her legs. She sat motionless, willing it to stop, but the ache became a burning pain and the trickle of blood a river. She was losing the baby, and there was nothing she could do to stop it. Her promise to Isaac, which she had made just moments earlier, to protect their child, was already broken. It seemed then that Isaac's death had been in vain because the baby was gone, and without the child or Isaac himself, her own life was worth nothing.

Hannah had left Berlin the next day, setting out covertly for Hamburg hidden in the back of a car, transport arranged by one of her few remaining resistance contacts who had not been arrested. She needed to leave Germany, but it had at first proven impossible, and she had hidden in the port city for several months, certain she would be discovered and arrested. For weeks after losing the baby, she had fever and chills that made her worry about infection. Her body ached, as did her heart. She could not outrun the memory of the man she had loved. Even more painful was the loss of their child, crushing her in a way she could not have imagined. Once she had eschewed things such as marriage and children. But with Isaac it had almost seemed possible. Now with the dream shattered, she saw the promise as a kind of hubris: What had made her think that she deserved the same happiness as everyone else? By nature, she was solitary, and that was how she would now remain forever.

Finally, she had been able to use her reputation as an artist and a favor from an old friend to arrange scarce, precious papers and secure a place on the *Brittany*, a ship headed for Cuba, and one of the last to carry Jews, since Hitler had issued a prohibition against their emigration. She would arrange passage from there to America. But the trauma still loomed large.

A shuffling noise from across the room stirred her from her thoughts. Hannah had wanted a first-class cabin to herself and could afford to pay for it. But there was simply no such thing on the dilapidated ship, and so she had had to settle on the next best thing, a tiny stateroom shared with two spinster sisters from Sopot who were trying to get to their cousin in the Dominican Republic.

Hannah had bigger problems than her cabinmates, though. Official word had come that no one would disembark from the *Brittany* in Havana. The ship would depart for Europe in the morning. The passengers had reacted with disbelief, followed by anger. Their papers were entirely in order. Many had spent their life savings on the visas that promised to get them in. But it had all been a scam. There was simply no place for the ship full of refugees to land.

"Where are we to go?" an elderly man had demanded. They were Jews, hunted by the Reich. They could not possibly return to the countries from which they had fled, steps ahead of arrest or worse. Surely there would be even more horrible reprisals for them now because they had tried to escape.

Unable to sleep, Hannah walked up onto the deck. They had been at sea for so long that she scarcely smelled the salty air anymore. But its brackishness filled her lungs now, thick and stifling. She pressed herself close to the rail, as if leaning closer to shore might actually bring her there. Like Moses, she could see the Promised Land but was unable to enter it.

"Careful," a voice behind her warned. Hannah turned to find one of the ship's security officers, making rounds of the deck. The light of his cigarette glowed in the darkness. She expected him to scold her for being out and usher her back to her cabin. Instead, he simply held out a pack of cigarettes, offering her one. She waved it away. "Hell of a thing," he said. Hannah knew enough English to understand his words, and that he was talking about the passengers' situation.

"What do you think will happen next?" she ventured. He shrugged. "Will we go to America?"

He shook his head. "Nah. Roosevelt is too much of a politician." The price of saving a ship full of Jews was too much for even the president of the United States to bear. "Other countries will let some people in, though." She tilted her head. "Belgium and Holland have agreed to take a number of folks." Hannah's heart sank. They would be going back to occupied Europe after all. "Priority will be given to those with a relative to vouch for them." So their salvation would not come through some sort of collective rescue. It would be every person for themselves, using whatever connections and resources they had. "We set sail for Antwerp in the morning."

Lily, she thought suddenly, remembering her doe-eyed cousin, the closeness of their youth. Just months apart in age, they had been almost like sisters, reunited each summer at their family cottage by the Baltic Sea until Lily's family had moved to Belgium when she was ten. They had kept in touch more regularly by letter when they were younger but had not spoken often in recent years. Hannah somehow knew, though, that Lily would help. Belgium, occupied by the Nazis, was hardly safer than Germany was. Still, it was her only chance.

"I don't suppose I could send a telegram," she said to the steward.

He looked at her dubiously. "The wire is only for official crew business, ma'am."

"Then, perhaps you could send it." Hannah tried to think of a way to persuade him. Another woman might try to flirt, but it was an art that had always been lost on her. She reached into her pocket, feeling for the remaining cash she had with her. She had been hoarding it, and more than ever she hated to part with it now, not knowing if she might need it wherever she finally landed. But she had no choice.

The guard palmed the money and shoved it in his pocket, then produced a small notebook and stub of a pencil. "Write down what you want to say and the address, and I will make sure it is sent. Keep it short."

Hannah hesitated. She wanted to see the message sent personally to make sure he followed through. She was hardly in a position to negotiate, though. She took the notebook, the pencil hovering in her hand above it as she tried to figure out what to say to the cousin she had not seen in more than two decades, who was now her best and only hope.

Arriving in Belgium on the MS Brittany. *Please come for me. Your cousin, Hannah Martel.*

She included her surname, as though Lily might have forgotten over the years who Hannah was. She felt as though she should write something more, perhaps tell her cousin when and in which port she would arrive. But there was so much she did not know—including Lily's address, which she'd left buried in her things back in Berlin. Hannah recalled, though, that Lily's husband, Nik, was a professor at the Universitair Ziekenhuis in Brussels (or at least he had been before the war), so she wrote down the address in care of him at the hospital there and hoped that would be enough.

She handed the paper to the officer. "Please send it as soon as you can." He turned and walked away without agreeing to her request.

Hannah slumped against the rail of the ship, shaken by the turn of events. The last thing she wanted was to return to Europe. But right now she just needed somewhere safe to land so she could start over and try again.

The next morning, the ship pulled from the harbor before dawn, like a lover leaving without saying goodbye. Hannah remained in bed, skipping breakfast. She could not bear to look at the shoreline as it receded in the distance. She wondered if Lily had received her message, tried to imagine her reaction. Even if the telegraph had gotten through, she was unlikely to receive a response onboard.

As the ship churned out through rougher waters, Hannah's insides quaked. It was not merely seasickness. What if she arrived in Belgium and there was simply no one there to meet her? She would die before she would go back to Nazi Germany. She vowed to throw herself clear overboard into the Atlantic before letting that happen. Return was simply not an option.

But even in her despair, she felt a flicker of hope. She still saw Lily as a girl with her long black braids, elegant and refined in a way that Hannah had never managed. Hannah's childhood had not been an easy one: her father drank himself to death when she was sixteen. Her mother, who had never been able to protect Hannah from her father's drunken wrath, died a few months later. Lily and their summer visits had been a light in that dark world. Lily had been, quite literally, a lifeline, the only friend she had. At their last tearful farewell when Lily's family left for Belgium, they had sworn to always remain close and be there for one another. The first part of that pledge had failed; they had grown distant and all but lost touch. But the second part remained a prophecy unfulfilled, and she hoped that Lily remembered.

Now as the she lay bobbing with the ship, she squeezed her eyes shut. If she were a religious woman she might have prayed, but instead she just desperately hoped and wished their promise would be true so she could reach Belgium safely and begin to look for another way out.

Her very life depended upon it.

3

Lily

The *MS Brittany* was already docked as Lily reached the port of Antwerp. The dilapidated steamer was indistinguishable among a cordon of great hulking ships, save for the cluster of passengers waiting to disembark. A sharp wind cut across the harbor, causing Lily to draw her coat more tightly around her. Though the February air was not bitterly cold as it might have been, dark clouds signaling a late-afternoon storm gathered across the horizon.

Seeing her cousin's ship already at port, Lily rushed forward. Her toe caught on a loose board on the dock. She reached for the railing, and a splinter sliced through her fine kid glove, cutting her finger. She brought her hand to her mouth, stifling a yelp. Then she removed the glove to inspect the wound. Lily prided herself on calm and order, but everything seemed askew now, out of place.

Of course, she was not late. Though the ship had already arrived, it would take hours to process and disembark the hundreds of passengers. She had checked in at the port office, signed a voucher claiming her cousin, whom she had not yet seen. Each passenger had to be checked, the clerk had told her officiously, to make sure they had someone to vouch for them and provide a place to live in Belgium. There was nothing to do now but wait.

Clutching her scalloped purse and a small cardboard gift box against the waist of her fashionably trim skirt, Lily looked back over her shoulder at the Antwerp skyline. She reacquainted herself with the delicately sloping baroque and neoclassical architecture of the city, a sea of red rooftops broken by the Gothic tower of the Cathedral of Our Lady, which rose over the city like a scepter. Antwerp was the city of her childhood, and Lily might have expected to feel more fondness and nostalgia for it. She had roamed its winding streets endlessly as a girl from the diamond district where her father's shop had been to grassy paths of Nachtegalen Park. The whole city seemed smaller now, provincial compared to Brussels, in a way she had not noticed as a child.

Lily had left Antwerp for Brussels nine years earlier to marry Nik, more than a decade her senior, fleeing the grief of losing her mother and the pain of a broken heart with the very doctor who had treated her. She had not been back to Antwerp since her father's funeral three years ago. She had planned to stop at her parents' graves in the Jewish section of the Putte cemetery earlier today, but there hadn't been time.

Lily thought with longing now of their home in Brussels with its pleasant garden and late-afternoon sunlight slatting in through the paned front window. Georgi would be finishing his homework, and she hoped that the governess Camille, who had stayed with them out of a sense of loyalty and her love for Georgi, despite the German prohibition against Jews having domestic help, had checked his sums. Even more so now, when Belgium was occupied by the Germans, their house was a refuge from the outside world.

She remembered Nik coming home early from work one morning nearly two years ago, his normally calm face now ashen. "Darling, are you ill?" He had left for work not an hour earlier and was not expected back until evening. "Did you lose a patient?" Nik shook his head. "Is everything all right?"

"No, I'm afraid not." He had come and sat down beside her, putting his arm around her in a way that had always managed to make the world feel safe, at least until now. Then he looked down at her, his somber blue-gray eyes meeting hers. "Germany has invaded Belgium." The weight of his words came crashing down on Lily as all that she had thought impossible suddenly came true.

"Surely the Belgian army will resist." They had watched Germany roll over Czechoslovakia and Poland, though, and knew that their tiny country was no match for German strength either.

Eighteen days. That was how long it had taken for Belgium to fall. One day Belgium was neutral, the next day occupied by Germany. In the early months immediately following the invasion, things had not changed much. The occupation at first felt like an unwelcome houseguest, a nuisance and inconvenience that would soon leave. Lily had hoped it would not turn into something more. Her family had emigrated to Belgium after the Great War, and she had no personal recollection of the horrors of the first German occupation. *The rape of Belgium* some called it. She could see it on the faces of those who were old enough to remember, the fear that it was happening all over again. Surely this time could not be that bad, Lily thought more than once. Not in modern, civilized Brussels.

The initial changes had come almost too slowly to notice. The signs on the street and in the shops had changed to German only. Then the Jewish businesses had been expropriated. There were curfews now and requirements to turn in radios. The food shortages seemed to grow worse by the week.

"There's a registry for Jews," Nik had announced one day after work. "I've entered our names."

"Perhaps we should have discussed it first," Lily said.

"I know. I'm sorry. But I was asked to do it, and so I did. It wasn't as if we had a choice." *There is always a choice*, she wanted to say. Nik was not one to break the rules, however. Nor was she, at least since she had married him. Anyway, it was too late now. They were officially listed, unable to avoid detection. An indelible mark. They each had an identity card marked *Juif-Jood*. She had not been asked to show it yet, but she could feel it burning a hole in her purse.

Then one day Nik came home early from the university, just as he had the day the Germans had invaded Belgium. "I've been dismissed," he said, his voice aghast, almost embarrassed. There was a scratch beneath his eye which had not been there when he'd left that morning.

Lily was devastated. "That's impossible." Nik was one of the most highly respected doctors in the city, winning accolades from the university year after year for his medical research as well as his clinical work with patients. "They adore you. They would never let you go."

"Not just me. All the Jews." Being Jewish in predominantly Catholic but tolerant Belgium had never been an issue. Now it was a liability, and one that made their futures uncertain.

The sea of passengers on the deck of the ship began to move, sidling toward the gangplank like the tide coming in. German soldiers flanked the dock, scrutinizing the new arrivals. Most of the passengers moved slowly, finding their legs for the first time after weeks at sea. Lily watched a woman try to corral three children and wondered where the woman's husband was, why she was alone. It had been just over a month, Lily knew from reading the paper, since the ship filled with Germans and Poles and other East Europeans had set out from Hamburg. The passengers were turned away from Cuba where they had been promised entry, then foundered at sea while the United States and other countries refused to let them in.

Others who did not have permission to disembark in Belgium lined the railing of the ship watching forlornly. Of the hundreds of passengers on the ship, only a few dozen would be staying in Belgium; the others were to be divided up among countries who had agreed to take them, a number to Holland, others to England. It was sensible, Lily reflected: no one country could be expected to absorb so many. However, as she watched, she felt a pang of sympathy for those who still had not reached their final destination and had hundreds of kilometers yet to journey. She could not imagine what these poor souls had been through, losing everything and everyone they ever loved.

Hannah's telegram, forwarded to Nik from his former office at the university, had been brief, just the name of her ship and the fact that she was arriving. No explanation why. *Arriving in Belgium on the* Brittany. *Please come for me.* It was the *please* that had tugged at her. Her cousin had always been a commanding presence. Fearless. Now she sounded desperate. The message had contained no arrival date either, so it had fallen to Lily to ring the port to learn the ship's arrival date.

Hannah appeared above the bobbing heads. Hannah was about thirty years old as well. Though they were just a few months apart in age, Hannah had always seemed more mature, and Lily envied her bold, confident ways. In her mind's eye, Hannah had always been breathtaking and cosmopolitan. Now, though, Hannah seemed ill at ease, her eyes wide and darting like a hunted animal. Lily was seized with the urge to protect her.

Lily's and Hannah's fathers had been brothers, and for many years the girls, both only children, had been as close as siblings themselves. They had met each summer by the Baltic Sea, Hannah coming from Berlin and Lily from southern Poland, with their families to a cottage near Gdansk. While the adults drank and sunbathed, Lily and Hannah were free to roam the shores on their own adventures, sharing stories and dreams. In a world where little girls were seldom noticed, she and Hannah had seen, really seen, one another. They dreamed of traveling together, Hannah painting and Lily writing. Hannah had gone on to become a painter. What, Lily wondered now, had happened to her own dream?

Lily's family had left Poland when she was ten, after a colleague had invited her father to join him in his diamond business in Antwerp. He had done well here and created a life for Lily and her mother. Though the two families had the best intentions of staying close, the greater geographic distance and demands of her father's business kept them from meeting up in the summers as they once had. Lily had not seen Hannah since the move and had corresponded infrequently. Now as she waited for her cousin, she felt an odd mix of anticipation and unease. She was excited to see Hannah after all these years. But would she be the same after so much time? Could she be?

Hannah paused and stood awkwardly among the surging cluster of arrivals. Lily waved a hand to get her attention, but the gesture seemed somehow silly. Hannah nodded. Lily had expected something more, a wave back or perhaps a smile. Hannah started slowly in her direction. Lily had remembered her older cousin as beautiful, but *handsome* seemed more the word now. Though she still had the same high cheekbones, her features were pronounced in a way that was not altogether feminine.

Lily wanted to hug her cousin in greeting, but something stopped her. "*Wilkommen*," she said, assuming that was the language with which Hannah would be most comfortable. Hannah's skin, when they exchanged kisses, was papery and dry. Her chestnut locks, once luminous, were dull and limp, flecked with a few strands of gray. Hannah's dress was modern, last year's fashion at worst. Were it not dusty and wrinkled from the trip, she might have fit in wearing it on the streets of Brussels. Then Lily glimpsed her cousin's shoes, the simple peasant style. She was hurled back to a childhood of doing without, of toilets not in the house and crude, simple ways she had tried so very hard to forget. It all came back now, uncomfortably intruding on the very neat life she had created.

"Thank you for meeting me," Hannah answered her smoothly in French. Of course. Lily knew from the few letters they had exchanged over the years that Hannah had lived all over Europe, studied at the Sorbonne to become a successful painter and spoke several languages. She was, in her own way, every bit as sophisticated as Lily, perhaps even more so.

But Hannah's voice was without warmth now, and her eyes hollow. It was the journey, Lily decided instantly. Hannah had been bobbing around like a cork on the *Brittany* for weeks. Lily couldn't imagine leaving everything behind as her cousin had, much less being forced to turn back. "How are you?" Lily asked. The words seemed inadequate to express her concern. "I mean, your journey was horribly long." Hannah nodded.

"I brought you these." Lily held out the box, wrapped in brown parcel paper. They were the finest chocolates in all of Belgium from the confectionery in the Galeries Royales Saint-Hubert. Lily's mouth had watered as she had carried the dainty sweets, not daring to touch them. Now as she offered the gift it seemed frivolous, even silly.

"Thank you." Hannah took the box but did not open it to eat or offer one. Instead, she tucked them away for later.

There were so many questions Lily wanted to ask Hannah, not just about her failed journey to America but the years between and all that had happened while they had been apart. But now was not the time. "Are you hungry?" Lily asked instead. "We can have a meal before starting back, if you'd like."

Hannah glanced uneasily over Lily's shoulder at the German soldiers. "I'd just like to go."

"Of course," Lily replied. "Let's get your bags so we can start home."

Hannah pointed down at the small satchel she carried. "This is all that I have."

Lily's eyes traveled to the tiny bag. How was it possible to survive so many weeks at sea with almost nothing? She wondered whether that was all her cousin had brought with her from Germany, if her belongings had been lost or taken along the way.

Lily's hand rose instinctively to her throat, touching her fine silk scarf. Normally, she found the texture soothing, but she felt guilty now about all that she had that her cousin and the others coming off the ship did not. The magnitude of what Hannah had been through washed over her. There was a vulnerability about Hannah that Lily had never seen, and she found herself drawing her in protectively, suddenly the older, stronger one. "Never mind," she said, putting her arm around Hannah. "We will get you everything you need when we get to Brussels." Hannah's face seemed to brighten.

"I've set up a studio for you on the fourth floor of the house," Lily added. She could feel the words coming too quickly now, as they often did when she was nervous. Lily wanted her cousin to be happy about the decision to live with her. "It's not much, but it has a good view for paining."

The light evaporated from Hannah's eyes as quickly as it had come. "I don't paint anymore." Hannah had been a gifted artist. Lily's earliest memories of her cousin were with stained fingers and a paintbrush in her hand. Indeed, it was hard to picture her without one. What had happened to make her stop doing something she had loved so much? Lily realized she had much to learn about her cousin. "And I don't think I'll be here that long," Hannah added. "I'm very grateful to you for taking me in, but I still need to leave Europe as soon as I can." There was an ominous note to Hannah's voice. Had Hannah tried to emigrate because she was Jewish, or was there something more to it? Lily made a note to ask her about it once they were home.

"I understand," Lily replied. Her cousin was not here by

choice and would be on her way as soon as she could. "Still, I'm glad to see you. You'll be safe in Belgium." Hannah looked as though she wanted to argue, but she did not. "And it has been too long." Lily squeezed her cousin tighter.

"Yes. Yes, it has." Hannah relaxed in her arms and a smile seemed to flicker across her face. She looked in that moment like the cousin Lily remembered from childhood, who showed her how to climb trees and swim in the stream.

And having Hannah here would be a good thing for her too, Lily realized. Though she traveled easily through the city's upper-class social circles, Lily did not have anyone she could call a close friend. Nik, though sweet and thoughtful in many little ways, was so busy with his work. It was mostly just her and Georgi, and even he was growing older now, interested more in the outside world than in his mother with each passing day. Hannah would be good company. She was not just her cousin but her friend.

"Oh, Hannah!" Lily cried. "I'm so glad you're here!" She hugged her cousin then, no longer holding back. Hannah had been through so much on her journey, and it was up to Lily to help her and make her feel at home. Hannah wrapped her arms around Lily, wordlessly returning the embrace. Things would be wonderful between them again, like no time had passed at all.

"Come, let's get to the car." Lily took her by the hand, and together they started the long journey home as the first raindrops began to fall.

4

Hannah

Hannah awakened to the sound of crying. The sobs were her own, and her pillowcase was wet with tears.

She sat up, getting her bearings, and remembered that she was no longer in Germany. *Safe in Belgium*, her cousin had said the day she arrived. Hannah had fought the urge to laugh. As if anywhere, especially in occupied Europe, would ever be safe again. It was the little things that took her back—the sound of a police siren, a too-large crowd. Suddenly she was there once more, pressed against the floor of the butcher shop, feeling the glass cut into her skin as she hid. She had hoped to outrun her painful memories and her past to get somewhere, anywhere. Yet here she was, back in this godforsaken cesspool of a continent.

Hannah felt a pang of embarrassment now. She hoped that her cries had not disturbed Lily or her family. She blinked to adjust her eyes to the predawn darkness. The bedroom was elegant, with fine mahogany furniture, the rose carpets and drapes and duvet all matching. The easel Lily had set up for her stood untouched in the corner, the white canvas still blank. Her cousin had meant it with the best of intentions. How could she possibly understand that, after all Hannah had been through, art and beauty simply no longer existed?

Hannah stood and dressed, then tiptoed into the hallway. The rest of Lily's house was as meticulous as the guest room, polished wood floors covered with silk rugs, no sign of the toys or clutter one might expect from a home with a child. The house was well-designed, with every comfort anticipated, from the warmers in the bedrooms that had come in handy on colder nights to the window catches which allowed them to open just enough for fresh air without letting in bugs or dust.

Hannah slipped downstairs, sniffing in the hall a hint of Nik's pipe smoke that lingered from the previous evening. She went to the door, looking both ways before leaving the house. She walked silently along the row of wrought iron fences that separated the elegant houses from the street. The Germans had imposed a curfew, and technically being out before dawn violated that. Hannah, more so than anyone, had reason to be careful not to get caught. But her solitary morning walks were like oxygen to her and she could not bear to give them up. So she walked stealthily, keeping her footsteps light and clinging to the shadows of the buildings.

She made her way toward the main boulevard, Chaussée d'Ixelles. The streets of the upscale neighborhood were deserted at this early hour, and for that Hannah was grateful. She had been in Belgium for almost a month, and she still marveled at the easy, unafraid way people smiled and greeted one another—as if they were unwilling to let the German occupation dampen their amiable spirits. Hannah remained guarded and bruised from her time in Germany, and she found the familiarity of complete strangers unsettling.

She turned onto the Rue Gabrielle, the scraping of her footsteps against the cobblestones breaking the silence as she steered toward the city center. At the top of the avenue, the sight of the

Palais de Justice, its neoclassical dome silhouetted against the brightening sky, was undeniably appealing. She started across the Place Royale, past the flower stalls. The square was ringed by steep gabled guild houses, their gold trim weathered and faded.

A flag bearing a large swastika billowed from the front of one of the buildings. Unnerved, Hannah stopped. Life had gone on much as it had for ordinary Belgians during the occupation. The Germans attempted to maintain the thinnest pretense of civility. Sometimes in the elegant city, it was possible for even Hannah to forget for a few moments the reality of the dangers that loomed everywhere. But she had seen too much in Germany, and she knew that even here, the status quo would not last.

Her personal situation was precarious as well. The Germans had not realized who she was or that she was in Brussels—yet. Sooner or later, though, they would. She needed to leave as soon as possible. But the embassies were not receptive, and visas for non-Belgians were unavailable. She had quickly realized that official channels were closed and that she would need to find another way to get out. She did not have Isaac's underground contacts here, though, as she would have in Berlin. She had to make inquiries discreetly: one could not simply ask a passerby on the street where to find the resistance, as if trying to find a shop to buy milk. Asking the wrong person could result in arrest or worse.

Hannah started back south toward Ixelles, bypassing Lily's street for a quick stroll around the Bois de la Cambre. She was not eager to return to the house. Though Lily tried hard to make her feel at home, Hannah felt like a perpetual stranger there, like a hulking piece of furniture, taking up space. It wasn't that Lily had been inhospitable. To the contrary, her cousin was kind and thoughtful, the perfect hostess. She seemed to genuinely like having her there. Hannah loved Lily and enjoyed getting to know her again after so many years and regaining some of their earlier closeness. But Hannah felt as though she was accepting charity. Beholden. She had spent her whole life making sure she did not have to rely on others. Only now, she found herself in that very place—and she hated it.

Hannah had considered briefly trying to find work in Brussels to earn her keep. But most positions were off-limits to Jews, and she didn't have the papers to work. Lily had never asked Hannah to pay room and board, and she and Nik certainly didn't need the money. And getting a job felt like a sign that she wasn't going to be able to leave Belgium any time soon—something that she was not ready to admit.

Soon Hannah reached the expansive parkland of the Bois de la Cambre. Fog hung over the bare oak branches that lined the pathway, moistening them. She walked in the park with Georgi most afternoons. Watching the child, she was often distracted from the environment around her. Now in the early-morning stillness, she sensed the quiet beauty of the park.

Hannah saw something move by the duck pond, and a twinge of uneasiness passed through her. She wondered if it was safe to be alone in this dark, deserted space. Still, she was curious who else was here at such an hour. Closer now, she could see it was a man standing close to the pond, staring at the water. He had his hands in his pockets, drawing his shoulders low. He sported a goatee, though it was not the fashion of the day, and wore an Eden hat, a jaunty fedora. There was a guarded look about him, a kind of haunted air. He didn't strike her as dangerous, and he was too intent in whatever he was doing to notice her. He crouched low by the pond, studying one of the rocks, running his hand over it.

Hannah watched the man for a few more seconds before turning and slipping away. It was daylight now, and she started back to the house so Lily would not miss her. But the image of the man near the duck pond lingered. What was he doing there at such an hour?

Hannah felt an unexpected urge to capture the scene. To

paint it. The yearning, which she had not felt in months, came back to her then like an old friend. She immediately began envisioning just how it would look, the way the moonlight reflected upward from the water, illuminating the curious man who knelt over it. She left the park and hurried back to Lily's house, eager to get started.

When she reached the house, she hurried up the stairs to her room and went to the easel. She opened the paints now, the sharp, familiar scent filling her nostrils.

She worked steadily for more than two hours until a knock interrupted her. Lily pushed the door open and stepped in. "Breakfast and oh—" She stopped, noticing the image Hannah was painting.

Hannah wished she had moved more quickly to prevent Lily seeing her work in its early stages. "I hope you don't mind me painting. You left me the supplies so I thought it would be all right." She was glad she had thought to roll back the carpet and lay down a cloth so as not to stain the fine wood floors.

"Of course. I'm thrilled that you are painting again. Who is he?"

Hannah shrugged. "No one in particular, just someone I saw at the park."

"Anyway, there's breakfast if you want to eat before it gets cold."

Hannah hesitated. Back home, she had always painted in great streaks, nothing for days and then a fit of long, sleepless nights, not even breaking to eat but taking small bites while at the easel, the crumbs mixing with spilled paints on the floor. But she was a guest here and did not want to be rude. "I'm coming." She left the painting midstroke, feeling as though she had been awakened from a dream.

She reached the dining room just as Georgi was finishing up a slice of *cramique*, raisin bread with butter. "Good morning, Tante Hannah," he said politely.

"Good morning." She could not help but smile at him. Georgi had jet-black hair that matched his eyes, set deep like two coals. His porcelain skin was perfectly pale but for the faint rosiness of his cheeks. He had received the best of his mother's features, though where he got the curly hair from Hannah could not quite say.

"Nik's already gone to the clinic," Lily said, gesturing with her head toward the small office adjacent to the back of the house where Nik saw patients since he and the other Jewish doctors had been dismissed from the university hospital.

"I'll take Georgi to the park after his lessons, if that's all right," Hannah offered. Lily nodded. The first time she had offered, there had been an unmistakable hesitation before Lily responded, as though she had not thought Hannah capable of minding a child. In fact, Hannah watched him carefully, perhaps even more so than a parent, as though afraid something would happen and Lily would be proven correct in her mistrust.

Hannah picked up the newspaper. "The Germans are requiring all Dutch Jews to wear a yellow star," she noted. Lily looked down at Georgi, distressed that she would speak of such things in front of her child.

Georgi's eyes widened. "Will they do that here too, Mama?" Hannah shot her cousin an apologetic look, and Lily shrugged, forgiving her missteps as she always had.

"No, darling." But she was not just saying it for Georgi. Two years into the occupation, Lily really believed that, despite the war, Belgian Jews might be permitted to continue life much as it had been. Hannah knew better: she had witnessed firsthand how everything could be taken in an instant. She looked at her cousin with pity. Lily simply had no idea how bad things could get.

The moment seemed opportune to be more direct with her cousin than she had previously been. "You know as grateful as I am to you for having me, I still need to get out of Europe," she said, hedging the subject. "And I've had no luck with the embassies."

"I know. I've had Nik ask his colleagues if they know anyone in the government who could help, but so far nothing."

Hannah paused, weighing her words carefully. "The Nazis… Do you know anyone who is working against them?" she asked in a low voice.

"No, of course not," Lily replied, her voice aghast at the notion.

"I'm sorry for asking. I just thought if I could make contact with the underground, they might be able to help me find a way out."

"That sounds so dangerous."

"It is. But I don't see another way."

"Do you really have to go?" Lily asked. "I mean is it so bad here?"

Yes, Hannah wanted to scream. *Or, at least, it will be.* "For me it is," she replied, then paused, wondering how much to say. "You see, I didn't just leave Germany because I am a Jew. I was working on political cartoons against the Germans. I drew them under a pseudonym, but when the Germans raided the shop and found our printing press, they discovered my real name."

"Oh!" Lily said, clearly taken aback by the information. "I had no idea."

"So you see, that's why I had to leave."

Lily's eyes grew dark with concern as she processed the danger Hannah was in—and that she had brought with her to Lily's house. Hannah wondered if Lily regretted allowing her to stay. "You see now why I must leave. That's why I asked if you knew anyone. I thought you wrote to me once about some friends in the old days who were involved in political matters," Hannah said.

Lily shook her head. "That was when I was a student. I've left all of that behind." Hannah tried to imagine Lily's younger years, but the image in her mind was blurred like smudged ink.

They ate in silence. When they had finished, they moved to the sofa in the sitting room, watching Georgi talk to himself as he played alone. "I often feel bad," Lily confessed in a voice too low for him to hear, "that he doesn't have a sibling."

Or a cousin, Hannah thought, feeling the empty ache at her midsection. "Why didn't you try for more?" she asked bluntly.

"We wanted more," Lily said sadly, "but it just didn't work out."

"Perhaps you still can," Hannah offered, trying to be helpful. Lily was not so very old.

"Once I thought so too." The corners of her cousin's mouth turned downward. "But never mind. Georgi is everything to us."

"Georgi's a wonderful boy," Hannah said, both to offer comfort and because it was true.

Lily nodded. "We're very fortunate. And it's nice to have you here, to be able to talk about these things. I feel less alone, you know?"

Yes, Hannah thought, she did. "I lost a child, before I set sail for America," Hannah said. It was the first time she had spoken the words aloud.

Lily touched her arm. "I'm so sorry." There was a silence, Lily inviting her to say more if she wanted to. "That must have been so painful. I wish I had known, that I could have been there for you."

"Me too. But you're here now." Hannah leaned her head against Lily's shoulder, and the two women sat close, neither speaking further.

Later that morning when Georgi had finished his lessons, Hannah nudged him out for a walk.

"Come," she promised. "I will buy you some salted nuts." She wanted to take another look at the spot by the pond that she was painting.

They started out. The midday March air was cool and damp, but not cold. Georgi did not run ahead but walked pleasantly alongside her. Hannah had not spent much time with children, and she was not particularly comfortable with them. But Georgi

was not like other children. He was a quiet, inquisitive boy—
still waters running deep. Hannah found herself working hard
to win his smiles. Often, he seemed lost in his own world. He
had a penchant for counting and organizing things. Lily said he
got that from Nik, but Hannah sensed it was more than that, an
almost compulsion. Now as he walked he surreptitiously stepped
over each crack in the pavement. Hannah wondered what he
thought would happen if he stepped on one.

As they neared the park, a group of German soldiers spilled
from a café onto the pavement in front of them. Hannah froze.

Hannah forced herself to keep walking past the Germans,
trying to breathe normally. She felt the eyes of one of the soldiers on her. It was because she was a woman, she told herself.
Nothing more.

At last she and Georgi reached the park. Children played mer-
rily in the grass, and nannies pushed prams along the winding
path. "Tante Hannah, the salted nuts," Georgi reminded gently.
"Please." She fished in her purse for some coins and handed them
to him. He raced off across the park in the direction of a vendor.
Hannah let him go but craned her neck to keep him in sight.

When she saw that he had reached the nut vendor safely, she
started in the direction of the pond. Then she stopped. The man
she had seen there in the predawn hours was there again, standing by the pond, as if he had never left. He had left, though,
she could tell, because the heavy overcoat which he had worn
previously was gone, replaced by a lighter-weight jacket. He
crouched low as he had done that morning, running his hand
over the same rock.

Hannah looked across the park once more to check Georgi,
who was eating nuts as he played by the fountain. Then, curious,
she moved closer to the man. Still kneeling, he lifted the rock
and took something from beneath it. Had he left it there when
she had seen him earlier that morning? Peering closer, she could
see that it was a piece of paper. He was sending and receiving

messages, she recognized from her days with the resistance in Berlin, using the place beneath the rock as a kind of drop box.

The man straightened and turned, sliding the note into his pocket. Seeing her, alarm flickered in his eyes, and she wondered if he was angry she had been watching him. Then, to her surprise, he took a step toward her and smiled. "So you come here during the day as well."

"Excuse me?" she stammered ungracefully. It was not like Hannah to be thrown off-kilter. She could not fathom how the man had recognized her from earlier that morning when he had not even looked in her direction.

"I often walk here in the early morning, and I've seen you more than once." His voice was smooth, and if he knew she had seen him take the paper, he gave no indication. "I'm Matteo," he said.

"Hannah Martel." She extended her hand. He wore horn-rimmed glasses and had thoughtful brown eyes.

"You're an artist?" he asked, and for a moment she wondered if he might have heard of her work. But he was gesturing to the paint stains on her hand.

"Yes..." She paused. "That is, I was." It was not that she was insecure or even modest. She was an established painter, her works featured in some of the finest galleries in Europe. "I was an artist in Germany," she continued. "I arrived here a few weeks ago."

There was an awkward pause between them. "Well, nice to meet you, Hannah from Germany." Matteo touched the brim of his hat, not quite tipping it, then started away.

"Wait!" she started. He turned back. She faltered. Matteo was clearly doing some type of covert work. But that didn't mean he was working for the resistance. He could be collaborating with the Germans, for all she knew.

But she needed to get out of Europe. Every day she remained in occupied Belgium meant a greater risk that she would be recognized and arrested. He might be able to help.

"Is there something else?" he asked politely.

"You aren't as good as you think," she said. He looked surprised, then angry. "I saw you leave the message under the rock." It was a calculated guess. She did not, in fact, actually know what the paper was. But color rushed to his cheeks, confirming her suspicions.

Alarm crossed his face, quickly replaced by anger. "What do you want?" he snapped. "Money to keep quiet?"

"No, no," she protested, realizing it had come out all wrong. "I have no intention of telling anyone."

"Then, why are you trifling in my affairs?"

"Because I need your help," she said.

"I don't understand."

"I have to leave Europe as soon as possible, and I've had no luck through official channels. I'm trying to make contact with people who might be able to help."

"Why do you have to go?"

She hesitated. *Trust no one*, she could hear Isaac say, his dark eyes burning like coals. "I'm sorry, I can't tell you."

"Then, I can't help you." They stood staring at one another, having reached an impasse.

"How do I know you are on the right side?" she asked.

"You don't. But I'm guessing you don't have a lot of other options." He placed one hand on his hip. "So do you want to tell me why you have to leave, or should I be on my way?"

"I need to leave Europe because of this." She pulled out a folded piece of paper from the lining of her sleeve and passed it to him.

Matteo unfolded it and held it up to see with a practiced gesture, taking care not to be conspicuous. His fingers were long and delicate, like a pianist's. "It's a political cartoon by Maxim," he said. Clearly, he had heard of the artist. "But what does this have to do with you?" She raised her ink-stained fingers, waiting for him to make the connection. "You're Maxim?" She nodded, feeling a tug of pride that her political cartoons had reached Belgium and were known here. Matteo's eyes widened with disbelief. "I thought Maxim was a man."

It was a common misperception, and one that had served her well during those dark days in Germany when the *Gestapo* hunted far and wide for the artist who had drawn the popular subversive cartoons. But then they had found out and come looking for her. Isaac had died that night trying to protect her.

"Because only a man could do this kind of work?" she asked with more than a touch of sarcasm.

"No, because Maxim is a man's name."

"That's fair," she conceded. "I can draw you another if I must prove it."

"No, I believe you."

"You see now why I need to get out of Europe. Can you help me?"

He shook his head. "This sort of thing…it isn't what I do. I work with the resistance, sabotage, liaising between groups, that sort of thing."

She eyed him skeptically. "You don't look like a partisan," she remarked, hoping he did not also find this comment rude.

A faint smiled played about his lips. "That's the best way, isn't it? I'm afraid that helping people escape isn't my thing. But I know someone who might be able to assist you."

Hope rose in her. "Really? Who?"

"The head of one of the escape lines here in Brussels. The name isn't important."

"You must take me to him right away. Time is of the essence. Can you arrange a meeting?" He did not answer right away.

"Meet me at 17 Rue du Champ de Mars tonight at nine. The building serves as a canteen during the day, but we are able to use it in the evenings. There's a salon then, a gathering of some friends. My contact will be there."

"But if there's a party…" How could they meet in secret with so many people there?

"Trust me. I can introduce you then. I will see you tonight." Before she could protest or ask further, Matteo turned and started away. Still puzzling over who he knew who might be able to help her, she went to fetch Georgi, and together they started for home.

That night at a quarter to nine, Hannah walked through the wrought iron gate at the address Matteo had given her, a stately *maison de maître* or sort of minimansion in one of Brussels's old, upscale neighborhoods, not far from Lily's house. She rang the bell and waited. No one answered. She tried the handle, which was locked. Hannah thought she had made a mistake regarding the address, but inside she could hear music and laughter. She knocked on the windowpane, and the curtain drew back just a bit to reveal a yellow patch of light. Through the gap, Hannah could see at least a dozen people. She hesitated. Large crowds were never her thing, especially since the night of the attack in Berlin. The very sound of people gathering could make her run for cover.

A moment later, the door to the house opened, and Matteo appeared. "Good evening," he said, taking her in. She had changed into a brightly colored peasant's skirt and blouse, and her dark blond hair, normally cowed in a messy bun, fanned out around her face like a lion's mane. The change was not for his benefit, though, but for whomever she might have to impress to help her leave.

Matteo led her into the main room where there were even more people than she had seen through the window. They sat about a few small tables, drinking Duvel ale straight from the bottle and another amber liquid from low glasses. Several people smoked, billowing great clouds into the air above them that formed a collective wreath around the room. A man in the corner played a Django Reinhardt tune on a worn guitar. Matteo introduced her around the gathering, and she tried to memorize the sea of names and faces before giving up.

Hannah turned impatiently to Matteo. "Really, this is lovely, but I didn't come to socialize." He raised his finger to his lips, gesturing for her to be quiet. A man poured her a snifter of Jenever liquor, and someone else offered her a cigarette. She took it and inhaled too sharply, already regretting the sour, burnt taste it would leave in her mouth the next day. She felt in that moment not like herself but rather as if impersonating someone else for a time. Part of her readily welcomed the escape.

A minute later, Matteo looked toward the doorway, a more serious look on his face, seeming to have heard or seen something. He stood abruptly. "Let's go. It's time." He led her down a dilapidated hallway, past the darkened rooms smelling of smoke and dust. When they could go no farther, he turned to the last door on the right. He knocked softly, as though not wanting to disturb whoever was on the other side.

"Come in." The voice that answered was brusque and businesslike.

He opened the door to an office, high bookshelves lining the walls. Someone sat at a mahogany desk in a large leather chair, facing away. "Hannah, come in and let me introduce you."

Hannah stepped through the doorway. Then, as the person in the chair swiveled toward her, Hannah stopped short. She had made the same mistaken assumption that people so often made about the creator of her political cartoons.

The head of the underground cell was also a woman.

5

Micheline

Earlier that day...

Micheline entered her fourth-floor flat on the Rue Saint-François in the Schaerbeek district, a quiet residential neighborhood on the outskirts of northern Brussels. Her clothes were soaked with rain. She shook her damp curls loose. Her red hair was not ideal for the work. It stood out too much, made her instantly recognizable. But she refused to color it, instead wearing it in plain sight.

Micheline proceeded to draw a bath in the claw-foot tub. After more than a month of work in Paris with its thieves and spies, she was glad to be home. She removed the radio from its hiding place and tuned it to the BBC before getting into the bath. She scrubbed hard, as if trying to wash the filth of the city from her skin.

As she listened to the broadcast, the accented voice reminded her of the hapless airman she had left behind at the safe house weeks earlier. She had received word he'd made it from the city, but she had no idea if he had crossed the border safely. She pushed the worry from her mind. He wasn't her problem, not anymore. That was one of the things she liked best about escorting airmen, other than helping to defeat the Germans. The job was discrete and finite. The *passeur* took an airman from point A to point B and handed him off and was done. There were no messy entanglements, no ongoing commitments—or at least there hadn't been, until she'd found herself in charge of the whole godforsaken thing.

Micheline had not set out to lead the Sapphire Line. She had tagged along with her older brother Matteo to his resistance gatherings in the early days of the war. The siblings had been orphaned by a car accident when Micheline was four and had spent their childhood shuttled between relatives. All they'd had was one another, and except for a short period when Matteo was old enough and went abroad, they were inseparable. She stood in the shadows, listening as young people, men mostly, planned raids and other ways to fight the enemy.

Then one day, the call came for a new type of work: British airmen who had been downed while flying raids over Germany needed to be secretly led out of occupied Europe. Micheline had volunteered. At first the men were skeptical: she was barely more than a girl. "Exactly," Micheline countered. "I'm less likely to be noticed or suspected." She learned the route through southern France to the Pyrenees, made contacts among the Basque villagers who could help them over the treacherous mountains. She was good at planning—and thinking on her feet when the plan needed to change—and she found herself quickly rising through the ranks of the network.

Then a few months earlier, two German agents posing as evacuees had infiltrated the network, resulting in the arrest of more than a dozen men, including their leader, Andree. Micheline never wanted to be in charge. She preferred working behind the scenes, quietly operating. But the others who remained after the arrests seemed to lose their nerve. If she had not stepped up to lead and rebuild the network, it simply would have crumbled to dust.

So Micheline took over operations for the Belgian segment of the line. She owed that much to her predecessor. And once in the role, she found she liked the sense of control. Being in charge was the only way she could ensure that things went smoothly.

After she dried herself and dressed, Micheline picked up the copy of *Le Monde* she'd brought with her from Paris and studied the weather forecast for the south of France, thinking of the group she had sent south three days earlier that would now be nearing the border. The rain was important. It had to be just hard enough to keep the police from patrolling, but not so torrential enough to make the final crossing of the Bidasoa River impossible.

As Micheline set the newspaper down, she noticed an envelope on the table. She tensed. This was not a safe house, used by others, but her own, private flat, and the notion that someone else had been here was alarming. She wished, not for the first time, that she had a gun. But the handwriting, long and looped, was familiar. It was only Matteo, she realized, relaxing slightly. She had given him a key. Thinking of her older brother, she felt a pang of affection. With their parents long gone, it seemed it had always been just the two of them.

Still, it was unusual for him to come here, much less leave a note. She wondered at first if it was another airman in need of rescue. The British were increasing their air campaigns, and there were more fliers literally falling out of the sky every single day, almost faster than the battered network could handle. But there was no pressed flower in the envelope, which would have signaled an airman in need of rescue. Instead, there was just a scrap of paper with two numbers, *24* and *9*, representing the date and time, scrawled on it. A request to meet him this evening. There was no location; that was understood. She wondered what Matteo wanted.

That night she set out from the flat, wearing her long blue cloak. Other than her red hair, it was her one impracticality. The cloak was odd and unfashionable and made her stand out too much.

Outside Micheline walked to the motorbike that was chained in the archway of the apartment building. She drove south through the darkened streets, the red-roofed townhouses looming close over her.

Twenty minutes later, she reached the meeting place, the canteen on the Rue du Champs de Mars. By day it served as a kitchen sponsored by the Swiss Red Cross, where boisterous youngsters from poor families all over the city gathered in a cafeteria-style setting with long wooden tables for a hot lunch of potatoes and carrots. Now, the long wooden tables where the children ate were pushed aside, and a dozen or so young adults sat on the benches or chairs smoking and drinking. Micheline didn't mingle with the others but said hello and went into the back room that served as their headquarters to go over the latest information from the field.

"The airman in Paris I rescued?" she asked Pascal, a young aide, who was studying a map flattened across the desk through thick glasses. The botched rendezvous and the airman's unknown fate still nagged at her.

Pascal stepped aside now to make room for her behind the desk. A priest who had left his religious order to fight, he was quiet and thoughtful, the very opposite of what you expected in the underground. "Made it safely over the mountains and delivered to our contacts in Spain."

Micheline exhaled with relief. That was the name of the game: get as many airmen out and feed them back into the pipeline of fighters. Some would never fight again. They were too injured or scarred. Others would jump back in as soon as they could.

One airman from Newcastle had crashed and had to be rescued a second time after she had already returned him once to England.

There were so many perils along the escape route other than being caught, though. The physical elements were perhaps more treacherous than the Germans. The high mountain pass through the Pyrenees was dangerous in normal circumstances, made worse now when the rocks were slippery from the spring rains. Then there was the difficult river crossing, which so many had to undertake when other routes were heavily guarded. Xavier, their best Basque guide—and the only man Micheline had ever loved—had been lost in just such a mishap in a strong current when the river swelled from melting snow.

It was too easy to get caught up in the losses. Stepping back now, Micheline could see all they had accomplished, the dozens of airmen they had gotten safely across the border since the evacuation work had started. She felt a tug of satisfaction. When the line worked, it was glorious.

But Micheline was not one to dwell on her successes. "And Renee?" Her thoughts turned to the *passeur* who had abandoned the airman in Paris, nearly causing his arrest.

Pascal hesitated. "No word." Micheline had almost hoped that she had not arrived to escort the airman because she had been arrested. Better that than to worry she had been a traitor all along.

Micheline studied the map, overwhelmed as ever by the scope of the operation she oversaw. Sabotage might be undertaken with just a few people. But escape work was different: it required hundreds of workers across four borders and seven occupied zones, plus at least three languages and four currencies.

"There's something else…" Pascal said. "Two airmen were taken from the safe house in Ghent."

"How?" Micheline demanded. "That was one of our most secure locations."

Pascal shrugged. "I don't know."

Micheline looked at him, an uneasy sense welling up inside her. That they lost two airmen was bad; that they did not know how it had happened, catastrophic. When the network had been compromised and Andree arrested, there were some who thought they should go smaller or perhaps stop altogether. But Micheline had done just the opposite. She seized the moment as a chance to seed new contacts throughout France and Belgium. She worked painstakingly to rebuild it, to recruit new volunteers and find new safe houses, and to gain the confidence of their liaisons in London and some of the wealthy local benefactors who financed their operations. New arrests and breaks in the line would undermine all of that.

Micheline pushed aside her concerns and focused on the map. The escape line operated like a secret railroad of sorts. And no matter what, the railroad had to keep running. "We're expecting a package tomorrow," Pascal informed her. That was code for *airmen in transit*.

She frowned. With the safe house compromised, they would need to find somewhere else to store the new arrivals. "Any word on a new safe house near Hasselt?" she asked.

"Nothing yet. I've found a clerk in the town hall who might be able to help us." There were people who held official positions by day but supported the underground by night, straddling the line between sanctioned and clandestine. "For a price." Micheline groaned. She had learned from the earliest days of the war that every good network needed three things: information, communication and money. Money was often the hardest. Some workers helped out of a sense of patriotism, others were more mercenary. But almost all, save for the most principled, wanted to be paid for risking their lives. Money was scarce right now, with every spare bit going to food and supplies needed for the airmen to make the crossing. There was simply no extra lying around for bribes.

"Have you seen Matteo?" she asked, looking at the clock. She asked not just because of their scheduled meeting. Matteo had a gift for finding resources the network needed, new safe houses, food, even money. Micheline herself was more blunt and could be off-putting, but her brother could charm people into helping and giving who otherwise might not.

"I haven't seen him. But he might have come in while we were talking."

Micheline was annoyed. She herself was always early, but it was just like Matteo to summon her and then make her wait. "Go check the front room for him, please."

A minute later, the door to the office swung open. Matteo walked in, followed by a woman whom she did not recognize. "Hannah, this is Micheline."

Micheline was instantly on guard. Strangers were not permitted among their gatherings, especially not in this office where so many operations were planned.

"Micheline, this is Hannah. She came here from Berlin."

She looked at her brother with disbelief, annoyed that he was taking up her time with the pointless introduction. Was Matteo, ever the loner, on a date? Surely he had not summoned her here for this. She waved him over closer. "What were you thinking, bringing some woman here?"

"She can be trusted. She's not just any woman. She's Maxim."

"The political cartoonist?" Micheline asked. "Are you really certain?"

"I am." The admission was in itself deadly, Micheline recognized; no one would claim to be the fugitive satirist unless it was true. The woman stepped forward, her expression earnest. "I fled the *Gestapo* in Germany for America, but our ship was turned back when it reached Cuba. Your brother said you might be able to help me." She was maybe a decade older than herself, Micheline guessed, with strong features and a careworn face that showed she had seen hardship. She was striking, though, her blue eyes and high cheekbones giving her a leonine appearance. "I have to get out of the country before the Germans realize I am here."

"I don't have those kinds of contacts."

"But your network delivers people."

"British airmen. The people we evacuate are trained servicemen, who can come back to fight the Germans once more. We can't take anyone else." This was the truth. There were tens of thousands of ordinary citizens trying to escape occupied Europe as well. Not just Jews but young men hoping to avoid conscription or the labor draft. The line had to prioritize those who could do the most good for the war. They could not save everyone.

"Please," Hannah said. "I lost my fiancé and my unborn child. The work I do fights the Germans too, in a way."

The truth of the statement was undeniable, yet Micheline remained unswayed. "I wish I could help you. I'm sorry. I can't."

Hannah started to turn away dejectedly. "Would you excuse us for a moment?" Matteo asked Hannah, gesturing to the other room. When Hannah had left, Matteo walked over to his sister. "Isn't there someone who can help? What about one of the other lines? Pegasus?" he asked referring to the much larger line that helped evacuees. "Maybe Dutch-Paris?" Micheline considered the idea. There were other networks which transported out of occupied Europe those civilians who did not have the papers to leave. They might be able to help this woman. But that was not Micheline's work, and she wouldn't call in favors for someone she didn't know or trust. Even if she was inclined to reach out to another line, she would have to make contact, convince them to help. There simply wasn't time with all of the other work Sapphire needed to undertake now.

"Even if there was, why would I risk it?" Her annoyance rose. Her brother had always been naive. "Teo, you don't know her at all. She is a stranger, could be a spy. You would risk everything we have built for this woman. Why?"

"She's a political cartoonist, and she's done important work for the underground. The work she does reaches thousands. She deserves our help."

"We can't risk the entire network based on your gut instincts. You just met her. How can we be sure?"

"Put her to work. Make her prove herself." He had a point. Teo might be gullible, but he was smart—sometimes frustratingly so. Now after losing so many workers, Micheline needed help more than ever. There were a million small jobs to be done: checking safe houses, procuring identification cards and distributing train tickets and money. Except none of them were small, because any misstep could result in the volunteer's arrest and compromise dozens of others. If the woman worked for them, that would show she was committed.

Matteo was right: Hannah could be of use. Micheline felt herself start to relent. "If we are to manage it at all, it will have to be through our own network." She regretted the words immediately, but it was too late to recant. They would make an exception just this once to help Hannah and then be done with it. "Bring her back in." Matteo opened the door and motioned Hannah into the room. "I will work on a way for you to leave. And in the meantime, you can help us."

"Help you?" Hannah needed to get out of Belgium as quickly as possible. She clearly did not plan to get involved here.

"You worked with the resistance in Germany, no?"

"I drew cartoons for the paper. Sometimes I delivered messages."

Micheline considered what she was about to say next. Hannah might be of use to the organization. Her German was native and unaccented, a trait which might serve well in operations near the border. There was a steeliness about her, born of all that she had been through. She might be just what the network needed—if she was willing. "For now, we need your help around Brussels. Eventually we might need you to operate close to the border and hand off the servicemen to the next person. It is a short trip, no more than two days."

Apprehension flickered across Hannah's face at the notion of going close to Germany once more. Micheline studied her, wondering if she could do it. She'd heard of resistance fighters who had trained in Britain or in the woods to prepare for missions. But there was no formal training for the Sapphire Line. Ferrying soldiers was just a kind of instinct. Would Hannah be up to the task? "You wouldn't go right away, of course. We would need to prepare you and see where you could be of greatest use."

"That sounds like it would take time."

"Everything takes time in this line of work. Nothing is easy."

"But I have to get out of Belgium right away. Every day that I stay is another day I risk arrest."

Hannah's statement was undeniably true, and Micheline felt a tug of guilt that she could not do more. "You have a better option?" she asked tersely. Hannah did not answer. "This is the only way. I will work as quickly as I can, but you have to trust me."

Hannah did not answer, and Micheline could see her wrestling internally. She had given everything to flee Germany, and now Micheline was asking her to dive back into the work and life she had left behind. It was a test. "Do this, and I will see that you get out."

Hannah dipped her chin slightly. "Okay, I will help."

"Can you do it?" Matteo asked quietly. Usually his faith in his sister was unshakable, but the war had made them all realists, and some things were simply not possible. "Get Hannah through, I mean."

"If I say I will do it, then I will," Micheline replied, though if she was being honest, she was not entirely sure how she would manage it. She turned to Hannah. "You will need a cover. Matteo will give you further instructions." Matteo was good at the tasks that she was not, the details of procuring what the network needed. He had a charming way with people, the financiers, for example, wealthy Brussels families who might be persuaded to slip a few thousand Belgian francs into an account to cover the expenses of housing and feeding the airmen. He would find the right cover story for Hannah.

If there was such a thing. Studying the woman, second thoughts crashed down on Micheline. Trusting others did not come easily to her. She took care of people, held the lives of hundreds of evacuees and helpers in her hands. Still, she could not depend on anyone but herself.

Micheline turned her back on Hannah, hoping she had not made the biggest mistake of her life.

6

Lily

Lily stepped off the curb outside the Palais des Beaux Arts, and Nik reached out reflexively, seeing a puddle before she did. He stopped her from stepping in it and ruining her dress shoes, a fine leather pair of heels. Their monthly night at the symphony was a tradition dating to before Georgi was born, and she had come to look forward to the few hours when Nik could leave his work behind and they could enjoy one another's company. Things were different now, though, since the occupation. The program of music had fewer musicians, and the applause of the audience had seemed subdued.

Tonight Lily had been distracted and restless too, her mind wandering to the things she had to do the next day. She thought more than once during the concert of Georgi. Bath and bedtime were among her favorite daily rituals, and though she might have tasked the governess Camille with them, she loved rolling up her sleeves and playing with her son in the warm soapy water. She wished now she was at home to tuck him in. Lily often missed the days when it was just her and Georgi, first when he was in her belly and later when he was an infant and Nik worked long days. There was a connection between them that made her feel whole. Georgi was a sensitive child; he didn't like bright lights or noises, and certain fabrics bothered him. She cut his food down and avoided the textures that made him gag.

Georgi was growing in that way boys did, toward his father and away from her. He followed Nik, looking for a male role model and wanting to be like him. For the first time in Georgi's life, there was a need which she could not fill. It was natural, she told herself. But it still stung.

Lily looked around the square at couples having drinks inside the cafés. If one did not look too closely, it might seem as though everything was normal. But upon closer examination, it was apparent that nothing was the same. There were high-ranking Nazis occupying many of the best tables. Once-affable waiters scurried to get what they needed, heads low. How long, she wondered, before she and Nik, as Belgian Jews, might be prohibited from enjoying the symphony and the cafés at all?

"Do you feel like having a coffee?" she asked.

"I have to see patients early in the morning."

"Yes, of course." Once they would have stopped for a coffee laced with something stronger and talked and laughed until the waitstaff began putting up chairs and sweeping the floor purposefully around them. But they were different people now, with a child to care for and Nik's work in the clinic at the rear of the house. When he had been dismissed from the university, Lily wondered if he might have lost his passion for medicine. But to the contrary, he was more committed than ever to helping people, particularly Jews who had so few options left for medical care and paid what little they could for his services. Lily often wished that she still worked as a nurse. There was something so fulfilling about healing people. But women of her station simply did not work, and though she had sworn to go back after Georgi was born, it had somehow never happened. She helped Nik out in the clinic from time to time, but it was not the same as having a job of her own.

"I treated an English airman today," he confided to her when they were well away from the crowd. "Secretly, of course." She looked over her shoulder, wondering if it was safe to speak of such things on the street. But they stood on a deserted stretch of the avenue with no possibility of being heard.

"Oh?" It felt intrusive and alien to think of a foreign airman here, much less one wounded and cared for by Nik. "I had no idea."

"Yes. You were out at the time. He was wounded in an air drop, and someone found him and brought him to me. I couldn't say no."

"Of course not." But she wished he had. Jewish doctors were not permitted to treat non-Jews, and certainly not foreign airmen, categorized as enemies of the German state. She loved and admired his caring nature. But she had wondered more than once if his inability to turn anyone away was going to spell larger trouble for them all. Now there seemed evidence of this before her eyes. She fought the urge to scold him. "I treated him, and they took him on his way," he added. He did not say who *they* were. "But the airman, Fergus Dunlop was his name, was very grateful. When he realized I was Jewish, he asked if we wanted to leave."

"Leave?" The word felt unfamiliar on her tongue. Lily knew people, not just Hannah, but some of their neighbors in Brussels, who had fled when war broke out in Europe, to the south of France or England or even America, if they had money and connections. But she was Belgian, and starting a new life elsewhere as Hannah had tried to do was unfathomable. "Where would we go?"

"England at first. He was offering papers for us to stay there, at least temporarily. I supposed we would have to apply for permission to remain permanently or for visas to somewhere else."

Visas. Permits. Lily's head swam at the notion of such things, which just moments before she had never contemplated. "But why? Why would we leave?"

"He seemed to think Europe would not be safe for Jews much longer." A chill went through her. Lily seldom thought of her religion. It was part of who she was, of course, like dark hair or petite stature or the fact that she didn't like eggs. She made a special dinner twice a year for Rosh Hashanah and Passover. But her Jewish heritage did not define her. She was, first and foremost, a Belgian, like everyone else around her.

"We are Belgians," she replied crisply. "We will see out the occupation here."

"That's what I told him. That I appreciated the offer, but we were going to stay." There was a finality to his voice, and she knew that they need speak no more about it.

As they neared Ixelles, the neighborhood they called home, they passed an elegant mansion. Once a stately home, it was a canteen now, providing breakfast and lunch to poor children. Lily had meant to volunteer there but somehow never found the time. It was too late in the evening for the canteen to be open for children. But lights on the ground floor peeked through a gap in the curtains, and the window was just slightly ajar. Inside, there was a gathering of some sort, young people, artists or bohemians she guessed, because their clothes were just a touch avant-garde. Socialists, undoubtedly, still clinging to the impractical ideas she had left behind at university so many years ago.

Lily glimpsed a familiar figure through the window. *Hannah*, she realized with a start. Peering inside, she saw her cousin seated between two men whose faces were turned away, talking earnestly, their expressions serious. Lily could tell from the way that Hannah tilted her head toward one man in particular that she was fond of him.

Lily was more surprised than she should have been. After all, Hannah went out sometimes in the evening; it had never occurred to Lily to ask where. Watching her cousin, Lily felt a sting of surprise, almost betrayal. She swatted it away. Hannah was an adult and could go out, of course; she didn't owe Lily any explanation. Still, it suddenly seemed that Hannah had a whole secret life which Lily knew nothing about.

The man to whom Hannah was speaking shifted slightly, and his face came into view. Lily gasped. *Matteo.* It couldn't be. A lump formed in her throat. She had last seen him nine years ago that final night in Antwerp before her mother died. She knew he was still out there somewhere. But she had forced him from her thoughts, like the part of a story that happened off the page. Once he had left her world, he simply ceased to exist.

Except if she allowed herself to admit it, she would be forced to acknowledge that it wasn't like that at all. She thought of him still in the dark and lonely moments. She had pictured him in faraway places, America maybe, or off in the South Pacific fighting, living the principles he still believed in, the same ones she had abandoned when she married Nik and settled into their safe and comfortable life. She would not in a thousand years have imagined him here just blocks away in her own neighborhood. She wondered how long he had been here and how it was possible that they had never seen one another.

Seeing her expression, Nik touched her arm protectively. "Is something wrong?"

Lily was uncertain how to answer. "N-no," she managed. Lily was torn. She stared at Matteo, drinking him in. He had aged a bit, gray now at the temples, a line or two around his mouth where there had only been a suggestion of them before. It all served to make him more handsome. Part of her wanted to run and fling open the doors of the party and wrap herself in Matteo's arms, or at least let him know that she was here.

That was the thing about her relationship with Matteo. Theirs had never ended with all of the messiness and regrets of a breakup. Rather, it had cut off suddenly like an unfinished sentence, all of the uncertainties and feelings still lingering on the blankness of the page. She had never allowed herself to consider what life might have been like if she had gone with him. It was a dangerous door that, once opened, might not easily be shut again. So she had put away the thoughts like childhood mementos, never to be reopened. Until now. Now the what-ifs spiraled out and loomed like a cloud of billowing smoke so heady it threatened to take the very air she breathed and swallow her whole. The loss of what she and Matteo had once shared was simply overwhelming.

"Are you certain you're all right?" Nik pressed, his expression concerned. "You look as though you've seen a ghost."

Which was exactly what had happened. "I—I'm fine," Lily stammered, though of course that was the furthest thing from the truth.

"It's good that your cousin gets out and meets people," he said, noticing Hannah and mistaking the cause of his wife's distress.

"Yes. Yes, it is."

Lily steeled herself. She would not, of course, walk in there. Because seeing Matteo again, having him know that she was here would upend her world which, thanks to the Germans and Hannah, seemed to already be teetering on the brink. Additional chaos and disruption were the very last things she needed. She took a breath and turned away, letting Nik lead her home.

The next morning, Lily waited until Hannah came down to breakfast before saying anything. She sniffed, detecting the odor of cigarettes that still clung to Hannah's hair from the previous evening, despite having washed and changed her clothes. "Have you been smoking?"

Hannah shifted guiltily. "I only had one."

"It's just so bad for you and unladylike. And a bad example for Georgi. Speaking of which…" Confrontation was one of the things she liked least, and she avoided it whenever possible. She loved Hannah and was glad to have her here. The last thing she wanted to do was quarrel with her. But Hannah's activities could endanger her family. She had to say something. "I saw you at the canteen last night."

Hannah's face registered surprise before she feigned normalcy. "I was having a drink with friends. Camille was watching Georgi. I didn't think you would mind." It was not her place to mind, Hannah's tone seemed to suggest.

"But those people…they aren't just artists, are they? They're socialists."

"And your point?" Hannah crossed her arms. "Are we meant to not associate with people because of their political views?"

Lily hesitated. Once she would have said no. Though she was always sensitive to the opinions of others, she accepted a wide circle of people. This was about more than social standing, though. With the occupation, politics and affiliations had taken on a meaning of their own. "Have you considered what your associations might mean to our family, the danger they might bring?"

"That's a bit dramatic, don't you think?" Hannah asked.

"I don't. We are at war, and I think this is deadly serious."

"Are you asking me not to see them anymore?" Hannah asked.

"I'm asking you to think carefully and be mindful of our family's safety. I'm worried about your safety as well. You're already in danger because of your work in Germany, and you don't need to get caught up in matters here." Neither spoke for several seconds. "And that man who was seated next to you, is he a friend as well?" Lily could not help but ask.

Hannah's pale cheeks flushed. "Yes. He's called Matteo." Lily thought she detected a note of affection in her cousin's voice. "Why do you ask?"

"He looked familiar, like someone I knew in Antwerp."

"Would you like me to introduce you?"

"No!" Lily's response came out too sharply. "That is, it was so long ago. He might not be the same person. And even if he is, I doubt he would even remember me. You looked as if you were fond of him, though." The previous night, Lily had been too surprised at seeing Matteo to process fully her cousin's affection for him. Now it was clear, undeniable.

"I suppose I am," Hannah confessed. "Only I put that part of me aside entirely when Isaac died. I have no intention of getting involved with anyone. Which is just as well because Matteo doesn't notice me at all."

"Does he have someone else?"

"Not that I know of." Did he still think of her? Lily wondered. It hardly seemed possible after all of these years. Lily wondered if she should tell Hannah the truth about what had happened between her and Matteo. Hannah continued. "Anyway, I'm leaving, so what would be the point?"

"True. You're getting involved with this group now, though. It's too dangerous."

"But they're doing such important work getting downed airmen out of Europe. Micheline, who leads the group, is incredible." Micheline was Matteo's sister, Lily recalled. She had been just a girl and Lily had never met her, but Matteo had always spoken of her with fondness and admiration. "She's younger than us, and she's so strong and brave. She's promised to try and help me leave as well, if I help them."

Lily was unconvinced. "I don't like it. You shouldn't get involved."

"That's the thing, Lily. We're at war. We are *all* involved, whether we like it or not." Hannah's spine stiffened, and she stood taller with a stubbornness that Lily recognized from her cousin as a child. Hannah had spent her entire life resisting any-one telling her what to do. She certainly wasn't going to start now. Hannah was going to keep seeing Matteo and the others.

"Please," Lily said finally, "just be careful." She wanted to tell Hannah that Matteo would surely bring trouble for her, as he had for Lily so many years earlier. But she couldn't, not without telling Hannah everything.

7

Hannah

Hannah studied the canvas in front of her critically, trying to finish the painting of Matteo in the park which she had started weeks earlier. She found herself focusing on little details like the contour of her subject's jaw and the gentle way his neck sloped into his shoulder at the collar. A moment later, she looked up. She wished for a cigarette like the ones she sometimes enjoyed during her evenings at the canteen. Even if she had one, though, she wouldn't dare smoke it in Lily's house.

Hannah gazed out the bedroom window, which faced a tiny courtyard with a trickling fountain. The Brussels skyline was just barely visible over the gray-slated rooftops. A spring rain had fallen earlier, leaving the cobblestones wet and a dampness in the air that seemed to seep persistently through the cracks. The house was blessedly still, with Lily out on errands and Georgi practicing his lessons with his governess. Though it was already midafternoon, the day seemed to stretch long until she would see Matteo and Micheline again.

Since agreeing to work with the Sapphire Line in exchange

for help leaving, Hannah had visited the canteen nightly. The gatherings had in the beginning seemed social, people bringing half-drunk bottles of wine and whatever food they could scrounge to share. The women who attended were sophisticated with their short, pleated skirts and oversize belted jackets, imitating the style of the *zazous*, the punklike culture coming out of Paris. Often one of the men would play guitar and occasionally someone would read poetry.

But as she attended the gatherings more frequently, Hannah discovered that beneath the convivial atmosphere, the meetings at the canteen were purposeful. Some people clustered in small groups, working on articles for *La Libre Belgique* and other anti-German underground newspapers which had popped up during the occupation, or conferring about other plans of which Hannah was not a part. Micheline prowled the room like a lion, consulting on one project, directing another. Seeing their passion and determination stirred memories in Hannah of her time with Isaac in Germany, when causes like this had meant something to her as well.

"Can I help?" she had asked more than once, including the previous night as a group of women prepared to distribute leaflets.

But Micheline had shooed her away. "You're needed for other things." But Micheline had not said what those might be or called upon Hannah yet to help. Hannah wanted to fulfill her end of the bargain so that Micheline would assist her in getting out of the country. Each day that passed brought greater risk that the Germans would discover her past and punish her for it.

Hannah looked over her shoulder around her cozy bedroom. Even as she was eager to leave Belgium, Hannah knew she would miss being here with Lily and her family. She had grown fond of Georgi, and she and her cousin had reconnected and regained some of the closeness they'd once shared.

A few weeks earlier, as she had gotten ready for bed, there was a knock at the door and Lily appeared, carrying a bowl of dried fruit and nuts. "Can I come in?" Hannah waited for her cousin to say what she needed, but instead Lily just sat on the edge of the bed in the corner close to the heater and tucked her feet under her nightgown for warmth. Lily was lonely, Hannah understood then. Despite her husband and child, there remained a void.

"Nearly April," Lily had remarked, "and still so cold."

"Yes. It will be Passover in a few weeks. I can help with the seder, if you'd like." The Jewish holiday had always marked the start of spring in Hannah's world, and whether with her family or later with Isaac in Berlin, they had marked it with a large festive dinner and all of the holiday rituals.

But Lily looked puzzled at the notion. "We've never observed it. Of course, if it's important to you, we can find a way. But I think with everything going on, it would be best not to." Lily had always clung to her secular lifestyle and never more so than since the occupation.

"That isn't necessary," Hannah said quickly. Lily had already done so much for her, and she didn't want to be a bother. "I was thinking of taking Georgi to the zoo tomorrow, if the weather is good," she added, changing the subject.

The two had sat and talked long into the night, and Lily had returned for late-night chats several times since.

A knock at the front door of the house jarred Hannah from her thoughts. She assumed it was a delivery and considered ignoring it. Then she peered over the window ledge. She could just make out the top of Matteo's navy felt hat. She felt a twinge of excitement. Though she did not care to admit it, what she liked most about the canteen gatherings was her time with Matteo. She enjoyed his humor and his quick mischievous grin that flashed without warning at a joke or wry remark. But it was more than just his mercurial wit and charm that drew him to her. Beneath the surface, she sensed a darkness, a pain that he was covering up, that reminded her of her own.

Hannah pushed her feelings down. She had not intended to ever become interested in a man again after Isaac, certainly not here and now. Help Micheline and get out of Europe, that was the plan. She had no room for messy entanglements.

Matteo was here, though, standing at the door. He had never come to her house before; she was not entirely sure how he even knew where she lived. He knocked again, and she hurried down the stairs to answer before the noise interrupted Georgi's lesson.

"Hello," Hannah said.

"Hello. I'm sorry to call unannounced. I hope I didn't interrupt."

"It's fine," Hannah replied. "I was painting."

"Yes, I see." Matteo's hand reached out toward her cheek, and she froze uncertainly, caught off guard by the unexpected and intimate gesture. "You have paint…" he said, wiping away the smudge of blue that now stained his fingers as well. Hannah's face flushed as she realized she had misinterpreted the gesture as something more. She was suddenly mindful of her paint-splashed smock and her hair which spilled out from a messy knot. She waited for him to say what he wanted.

"Is there somewhere we can talk?" he asked.

Over Matteo's shoulder, she could see that the street was lively with passersby going about their business, women headed to the shops, the letter carrier delivering the post. Conversation out here would not be safe. She turned behind her toward the study, but Georgi and his tutor were working there. "Come," she said, leading him up the stairs, only thinking once they had reached the third floor about the impropriety of bringing him to her bedroom. He stood awkwardly in the too-close space as she cleared a chair. She was self-conscious about having this man, whom she did not know that well, in her personal space. It was not the pile of clothes, though, or the rumpled duvet on the bed that gave her pause. Rather, it was the half-finished canvas on the easel. The portrait of him. She moved to step in front of it, cheeks burning.

But it was too late. Matteo leaned forward, drawing even closer to her as he peered over her shoulder. "Me?" he said, his voice pleasantly surprised.

"Y-yes," Hannah said. "I started it after the first time I saw you at the park. Before we formally met," she added, as if that made things somehow better. "I wanted to paint the scene at the duck pond, and you happened to be in it."

Matteo studied the canvas behind her, and she felt exposed, as though caught naked. "It's excellent," he commented, then stepped back to meet her gaze. "Of course, you could be using your talent for real good."

"Pardon me?" She made no effort to keep the indignation from her voice.

He gestured to the underground newspaper that she had left too carelessly on the nightstand after reading it earlier that morning, a cartoon of a German soldier in a gorilla suit printed in a square at the bottom of the page. The drawing was crude, and Hannah knew she could do better. "You could be drawing cartoons for the underground." She shook her head. It was true that sometimes at night she lay awake playing out satire on the page in her head. But she could not bear to work in the medium again.

"Anyway, I'm certain you didn't come here to view my work." She removed her painting smock and crossed her arms expectantly.

"Micheline sent me."

"Oh?"

"She asked that you deliver these." He held out a slim packet of papers. "There is a printer on the northern edge of the city who is sympathetic to our cause. We need you to take these ration cards to him."

"An errand?" Hannah asked in disbelief. "I'm not some sort of assistant." Hannah knew she should have been relieved that Micheline was not asking her to do something more dangerous. "Micheline said she needed me to help extract airmen near the German border."

"This is important work. We need to get the ration cards to the printer so that he can affix the proper seals and enable us to get food for the line. There are a dozen small errands that go into what we do," he added, lowering his voice. "Finding hiding places, procuring clothes and identification, providing money and supplies. Each of them is critical to the line's success. We all find ourselves helping in ways we never expected. You must be very good and very careful not to get caught. If Micheline asked you, she thought you were the right person for the job. Do you want to help or not?"

"Yes, of course. Let's go." She started for the door, eager to be freed from the intimate confines of her bedroom.

But Matteo lagged behind, stopping once more before leaving her room. He was staring at her easel again. "Your painting," he said, and she braced for him to tell her again that it was a waste. "I wonder if it could be somehow of use."

She cocked her head. "Of use?"

"For transmitting messages. Perhaps you could paint them into the picture and then paint over them."

"It won't work. It takes me too long, and whoever receives it could destroy the message when scratching off the paint. How about this instead?" She turned over the canvas to the space where it was stapled to the frame and pried the wood back off a bit. "We could hide a message in there," she said, running her hand over the flat space.

He bit his lip, accentuating the curve of his cheekbones. "That might do. But won't it look odd, carrying a painting around town?"

"There are reasons. I could be taking it to the store to get more paints or to a class at the art school or back to the park to capture the scene."

"Creative," he said with admiration. "Shall we try it with the ration cards?"

Hannah paused. She had not imagined attempting this so soon, but it would be better than carrying the ration cards in her purse or pocket, where they would be more easily discovered. Together they spread the cards flat along the back of the canvas, their fingers bumping against one another. "No good," she said. When they tried to replace the back of the canvas, it bulged too conspicuously.

"We will use it another time, then," he replied. Hannah started to tell him that there would not be another time, that she would do the errand for Micheline before leaving for America. But Micheline had never said how much she expected Hannah to help before fulfilling her end of the deal and helping Hannah to go.

Matteo started down the stairs, but instead of walking to the front door he went to the kitchen and opened the refrigerator. "What are you doing?" Hannah asked, startled by the intrusive gesture. She imagined Lily's reaction at coming home and finding a man she did not know rifling through her kitchen.

"Here, use this instead." Matteo pulled out a package of butter and handed it to her.

Hannah was confused. "You want me to put the ration cards in the butter?"

Matteo laughed aloud, the corners of his eyes crinkling. "No, but you should carry the package with you in case you get stopped and searched." She blanched at the prospect. He continued, "You can confess to buying butter on the black market which is a minor offense and better than what you are actually doing. It will distract them from your real purpose." It was clever, Hannah had to admit, though it seemed like a waste of food. Feeling the softening butter in her hand, Hannah felt sure there had to be an easier, or at least less messy, alibi. She did not protest but put the butter in her bag and then tucked the passes in neatly beside it.

"Why didn't Micheline come to give me the errand herself?" Hannah asked as they started from the house.

"I offered," Matteo replied mildly. Had he wanted to come see her? Hannah wondered. "Anyway, she's been called away on business." Hannah wanted to ask where and why. Even if Micheline had shared that information with her brother, though, Hannah knew he would not say more.

They reached the front door and stepped outside. "Take the tram to Schaerbeek and then walk down Rue Rubens for about four hundred meters to the printshop," he said. "Deliver the ration cards only to Herr Kunst. Tell him that Safir sent you. That's Micheline's code name, and he'll know it." Hannah nodded, lingering awkwardly to see if there were further instructions. He kissed her farewell on the cheek. *For show*, she told herself. It was important to keep up normal appearances in case anyone was watching. A hint of his cologne lingered as he started away.

Hannah walked in the opposite direction toward the tram stop. Despite the seemingly mundane nature of the errand, her nervousness grew. It was as if everyone she passed could see the secret she carried. *Knew.* She was reminded then from her days with the resistance in Germany of what it took to do this kind of work: calmness under pressure, the ability to think on her feet. She only hoped she still had it in her.

Forty-five minutes later, she reached the printshop. The proprietor's name was etched on the glass window in faded gold lettering. Inside the narrow shop, samples of cards and programs which the shop had printed hung framed on the walls. The smell of printing chemicals burned Hannah's nose.

Hannah walked to the counter and waited until the previous customer had left the shop. "Herr Kunst?" she said to the man behind the counter. He had a thick mustache and wore a monocle at his right eye. "I've been sent by Safir." The man's eyes widened. She reached in her bag and pulled out the wrapped parcel of ration cards. He took the package with shaking hands and shoved it away under the front counter.

The cards delivered, Hannah hurried from the shop. It had seemed almost too easy, and Hannah wondered if there was something more that Micheline had expected her to do.

When she reached the corner, Hannah looked back over her shoulder and saw a police officer walk into the printshop. She ducked into a doorway, out of sight. She had made it out just in time. But the policeman might have seen her hand over the ration cards. She wondered if Herr Kunst was in danger and whether she should go back and help him. The shopkeeper seemed to talk easily with the officer, though, and his expression showed no sign of distress.

Herr Kunst peered out the shop window, as if to make sure no one was watching. Then he reached below the counter and pulled out the package of ration cards. He was a traitor, Hannah realized then. And he was about to turn over the package to the policeman.

Impulsively, Hannah leaped from the doorway and raced back into the shop. "Excuse me," she said to Herr Kunst, stepping in front of the police officer. "But I think I left something behind in the shop." The package sat on the counter between them. If she tried to retrieve it, the policeman might realize the nature of her errand and arrest her. But if she did nothing, the policeman would take the passes and they would be lost for good. She had to do something.

"Oh, there it is!" she exclaimed, feigning surprise. She reached for the package, certain that Herr Kunst or the policeman would try to stop her. Her heart pounded. But the officer appeared not to know what was in the package or that Herr Kunst was about to turn it over to him. And the shopkeeper, unwilling to reveal that he was a traitor, said nothing. "Thank you so very much."

She grabbed the package and sped from the shop and down the street, praying that the officer would not follow her.

Hannah did not dare wait for the tram, so she started back toward the city center on foot. But the journey was longer than she had imagined, and she became lost in the twisting streets of the unfamiliar neighborhood. She had been gone much longer than expected, and Lily would be home by now, looking for her and wondering where she had been. Her feet ached.

Nearly two hours later, she burst into the canteen. Though she was eager to get home, she needed to tell Matteo about Herr Kunst and the ration cards. When Hannah entered the back office, she was surprised to see Micheline at the desk reviewing papers. "I thought you were called away on business," she said, struggling to catch her breath.

Micheline ignored the comment. "Why didn't you deliver the ration cards?"

"I did, but then a policeman walked into the printshop. Herr Kunst was about to turn them over to the police. So I went back for them."

"You went back and took them with the police standing there?" Micheline asked, an unmistakable note of admiration in her voice.

"Yes."

"That was a brave thing to do. Foolish, but brave."

"I couldn't let the ration cards fall into the wrong hands."

"You could, actually. They were fakes."

"Fakes?" Hannah's voice rose with disbelief. "But why?"

"We were testing Herr Kunst, and you showed that he could not be trusted."

"Why didn't you tell me? I could have been arrested or worse." Understanding then, her surprise turned to anger. "You were testing me too."

"I had to see if you were up to the task. I could not possibly trust you without knowing."

"So the whole thing was a charade?"

"Yes." Micheline did not bother to deny it.

"And the policeman?"

"He was real."

"You risked my life for nothing." Hannah's anger grew.

"It wasn't for nothing. I had to know. And you passed. So let's go." Micheline stood from her desk and pulled a flowing blue cloak from the hook on the back of the door.

"Go where?"

"On my errand. You can come with me." She strode down the corridor and out onto the street, as Hannah trailed close behind.

Outside, Hannah faltered. In her anger, she wanted to tell Micheline that she was done and walk away. But she could not. It was not just that she needed Micheline to help her get to America. Oddly, Hannah was more determined than ever to prove her worth—and her trustworthiness.

"Well, are you coming with me or not?" Micheline demanded.

Before Hannah could respond, Micheline started off down the street.

8

Micheline

"So are you ready to give up now?" Micheline demanded, wanting to know the true results of the test she had given. Micheline had sent Hannah on the fake errand deliberately, knowing that the package would be intercepted. The ration cards were fake and could be taken without consequence to the network. She would never have entrusted a girl she barely knew with real documents, despite the fact that she claimed to have worked with the resistance in another country. There was too much at stake, too many lives, to put it all in the hands of someone she had not tested. Even if Hannah was loyal to the cause, there was simply no counting on her to have the skill or experience or grit. She wanted to see how Hannah would hold up under pressure. She had to know if she had the moxie to see it through. Micheline wondered if the fear of nearly being apprehended and the cold reality of the work and its possible consequences would make Hannah want to quit.

"No." Hannah shook her head firmly. "I'm more committed

than ever." The errand had been a small but important test, and Hannah had passed. She had demonstrated courage and the ability to think on her feet.

"Then, come." She led Hannah down the street to a nearby alleyway.

Micheline opened the door to a municipal van. "The Germans watch the roads in and out of the city carefully. This van is the perfect cover because we can claim to be on an errand for the city." Far from perfect, though Micheline dared not say as much. They could still be stopped and searched, apprehended.

"But where are we going?" Hannah asked. Micheline shook her head. She never told anyone more than they needed to know. "It's nearly dinnertime, and I'm expected at my cousin's. How long will we be gone?"

Hannah asked a lot of questions. Micheline might have been annoyed, but she was much the same way herself. "As long as we need to." She wondered again whether Hannah would lose her nerve and back out. But she simply nodded and climbed in the passenger seat of the van, which smelled of stale cigarette smoke and some kind of rot.

Micheline started the engine, and it grunted twice before kicking in. As she turned onto the wider thoroughfare of the Rue du Trône, Micheline felt a sense of familiar satisfaction. She had loved driving from the moment Matteo had taught her, just fourteen years old and barely tall enough to reach the pedals. She'd insisted on learning. "A girl needs to know how to get from point A to point B and back again." The clunky van was nowhere near as satisfying as the motorbike she normally loved to drive through the countryside when she traveled alone. Still, she enjoyed the control of being behind the wheel, determining where she would go next.

Neither woman spoke as they drove through the outskirts southeast of the city and the buildings thinned, giving way to sparse, darkened farmhouses and gently rolling hills. For a time, the road ahead was deserted and dark. Then traffic grew thicker and unusually slow for this time of night. Micheline pressed her foot on the break as the car in front of her stopped. She inhaled sharply. There was a police cordon, two officers checking papers and searching vehicles. "What is it?" Hannah asked with alarm.

"Just a routine checkpoint." Micheline felt a tug of unease. Their papers were in order. But if the police looked in the back of the van they would find the British uniforms and money stored under the floorboards. "Give me your papers."

When the car in front of her had been cleared, Micheline rolled their vehicle forward to the checkpoint. She handed over their documents. *"Bonsoir,"* she said in her most girlish tone.

The policeman did not smile. "What are you ladies doing in a municipal vehicle?"

"We're running an errand to deliver some supplies to Liège," Micheline offered, using the excuse she had planned. "My father, who works for the city, is ill, so we had to go for him." She hoped the explanation would be good enough.

"At this hour?" The policeman sounded skeptical.

"We had to make sure that someone was home to care for him before setting out," Hannah interjected without hesitation from the passenger seat. Hannah's expression remained natural as she conjured the lie, and Micheline marveled at her quick thinking. "We've also got some frozen fish we are carrying for a merchant friend in the back that is going to make a terrible mess if we don't get going soon," Hannah added, wrinkling her nose.

Micheline was certain that Hannah had overplayed her hand: if the policeman opened the back of the van, he would discover the lie and question the rest of their story as well. The officer hesitated a beat. "Carry on," he said finally, and Micheline exhaled as he returned their papers. She started the van once more and pressed the accelerator gently, fighting the urge to speed away.

"That was good thinking," Micheline said with grudging admiration. Hannah had, in that moment, been quicker to react than she.

Hannah shrugged. "I've always been able to think on my feet. It's gotten me out of scrapes more than once." Micheline wondered what secrets Hannah kept, the past she had left behind. Hannah had already told her about her fiancé. What other mysteries did she carry still?

They drove in silence for nearly an hour as darkness fell. The trees which lined both sides of the road thickened to clusters as they neared the woods. Micheline searched for a familiar break in the trees and then turned right off the main road onto an unpaved path. The Senzeilles was a dark and dense forest outside the city. The branches, a mix of oak and chestnut and beech, bowed low over the road. When she had driven as far as she could without the wheels getting stuck, Micheline pulled over and parked the van between some thick shrubs so it could not be seen from the motorway. Hannah followed her from the vehicle and down a path by foot. Bits of old snow still clung to the grass, and her boots sank deep into the sodden earth with each step.

The two women walked in silence through the woods. "Where are we going?" Hannah asked once more. Her words echoed against the trees, unanswered.

Finally, they reached a clearing. A young man stood there smoking, the tip of his cigarette illuminating his face in an orange halo. Seeing them, he dropped the butt and stiffened to attention. It was David, a recruit who had joined the network at scarcely sixteen. Micheline should rebuke him for being sloppy and letting his guard down, but instead she made a mental note to have Matteo tell him later.

"Is my brother here?" she asked, dispensing with formalities.

David nodded. "By the stream."

Micheline made her way through the darkened forest on instinct, feeling for the familiar turns in the path. Hannah followed. "A whole encampment," Hannah marveled softly, as she took in a cluster of makeshift huts. "And so close to the city. You might never know it was here."

Micheline nodded. That was the idea. To the outside observer, the forest was uninhabited, and one who passed by might never notice the simple shelters constructed from branches. But the secret encampment was, in fact, expansive. There were ten huts and even a pump with running water. Dozens of men could be housed here, at least until the deepest winter.

"This is the center of our operations, or one of them." Micheline looked Hannah keenly in the eyes. "Once you have been here, there is no turning back." Hannah nodded solemnly, and Micheline could see that even if she could have left, she would not.

Hannah's eyes traveled to a few men in foreign uniforms clustered around a low fire. "British?" she asked, incredulous.

"Yes. Downed airmen are sometimes kept here, either until a safe house becomes available or because they are too weak or sick or hurt to cross the border." Hiding wounded airmen was among the most dangerous work. The Germans searched furiously for the fugitives. *Luftterroristen* they called them. Reprisals for those who helped the airmen were severe. More than one Belgian family had insisted upon arrangements for their own children to go into hiding as a precondition of agreeing to help.

Evacuating airmen was some of the most dangerous of resistance work, but it was also among the most important. Saving an airman was more than just saving a life; it was returning him to the front so he could rejoin the fight. And sending those fliers back to Britain helped with the morale of those who were about to deploy. It signaled that there was someone to help them if they were downed, a chance that they might be rescued and brought to safety. Of course, Micheline had never seen the reunions, the faces in the barracks or mess hall when a soldier who was missing or presumed dead walked in alive and well. But knowing gave her purpose and strength.

Micheline raised her hand in a sweeping gesture. "You see now why I had to do it? Test you, I mean."

Hannah nodded. "I do. There's too much at stake not to." Micheline wanted to say it went beyond that: mistrust was not just how Micheline operated, it was part of her very nature. Overcoming it with Hannah went against her every instinct. "I'll do whatever I can to help." Hannah was part of the network now, at least for as long as she remained in Belgium.

Micheline exhaled silently. "Good. When we are ready, I will call on you again, this time for real. Now, come."

They started toward the bank of the stream where Matteo oversaw an operation of four men, packing weapons and munitions in disguised casings. The men were from the General Sabotage Group of Belgium, or Group G, an organization that specialized in sabotaging trains and other German assets. Matteo, with his winning ways, had always been a natural liaison to other resistance groups, like the fighters they shared space with here. His charm, a foil to Lily's own brusqueness, helped to build bridges and find the things that the Sapphire Line needed.

At the unexpected sight of Hannah, Matteo's face softened and he smiled. Seeing his warmth toward Hannah, Micheline's stomach clenched. It was not just that she was protective of her brother. Matteo had a long and disastrous history with romance, ending in heartbreak and tragedy. She did not want to see him suffer like that again. More importantly, the network could not afford any disruptions that might come from a messy entanglement between two of its operatives.

"Hello!" Hannah said, a little too loudly.

Micheline spun toward her. "Quiet! Do you want to tell all the Germans we are here or just a few?"

"Michou…" Matteo tried to intervene.

But Micheline would not be subdued. "You must think, or you will get us all killed." She was overreacting, and she knew it.

"I'm sorry," Hannah said quietly.

"Give us a moment, will you?" Matteo said to Hannah tenderly. He gestured toward a group of men, clustered around a small fire a few meters away. "There's coffee, if you'd like some."

"There's been an arrest in Bruges," Matteo said in a low voice when Hannah was out of earshot. "One of our *passeurs* who was on her way to extract an airman."

"Who?"

"Adele."

Micheline felt a pang at hearing the name, a valuable agent who had been with them since the start. Then she swatted it away; she could not afford to let emotion cloud her judgment. "And the airman?"

"Still at the safe house at the university there, but in urgent need of rescue."

"Dispatch Lissette to extract him," Micheline instructed smoothly. She tried not to focus on the pain of losing one of their own, a woman who would likely never return from German arrest. What she could not ignore, though, was another breach on the heels of so many others. Each was a tiny crack in the network's foundation. How many could the line withstand before collapsing altogether?

Matteo nodded, then went back to packing weapons with the other men. Micheline signaled to Hannah that it was all right to rejoin them. As Hannah walked back over, Micheline studied the weapons with unease. Their plan, to smuggle guns across the border into Germany to another group of fighters, made her nervous. She was concerned only with rescuing the airmen and getting them to freedom. A serious gaffe with missions of sabotage and subversion against the Germans could spell doom for her own line too. But the two groups worked in tandem, as concentric circles, sharing space like this camp as well as other resources.

Matteo held up one of the guns, a German Walther P38, carefully pointing it downward. "We can spare one if you would like it."

Micheline waved it away. Though she was an excellent shot, she didn't believe in carrying weapons. "You don't have a gun?" Hannah asked incredulously.

Micheline shook her head. "It wouldn't do any good. If you reach the point where you need a gun, you've already lost. Our real weapons," she added, "are our hands and our minds. Things that keep us out of trouble in the first place, and that no one can take away from us."

"What do we do now?" Hannah asked.

"We will stay the night."

"But I must go back to my cousin's this evening. She won't know what happened, and she will worry."

"There's no choice. We can't risk going through that blockade again."

"And no way to send word that I've been delayed?"

"I'm afraid not."

Hannah's brow creased at the worry she would cause by not returning, or at the questions her absence would perhaps raise. "What if my cousin comes looking for me at the canteen?"

"What if she does? No one there knows about our errand, and they wouldn't tell her if they did. Come." She led Hannah to one of the huts, crouching to get through the entranceway. It was a simple structure, no more than two meters in diameter, with makeshift pallets of straw to sit and sleep on.

As they settled into the hut, Micheline saw Hannah looking through the doorway in the direction of the stream. "He's still working." They both knew she was talking about Matteo.

"He doesn't sleep much," Hannah observed.

"Hardly ever." Micheline could sleep soundly just about anywhere, but Matteo was always up, moving and doing.

"But why?"

"I think he keeps moving to outrun his pain. Someone hurt

him long ago." Hannah watched, waiting for her to say more, but Micheline would not. There was an undercurrent to her message, equal parts warning and plea: *Do not hurt my brother. I won't let that happen to him again.*

Hannah's expression was troubled. "What is it?" Micheline asked.

"You can't outrun your pain. Sorry." Hannah gestured outside the tent. "Being here among all of the resistance work. It just brings up memories, that's all."

"It must have been difficult losing your fiancé," Micheline offered. Empathy was not an emotion that came easily to her, but she could relate to Hannah's loss.

"I loved him," Hannah acknowledged. "And you? Is there someone?"

Micheline might have taken umbrage to the intrusive question. Instead, she answered. "There was. He was a Basque guide who led our men courageously over the mountains." Her voice was hesitant. She had never spoken about Xavier to anyone. At the time, it would have seemed silly, compromised her leadership to have people know she had fallen in love with one of their guides. Afterward, it was just too hard.

But talking with Hannah now seemed to bring it all to life again. Xavier was a Basque mountaineer, tall and hulking, with craggy features and a ready laugh. The Basques had a strong patriotic tradition, and while their government had ceded willingly to the Germans, the citizens resisted. Xavier had taken great pleasure in navigating the airmen through the rugged countryside and using the terrain they had occupied for centuries to best the Germans. Micheline found herself venturing farther south than was normally her route in hopes of seeing him. They had bonded on their trip over the mountains, made plans together for the future. It was the only time she had let herself get close to a man.

"What happened?" Hannah asked, interrupting her memories.

"He drowned trying to take three men across the swollen Bidasoa River in a storm." The image faded, and she found herself hollowed out by the memory. She had not taken the route to the south of France since that night but had found others to do it. She told herself that, as head of the network, it was too dangerous for her to be on the line. The truth was she simply could not bear to go there and face her memories again.

"So what now?" Hannah asked. "Do I go through some sort of training?"

Micheline shook her head. "There is no training for what we do."

"Then, why bring me here?"

"So you could see what we do and why we are doing it." But that was only part of it. Once Hannah had seen all of this, she would be in too deep. There was simply no turning back. Still, Hannah watched her, as if looking for answers. Micheline searched for something she could give Hannah, tangible and real, to help her with the endless dangers she might face while working on the line. "Trust no one. Do and verify everything for yourself. Vary your route. Never stay more than one night in the same place. And always trust your instincts." Micheline leaned back, satisfied. The rest Hannah would just have to learn on her own.

Neither she nor Hannah spoke further, but they sat silently in the semidarkness, heads tilted back against the roughly hewn wall of the hut. Hearing Hannah's breath grow long and steady, Micheline knew she was asleep.

As she watched Hannah, illuminated by a thin shaft of moonlight, a wave of affection rose up in Micheline. She had never sought out the company of women, and having sisters or female friends was not something that she had particularly missed. But there was a quiet comfort in Hannah's presence that she welcomed.

Micheline pushed the sentimentality aside. Hannah was nothing more than an asset, and one who planned to leave as soon as she was able. For that reason alone, Micheline could not become close to her. It was not worth getting attached if the girl was going. *If.* Micheline had only agreed to try and find Hannah a way out. Her inquiries so far had not yielded a solution. She would keep asking; that was all. Helping Hannah was not her primary mission, and it would not be done at the expense of other, more important work.

Unusually restless and unable to sleep herself, Micheline stood quietly and stepped out from the hut over to the bank of the stream where Matteo, now alone, was packing the last of the weapons. "Hannah?" he asked, and she could hear the affection in the way he said her name.

"Sleeping." Matteo's gaze traveled in the direction of the hut, and Micheline's concerns redoubled. *Not this.* She and Matteo had both been hurt before. She had sworn to never love again. But Matteo, with his big, open heart, was prepared to swoop back in and risk everything. She admired and pitied him at the same time.

"You were rather harsh with her earlier for being too loud," Matteo observed.

"Would you say that if she was a man?" He did not answer. "You're fond of her, aren't you?"

"No," he replied, too quickly. Micheline realized that she needed to find a way to get Hannah out, not just to deliver the information she carried or to fulfill her own promise to Hannah but to get the woman away from her brother as quickly as possible, before he could develop stronger feelings and risk further harm.

"The British reached out again," he said, changing the subject. "They want to use the encampment as a holding ground." She had heard this before. Things had gotten so much busier with the increased air raids, the trickle of airmen in need of rescue now a steadily growing stream. Sapphire and the half-dozen or so other networks evacuating them couldn't keep up. The British had grown impatient, and they thought the route through Spain was too long and protracted. Instead, they wanted to gather them and evacuate the soldiers to the coast of Brittany from a rocky outpost called Bonaparte Beach and ferry them across the channel.

It was a far cry from two years ago when Micheline had turned up at the British consulate in Lisbon with two airmen. An unknown to them, the British officials had eyed her skeptically. Now, more than a hundred safe extractions later, the British government not only knew that the Sapphire Line was for real, it wanted to take it over and run it. Better protection, smoother lines, that was what they had promised. Micheline was having none of it. The network worked so well because it was run on the ground with decisions made in real time based on the situation. The last thing she wanted was for it to get bogged down in bureaucracy and political infighting, driven by men who had not once worked with her on the ground.

She shook her head. "Impossible. It's too dangerous. There's a German post not a thousand meters inland. The nights are shortening." It was not her business to tell them what to do. No one was going to listen. But she would be damned if she was going to let them jeopardize her camp to do it. The network had almost been obliterated before by getting too big and trying to do too much. They had worked hard to come back from that and restore operations, rebuild when so many thought it was over. She would not—could not—have it fall apart again.

"We can't hide any more people. We don't have enough safe houses to hide the airmen we already have."

"Pascal said he has a contact who might be able to help. A Frenchman who has resources and connections to wealthy donors."

Micheline cringed. "You know I don't like relying on outsiders. And Pascal never mentioned this to me."

"Because he knows you don't like relying on outsiders. And you can be a little, well, intimidating. Especially when we're telling you something you don't like," he chided, and they both laughed.

"You know me too well," she conceded.

"You said yourself we need more money," Matteo pointed out. Money was a part of it, more than Micheline cared to admit. They needed food and rail tickets and rented flats, and also to pay those who forged documents. And not everyone worked free for love of country.

"I'll talk to him about it," she agreed reluctantly. Then she changed the subject. "This latest arrest, after the *passeur* didn't turn up in Paris… Something isn't right."

"Just a coincidence, I'm sure."

"Maybe." Micheline tried forcing certainty into her voice, wanting desperately to believe it. But a nagging feeling told her otherwise. One misstep might be written off. But two spelled a kind of trouble she wasn't ready to consider.

Micheline wrapped her arms around herself against the chill. She was a solitary creature by nature, working and operating best on her own. But the entire network was hers now, and the agents were connected in purpose and spirit. She felt them now, spread out across three countries spanning from the English Channel to the south of France like a constellation of stars.

"I have to go," she said.

"Where?"

"Away." Though there were never secrets between them, even Matteo did not need to know the full extent of her business.

"So soon? You just got back." She nodded. The work came faster and faster these days. "I wish you wouldn't. Things are so unsettled now, and nothing is quite right when you are gone."

"I know, but there is no other way."

"You take on too much where you could send someone else."

"I could say the same to you, big brother," she chided.

Matteo did not join in their usual joking. His eyes remained grave. All they had left in the world was one another. Neither could imagine losing that. "At least let me come with you."

Still the Matteo of her youth, she mused. Older, yet always close on her heels. She shook her head. "You're needed here. You know that." He looked as though he wanted to argue but could not. Though their hearts as siblings were intertwined, their work was separate, each to their own strengths. "Tell Hannah I had to go."

"I shall. And I will make sure she gets back safely."

Micheline wanted to remind him that his first obligation was to the network—Hannah would have to learn to take care of herself. But Matteo always had a heart too large for his own good, and the words would be wasted. "Be careful," she said instead. She gave her brother a peck on the cheek and turned to go.

She started through the darkened woods, feeling the path back to the van on instinct.

An owl called out unseen, and its hoot seemed to echo Matteo's earlier caution: *Send someone else.* As she reached the spot where the van was parked and climbed inside, she swatted the idea away.

After all, there were some jobs you had to do for yourself.

9

Lily

One bright spring morning when Georgi's tutor had not come due to illness, Lily set out with him from the house. "Come," Lily said. "Let's go to the market and then the park."

Georgi, carrying his favorite ball, turned eagerly in the direction of Place Sainte-Catherine and the market they usually frequented, anticipating the chocolate-covered waffles at the patisserie stand. Lily turned him away gently with a pang of sadness. Jews were not permitted there anymore. "Why don't we try a new market?" she said, forcing excitement into her voice. But the place where Jews were allowed to shop was outside of the city center, in an immigrant Jewish neighborhood close to Gare du Nord. She had never once been there in her whole life.

As they started in the direction of the new market, Lily recalled how she had looked inside the cupboard a few days earlier to discover they were almost out of flour and milk, both of which were hard to come by. "That's all we have?" Hannah had asked in disbelief, standing behind her and peering over her shoulder. Lily nodded, equal parts embarrassed and annoyed. She always bought groceries fresh, never keeping food around more than a few days. It had never occurred to her to stockpile or hoard. "I'll find us food," Hannah said confidently.

"How?"

"There are ways."

Lily had narrowed her eyes suspiciously. Surely Hannah's *ways* involved the friends she'd made at the canteen. And if they were getting food on the black market, it would only spell trouble. Still, when Hannah returned home the next day with an armload of leafy greens and crisp apples, Lily had accepted it gratefully. But even with Hannah's contribution, Lily still needed to find a more reliable source of food, and the permitted market, though inconvenient, was their only option.

About thirty minutes later, they reached a downtrodden neighborhood where the buildings were unkempt and trash was strewn on the sidewalks. Lily kept her head low, hopeful she would not see anyone she knew. The crowded streets felt like a foreign country, reminiscent of her early years in Poland or what little she remembered from them. The smell of cooking, heavy with garlic and onions, wafted unpleasantly through a half-open window.

Though she had lowered her expectations, the market was even worse than Lily had imagined. She peered with distaste at the spoiled meat and mottled vegetables. Just a few months ago, she had shopped on the Grand Place at the finest food hall in Belgium for salmon and caviar and fresh fruit even out of season, all to her heart's content. Now she was forced to go to the Ration Office—a risky proposition in itself—just to procure the stamps to be allowed to purchase this trash.

"Pastries?" Georgi asked hopefully.

Lily shook her head. "I'm afraid not, darling. But let's make some *oliebolen* when we get home." She prayed the promise of warm doughnuts with powdered sugar would entice him and that he would not make a scene. "We can go to the park now, though," she added, forcing brightness into her voice.

Turning away from the market after managing to buy just a few turnips and carrots, Lily started past the rail station. Then she stopped again. There was a gathering of several dozen young people, in their late teens and early twenties, clustered by the side entrance to the station. She might have mistaken them at first glance for a youth group, off for a weekend camping trip. But their clothes were out of season, and they wore heavy winter coats and carried overstuffed backpacks. Their expressions were grim, with no excitement or anticipation about the journey they were about to undertake.

"A call-up," a woman beside her on the pavement said in a low voice, her tone ominous. "Young people, given notice." Lily was shocked. There had been rumors of Jews who were not Belgian citizens being called up by the Germans to report to the labor camps. But Lily did not personally know anyone who had received a summons, and she had found such an idea unbelievable.

"What if they don't show?" she asked. Would the Germans go after them? She imagined how the immigrant neighborhoods, narrow and tightly packed, would have been ideal for the Germans to corral the Jews who were undoubtedly caught unaware, trapped.

"They call up more, I suppose." The woman shrugged matter-of-factly. "It's fine. They're only taking the foreigners. And the trains must be filled." She made it sound as if she was talking about a shipment of cattle or grain. In fact, the very opposite was true: the trains could not, should not, be filled with people whose only crime was to be born in the wrong country, not unlike Hannah—and Lily herself.

Lily, appalled by the woman's dismissiveness, turned Georgi away from the station. She had often regarded those who had emigrated to Belgium as different and strange. But Hannah was a foreigner, and the threat was personal and real now. What made one native? Lily's family had come here when she was a girl, long enough ago that she appeared in every way Belgian. But her origin was still discernible if anyone cared to check. And what would the Germans do when the foreign Jews were all gone? Surely the Jews who were Belgian citizens could not be taken just as easily.

Lily led Georgi toward the Parc du Cinquantenaire. As the walk dragged on, Georgi's pace slowed and Lily feared he would refuse to continue. But he pressed on, seemingly enticed by the prospect of playing.

When they reached the park, she scrutinized it carefully. Once the park had been a safe place. Now nearly two years into the occupation, it was not at all the same. The green leaves bowed in heavy canopies above as they always had, and children's laughter rang out as they played around the fountain. But there was a military car at the corner and a pair of German soldiers watched the people intently. Deciding they were sufficiently far away from the spot where she and Georgi stood, she released him to go play with his ball.

Her mind reeled back to the troubling sight by the station of the young people gathering for deportation. Surely someone would do something to help them. But who?

Lily was drawn from her thoughts by Georgi's cry. Her head snapped in his direction. She was relieved to see that it was only his ball that had rolled out into the road. She leaped up, but before she could get it, one of the Germans retrieved the ball. He looked down at Georgi. Lily's breath caught. Georgi was not wearing the yellow star as they were all required to now. It was affixed to his jacket, which he had cast off and that his mother now held. She had not had the chance to sew one onto his shirt, and she worried that the German would somehow know that he was Jewish and notice it was missing. But the soldier returned the ball to him, then ruffled his hair. The touch sent chills down Lily's spine.

Stay silent, Lily thought as Georgi took the ball and continued playing by the fountain. That was the lesson of the war and the only way to survive it. She knew that now more than ever. If only she could make Hannah, with her wild parties and troublesome friends, see that. Because Hannah's friends were not limiting themselves to late nights and loud parties, not if Matteo was among them.

Matteo. His face appeared in her mind as she sat down on the park bench, not the fleeting image that she had seen at the art school but the young man of a decade earlier. They had just finished making love in his bare attic apartment, the sweat of one another still clinging to their entwined naked bodies.

"I'm leaving Antwerp," he said. "Going abroad to see the world."

Her heart ripped wide open. He had talked before of going. But the reality of it knocked the wind right out of her. "Come with me," he added.

She was stunned by the idea. "Me?"

"Yes. We could have wild adventures and make a life together. It would be so much better with you. What do you say?"

Lily had never thought of leaving Antwerp or her parents. But the whole wide world seemed to lie before her at that moment, and she knew this was her one—and maybe only—chance to be free. She had to take it. "Yes." She threw her arms around him.

An hour later, she had arrived home, still aglow. She braced herself to tell her parents that she was leaving. They wouldn't approve, of course. They had never liked Matteo, not so much because he was not Jewish but because of his wild views and lack of a traditional career.

Lily raced into the house. "Papa? Mama?" She found her parents sitting in the parlor, their faces grave, with news of their own to share.

"Darling, your mother is sick," Papa had said, his voice breaking.

Lily had rushed to her mother to comfort her. "Surely the doctors can do something?"

Papa shook his head. "It's cancer. There is nothing to be done." Her mother folded into her, and suddenly they had switched places, Lily the one who needed to be strong, who would act and make decisions when her parents could not.

There was never a hopeful moment after that. Lily stayed by her mother's bedside, and two weeks later, the once-vivacious, brilliant woman Lily had idolized was gone. The days which followed were a blur, and only for a second that night as Lily looked out across the starless sky above the harbor did she imagine Matteo waiting for her, wondering why she had not arrived for their scheduled meeting to depart from Belgium. She wished that she had sent word explaining that she was not coming and why. But she had been too caught up in the shock and grief of her mother's sudden diagnosis, and by the time she thought of it, he was already long gone.

Lily never heard from Matteo again. Once he left Antwerp, she had no way to reach him. Why hadn't he come looking for her or at least sent a letter? Perhaps he had been angry. She might have followed him if she had known where to find him. But she couldn't have gone anyway and left her father alone in his grief. She had resigned herself to the fact that she would never see Matteo again and opened her heart to Nik, the doctor treating her father, shortly thereafter. Matteo was gone from her life forever.

Until now.

Though she had not seen him since that spring evening at the canteen, she thought of him ceaselessly. Hannah had not mentioned him again, though, and Lily had not asked. It was just as well. His return to her life could only spell trouble. Not just the feelings he stirred up in her—she could manage those. But Matteo was surely working with the resistance and drawing Hannah in as well. Her cousin didn't think Lily had noticed that she was gone all night and crept in before dawn, nor had seen the anti-Fascist newspapers peeking out from underneath the art supplies in her bedroom. This was about more than just parties now. Hannah had become involved in ways that were dangerous to all of them, and it had to end.

Lily despised conflict, avoided it at all costs. But more than once, she yearned to say something to her cousin, to ask—no, demand—that she stop associating with Matteo and his friends. The risk was simply too great.

Just then Lily noticed a familiar figure across the park. "Hannah!" she called. Her cousin appeared, as if conjured by Lily's thoughts. They were not far from the house, the park on a route they both frequented for errands. It was not so very strange that they should meet here. Still, Hannah turned and her face registered surprise and something else: discomfort maybe, or alarm. "What are you doing?" Lily asked, curious.

"Just out for a walk," Hannah replied, but Lily had seen her purposeful gait as she neared the park. Hannah was doing something more than that. "And some errands. Here," Hannah added, reaching in her pocket and pulling out a small box. Inside was a necklace with a blue stone. "I remembered you having one just like it when you were a girl. You were so upset when you lost it. So when I saw this in one of the shops, I thought of you. Plus it's your birthday next Tuesday."

"Thank you," Lily said, touched that Hannah would remember the necklace and her birthday. She took it from the box and put it on, fumbling with the clasp.

"Let me help," Hannah offered, and Lily turned, lifting her hair from her neck so that Hannah could fasten the clasp for her. "There."

Lilly adjusted the necklace so that the stone was centered. "It's beautiful."

"It's secondhand, I'm afraid. But when I saw it, I thought of you. I've been wanting to get out and find something for your birthday for quite some time, so when you took Georgi this morning, I saw my chance." Lily felt guilty for assuming her cousin had been doing something more suspicious. "I should have waited until your birthday to give it to you, but you know I can never wait."

Lily smiled. "I know. Thank you for the early gift." She had nearly forgotten her own birthday, with all that was going on. Nik would remember, of course, with a cake and a present and flowers. Georgi would surely make her something as well. But Hannah's unexpected gift made this birthday special.

"Look!" Lily pointed to a sparrow flying overhead. "Do you remember?"

"Of course." The summer vacation when the girls were nine, they had found a wounded sparrow lying on the beach. At first, Lily had been afraid to go near the bird, but Hannah had gently lifted it and put it in a box, and together they nursed it back to health. "We called it Estelle." The French name meant *star.*

Georgi walked up then. "What are you talking about?"

"When Tante Hannah and I were about your age, we found a sparrow and nursed it back to health, then set it free."

Hannah frowned. "We didn't nurse it back to health. It died."

"No, we released it into the wild." Lily could see the bird, hovering overhead before flying away once more.

"The bird didn't survive. We buried it in the yard beneath a stone." They stared at one another, puzzled. How was it possible to remember things so differently?

"Tante Hannah, come and catch me!" Georgi called, losing interest in the conversation. He set off across the park, and Hannah followed, chasing him around the fountain and letting him get away for a few seconds, before catching him and tickling him until he squealed. Watching, Lily smiled. She and Hannah might remember the sparrow differently, but it was a memory they shared nonetheless.

"We're going home for lunch," Lily said, when Hannah returned to her side, breathless from the chase. Georgi was playing with his ball by the fountain once more. "Walk with us?" She worried that Hannah might say no and head off on whatever errand she had been running. But her cousin nodded and held out her hand and together they started toward Georgi.

"Mama!" Georgi cried. She looked up to find that his ball had rolled into the street once more. The same German soldier retrieved it, and Lily hurried over. He held it out to her, and his eyes traveled from the star on her dress to the meager satchel of vegetables from the Jewish market which she carried. Something in his expression seemed to harden. She held her breath, waiting for him to hand the ball to her so she could turn and go. For an instant, she thought he might refuse to give it back because he knew that she was a Jew. *One, two…*

The soldier's eyes flickered. Then he handed the ball to her, and it was as if it hadn't happened at all.

10

Hannah

One morning Hannah returned to Lily's house and crept inside before dawn, hoping her cousin would not hear her. She had run another errand to the encampment in the forest to deliver a parcel to Matteo, only this time she had gone alone.

As she washed herself and changed her clothes, Hannah felt a tug of pride that Micheline now trusted her. She thought about how strong and fierce Micheline was. She was not just a helper on the sidelines but led the whole group. Hannah had seen how the volunteers of the Sapphire Line admired her. Though brusque, she had inspired deep devotion. She had a singular sense of purpose, and she approached the work with a passion and intensity that drew others in and made them believe.

Hannah started back downstairs for breakfast, trying to think of an excuse if Lily noticed she had been gone all night. A man, she decided. Promiscuity, though distasteful to her cousin, would surely be more palatable than knowing Hannah had been on an errand for the resistance.

When Hannah entered the dining room, Lily was gone and the breakfast table cleared, save for a plate of toast and marmalade she had left for Hannah. Relieved, Hannah ate alone, then started back upstairs to paint. In the foyer, she stopped. There was an envelope lying on the front table which Hannah had not seen earlier. She went to inspect it more closely and realized it had her name on it, the address typed and formal. That was strange, she thought. There was no one who knew she was here in Brussels, much less who would think to write to her.

Hannah reached for the envelope, then tore it open. It was an *Arbeitseinsatzbefehl*, call-up notice, instructing her to report to the rail station for deportation to a labor camp. At first she froze: Had the authorities realized who she was and that she was here? The order was perfunctory, though, matter-of-fact, listing the time and date she was to report and everything from the sheets to the work boots that she should pack. She had not been called up as a political subversive but an ordinary, non-Belgian Jew. Her blood chilled. She had known about the call-ups and worried that, as a foreigner without permanent papers, she might be susceptible to them. Only she had not imagined it would happen so soon.

Half an hour later, she arrived at the canteen, still shaken. Matteo was there looking equal parts surprised and pleased by her unexpected arrival. Then seeing her expression, his smile faded. "What is it?" he asked.

"Is Micheline here?"

He shook his head. "Away on an errand, I'm afraid. Can I help?"

Hannah handed him the letter. "I've been called up. What am I to do?"

Matteo scanned the order. "You won't go, of course. You'll ignore this like hundreds of other people have."

"Ignore it?" The idea was not one she had really considered. "But what if they come looking for me?"

"They won't." He shook his head firmly. "The Germans are calling up thousands of people, hoping to get a fraction of those. They know not everyone will comply, and they simply don't have the resources to come looking for those who don't. Plus, if you go, it is only a matter of time before they discover who you really are."

And then, Hannah acknowledged, things would be much, much worse. She reread the notice, aghast. They were taking people for labor in the east. "I'm an artist, for goodness' sake. I've never done anything more strenuous than knead clay. Surely they can't mean for me to comply."

"And you won't."

"If only Micheline had arranged for me to go by now..."

"She's working on it," Matteo reassured. "My sister always keeps her word. Not that I want you to leave." He smiled, and Hannah could not tell if he meant it as a joke or genuinely wished she would stay. "You can't use your own identity now that you have been called up, though," he added, his voice turning more serious. "If they run your card, they will know. You were meant to have a new identity anyway for the work you are doing to help us, but I was waiting until we could get you true-false papers." *True-false* meant that the identification papers were actual government-issued documents, procured from a local or state official who was sympathetic to the cause and willing to process them without looking too closely. They were better than forged documents, which might be more easily spotted upon inspection, but harder to get. "They've been delayed because our contact in the mayor's office was nearly arrested and has become too scared to help. Hopefully they will come through soon."

Not soon enough, Hannah thought as she made her way home from the canteen. If only there was another way for her to get papers. *Lily*, she thought suddenly. Lily had worked as a nurse and still helped Nik in his medical clinic from time to time. She had a uniform which hung neatly in her armoire and, Hannah recalled, a separate identification card that gave her medical privileges to move about the city more freely on errands, even now. If only she could borrow those.

The uniform might be too much, but using Lily's identification card, which gave her professional status as a nurse, would be ideal. There was another advantage to masquerading as Lily: her papers showed that she was a Belgian Jew, one who received preferential treatment. It often nagged at Hannah, seemed unfair. Lily had been born elsewhere and come to Belgium the same as she had. Yet somehow because she had done so years earlier and been naturalized as a Belgian citizen, Lily was treated better. Now Hannah could use that difference to help in her work.

Of course, Lily would never agree. Lily didn't even want Hannah involved with the network, much less using her name. But what if she didn't know? Hannah stopped, caught off guard by the idea. She would be stealing her cousin's identity. Not stealing, she corrected herself. *Borrowing.*

Still, to deceive Lily seemed wrong. Hannah felt a tug of guilt. Lily had opened her home to her, given her a place to live. To secretly take her identification card would be a betrayal.

And dangerous. Lily's identification card bore her name and address, and if Hannah was caught using it, she would put Lily and possibly her family on the Germans' radar. That would place them in danger against which even their Belgian citizenship would not be able to protect.

When she returned home from the canteen, Lily was at the table sorting through buttons. "You didn't come home last night," she observed mildly, not looking up.

Hannah ignored the question, which just hours ago seemed so important but now didn't matter at all. "I've been called up."

Lily raised her hand to her mouth. "What ever will you do?"

"Ignore it. Did you expect me to do otherwise?"

She saw the conflict on Lily's face. "No, of course not." Lily was clearly horrified at the notion that her cousin had been called up. At the same time, Hannah sensed that she was weighing the risk to her own family if Hannah did not comply. "You're an artist, a person of importance," Lily said insistently, as if by emphasizing the phrase she could make it true. "Not someone who can just be taken." *No one should be just taken*, Hannah wanted to point out. But she saw that Lily was only trying to help make the news less awful. "Still, if you hadn't been socializing with that lot…" Lily's voice trailed off.

"That lot?" Hearing how Lily referred to Matteo and her other friends, Hannah bristled defensively. "You can't possibly blame my friends for me for getting called up." She felt as though Lily had slapped her.

"No, of course not," Lily retreated quickly. But Hannah saw the message, too big and indelible to be ignored. To Lily there were two kinds of people: *us* and *them*. She had put Hannah in the second category, separate from herself and her family, and Hannah would have to fend for herself because no one else, including her cousin, would do it for her.

Hannah's indignation grew. The call-up notice had come because she was a foreigner and a Jew; it had nothing to do with her social life—or her resistance work. "They called thousands, young people minding their own business…all because they came to Belgium more recently than you and don't have the luxury of pretending," Hannah spat back.

"I'm sorry. That isn't what I meant at all," Lily said, trying to correct the statement but failing.

"You can't keep your head down and hope they won't come for you. Sooner or later they will come for everybody." Hannah walked away, stung by her cousin's allegations. Though Hannah was not averse to conflict, the last thing she wanted to do was quarrel with her cousin, who had done so much for her. She wanted to tell Lily the truth about her work, that what she was doing mattered and might save the lives of thousands if she succeeded. But she could not.

Hannah stormed from the room and up the stairs. On the

landing she stopped, looking through Lily's open bedroom door. There was nothing halfway in this war. She had learned that much in her short time working with Micheline. Hannah's eyes traveled to the armoire in the corner of the room where Lily's nursing uniform hung. She considered again the idea of taking her identification. Her doubts resurged. She didn't like it. It was lying to her cousin who had given her everything. She loved Lily and was so grateful for all that she had done for her, the last thing she wanted to do was to hurt her. But Hannah needed a different identity if she was to help the network and fulfill her promise to Micheline in exchange for help in leaving. She would borrow it just briefly, she decided. She would be careful and not get caught. Then she would return the card, and no one would be the wiser.

Hannah started back down the stairs. Lily's purse sat by the front door. She looked uneasily around the corner, but Lily was engaged in a debate with Georgi over taking his bath. She sidled closer to Lily's purse and felt inside, expecting to be caught at any moment. Lily's nurse identification was in her wallet, along with her regular identification card and other documents. Hannah would just borrow it for a bit. Lily would never miss it—or, at least, she prayed she wouldn't. Hannah slipped the card out and put it into her pocket.

11

Hannah

Hannah crossed the Square du Petit Sablon on a bright spring afternoon, carrying a canvas. More than six weeks had passed since she'd met Micheline and promised to work for her in exchange for help leaving the country. Micheline had called on her for the occasional errand, delivering documents or messages, which she had completed without incident. Having kept up her end of the bargain, Hannah was growing impatient. Micheline had not said anything further about getting her out of Brussels, and Hannah questioned whether she was stalling because she needed her. Or perhaps she simply could not do it.

Then the previous night at the canteen, Micheline had summoned her to the back office.

"We need a message delivered tomorrow."

"Delivered where?"

"The message is going to Our Lady of Victories. Do you know it?" Hannah nodded. She was familiar with the large Gothic church in Sablon Zavel district, close to the city center. "It should be straightforward. Just drop the message in the alms box. I don't like asking while your papers are not in place, but there's no one else."

"I can manage."

Micheline handed her a folded slip of paper. "This contains vital information about a delivery of airmen to a safe house." Hannah was surprised: usually Micheline said nothing about the contents of the messages Hannah carried. She continued. "If discovered, this could cause not only your arrest but the deaths of the very men we are trying to save." It seemed like a simple task, but clearly an important one. Hannah concealed the message in the sleeve of her blouse and then turned and left.

The next morning, Hannah waited until her cousin had left the house, slipping out the back door with the painting so that the maid would not notice. She started down the street, still smelling the just-dried paint, the square edge of the canvas tucked in her palm. It was more conspicuous carrying a large painting across town than simply carrying the papers themselves. But Matteo was right: as an artist, she had an alibi for the painting, and no one would think to search the backing. The canvas seemed to burn red-hot in her hands. She had the perfect explanation, an artist taking her work to sell at the art gallery near the church on the Place du Jeu de Balle.

Hannah neared the open-air market on the square and pretended to study the meager vegetables one of the sellers offered, while peering out beneath the awning at the church. The alms box was affixed just inside the front door of the church. She simply had to cross the square, dislodge the message from the painting and drop it in. What happened from there she did not know. Did a priest take it and deliver it to someone else? Or did he simply leave the box unlocked for someone else to retrieve the message? Though the clergy gave the appearance of neutrality, Hannah had heard stories of heroic acts of rescue and assistance by priests and nuns alike. What if someone else came along to make a donation or even, as sometimes happened, steal from the box and discovered the message?

This was not her problem, though. Her only job was to get the message into the box. Pushing aside her doubts, she started forward. She would need to find a quiet corner, perhaps inside the church, to dislodge the message from the back of the painting. As she neared the building, she stopped in her tracks. There was a German officer, his uniform decorated with the insignia of the *Luftwaffe*, standing near the steps of the church. Normally the presence of a German air officer would not have been very concerning, as they were not the ones who patrolled the streets of Brussels. He might simply be on leave in the city. But Micheline had told her once that the *Luftwaffe* considered hunting down Allied airmen and those who helped them to be their special province. She could not let the message she carried be taken by this man.

"*Guten Tag,*" he said, greeting her in German before she could turn away.

"*Guten Tag,*" she replied, feigning a smile. She started into the church.

"Wait!" She turned back, a pit of dread forming in her stomach. "That painting, may I see it?"

She turned it toward him reluctantly. "It's mine," she said.

"You painted it?" His voice carried an unmistakable note of surprise.

"Yes. Painting is my hobby." It felt odd, but necessary, to downplay her skill.

The German appraised the painting critically. "It is quite good." He had no idea that the painting in fact depicted Matteo, a resistance fighter, on some sort of covert errand. He reached for it. "I'd like to buy it. I can give you five francs." She tensed. "Ten," he said, mistaking her apprehension for offense at the low price. When she did not answer, his face tightened. "Of course, I could just take it." He reached out. It was not a question of price.

She could not let the painting with the secret message hidden inside be confiscated.

She stepped back. "I-it isn't that," she stammered, thinking quickly. "It's just that it's not finished. In fact, I'm taking it to an art-supply shop because I need more paint, and I'm trying to match the color. I would be embarrassed to have this hang in a fine home of the officer of the Reich before it's done. If you wait for the finished work, it will be done in a few weeks."

"Two weeks," he said firmly, then handed her a card. *Gruppenführer Otto Helm*, the name read. *Abwehr.* He was part of the German intelligence service. "Deliver it here, please."

She wanted to tell him that you could not order art like a meal at a restaurant. But the message would be lost on this brute. No, agreeing was her only hope of getting away from this man so there was no point in arguing. "Fine." She had no intention of actually returning with the painting. She started away.

"One more thing." He held out his hand. "Papers, please." His voice now carried an edge.

Dread rose in her. He was not going to let her get away without knowing who she was. She hesitated. Did she dare give him Lily's identification card? She had no other option. She moved slowly, reaching for Lily's card. As the man studied it, she braced for discovery, suddenly mindful of the differences between Lily's image in the photo and her own appearance. Surely he would realize that she wasn't the woman on the card.

She handed him the card. "Nurse…" He said the word as if he didn't believe her.

"Yes. I work with my husband in his clinic, and I'm late, so if you'll excuse me…"

He looked her squarely in the eyes. "I know who you are now, Lily Abels," he said. His voice was menacing and cut through her like a knife. "I'll be seeing you again." The card contained more than Lily's name: it had her home address as well. Using it had been not just foolish but dangerous. Whatever had she been thinking?

"Two weeks." She tucked the painting under her arm and started quickly toward the church door.

Inside, she paused to catch her breath. Her heart raced. At the wide carved entrance, she crossed herself surreptitiously for appearances' sake, feeling as she did the betrayal of her own faith. She stepped inside uneasily. Hannah had never felt comfortable in churches. It wasn't the religious doctrine that offended her; she was not particularly observant as a Jew. But from the high, dark eaves it was as if someone was staring down at her, judging.

She walked to the alms box, but she didn't dare leave the message now. Instead, she fished around in her purse and then slipped a few coins though the slot. They rattled too noisily, echoing off the walls. A man looked up. She sat in a pew for several seconds, pretending to pray. Then she stood and walked through the nave and slipped out the side door. Outside she fought the urge to pick up her pace, keeping her steps even.

She walked away shaken. The encounter had been close—too close. She would have to find another way to deliver the message, and she would tell Micheline she could not undertake any more deliveries until she managed a new identity. She would be angry, but Hannah simply could not risk Lily and her family any more than she already had.

It was late afternoon when she reached the canteen, still carrying the painting. The room on the main floor where they normally gathered was still set from lunch, and Hannah could imagine children laughing over bowls of warm soup. The lingering smell of the tomato broth and cooked vegetables tickled Hannah's nose as she walked down the hallways to the back office.

Matteo sat behind the desk in the office. Seeing her, he stood and smiled warmly. "Hello. Did you deliver the message?"

"I couldn't do it," she said. His brow furrowed. "There was

a German officer standing at the front of the church, and he questioned me about the painting. There was no way I could leave the message in the alms box." She omitted the part about showing the officer Lily's identification card, not wanting to worry him further.

Hannah held her breath, concerned that he would be angry, as Micheline surely would have been. But he nodded and stood. "Come."

"Where are we going?"

"To deliver the message ourselves." He took the painting from her and dislodged the message carefully from the back. Then he took her forearm and led her from the canteen and down the street to a Citroën parked at the curb. He held the passenger-side door open for her.

"Where?" she asked as he started the engine.

"To a safe house outside the city near Bruges."

"But that's so far. My cousin expects me at home within the hour." She was a guest in her cousin's house, and disappearing and worrying her again like she had the night at the encampment would be rude.

"We missed the courier at the church, so there's no other way. If you want to go home, I will take the message myself," Matteo said.

Hannah considered the offer. It would be all too easy to leave the task to him. But it was her errand, and she was the one who had failed. She needed to see it through. Plus, if she was being honest, she did not entirely mind spending the time with him.

"I'll go with you. But I should let my cousin know."

Matteo pulled up at the corner and gestured to a phone booth. Hannah fumbled in her purse for a coin as she climbed from the car.

"Yes?" Lily's voice was harried, and she could hear Georgi fussing in the background. A pang of guilt shot through her. She should have been there to help.

"Lily, it's Hannah. I've run into my friend from the canteen, and he's asked me to have dinner with him." She did not say *coffee* in case the errand took a bit longer.

"Oh." She heard an odd twist in Lily's voice, disapproval maybe, or something else.

"I'll be home late," Hannah added.

There was a pause. "Be careful" was all Lily said before signing off. Hannah climbed back in the car, and they started off once more.

An hour later, Matteo pulled the car along the side of the road, seemingly in the middle of nowhere. The snow was untouched here and so deep it seemed the car might get stuck. He parked in an alcove that obscured the car amid a copse of trees. "Come," he said, and she got out and followed him down a path into the forest, cold seeping through her boots. They reached a small cabin, and he unlocked the door. Inside, it was modestly furnished with a few chairs and a tattered rug, with the feel of a rustic family getaway.

"What now?" She had expected a contact or meeting of some sort. But there was no one there.

"Now we wait." She wanted to ask for whom they were waiting and how long this all might take. But he disappeared outside and returned a moment later with some kindling for the fireplace, making clear that whoever they were waiting for was going to be a while.

Not that she minded entirely, Hannah reflected as she watched him build a fire. Her feelings for Matteo, no matter how hard she tried to deny them, were unmistakable. But he did not seem to notice or return the sentiment. There was something steely and closed-off about him at times. Micheline had mentioned a woman who had broken his heart. It was just as well, she decided. When she had lost Isaac, she had sworn to never love another man and let herself feel pain like that again.

Still, watching him now, she could not help but be curious

about his past. "Do you have family?" she ventured to ask. "Other than Micheline, I mean."

"No, it's just the two of us. Our parents died when Micheline was very young." Though she wanted to ask more about their parents, his clipped tone seemed to fend off any further questions.

"What did you do before the war?"

"I ran guns against Franco," he said. Hannah had heard of young men flocking to Spain to defend against the Fascists, but she had not imagined Matteo to be one of them. "Or do you mean *before* before?" He paused. "I was not a good person before the war," he said, his head hung low. "I had lost my way at university and dropped out. I became a racketeer. Small operations, mind you. Stealing papers, selling things on the black market. Then one day, I supplied some glass jars for medicine that did not really work. On the corner I saw a woman crying. She had used her savings on the fake medicine and would not be able to help her dying mother. It was the low point of my life. I had caused that woman's pain. It was unforgivable."

"And still I did not change," he added. Hannah was surprised. How could one possibly go on after that?

"What happened?" she asked. There had to be something that had brought him to where he was today.

"One day as I was fleeing the police, trying not to get arrested for stealing something, I stumbled upon the fort in the woods and the men who were preparing to resist the Germans. I claimed that I was a resistance fighter, but really I was just looking for a place to hide. But being among those brave men and learning what they were doing, I became genuinely committed to the cause. I changed. It was sheer chance that brought me to the fort as I fled through the woods."

"You still made the choice to change."

"Are you appalled?" There was a catch in his voice, a bit guarded. He tried to sound light.

"A little," she admitted. But it made her feelings no less strong.

Matteo had not been born with a passion for this the way Micheline had. He had come to it, earned it and changed. In some ways that made her respect him more.

"Who I was is not who I am now," he said.

"I understand," Hannah said. She moved closer to comfort him, and he wrapped her in his embrace. They sat silent and motionless for several minutes. She pulled back slightly to look up at him, and their eyes met. "Hannah…" She saw then in his eyes that he had feelings for her and realized how very deeply she cared for him as well.

He kissed her then, tentatively, as if asking a question. Hannah had not been held by a man since Isaac died, and at first the kiss felt alien and strange. She started to pull away. This could not, should not, happen, especially not now, when they were on a dangerous mission and their contact might arrive at any moment. But then her lips responded, and she was kissing him back, drawing him closer. His fingers traced her jawline, then ran down her neck and shoulders.

She leaned back, his hands cradling her head to shield them from the roughness of the floor. Their clothes seemed to peel back then, as if of their own accord. The weight of him atop her was bittersweet, a reminder of the love she had shared with Isaac so long ago. At the same time, it was wholly different, a passion so raw and consuming. She had never felt like this before, and she did not want it to end.

Afterward, as they lay entwined, Hannah tried to process what had just happened. Letting herself get so close to Matteo now was a mistake. Yet even as she thought this, she savored the lingering waves of passion. It was just a moment, she told herself, trying to minimize the magnitude of it and how vulnerable it made her feel.

Matteo pulled away from her and sat up, his head in his hands. "I'm sorry."

"Don't be," she said, trying to make light. "We both had a

part in it." But her heart sank. How could he regret the moment so readily?

"There was someone else," he confessed. "Many years ago. I've never quite freed myself." She understood his message all too clearly: despite the passionate moment they had just shared, his heart still belonged to the woman who had broken it. That explained Matteo's pain which always seemed to be lurking just below the surface. She marveled at a love so deep that it had still left him broken years later.

Broken…and unable to be with her. "I understand." She stood up, buttoning her blouse, feeling foolish and ashamed. He also dressed swiftly. "I should go," she said. Their contact had not arrived, and Hannah had no idea how to make it back to the city on her own. But she simply could not bear to stay here with him a minute more.

"Hannah." Matteo reached up for her, as if to stop her from going. She hoped for a moment that he might change his mind and admit that this was something more. But as he pulled her back to the ground, she understood why. There was a noise outside the cabin. The person to whom they were delivering the message had arrived.

"I need to give the all clear." He stood and walked to the door. But as he was about to open it, there was a loud cracking sound outside. Gunfire. Whoever had come to meet them must have been followed.

"Quickly!" He grabbed her and dragged her to the back of the cabin. There did not seem to be another door, and she worried that they were trapped. He led her to cellar stairs hidden behind the fireplace, closing the door behind them after she had gone down. Below there was a small crawl space and a tunnel that led away from the cabin, so narrow they had to squeeze through crouched and single file.

The tunnel ended about fifteen meters from the cabin. They knelt in the dark underground space, their bodies pressed close out of necessity and not passion now. Above, Hannah heard someone rustling in the cabin, the fire they had built a dead giveaway of their presence. Whoever had come would find the tunnel.

But a few minutes later, the cabin door slammed shut once more. Matteo led her farther down the tunnel, then stopped before a series of notches in the wall that seemed to form a make-shift ladder. Matteo scampered up it to the top of the tunnel and cleared an opening above them, revealing a hole that she had not previously seen. He climbed through the hole to the ground above, brushing back the snow, and then reached in to help her. They were outside, well behind the cabin. Her hair and clothes were caked with dirt from the tunnel. The woods were silent. Matteo gestured her to stay back as he crept closer to the cabin. On the ground a few meters from the cabin door lay a wounded man Hannah recognized from the canteen.

Matteo knelt beside him, checking his wounds, which bled into the snow. "Go get the car," he instructed, tossing her the key. "Bring it as close as you can." Hannah raced through the woods to the spot where he had parked, terrified that she herself might be shot or caught at any second. The icy air burned her lungs. She started the ignition, hesitating before putting the headlights on. She steered the car carefully through the trees toward Matteo and the wounded man.

Before she neared the cabin, she heard the unmistakable cracking of gunfire once more.

She gunned the engine and pulled up just in time to see Matteo falling to the ground in a halo of yellow light.

12

Lily

A loud knock jarred Lily from sleep. She sat up, feeling for Nik in the space beside her, but instead her hand rested on Georgi who had come in unnoticed in the middle of the night. Nik was already up, tending to whatever was transpiring below. Was it the Germans? Though Lily never expected to leave, she had begun packing things in a bag under the bed just in case. Her hand reached for the bag now instinctively.

She drew her robe more tightly around herself to ward off the chill that seemed to be ever present with the cheaper oil they had to use now to heat the water for the radiators. The voices below were urgent, but not hostile. Quickly so as not to wake Georgi, she dressed and started down the stairs, inhaling the lingering pine scent of the fir sprigs she had used to make the house festive for the holidays, though they did not celebrate Christmas.

On the landing, she stopped, still out of sight. Hannah was saying something to Nik. Alongside Hannah's voice she heard another. *Matteo*. The realization that he was in her house stopped

Lily cold. Since seeing him at the gathering with Hannah, she had managed to avoid him and not cross paths. To know that he was here in the same city was one thing. Now her former lover was here, unannounced, in the very house she shared with her husband and child. Lily felt violated.

Taking a breath to compose herself, she continued down the stairs. Hannah stood in the doorway. Behind her was Matteo. As she stepped into view, her eyes locked with his, and the world froze. Everything else faded away, and there were just the two of them.

"Lily," he breathed, the shock on his face impossible to hide. There was a gash on his forehead, as though he had been wounded.

"Mattie," she said, inadvertently using her pet name for him.

"You know each other?" Nik asked.

Matteo opened his mouth to reply, but no sound came out. He seemed unable to speak, the words cut out from under him. "We are acquaintances from a long time ago, in Antwerp," Lily jumped in. Of course they were much more than that, but this was hardly the time to explain. Hannah squinted her eyes, and Lily was unsure if she believed the explanation. "So very nice to see you again." Lily could feel Hannah watching, quickly putting the pieces together.

Hannah turned to Nik. "We have a man outside, wounded. Can you see him in the clinic?"

"Of course," Nik replied without hesitation. "Bring him around."

Hannah and Matteo disappeared through the door, Nik following closely behind. Lily went through the house to unlock the exterior door of the small office Nik kept at the rear of the house. It was spartan, with just an examining table and a chest of supplies. They had only meant it for occasional use, but Nik saw patients there daily since he had been dismissed from the university and Jews had been denied treatment at hospitals and other doctors' offices.

Lily opened the door to the clinic. Between them, Matteo and Hannah held a man who was nearly unconscious. The front of his shirt was torn open and stained red from a gunshot wound to his stomach. They managed to get him into the clinic and, with Nik's help, onto the examining table. Blood seeped from his clothing onto the white sheet.

"What happened?" Nik asked.

Matteo shook his head. "Best that you don't know too much. But we were to meet him at a safe house, and someone followed him there. He was shot."

"When I saw you go down, I thought you were hit as well," Hannah interjected, her voice still heavy with worry.

Matteo shook his head. "I dropped low when I heard the second shot, and it fortunately missed and hit a tree behind me. I was just grazed by some shrapnel." Lily felt her own sense of relief that Matteo had not been badly injured. "But Tomas was shot, and we had to wait until we were sure the forest was clear before bringing him to you. He's lost a lot of blood," he added, turning to Nik. "Hannah said you are an excellent doctor. Please, you must help him."

Nik studied the man's wound. "He should be in a hospital." Of course, that was impossible. The Germans watched them closely for just this sort of thing. He looked up at her. "Darling, some liquor please."

Lily ran back into the house to the liquor cabinet in the dining room. Nik was not a big drinker in normal times, but he had taken to having a cocktail with his evening pipe to counter his depression and the stress of the occupation. Their liquor supplies had dwindled, and replacements were scarce. The only thing left was a bottle of cognac they had been given as a wedding present and were saving for their upcoming tenth anniversary. It was all they had, though, and she hesitated just a second before grabbing it. Breaking the seal and spoiling the promise of a future celebration felt like an ominous sign.

Lily returned to the clinic and handed Nik the bottle. "I need more antibiotics," he said. The very thing the clinic had run out of the day before. "We must try the pharmacy, at least."

"I'll go," said Lily, eager to escape. She walked through the house and grabbed her coat before stepping onto the street. The pharmacy at the corner was dark and shuttered at this hour: Nik meant for her to wake the pharmacist. Lily hesitated for a beat, then rang the bell alongside the shop door, the one that rang in the pharmacist's apartment above.

A minute later, the door opened, and the pharmacist, an earnest young man, appeared. He had recently taken over the shop from his father. Lily did not know him as well as she had the older man, but his expression was neither alarmed nor annoyed. Clearly, it was not the first time he had been awakened in the middle of the night for help. "My husband, Dr. Nik Abels, sent me. He needs antibiotics." A knowing look passed over the pharmacist's face, and for a moment, Lily thought he might refuse or, worse yet, report her. But he disappeared, and a few minutes later produced a small vial. "I'm afraid that's all I can spare." He accepted only half of the coins she offered.

Lily rushed back and handed the vial to Nik. "That's it?" he asked with a note of dismay.

"I'm afraid so." She stayed close as he tended to the wounded man in case he needed her help. She had assisted Nik many times with surgeries over the years, and they moved in a familiar, coordinated way, like two limbs of the same body. She was surprised to see Hannah turn away. She had not imagined her cousin to be squeamish about the sight of blood. Matteo stood on the other side of Tomas, holding his hand. Lily could feel him watching her but tried to avoid his gaze.

There was a clinking sound as Nik dropped the shrapnel in the metal pan. He proceeded to close and dress the wound. "He won't need further surgery, thankfully. But he has to rest. Do you have somewhere safe?"

Matteo shook his head. "Not after tonight." Lily wanted to know what had caused the man's injury and how Hannah had been involved. Matteo continued. "Our only hope would be to reach an encampment outside the city. But we wouldn't make it through the checkpoints."

"He would never survive the trip," Nik fretted. "He will need to rest here for a while, then."

Lily pulled Nik aside. "Do you really think that is wise?" she asked in a low voice. "He was clearly doing some sort of resistance work, and if the Germans find out we are harboring him, they will arrest us all." Treating the man was one thing, hiding him for an extended period quite another.

"If we put him out now, he will bleed to death." Nik's voice was steely, his expression resolved. Nik had always been a devoted doctor, but how could he risk their safety for this man? Though Lily loved her cousin, she wished for the hundredth time that Hannah had not come and brought such disruption and danger to their world.

"He is going to need more antibiotics than the pharmacist gave us," Nik added.

"The pharmacist said that was all he could spare."

"I can get some from my old office at the university hospital."

"Darling, you aren't permitted," Lily said. "It isn't safe."

But Nik would not be dissuaded where saving a life was involved. "I have to go get the medicine, but we need to be swift." He turned to Matteo and Hannah. "You have a car?"

"Yes, but…" Matteo looked at the wounded man, not wanting to leave him.

"I can take Nik," Hannah interjected. "You stay here."

"I shall," Matteo said, "and please phone Micheline, if you can, to let her know where we are and what happened."

Lily opened her mouth, but no sound came out. Being left alone with Matteo was unfathomable. But before she could think of a reason to object to the plan, Nik picked up his medical bag, and he and Hannah were gone.

She looked over the injured man at Matteo, noticing once more the gash on his forehead. "You're bleeding." She reached out without thinking. For a second, he pulled back. Then he let her examine the gash.

"I'm fine," he said. His breath was warm on her cheek as she leaned close to clean the wound. He cringed as she bandaged the wound, but whether from pain or her touch she could not say.

"There. Nik can look at it when he returns."

"Your husband is a very good doctor."

She wondered if Matteo was as uncomfortable discussing her husband as she was. "He is a very good man." She loved Nik. Matteo being here might complicate things, but it did not change that.

"Is that why you never came?" Matteo asked. "Because of him?"

She paused, caught off guard. "No, I met him after." Was that true? The timeline was jumbled like scenes from a movie she could not put in place. "The night before I was supposed to leave with you, I learned that my mother was sick. After my mother died, I couldn't leave my father." She was all her father had left in the world. Her place had been with him. So she had abandoned Matteo and walked away from that whole life, from the promise of seeing distant lands and living wild adventures. And then Nik had come and cared for her father and loved her, given her a safe and beautiful home as the last of her childhood disappeared forever. She had never looked back.

Until now. Now her whole past loomed before her, demanding answers she did not have. "When I saw you at the canteen…" She paused, realizing her mistake.

"You knew I was here? Why didn't you say anything?" His face registered disbelief.

Why, indeed? Because she had hoped that, by not speaking

aloud the fact that Matteo was back or making contact with him, she might avoid acknowledging all of the feelings that realization brought with it.

But it had not, and he was here before her, demanding answers. "I didn't want to complicate your life or mine."

There was a moment's silence between them. "Tell me about your life after you left," she said finally. She yearned to know what had happened, like discovering there was a sequel to a book she finished long ago.

"I traveled for a while, and then I came back to care for my sister. Later I went to Spain to fight Franco, and I was badly wounded." He held up his arm to reveal a scar running the length of the underside. "When I was strong enough, I made my way back to Belgium and connected with the resistance, which was just forming. We are a small organization under the Front d'Indépendance. Then Micheline joined me."

"You two are close."

"Neither of us has anyone else." The words hung between them, an accusation. Lily shifted uneasily. "We've both been through a lot. We believe in the same things."

"She doesn't like me, though," Lily said wryly.

Matteo did not deny it. "She doesn't want me to get hurt again." There was an unmistakable note of recrimination in his voice. "I always hoped I might see you once more—even though you didn't want to hear from me."

"That isn't true," she replied.

"You didn't come to meet me. You never told me why."

"I always thought…" *That you would come for me.* She was unable to finish the sentence.

"But I did. I sent letters, more than one, telling you that I would come back if you still wanted me."

"I never received them." They stared at one another, genuinely puzzled. Had her father, wanting someone else for her, kept the letters from Lily? He made no secret of his dislike for Matteo.

He thought she deserved someone traditional, more successful. She had always wanted to know what had happened. She saw it clearly now. Matteo thinking she had abandoned him; Lily having no idea. What might the other life have looked like if they had found one another?

Then she looked around the clinic, through the door to her home on the other side. Guilt rose, eclipsing the possibilities. She had Nik and Georgi now, a family that loved and counted on her. That was more than enough.

Between them, the wounded man stirred. Matteo turned toward him, the lines in his brow deepening with consternation. He reached for the bottle of liquor Lily had brought Nik earlier and poured some onto a cloth, holding it up to the man's lips. The man gagged and spat. But then as the strong liquid went down, he seemed to ease into a bit of sleep.

"I never expected to see you again," Matteo said. "Especially not here of all places with Hannah."

"You didn't know?"

"How could I?" He shook his head, his eyes sincere. "I had left you in Antwerp, and I had no idea you'd moved to Brussels. Hannah said that her cousin was named Lily. There was so much else going on, though, that I didn't give it much thought. And then I walked in tonight and saw you..." He, too, was as perplexed by the odd twist of fate. "Anyway, I met your cousin, and here we are."

"Yes." Far more than a casual meeting, their lives were now inextricably intertwined. "I think she cares for you." The words slipped out too easily, a betrayal of Hannah she had not intended. "Do you have feelings for her as well?" Lily hated how jealous her question sounded. Of course, she did not mean it that way. She had no claim or hold on a man she had not seen for nearly a decade. Rather, she wanted to know that his feelings for her cousin were real and that he would not hurt her.

"I like her," he admitted. "A lot." He had stopped short, she noticed, of saying he loved her. "I thought I might have a real chance at being happy again. Only now…" He gestured his hand between the two of them. "Knowing you are here… I couldn't possibly."

Lily decided to change the subject. "I worry about Hannah working with your group. She's reckless and headstrong."

"Your cousin is strong," he corrected. "She is what you should have been."

"How dare you judge me?" she asked indignantly.

Between them, the wounded man groaned in pain again. Lily went to feel his brow at the same moment that Matteo reached out, and their fingers brushed. "Lil," he said, almost pleadingly. He was the only one who had called her that.

He reached for her, and she pulled back instinctively. A voice inside of her screamed for her to run. But her hand reached out as if by its own accord, taking his. Their fingers laced, the electricity surged like a current between them. Her head swam, and she fought for breath. This was wrong. She was in the very house she shared with her husband and son, and holding hands was a betrayal, not just because of where it could lead but also because of all that it represented.

"Matteo, please," she said, begging him to be strong where she could not. But he took her plea as something else entirely and leaned in closer, lips nearing hers. She was frozen, unable to move away.

Just then, there was a creaking noise outside the door. "They're back," she said, pulling away, equal parts regretful and relieved. Though just over an hour had passed, it felt like much longer.

"Meet me," he said, his voice urgent.

"What?" Lily prayed that she had heard him wrong.

"Tomorrow. Meet me. Just to talk," he added.

"I can't. My family—"

"Please. We can't leave it like this, not again."

There were footsteps in the hallway now, Hannah's and Nik's, growing louder as they neared. Lily was eager for them to arrive so she could escape. At the same time, she wished to freeze time and live in this moment forever. "I will be at the café on Square de l'Aviation tomorrow at three," he whispered. She knew the place, public but out of the way, discreet. "Come if you can."

Before she could reply, the door opened, and Hannah rushed in, followed by Nik. "How is he?" she asked.

"The same."

Nik rushed to check the wounded man. A moment later Lily heard more footsteps outside the doorway. Lily started, worrying that the police had somehow found them or followed them here. A young woman appeared, pushing past Hannah and into the clinic. Though she had never met her during her relationship with Matteo so many years ago, Lily knew instantly by the resemblance that it was his younger sister, Micheline. The woman Hannah spoke of with such reverence was in fact barely more than a girl.

"Teo?" Micheline looked from the bed to the chair where her brother sat. Her body relaxed with relief. "Oh, thank God! I heard someone was injured, and I thought it was you. What happened?"

"I wasn't able to leave the message in the alms box because there was a German officer near the church," Hannah explained. "So Matteo and I tried to complete the errand ourselves and meet Tomas. Someone must have followed him." Lily could tell that Hannah was being purposefully vague about what she had been doing because she was speaking in front of her and Nik. But she could glean enough to know that it was something for the resistance and that it was dangerous enough to get a man shot. What in God's name had Hannah been thinking?

Micheline started forward, her concern now focused on the man on the bed. "Tomas is one of our best men. What happened? Will he be all right?" Her questions were rapid-fire.

"Still sleeping, but his heartbeat is strong," Nik replied. "He'll make it."

"He's getting the best care," Lily interjected. Of course, this was untrue. The best care would have been in a hospital with sterile equipment and good technology, but that was impossible.

"Lily's right," Matteo added. "The doctor is doing everything he can."

Hearing Lily's name, a light of recognition dawned in Micheline's eyes. Her head turned in Lily's direction. Her eyes locked with Lily's for a fleeting second, and Lily hoped she would not realize who she was. But the daggers she stared indicated that she knew—and remembered everything. "Lily from Antwerp?"

"Michou…" Matteo said pleadingly, begging her to leave it alone. "Not now."

Micheline seemed to blink back her anger. "The message, give it to me." She held out her hand low to Matteo, and he passed her a slip of paper. "We have to go," Micheline said. "There are police looking for us. I've secured a safe house on the outskirts of the city and arranged a car to take Tomas there."

"I'll help you get him to the car," Nik offered.

"Thank you." Matteo shook Nik's hand. Lily's worlds collided, and her breath stopped. Together Matteo and Nik lifted the wounded man and carried him with effort from the room, Micheline and Hannah following behind. Lily did not look up as Matteo turned back to her one last time, silently entreating her to meet him.

And then he was gone.

She sat alone in the empty clinic for several minutes. Matteo's unexpected appearance and the feelings it had brought ricocheted around her head. And she had agreed to see him again. What on earth had she been thinking? Her life, well-ordered just a few hours earlier, now seemed thrown into chaos.

Nik returned, pulling her from her thoughts. "They're gone." He crossed the room and put his arms around her.

She looked up at him. "The man, will he be all right?"

"I hope." His words stopped short of a promise. "Hannah's friends, the man who brought him here and the woman who came after...you knew them?"

"The woman I never met. Her brother I knew briefly in Antwerp when I was much younger." Lily hated lying to him, but it would be too hard to explain to her husband what had been between her and Matteo. Seemingly satisfied with the explanation, he started to clean up the instruments he had used to treat Tomas.

"I'll do that," Lily offered. "You must be exhausted."

"I am," he admitted. "Are you certain?"

Lily nodded. It wasn't as though she could sleep anyway. "You go to bed. I'll finish and join you shortly." He kissed her on the cheek and then started for the stairs.

After Nik left, Lily began to clean up the soiled sheets and towels. When she had finished, she left the clinic and returned to the house. The night had passed, and it was too late for sleep, so she busied herself with a half-dozen tasks, preparing cereal for breakfast, organizing bandages for the clinic. All the while, she tried to push thoughts of seeing Matteo again from her mind.

Hannah appeared at breakfast, freshly dressed. Seeing her, Lily was thrown back to the previous night. She gestured angrily toward the clinic. "This, this is what you've been doing?" she demanded. She was unchained now, all pretense of civility gone. "You might have been wounded as well."

"I'm fine," Hannah said dismissively.

"You aren't, and neither are we. If you keep this up, you are going to get us all arrested."

"You care nothing about the lives of those who fight for us," Hannah accused.

"I care about the safety of my family," Lily said defiantly. "Your actions are risking that."

"Then, I'll go."

"No," Lily said softly to her cousin. The truth was Lily loved having Hannah in her life again. With Hannah here, she somehow felt stronger and less alone. It was the one thing she needed, though she hadn't known it at all. Despite everything, she did not want her cousin to leave. "Stay. But please be careful."

The two spoke no more about it over breakfast. Georgi came down late. His hair was tousled and his eyes still thick with sleep. "There were people in the clinic last night," he said, his brow wrinkled with confusion.

Lily had not realized that her son had woken during the night. How much had he heard? "Just a patient who needed urgent care from Papa," she explained.

"But Papa wasn't there, just you and a stranger. Who is that man you were talking to last night, Mama?"

She considered telling Georgi that it had been a dream, but she did not want to lie to him.

Her eyes met Hannah's uneasily across the table. "He was no one, darling. No one at all."

13

Micheline

It was nightfall when she reached Amsterdam.

Micheline stepped off her motorbike. Her pants were tucked in her boots, and dust covered her cloak. She had slipped across the Dutch–Belgian border by cover of darkness through a wooded route known only to her, stealthy as a cat. She made her way as she always did to one of the rail stations in Osdorp, a suburb of the Dutch capital. Boarding there and taking a local train would attract less attention than entering the city directly. When she reached the small station, she hid her motorbike in a cluster of trees and walked to the platform.

Micheline boarded the arriving train and moved swiftly toward the center railcar as was her habit. The middle was the least likely part of the train to get hit during a bombing raid. Plus, it provided the most time to react should the Germans board and start inspecting papers. She found a compartment that was empty except for a sleeping businessman. She would have preferred to stand in the corridor, or at least find a carriage to herself, but she didn't want to attract attention as a woman traveling alone.

Micheline was going to Amsterdam to meet with Pascal's contact, the Frenchman who might be able to help with resources for the line. Though she had resisted the meeting for some time, she had finally acquiesced. The Sapphire Line simply did not have the resources, volunteers, safe houses or money to keep up with the growing number of airmen in need of evacuation. A new contact, who had donors willing to help their efforts, might be just what the line needed.

As the train clacked through the Amsterdam suburbs toward the city, Micheline's mind reeled back to a few nights earlier, Tomas lying wounded in the medical clinic. She had received word before leaving today that he should survive. *Should* survive. There were so many uncertainties in this line of work.

The train neared the capital. The houses on either side became more congested, replaced by sloping buildings that seemed to lean upon one another. Micheline did not ride the train all the way to Amsterdam Centraal but got off a few stops early and made her way to the city center by foot, navigating through the throngs of pedestrians taking advantage of the warm summer evening.

She passed a park that had a public toilet, and checking to make sure no one noticed, she slipped inside to change. Micheline was like a chameleon, Matteo had joked more than once. Normally she wore schoolgirlish clothes in order to pass on the street without suspicion. But today her look was designed to blend in with the other women in the café, a sophisticated but understated dress, high heels and stockings with a seam up the back.

She walked to the entrance of the Café Grand, a modest establishment along one of the canals in the tightly packed Jordaan district. From the doorway, live music blared. The café harkened back to happier times, with a small band playing in the corner and a case of mouthwatering cakes in the front. Of course, it was all for show. Here, as in Brussels, the markets were largely empty, and the ordinary people suffered daily hardships of hunger and other deprivation. The Germans kept a few nice spots open in the crown jewel cities like Paris and Amsterdam so they could take dates there and show off as if nothing had changed at all.

Micheline spied a woman with too much makeup sitting close to a German officer. *Collaborator,* she spat inwardly, scarcely able to mask her disdain. Who were these people? she wondered, not for the first time. Locals who drank and dined elbow to elbow with the enemy as though there was not a war raging outside. Was it actual complicity, or a desire to stick one's head in the sand and pretend that the war did not exist?

She did not see any *Gestapo,* although this was not entirely reassuring: they could be wearing civilian clothing. She crossed the café, her head high. Her reflection flashed across the mirrored walls. Her normally wild red hair was swept up into a sophisticated knot, and her dress was the latest style. It was as if she was someone else entirely.

Across the café, she spied a familiar figure at a table. Pascal. The former seminarian seemed out of place in the chic space, and she suspected that the choice of location was not his but his contact's. Men often wanted to meet in restaurants and bars, amid the wine and food. Micheline found it too visible, the bill of their meal easy to trace. But she had learned that giving people a little bit of control made it easier for her to take charge of the overall situation, and so she acquiesced.

She started toward Pascal's table, then stopped short. There was a man sitting next to him, older and too formally dressed in a silk cravat and scarf. Micheline was generally wary of new people, especially those that she herself had not vetted. Something about this man, though, made her particularly uncomfortable.

Leave, her instincts wailed. But it was too late now. Pascal had spied her and was gesturing her over. The other man had clearly seen her as well. He was slight and sinewy with a mustache and pale blond hair. He stood as she approached and gave a slight bow. Pascal remained seated. "Micheline, may I introduce Monsieur Anton Labeau from Paris." The name was not familiar to Micheline. The stranger held out his hand, and she took it reluctantly. His fingers were cool and limp to the touch. He raised her hand to his mouth, but she pulled back before he could kiss it. She noticed that his front teeth were capped in gold.

Micheline tried not to recoil further as the man pulled out her chair and put his hand on the small of her back with a too-familiar gesture, urging her to sit. This was the business, though: smile and get them to do what you needed them to do, to tell you what you needed to know. She sat down and looked at Monsieur Labeau squarely.

"There is a group of airmen in need of rescue," he announced without pleasantries.

Micheline was caught off guard. Matteo had said that Pascal's contact might be able to help them. Instead, he was asking for her to take on a mission. "Why did I not receive the request directly?" she demanded. Usually news of downed airmen came from the British government through the radio or other established channels.

"The request came from Bellweather."

Micheline's eyes narrowed. Bellweather was a separate network in France. Why were they asking Sapphire to take this on? "I don't like it." Accepting airmen from insecure sources was one of their greatest vulnerabilities. "Who's the contact?"

"Marceau Benoit." Micheline had never heard the name, but that was not unusual. At least a half-dozen or so separate networks running escape routes out of Europe had sprung up since the start of the war, and outside of her own there were many people that even she did not know.

"You said a group of airmen. How many?"

"Six."

Micheline tried to conceal her surprise. She had rescued two or three before, and it had been much harder than transporting a single airman because it was so hard to blend in. Six was more than they had ever attempted at once. "How is that possible?"

"A single downed aircraft near Leiden. They've been brought across the border at Maastricht and are hiding in a deserted barn in the woods near Lafelt. You know it?"

Micheline nodded. "So we have to get them over the Pyrenees?"

"Five of them, yes. But one is wounded, too sick to go that far. He would never make it." She nodded. The Pyrenees crossing was treacherous under normal conditions, and it would be impossible for one who was ill or wounded. "I will arrange for those who are able to be brought to Brussels and escorted to Gare du Midi."

"Not Gare Centrale?" She was puzzled by the change from their usual point of embarkation.

"Not this time."

"Why the switch?"

Monsieur Labeau shrugged. "Why anything? I don't set the plans. I just relay them." She wanted to press further but could tell from his brusque tone that he would offer nothing more. The changed location was odd, but not so odd that she would balk and compromise the extraction. "I will personally escort the five from there to Paris. I need you to get the other one who is recuperating close to the German border." Micheline understood then why he needed her to help. The border region between Belgium and Germany had gone back and forth between the two countries throughout the centuries. Though it was part of Belgium since after the Great War, it was home to a great many ethnic Germans, some of whom were sympathetic to the Reich. This made it one of the most dangerous areas from which to extract airmen. The Sapphire Line was the best established in the region and most capable of taking on the dangerous plan.

"What do you want me to do with him once I have him?"

"Hide him until he is well enough for us to evacuate from Europe."

"Depending upon the extent of his injuries, that could take months."

"You could take him to the encampment," Pascal offered. Micheline hated that he spoke of the camp, the heart of their covert operations, in front of this stranger. At least he had not mentioned its location.

"These airmen, have they been screened?" she demanded. The network required downed airmen to be vetted for authenticity before being evacuated. Each one had to go through a thorough background check. It was a cumbersome but necessary step to ensure that they were not spies pretending to be downed airmen in order to infiltrate the network and find its safe houses and helpers.

"Of course," Monsieur Labeau said. She did not believe him but had no way of proving otherwise. "You will be well-compensated, by the way. My contacts can pay fifteen thousand francs. So you'll do it?"

"Yes." Micheline rescued airmen out of a sense of duty. But she was not too proud to accept the money much needed to run the line. "Am I to go now?"

"No," Pascal replied. "The wounded airman isn't strong enough to walk. He needs a few days to recover where he is. I will send word when it is time to go."

"I have a new guide who can join you at the station and help take the others south," Micheline said, a plan forming as she spoke it aloud. She was going to try again to make good on her promise to find a way to get Hannah out of the country. Micheline had tried several times to arrange for Hannah's departure, without success. It was harder than she had imagined to move a Jewish civilian, much less a wanted woman, out of occupied Belgium. All of her most promising leads had fallen through. But she was hopeful that Pascal's contact, in addition to offering resources, might have a way to help Hannah leave. Micheline hated to lose Hannah now that she knew how good she was, but she would keep her word.

Of course, she would not ask Monsieur Labeau for help getting Hannah out directly. Instead, Micheline would make her part of the solution.

"And then?"

She swallowed. "And then she will continue on to America." The answer had been there all along, so simple she had almost missed it. Hannah would escort the group of airmen to the border, only she wouldn't come back. She would keep going. "This particular woman needs get to America." She met his eyes squarely.

"You want me to extract a civilian, a woman?"

Micheline's anger flared. It was typical for a man like Labeau to look down on a woman. He would never see Hannah, or any woman, for the strong, intelligent fighter that she was. "It's important that she escape safely." Micheline wanted to tell him that she was not just a fugitive, but a woman wanted by the Reich for her political satire, but she did not dare say that in front of the newcomer.

"Now, now," Pascal intervened. "This woman can serve as cover for the airmen. A group of men traveling together will raise suspicion. But if she escorts one of them to the train, less so." Micheline appreciated his support but resented needing a man to reinforce her position. Why should the opinion of a junior aide carry more weight, simply because he was a man?

"You need my help. This is the price," she insisted. "This—and the fifteen thousand francs."

Monsieur Labeau hesitated, and she was certain he would refuse. Finally, he let out a long breath, almost a whistle. "Have her meet us at Gare du Midi, and we will get her out as well."

"If you'd like, I can help arrange papers onward for her in

Spain," Monsieur Labeau offered. For a moment, Micheline felt a flash of gratitude toward the newcomer. This was quickly replaced by doubt: no one helped without a reason.

"I will be well-paid by the British for the extraction," Labeau said, seeming to read her thoughts and making the scope of his interest clear. She hated mercenary people like this man almost as much as those who stood aside and did nothing. But he could deliver what she needed, and she did not have the time to quibble over his values. They would work with him on this one mission, and if he was not worthy, they need not trifle with him again. Except, there was no room for missteps or second chances in this work. She appraised him and decided he was just one of those bottom-feeders who profited off the war and went to the highest bidder. He was theirs—at least for now.

"I will rescue the injured airman," Micheline said. "And I will send the woman to the station to go with the others."

"Very well, then." Monsieur Labeau waved his hand dismissively. "Just make sure it all works."

"It will work," Micheline said icily. "It always does with me."

14

Hannah

Hannah was working on the painting once more. She had stayed up late the previous night and had nearly finished it. She felt a note of genuine pride. It was a good painting, one that had taken her longer than she expected to complete. She remembered the German officer and his instruction that she deliver the piece to him. She hoped that it had just been a passing interest and that he would have forgotten by now.

She put down her paintbrush reluctantly and went to the basin to freshen up and smooth her hair. Then she started out to the canteen. It was a cloudy spring day, the thick moist air carrying the promise of a storm. Micheline had summoned her, for another errand she assumed. It was the first time she had heard from Micheline or Matteo in the nearly two weeks since they had brought the injured fighter to Lily's house. She had started to go with them when they took him to the safe house, but Matteo had shooed her away. "It's too dangerous. You stay here." She had hoped that she might hear from him after that, but she had not. The nightly gatherings had ceased now too, since things had become more dangerous.

When she reached the canteen, Matteo was just leaving, coat buttoned high and a plaid scarf tucked beneath his chin. His hair, usually askew, was neatly combed. Seeing him, longing rose in her. She had hoped that the passion between them was real. But Matteo seemed distant, as if he regretted what had happened, or at least had no intention of letting it happen again.

Now Matteo smiled as she approached. "Hello…" His greeting was friendly, nothing more. The gash on his forehead was almost healed, a faint red line marking the spot where it had been.

"Your sister summoned me," Hannah offered. "Tomas. How is he doing?"

"Healing slowly. A bit better every day." An awkward silence passed between them.

"Hannah, is that you?" Micheline called from the back office.

"Yes, coming." Hannah walked to the office, still puzzled by Matteo's cool demeanor.

"I have a job for you," Micheline said brusquely from behind the desk, not bothering with greetings, as was her custom.

Hannah hesitated. Her encounter with the German, followed by the resistance worker being shot, had made the danger seem all the more real, the stakes higher. Of course, she still could not refuse to help. "What is it?"

"I need you to meet a group of airmen at the rail station and escort them to France."

Hannah's heartbeat quickened. Micheline was asking her for the first time to undertake the real work of the escape route. She had thought Micheline considered her too weak. Now she was finally being given real responsibility. "I'm picking up one of the other airmen from the group who was wounded and is too weak to travel," Micheline added. "I'm taking him to the camp to hide."

"What am I to do once we reach the station?"

"Get on the train and go south with the airmen across the border to Spain."

"Leave Belgium?" Hannah scarcely believed the words as she spoke them. "You mean, for good?"

Micheline nodded. "Just as I promised. It's all been arranged. Go to Gare du Midi today just before five o'clock. You will see a group of airmen, dressed in plain clothes on platform three. You are to join them, board the train and accompany them over the border. Here." She thrust the papers at Hannah. "You can use these to get across France and into Spain. A visa will be waiting for you at the British consulate allowing you transit to America. After that, you're on your own." Micheline was handing her freedom, fulfilling her end of the bargain.

Hannah stared at the papers, still not quite believing it. "Really?"

"Pack no more than you would for a short weekend trip. You will see a convoy of airmen changing trains. They won't be walking together, but spread out with a few meters between them. But you will be able to tell by their short hair that they are military. Join the very last soldier as if you are greeting him."

"Will he know?"

"I doubt it. But if you say the word *sapphire*, he will recognize that you are part of the network, or at least he should. You are to board the train south with them. Do you understand?" Hannah nodded. "That is all. You're leaving, so go." Micheline turned away, her voice hardened.

Hannah was perplexed. Micheline had arranged her safe passage and kept her part of the bargain. But she seemed angry at Hannah now for taking it. And if Hannah was to be perfectly honest, going did not feel quite right to her either. "You know, I could stay if you wanted. Help a little longer."

"We need you," Micheline admitted, then shook her head. "But this is what you wanted. What you were meant to do. And it is likely your only chance."

"Matteo…you'll tell him after." Hannah found the notion of leaving without saying goodbye unbearable. But she knew that if she saw him again, she might decide not to leave at all.

"Yes. I will take care of him. I swear it." Micheline took her cloak from the coat stand in the corner and put it on. She held out some coins. "For the train ticket."

"Thank you," Hannah said. The words, which seemed inadequate, were all she could manage.

Micheline nodded. "Godspeed." Hannah wanted to stay longer, but she knew there was nothing more to say.

With a confusing mix of sadness and excitement, Hannah left the canteen and started in the direction of Lily's house. She dreaded saying goodbye to her cousin, and not just because of the many questions Lily would ask about her departure. The two women had become close in the time since Hannah had arrived, recapturing their childhood bond that Hannah had thought was gone forever. She did not want to lose that again.

When Hannah reached the house, it was still, except for Georgi's high-pitched voice from the study. She pushed the door open and the tutor looked up from their lesson. "Lily?" Hannah asked.

The tutor shook her head. "Sorry, ma'am. She's gone out." *Again.* Lily had been away from the house more often than usual lately.

Hannah reclosed the library door and went upstairs to pack her few things. As she passed Lily's bedroom, she paused uneasily, remembering Lily's identification card. The night that she and Matteo had gone on the errand and brought the wounded fighter to Nik for treatment. Later, she had gone to return Lily's identification card to her purse as she always did after using it. But when she reached in the pocket of the skirt she had been wearing, the identification was gone. She had lost it somewhere that night, she realized panicking. She searched her belongings for it in vain. She didn't know if she had dropped it in the woods or at the cabin. She worried that Lily would notice it missing, but so far, she had not.

Hannah packed a change of clothes and a few toiletries, looking back wistfully at the art supplies and other things she would need to leave behind. She went back downstairs, hopeful that Lily might have returned, but she had not. Hannah would have to leave now, without saying goodbye to her cousin. Part of her was relieved. Lily would have asked a dozen questions about where she was going and how she would manage—questions to which Hannah did not have all of the answers. She would have argued that it was too dangerous. It was for the best that Hannah could not tell her.

But she could at least leave a note. She walked to the notepad on the table in the foyer and picked up the pen beside it.

Dearest Lily,
Micheline has found a way for me to leave, and I need to take it.
I'm sorry not to say goodbye, but it came up without any notice. I
am so grateful to you for letting me stay and for all that you have
done. I will send word once I reach America safely.
All my love,
Hannah.

She imagined Lily's sadness and surprise at reading it and finding her gone. But at least she would not worry about what had happened to her. Hannah took her small bag of belongings and started to go.

At the door to the study, she paused, wanting to go to Georgi and sweep him up in her arms one last time. But interrupting his lesson would raise questions. Instead, she peered fondly through the crack in the door at his dark curls bowed over a book, then turned and started from the house.

Hannah began walking in the direction of Gare du Midi. A light rain, almost a mist, had begun to fall. The station was on the western edge of the city center, farther and in a different direction than Hannah had normally ventured on her walks. As she crossed the Square de l'Aviation, she spied a familiar figure on the far side. *Matteo.* She thought fleetingly that he had learned of her departure and was coming to see her. He was not headed toward the station, though, but in a different direction, his steps purposeful.

Hannah watched him, puzzled. She had not expected to find him in this part of town. But thinking about it, what did she know, really, about how he spent his time when he was not with her? She wanted to call out to him but did not want to draw attention to herself. He was striding away from her now, with a determined gait. She found herself following urgently, distracted from her need to get to the station.

Matteo stopped in front of a café and stood expectantly, as though waiting for someone. Then his eyes seemed to light up. For a moment, Hannah thought he might have spotted her and been pleasantly surprised. But he was looking past her to the right. Hannah followed his gaze. A woman was approaching in the distance, her face shielded by a parasol. A pang of jealousy shot through her. *Relax*, Hannah thought. She could just be an associate, someone who helped the network. She could tell from Matteo's expression of unmasked affection, however, that the woman meant so much more. Matteo had claimed to be alone since losing his heart to a woman years earlier. He had told Hannah that he could not possibly love again. Yet here he was with someone else. Hannah's anger grew.

Then the woman lowered her parasol, and as her smiling face came into view, Hannah gasped aloud.

The woman Matteo was about to meet was her own cousin, *Lily.*

How was it possible? She recalled Lily's interest in Matteo when she had seen Hannah with him at the café, a vague mention of meeting him years earlier. That would have been just before Lily met Nik. The ground seemed to slide out from be-neath Hannah as the final piece of the puzzle clicked into place: Lily was the woman who had broken Matteo's heart. Lily and Matteo had been—and possibly were now—lovers.

Hannah stepped back, cheeks hot despite the cool rain that fell upon them. Her eyes stung. Lily and Matteo. Though she had not actually seen them together, the look of affection be-tween them as Lily approached spoke volumes about the feelings she and Matteo shared. They were having a secret affair. What other explanation could there possibly be? Her cousin already had absolutely everything. Must she take him as well?

But of course, she had not taken him. Lily and Matteo had been together long before Hannah came to Belgium, and it was just a terrible twist of fate that Hannah had seen him in the park and had fallen in love with him herself.

Still, Lily had kept it from her. That was what hurt the most about it—not Matteo's feelings for Lily but the fact that Lily had lied. She had betrayed her. Hannah wanted to storm across the square and confront them as they met. But something, pride per-haps, kept her from doing it. A church bell chimed, signaling a quarter to the hour. Hannah looked at the clock above one of the shops. Four forty-five. She had less than fifteen minutes to reach the station and connect with the departing airmen. Her future was in America, not here. So much the easier to leave now, knowing that Matteo was not really hers. She squared her shoulders and, heedless of the rain, started for the station with-out looking back.

Inside Gare du Midi, Hannah looked around, trying to get her bearings in the unfamiliar station. Platform three, Micheline had said. She located the platform and started toward it. From the opposite direction, she saw a group of men walking toward the train. Though they wore the simple clothes of Belgian la-borers, their too-short haircuts threatened to give them away as military. There was a man in front of them, French-looking, with thin sandy hair, who seemed to be leading the group. Hannah was certain those were the airmen she was supposed to meet. She started toward them, determined to leave Belgium and Europe and all of this pain behind forever.

The airmen walked at a quicker gait than she, and Hannah sped up as much as she could to fall in beside them without attracting attention. She needed to reach them before they boarded. Another ten meters and she would be there. But as she neared the group, two policemen stepped out in front of her, cutting off her path. For a moment, Hannah thought she had been apprehended. Her heart stopped. How could they possibly know she was trying to flee? But the police were facing away from her, their stances turned in the direction of the airmen. "Halt!" one of them cried. "You are under arrest!" The convoy had been detected.

The sandy-haired man was talking to the police, seemingly trying to explain something. He had gold teeth, which seemed to glint as he spoke. One of the policeman handcuffed him roughly. There were police behind the group of airmen now too, blocking their escape.

But there were none behind Hannah. Slowly, she turned and started walking away, certain that at any moment, she would be apprehended as well.

The police seemed not to notice her, though, and a moment later she stepped outside the station. She hurried down the steps, eager to get as far away as she could. Around the corner, she stopped, gulping great gasps of air. Her lungs burned. The airmen had been captured. Someone knew that they were coming and had intercepted them. They had been taken, and with them her chance to escape this wretched place was gone as well.

What now? She needed to tell Micheline that the convoy had been arrested. But Micheline had left (to save the injured airman, Hannah presumed, though Micheline had not said as much.) And as for Matteo… Well, Hannah could not possibly face—or trust—him again.

She raced back to the canteen, which was now deserted, and left a quick note for Micheline. "Flight canceled. Planes grounded." It was the only way she could think of conveying, without saying outright, that the men had been taken.

Hannah stepped outside, trying to figure out where to go next. Though the rain had stopped, her hair was still damp. She was exhausted from all that had happened. But she did not want to return to Lily's house, not after seeing her with Matteo. Hannah began to walk away from the station toward the park, trying to process all that had happened and figure out what to do next. As she wove her way through the commuters and other late-day pedestrians, Hannah's mind reeled. Lily had betrayed her, and the convoy, her best and only chance of leaving Belgium, had been apprehended. She was trapped, caught in a dead end as surely as she had been the night that the *MS Brittany* sat docked at Havana Harbor.

After nearly an hour of walking the city, Hannah slowed. Her feet ached. It was nearly dark now, and the streets nearly empty, with most of the people who had been out having made their way home. She couldn't remain outside forever. She needed to return to Lily's house, the closest thing she had in Belgium to a home. After what had happened, though, she could not stay there. She would find another place to live and continue to help Micheline until she could devise a different escape route.

But first, she decided, she would confront Lily about Matteo. Lily would deny it at first, of course, but then when faced with the truth, she would have no choice but to explain herself.

With grim determination, Hannah started for the house, her mind reeling. Within minutes, her entire world as she knew it had been upended.

She reached the house and hesitated, steeling herself to confront her cousin. It had been a few hours since she had seen Lily with Matteo, and she should be home by now. Then she stepped inside. The foyer was still. She listened for the usual sounds of the house at that time of day, Lily in the kitchen, talking to Georgi about his day as she made tea. Stillness. She walked into the study. The tutor had gone and Georgi sat alone on the floor, drawing with crayons. "Darling, is Mama here?"

Georgi shook his head. "She hasn't come back yet."

Hannah was puzzled. Lily had not returned home. Was she still with Matteo? She likely would not have remained out with him that long into the evening, though, and risked arousing suspicion. She should have been back by now, Hannah realized, suddenly uneasy. Despite her anger at her cousin, she was also concerned. Where could Lily possibly be?

"Who is minding you?" Hannah asked.

Georgi pointed in the direction of the dining room. "Papa."

Nik was home early, Hannah noted with surprise. Hannah had hoped to catch Lily before Nik got home so that she could confront her about Matteo without her husband hearing. Now she would have to wait until the next time they were alone.

Hannah walked into the dining room where Nik sat at the table, his head buried in his hands. "Have you heard from Lily?" she asked. "I thought she'd be home by now."

Nik looked up. His eyes were bloodshot and rimmed with red, as if he had been crying. For a second, Hannah thought that perhaps Nik, too, had learned of his wife's betrayal.

But something about his dire expression told her it was even worse than that. "What happened?" she asked, her concern growing to panic. "What's wrong?"

"Lily…she's been arrested."

15

Lily

Today was to be the last time.

It had been nearly two weeks since Hannah had brought Matteo and the wounded fighter to the house and since Matteo had asked Lily to meet him. At first, she had thought that she might not go at all. But she had stood him up once in Antwerp all of those years ago. She could not do it again. She would meet him just once. She told herself it would put things to rest between them. She dressed for the meeting without too much care, though going out in the middle of the day in Brussels one still had to look proper, she told herself as she fastened her pearl earrings with shaking hands.

"I'm going shopping at the Old England" she'd announced, referring to the downtown department store. She feared that Hannah would notice her dress, with its trimmer-than-usual bodice, and ask or suspect something, but her cousin was preoccupied. "Please feed Georgi lunch," she said, hoping Hannah would not be too caught up in her work to remember. She had taken to painting more lately, and while it was good to see her getting back into her art, it often meant she was distracted to the point of unreliability.

She had set out across the square nervously, taking the side streets to the café Matteo had chosen. As she neared, Matteo saw her, and his face broke into a wide smile. Their eyes locked. She knew in that moment that she never should have come.

They walked in the park, strolling beneath the bowed oak trees. The years peeled away, and it was as if nothing had changed. Only when she noticed how low the sun had dipped behind the fountain did she realize how long she had been gone from home.

The deception got easier after that. They met again, and then a third time. Each time Lily found an excuse to go out dressed a bit too nicely. Their meetings were innocent enough, always walks, usually through the Bois de la Cambre, but other days farther afield, like the Parc Reine-Vert, with its panoramic view of the city. Sometimes they talked about life or politics or their dreams that had not yet come true. Other times they strolled in silence, simply content to be in one another's company.

Lily had thought that by seeing Matteo just once she might ease the nagging feelings that had plagued her all these years, like scratching an itch. Or at least she had tried to tell herself as much. Instead, the itch had grown worse, demanding attention. She needed the visits now, like air or water. She found herself forgoing other things to meet him and lying to Nik to get out.

Nothing untoward had happened between them. A long look, a casual graze of the hand. But there was an unspoken intimacy between them. She was cheating with Matteo as surely as if they had made love under the trees where they walked (a thought she had shamefully entertained more than once before hurriedly chasing it away). And by cheating with Matteo, she was betraying not just Nik but Georgi as well. She came home from their walks feeling soiled and dirty. She felt certain that Nik or Hannah would be able to tell that she had done wrong. But no one seemed to notice, and so the secret festered within her.

And with every visit, the connection between her and Matteo seemed to grow, taking them toward the inevitable. The other day, she nearly slipped on a wet patch of pavement, and he reached out for her so that she did not fall. She took his arm to steady herself. And she did not let go. Instead, she slipped her hand into his, and their fingers laced. His arm circled her waist drawing her closer. With that one gesture, desire rose up and crashed down upon her like a wave. She saw then the full danger of what they were doing. She pulled away. It needed to stop.

She had not gone to their last meeting because she did not want to do something she would regret. But that did not erase the thoughts or feelings. And it did not stop him. He had sent a note to the house, unsigned, with just a single word: *Why?* She would meet him one last time, she decided, to tell him that it was over. He deserved that much. Today would be the end of the charade.

The rain began to pelt harder now as she approached, and she put up her umbrella to shield herself against it. She saw Matteo across the square, waiting at their arranged meeting place. His expression turned to joy when he saw her, as it always did. She was afraid that she would not be able to leave him, but remembering her resolve and her loyalty to her family, she steeled herself and started toward him.

Matteo's smile faded as she neared, and she thought that perhaps he somehow knew the grim message she was coming to deliver. But then she saw it, and she knew that his concern had nothing to do with her feelings.

There were two policemen standing between them. And they were looking right at her.

Lily's breath caught. The police were everywhere these days, and there was no reason to think they were looking for her. Then one of the policemen started in her direction, his focus unmistakable, and the other quickly followed. What could she have done to draw their attention? She turned sideways abruptly, looking in vain for an alternate destination. But the market stalls were too far, seemingly kilometers instead of meters away, and the shops were closing. Her sudden gesture had drawn the attention of the police, who continued toward her.

"Papers," one of the officers commanded.

It was a perfunctory check, a formality, she told herself. The targeted way in which they had approached her, though, told her it was something more. She calmly reached into her clutch purse for her identification card and passed it over.

"Lily Abels?" one of the men asked. The second man scanned a list that he carried and nodded, as if confirming what they already knew. She was stunned. For the first time in her life, she was seized with the impulse to deny her own name. How did they know her? She was quite certain that she had never seen these men before in her life. Yet something had drawn their attention to her.

"You are under arrest. You must come with us."

"But this is preposterous. I'm a Belgian!" Until now, only the foreign Jews had been taken. Why was she being treated like one of them? "There must be some kind of mistake. I'm sure if you call my husband..." Although she had come here to see Matteo, it was Nik's status in which she sought protection. "He's a professor at the university." *Was*, she reminded herself silently. Nik had been stripped of his title and with it any influence or import that might have helped in the situation.

"You're being charged with sedition," the first officer said. There had to be a mistake. She tended to her son, went to the shops, worked as a nurse in Nik's clinic when she was able. She had not engaged in any sort of treason or anything at all beyond caring for her family.

Across the square, Matteo watched with shock and horror. He took a step toward her, as if planning to intervene. Her eyes met his, and she shook her head slightly, willing him not to. Matteo was impetuous and probably known to the police himself for his work with the resistance. His involvement in this would only make things worse and get them both arrested.

The policeman reached for her arm. "One moment, please," she begged. Tears formed in the corners of her eyes. Needing a handkerchief, Lily reached into her purse. It fell to the ground, contents spilling. She was too petrified to bend down and get it. In other circumstances, she felt certain, a passerby might have stopped to help. But no one did, and her personal belongings remained splayed on the pavement for all to see.

Beyond the terror of the arrest, what Lily felt most in that moment was shame. People usually looked away from the Germans, averting their eyes so as not to get caught up in the trouble. Now it seemed that everyone, all of the pedestrians and patrons at the cafés, were staring at her and the melee of which she was a part. What had this fine lady done to be arrested? Lily lowered her head. Suddenly she was nothing but a castoff, someone to be avoided and shunned. Everything she had worked for her whole life, everything she had tried to be, disappeared.

Of course, social propriety was not her real concern, and all thought of it faded instantly as the policeman grabbed her roughly by the arm and led her from the square. She was being taken from the street, might never be heard from again. She'd heard stories of it. Part of her wanted to believe that it was all a misunderstanding that would be cleared up. She would be home by nightfall and with an apology from the chief of police. But if she was not... Her mind did the gymnastics of a mother reshuffling her deck of responsibilities. Hannah would be home with Georgi now and would see to dinner and bedtime, while Nik went searching for her. Only how would he know? He would think she was late, but then he would grow worried. Other practical concerns intruded as well, such as the bag she had packed in case of emergency, which sat uselessly beneath her bed at home. She had nothing with her that she would need if this took more than a few hours.

They reached the edge of the square and a waiting police car. Seeing the open door, Lily's terror doubled. She had never been in a police car in her entire life. But there was no other choice. She shook off the policeman's grip, insisting upon the dignity of getting in the car herself and ducking her head carefully so as not to hit it.

"Lily! Lily!" She heard Matteo calling her name over and over now, his voice high-pitched and keening, as she slid inside. She could not bear to look up. Then as the door closed, the sound was gone.

16

Hannah

"Arrested?" Hannah repeated after Nik told her, shocked. How was that possible? Hannah had seen Lily with her own eyes just a short while earlier meeting Matteo, though of course she could not say that to Nik. Except for Georgi playing in the study, the house was eerily still. Things seemed so ordinary and undisturbed that Hannah almost hoped that Nik was mistaken.

"Yes." Nik's face was pale, his eyes wide with panic. "Not an hour ago." It must have happened just after she had seen Lily, Hannah realized. "Our neighbor, Madame Zeigler, saw the whole thing and ran to tell me. I have no idea where she is, whether she is all right."

Before Hannah could respond, Georgi came into the room. "I'm hungry," he announced.

"Come," Hannah said, holding out her hand. No good would come of him seeing his father so distraught. "I'll fix you a snack." He followed her into the kitchen. She took a plate from the cabinet with shaking hands, nearly dropping it. As she prepared a plate of salted nuts and cheese, she worried whether Lily, wherever she was, had food.

And still the question nagged: Why had Lily been arrested? Lily was the most law-abiding citizen she knew. She did nothing more dangerous or controversial than trying a new brand of coffee at a café. Hannah felt with certainty that her own work had somehow gotten Lily into trouble. And she had been arrested at almost the exact same time as the convoy was intercepted by the police—which seemed too close to be a coincidence.

"Where's Mama?" Georgi asked as he ate.

"Mama's gone on a trip," she said.

Georgi's brow furrowed as he tried to process this. Except for short errands, Lily had always been there. "When will she be back?"

"Soon, I hope," Hannah offered, wanting to pacify him but not lie. Seemingly satisfied, Georgi finished eating and returned to his toys. She wished for her own distractions as well.

Hannah walked back to the dining room to Nik. "Sweet Lily," he moaned. "Why would anyone want to arrest her?"

Hannah could not bear to tell them her suspicion that it was her own reckless conduct which had resulted in Lily's arrest. "We have to do something," she said instead.

"I phoned the police. But they had no information on where she had been taken." *Or refused to give it*, Hannah thought. The police worked so closely with the Germans these days that they were really one and the same. Nik looked up at her hopefully. "You have friends who are involved with political groups. Please ask them if there is anything they can do. We must find her."

"Yes, of course. I was headed out to do just that."

Leaving Georgi in his father's care, Hannah sped toward the canteen. Her mind raced as she tried to figure out the events that had led to Lily's arrest. Her identification card, Hannah realized suddenly. Her mind reeled back to the day the German had stopped her on the street and checked Hannah's papers. By impersonating Lily, Hannah had put her cousin on the Germans' radar. And then she had lost it somehow that night with Matteo. Someone could have found it and seen Lily's name, thought she was working with the resistance. She stopped in her tracks, overcome with remorse.

Hannah needed to find Micheline, but it was Matteo at the canteen when she arrived, seated at the desk with his head low. Remembering what she had witnessed between him and Lily, a wave of anger and pain rose within her. Part of her wanted to run from the room, but none of that mattered now. She would have to push her feelings aside. "My cousin...she's been arrested."

He lifted his head sadly. "I saw it happen on the square. We were..." He paused before the confession could leave his lips.

"I know," Hannah said bluntly. He lowered his head. "About you and Lily." She thought he might deny it, but he did not. "Why didn't you tell me?"

"I never meant to keep it a secret. At first, I was just stunned to find her in Brussels after so many years. I hadn't seen her in almost a decade. I thought she was gone forever. And, well, I just couldn't. I was too embarrassed, and I didn't want to hurt you. Nothing happened between us. Still, I'm so sorry."

"It doesn't matter anymore. We have to help Lily. Do you know where they took her?"

"Yes, I followed them. She was taken to the *Sipo-SD* building on Avenue Louise." Hannah shuddered. The security police headquarters was the very heart of German operations in Brussels, a place notorious for its brutal interrogations. Lily had not been arrested for some petty offense and would not be released easily. "I tried to see her, but it was impossible."

Matteo pulled out a chair. Hannah did not sit, though. She paced the floor, thinking. "She was taken at nearly the same time as the convoy so..."

"The convoy?" Matteo interrupted. Hannah could tell from

his puzzled expression that he had no idea what she was talking about.

"Micheline had arranged for me to leave Belgium with a convoy of airmen. But they were arrested at the station before I reached them. I left a note earlier to tell Micheline. You didn't get it?"

"I didn't see any note." Somehow, inexplicably, it had disappeared. "But I don't see how the two could be linked. Lily has nothing to do with our work."

Hannah paused, flooded with guilt. "But she does, and it's all my fault."

"What do you mean?"

She had to tell him what she had done. "I took her identification card to use in my errands for the Sapphire Line."

Surprise, then anger crossed his face. "Hannah, how could you?"

"I was stopped by a German officer a few weeks back, and I showed him her nurse's card. That must have put her name on their radar. And then when we were fleeing the cabin, I must have dropped the card in the woods. I know, it was foolish and wrong, and I couldn't regret it more. If I hadn't done it, none of this would have happened."

"That was too reckless, risking Lily's life."

"I know that now. I'm sorry."

She watched his face as he wrestled with his anger. "You were doing what you thought you had to for the network," he said finally, but his words were no comfort. "Blame will not help Lily," he added. "We have to find her." His voice was grim with determination.

Hannah started for the door. "I have to go to her."

"Hannah, wait." Matteo caught her arm. "The building is heavily guarded. You'll be arrested if you go there, and what good will you be to Lily, then?"

He had a point, Hannah conceded inwardly.

"Perhaps if we ask the *Association des Juifs en Belgique* for help," she suggested tentatively. She knew little of the organization other than it was comprised of Jewish leaders and had undertaken ministerial work related to the community since the start of the occupation.

"The *Judenrat*," Matteo spat with revulsion. "They are nothing but collaborators who turn over their own people to the Germans." He paused, thinking. "Has Lily's family been taken yet?"

Yet. Hannah's throat tightened. That Lily had been arrested was bad enough. The notion that sweet Georgi might be taken as well was simply unfathomable. She was seized with the urge to return home. "No, but I need to get back to them."

"Go home. The best thing you can do is to take care of her family. Be there for your cousin's child. He needs you more than ever now." Matteo was right. Nik loved his son, but he simply didn't have the capacity to fill the void left by Lily's absence. "I will find a way to reach Lily, and I will let you know as soon as I learn something." Hannah wanted to protest. She had to do more. She could not bear to return to Lily's house without her, to look Nik in the eye and tell him she had failed and to see Georgi pining for his mother. But there was nothing else she could do. Hannah could see in Matteo's eyes the depths of his feelings for her cousin, and she knew he would stop at nothing to save her.

Hannah turned and started for home, hoping that it was not too late.

17

Lily

"Sortez!" The barking order to exit the barracks shattered Lily's sleep. *"Kommen Sie schnell!"* Lily clambered to her feet. She had been at Breendonk for two days, and she was still not used to waking up here, the moldy dampness like a slap in her face, reminding her how very far she was from home.

Lily had not been taken straightaway to the Breendonk prison camp. Instead, the police had brought her to an improbably elegant house in the heart of Brussels. *Sipo-SD, security police* headquarters was on Avenue Louise, a street lined with chestnut trees less than a half-mile from her own home, which Lily walked any number of times during her years of living in the city. She had been kept for nearly two days in the basement prison without seeing another human save for the set of hands that pushed a meal tray into her cell twice daily. During that time, she peered through the barred windows at the feet of passersby above, desperately wishing that someone might realize she was there. She could just make out the base of the bench across the street where she and Georgi had once stopped on a walk so that she might tie his shoe.

Finally she was brought from the basement, and for a fleeting second, she foolishly hoped she might be released. Instead, a guard took her to a study and tied her to a chair that was stained with what appeared to be blood. She was left alone with a man who did not wear a uniform like the others.

"You were seen delivering papers," the man said.

"No!" she cried. They thought she was some sort of resistance member. Alarm rose in her. Political prisoners were treated even worse than the foreign Jews. The man raised his hand, and she braced for the strike.

But he lowered it again. "Someone with your name and description was seen delivering a message."

Hannah, she realized. "Someone must have taken my identification card. I noticed it missing the day before I was apprehended."

The man's eyes narrowed. "Who?"

Lily hesitated. She should give Hannah up right then and put an end to the whole mess. Perhaps by doing so she might be able to bargain freedom for her and her family, or at least better treatment. But she could not betray her cousin. Even if she could bring herself to do it, turning in Hannah would send the police to Lily's own house to apprehend her, and she could not risk Nik or Georgi. "It must have been stolen," she finished weakly instead.

The man was not convinced. He questioned her endlessly about places and things she had never heard of. "I'm a housewife," she said. Once she had resented the term, but now she held it up like a shield. "I go to the market, care for my family." She feared that they would beat her. The notion was a terrifying one: she had never been any good at withstanding physical pain.

After a day of questioning, the interrogator seemed to believe her, that she knew nothing. They took her from the building and brought her to a truck just outside, a windowless cargo hold fashioned with two crude wood benches. She started to protest: surely they did not expect her to ride in there. But there was no one to hear her anymore. She climbed into the back, unwashed and aching. She leaned back wearily, looking outside through a fist-sized hole in one of the truck walls.

As the Brussels skyline faded in the distance, her heart ripped with sadness and longing. She was being taken from her family and home, and no one who loved her knew where she was going. When the police arrested her, she had assumed she would be detained a few hours at most, then permitted to return home. Instead, she was being taken from the city, farther from everything she knew and everyone she loved. The chance of returning to them seemed smaller than ever.

The truck traveled the motorway in the direction of Antwerp. They pulled off onto a side road, and barren hills rose on either side. Ahead stood a medieval stone fortress, with a broad front and two long wings fanning out behind it on either side to form a U shape. Though not more than a few kilometers from the main road, the camp felt as though it was worlds away from anywhere. A deep moat surrounded the fortress. Men in striped uniforms worked at a quarry alongside it, removing some sort of red clay with shovels and wheelbarrows. Their heads were shaved bald, and their uniforms hung limply on their skeletal bodies. Lily shuddered at the condition of these poor souls who lived in such misery so close to modern, civilized Brussels. Was she to live like this as well?

The driver did not escort her inside the camp. Instead, he let her out on the side of the road. A worn bridge with low stone walls crossed over the murky brown moat, leading to the arched entrance of the fortress on the other side. *Breendonk* read a sign on the structure. Lily recalled hearing of the former military base, but she hadn't known exactly where it was or that it was being used by the Germans as a prison camp.

"Schnell!" a guard barked at her from the entrance to the fort. Another guard with a machine gun stood in a tower high above, watching her. She had no choice but to go inside. Taking a last long look around, she walked into the camp.

The arched entranceway led into a poorly lit tunnel with curved, roughly hewn walls. The guard who had ordered her inside led her down the tunnel. It ran about a hundred meters before opening to a wide courtyard with a makeshift reception area at the center. She stood in a line of several dozen new arrivals. The others seemed to be working-class folk from Brussels and the surrounding towns, she guessed, although a few carried large suitcases suggesting they had come from farther away. Guards stood on either side of the queue. One held back a German shepherd who strained at its leash, mouth frothing, ready to lunge at anyone who stepped out of line.

Lily waited her turn fearfully, then stepped forward when summoned. At the first table, she had given her information and been registered. She moved to the second station, where she was meant to turn in her possessions. Lily hesitated. She had been taken from the street with only her purse, and that had been confiscated at Sipo headquarters in the city.

"I have nothing," she said. The guard checking her in, a woman, looked at her with disbelief, and Lily hoped she would not be searched. Finally, she was issued a blanket, a cracked plate, a cup, a spoon and two crude burlap uniforms.

That had been two days ago. Three nights (including the one she'd spent in the prison cell at German headquarters) of not tucking Georgi at bedtime and as many of not being there in the morning when he woke. That was how she marked the passing of time. She was reminded of it now as a young child walked past her between his parents, exiting the barracks as quietly and somberly as a grown-up. The Belgian Jews were able to lodge as families, and she could not see a small child without thinking of Georgi. As she imagined his warm little body still swathed in sleep, her arms ached. She hoped that Nik or Hannah had remembered to tuck his stuffed bear in beside him and went to him if he woke in his dreams. What had they told him about his mother's disappearance? Lily had not been apart from him a single night in his entire life until now.

She rose and made her bed. The inside of the barracks were more dreadful than Lily could have imagined, foul-smelling from too many bodies, with walls so damp they seemed to ooze. Then she dressed hurriedly into the second of her two prison uniforms, turning away for modesty. She was not sure she would ever get used to the lack of privacy, but there was really no other choice. The dormitory for Belgian Jews, which was housed in the eastern wing of the stone fortress, was about twenty meters long and half as wide, with wooden bunk beds, crammed into rows so close together only one person could squeeze between them at a time. The room had an arched ceiling so the top bunks had a bit of air. There was a small stove at the end, too small to provide enough heat if it had been winter. Each of the barracks had a *Kapo* or leader, a Jew who had been put in charge.

Lily walked outside. The dirt beneath her feet had been soaked by spring rains, and the mud seeped into her shoes. She made her way to the latrine, a separate building with a dozen toilets crammed inside. The air was choked with the overwhelming stench of human filth. They had no dividers for privacy, just one of a thousand little things that were intended to degrade the prisoners. There was one large shower room with several dozen heads. The room was empty, and Lily was seized with the urge to wash. Their turns to bathe might have been spread out through the week, but instead the prisoners were all made to rush through in the same hour on Sundays.

Outside it was still dark, but harsh floodlights illuminated the courtyard. Instructions blared over and over across the loudspeakers. There were wood gallows that had been constructed at the top of the square, a warning for anyone who might think about disobeying. She hurried to her place in line. Each morning was the *Appell*, the roll call in which prisoners were forced to stand like statues for hours in the cold or heat while every person was accounted for and their barracks inspected. Lily stood motionless, keeping her eyes down. The slightest infraction, moving or making a sound or having a poorly made bed, would bring swift punishment. In the short time she had been there, she had already witnessed men forced to face the stone wall of the courtyard for extended periods of time, sometimes in a painful squatting position, or holding a pickax or a boulder above their heads. They might be slammed into a wall for no reason or beaten with a whip.

When the roll call ended after what seemed like forever Lily followed the other inmates to the mess hall, a room that was identical to the one in which they slept, except it was filled with long wooden tables instead of beds. She waited in line and claimed her portion, an ounce of stale bread and some watery cabbage soup, then found a seat in the middle of a bench where she was less likely to be noticed.

Looking at the revolting contents of the bowl, Lily marveled: Was it really only weeks earlier that she had dined on salmon tartine? Making the delicacy with coarse, rationed flour had seemed an inconvenience, but now she would have given anything for a morsel of real food. Around her, the others ate, used to starvation, accepting of it. Hunger, once foreign to Lily, was now everywhere, and she found the deprivation, and the ways people found to deal with it, horrific. Some looked for scraps around the camp's pigsty or rabbit hutch; others ate grass. Lily found that drinking water helped ease the pains in her empty stomach, although she did it sparingly because the water was brown and polluted and smelled foul and might bring on a case of dysentery at any moment. After just a few days of being underfed, her stomach ached constantly. She could not imagine what would happen after a week, a month; though, surely she would not be here that long.

Trying to forget about her hunger, Lily looked around the room, careful to keep her head low. The others here were mostly women, foreign Jews and perhaps a few political prisoners like herself, arrested for some perceived transgression against the Reich. At the next table sat a woman with luminous olive skin and jet-black hair. A child about Georgi's age leaned against her. Lily had noticed her before, struck by her intensely dark eyes. In another place, Lily might have taken the woman for Indian or Middle Eastern, but the sign around her neck explained everything: *Gypsy*. Gypsies, or *Romani* as they were properly called, were people she had seen often in the streets of Brussels and Antwerp. They were nomads who did not keep a permanent house or job, instead playing music for a few coins. Lily found herself curious about the woman.

The bell rang, signaling the end of breakfast. Lily picked up her bowl and started for the door, hoping she might have time to wash and stow it among her few things in the barracks as they were required to do before going to work. Lily had been given a job in the garment shop, a low shed behind the fortress. There she and a half-dozen other women washed, sorted and mended used prisoner uniforms for new arrivals. She tried not to think about where the threadbare uniforms had come from and what had happened to those who had once worn them. Though not as harsh as some of the jobs that involved outdoor manual labor, work in the garment shop was grueling. The coarse uniforms grew heavy when wet, and her bones ached from lifting them, as well as the long hours of standing on her feet. The strong chemicals used to clean them burned and cracked the skin of her hands.

Lily started out for her job at the warehouse. As she passed the mess hall, she saw the Roma woman she had noticed earlier, protectively watching her son play from a distance. Lily should go to work, she knew. Being late would risk swift punishment for the infraction. But she found herself drawn to the woman, envious that she was with her child and wishing that she could see Georgi. "Hello," she ventured, moving closer. The woman's eyes narrowed, and her face grew guarded. "I'm Lily."

"Sofia."

"And that's your son?"

"Yes, he's called Dorin. He's eight."

"The same age as my son," Lily remarked. "Only he isn't here with me."

"That must be difficult," Sofia said sympathetically. She raised her hand to wave at Dorin, signaling that he should stay closer. Lily marveled at how Sofia's hands were perfectly soft and manicured. Her own nails were cracked, dirt lodged beneath the cuticles. Just a few days earlier, she would have been appalled to have her hands in such a state. "Coconut oil," Sofia said, noticing Lily's gaze. She reached into her pocket and pulled out a small vial. "Here." She sprinkled a few drops into Lily's palm and the warm, soothing moisture felt like luxury. "You are Jewish?"

"Yes," Lily replied. Though her tag denoted her as Jewish, it also bore a *B* for *Belgian*, an acknowledgment of her citizenship, which gave her a favored status. The other woman wore the dreaded *F* for *foreigner* alongside her Roma designation that put her among the most vulnerable in the camp, subject to harsher treatment and punishment. "I'm from Brussels. Where are you from?" She worried that the question might have been a mistake, since Romani tended to move continually.

"We were taken off the streets of Amsterdam. My husband Felix was caught working with the Dutch resistance and arrested first. He was sent east straightaway, and we've had no word. Then the police came for us."

"I'm so sorry."

"You're here alone?" Sofia asked.

"Yes. My family was not arrested." Lily longed to be with

her family, but even as she did, she thanked God that she knew where they were and that they were at home and safe.

"I have to go to work," Lily said nodding in the direction of the warehouse.

"Me, too," Sofia replied. "I will walk with you." They crossed the courtyard, Dorin following. A new group of prisoners was coming in now, and Lily recognized the dazed look from her own just days earlier.

Sofia gestured with her head in the direction of the camp overseer, a stout man who stood over a kneeling prisoner, brandishing a club. "Be careful of that one."

Lily was puzzled. She knew well enough to stay clear of the overseer, who had a reputation for cruelty even beyond the others.

"Just make sure you aren't alone with him," Sofia added finally.

Lily understood then, horrified. "Did he...?" She could not bring herself to finish the sentence.

"Rape me?" Sofia asked bluntly. "No, not yet anyway. Still, you must be careful until you go."

"Go?" For a moment, Lily felt hopeful. Perhaps Sofia knew of some sort of planned prisoner release. "Go where?"

"You don't know, do you?" Sofia sounded remorseful, as if sorry she had said anything.

"Know what?" Lily demanded.

Sofia did not answer right away, and the silence was deafening. "You won't be staying here long. None of us will."

"I don't understand."

"This is a transit camp, temporary. Everyone goes east from here."

Lily shuddered. She had imagined being here for a few weeks at most before her release. Surely then she would be sent back to the only home she had ever known. "You must be mistaken. They could never force Belgian citizens to leave the country." But even as she spoke the words, she knew that they were untrue. The protection of Belgian citizenship was a myth. It had failed her when she was arrested, and it would not save her from whatever fate lay ahead. She wrapped her arms tightly around herself and prayed that Matteo would be able to figure out some way to save her.

18

Micheline

Micheline sat alone in the rear office going over paperwork. She had returned from her errand, meeting with a contact near the French border about a possible new safe house, to find the canteen empty. Hannah had left with the convoy three days earlier. Matteo was nowhere to be found. There was a message waiting for her from Pascal that the wounded airman was almost well enough to travel, and she wanted to make sure that everything was in order here before she set off to rescue him.

She looked up from her papers, her thoughts turning to Hannah. Micheline had pretended to leave first after their farewell, but in fact, she had watched Hannah go around the corner with a sense of remorse. She hadn't planned to like or trust Hannah. Use her for some clerical work, she'd thought, a few minor errands, an extra set of hands.

But Hannah had proven to be good—better than many of the others. Micheline didn't want Hannah to leave. She needed her for the line. Even after she had found a way for Hannah to leave, she considered not telling her. But that would have been unfair. They had made an agreement, Hannah's assistance in exchange for Micheline helping her to get out. The decision, if Hannah had chosen to stay, would have had to be her own.

It was no matter now. Micheline would find other assets to cover the work. That was the thing about the line: it was made up of dozens of individuals. No one was irreplaceable.

Micheline heard a sudden clattering outside the rear door. She stiffened, then leaped to her feet. She was not expecting anyone. When she opened the door, she was surprised to find Hannah. "Hannah? What are you doing here? You were supposed to have left with the convoy."

"Didn't Matteo tell you?"

Micheline shook her head. "I just got back. I haven't seen him. Tell me what?"

"When I got to the station, the police had just stopped the airmen. They were arrested. They're gone."

Micheline let the information sink in. Bile rose up in her throat. She swallowed, forcing it down. This was the business. They got as many out as they could, but sometimes it didn't work. Still, the airmen placed their lives in her hands, trusted her to deliver them safely. She had failed.

"Get inside," she ordered, taking Hannah by the arm and pulling her through the doorway roughly. "What happened?"

Hannah pulled away. "I don't know." For a moment, Micheline thought she might be lying. But Hannah's eyes were wide, and it was clear from her expression that she was just as puzzled as Micheline herself.

"The police. How many?"

"Four or five."

"What color were their uniforms?"

"Light brown."

Sipo-SD. Her alarm grew. This was not a happenstance arrest by an officer on patrol. A group of Germans had known the airmen were coming.

"Someone knew about the convoy, and they betrayed us."

"How did you manage not to be taken with them?"

"I was a minute or two late, and when I got to the station, the police had already started toward them. But I had not joined them yet, so I was able to slip away."

Micheline let out a long breath like a whistle. "That was lucky. You would have been arrested as well. I'm glad you weren't with them."

Hannah pressed her lips together, the grim truth sinking in. "Not lucky. I have more bad news, I'm afraid. My cousin has been arrested as well."

Micheline was caught off guard by this unexpected development. "What happened?"

"She was arrested on the Square de l'Aviation."

"Arrested? But why?"

Hannah shrugged. "I don't know. I think it was because I had used her identification card. Matteo was there meeting her and saw the whole thing." This last bit confirmed what Micheline had suspected: her brother had become entangled once again with the woman who had broken his heart. "She was initially taken to Sipo headquarters." This, Micheline reflected, was very, very bad. "Matteo went to see her and said he would let me know. But it has been three days, and I've had no word. That's why I came here."

Because he hasn't found her, Micheline thought. "I'm sure he will come back soon," she offered. But her concern for her brother grew. If he had not returned, it was because he was trying to do something, anything, to find and help Lily. Matteo was headstrong at the best of times. That, combined with his passion for Lily, would surely spell disaster.

Micheline's mind whirled. "Two arrests. It can't be a coincidence."

"You think the two are related?"

"I don't know." Even if the arrests were somehow coordinated, the network was segmented, each person only knowing just enough. The traitor did not—could not—know everything. But Micheline's uneasiness grew as she contemplated the extent of the possible breach.

"Micheline, we have to help Lily." Hannah's voice was pleading and pinched. "It is my fault that she's been arrested. She has a young child."

Micheline straightened. Lily's arrest, while alarming, was the least of her worries. "I will make inquiries."

"Inquiries? That's all?"

"What else would you have me do?"

"I want to help her get out."

"Out? If she is still at SD headquarters, that's impossible. And if she isn't, she's been sent to one of the camps." The Germans had created a few internment camps outside of the city where they held people who were to be transported east. But those were political prisoners and foreign Jews, not native Belgians like Hannah's cousin.

Still Hannah did not back down. "Lily was arrested as a direct consequence of our work. With all of your connections, surely someone can help get her out." Hannah softened her voice. "You help people escape. That's what you do."

Micheline searched for the words to make Hannah understand. "We rescue downed airmen. Freeing a prisoner is something else altogether. There's no way to get anyone out of SD headquarters or the camps. And even if we could, the line only evacuates soldiers. Can't you see? If we opened this up to refugees, there would be a flood, the whole line would be overwhelmed and shut down."

"War forces hard choices about who to save," Hannah acknowledged. "No one knows this better than me. But how can you not save a woman who had been captured as a direct result of our work?"

"Your cousin is Belgian," Micheline pointed out, avoiding the question. "They aren't deporting Belgian citizens. She will be all right."

"You don't know that," Hannah shot back. "They were not supposed to be arresting native Belgians either. Plus, if they think she is me and charge her with sedition, they might kill her."

Seeing the anguish in Hannah's eyes, Micheline softened. "I wish I could help. My advice to you is to leave Belgium and secure your cousin's freedom from abroad." Hannah's eyes widened with surprise. "You can still go. The transit documents I gave you are valid. We can find another route out for you." She was giving Hannah another chance at freedom.

"Never. I have to stay here and help Lily, even if you won't."

"Can't," Micheline corrected. "You know you might be giving up your one and only chance to leave? I don't have to tell you the favors I called in to get those papers."

Hannah looked down. "No, and I'm forever grateful. But my cousin's arrest…it's my fault. I need to stay here and try to get her out."

"I told you, there is nothing to be done." Micheline wished she could offer some words of comfort or reassurance to Hannah, but there was nothing reassuring about war. Micheline hardened.

Matteo walked in then, his face grave. Hannah ran to him. "Have you found her?"

"She's been transported to the prison camp at Breendonk. There's no way to see her, but I was able to check on her through a contact. She is all right—at least for now." Over Hannah's shoulder, Micheline exchanged uneasy glances with her brother. That Lily had been sent onward from German headquarters at Avenue Louise was an ominous sign. The Germans had no intentions of freeing her.

"No!" Hannah cried. "The conditions are meant to be

wretched there. Lily will not survive. And your sister refuses to help," Hannah spat bitterly.

"I've explained to her that there is nothing to be done," Micheline said.

"Micheline is right," Matteo said gently. "We can't simply storm the gates and free her. I would do anything to help your cousin. But this is beyond all of us." There was a pleading note in Matteo's voice, asking Hannah to understand. "I will keep trying." He would not make promises he could not keep or raise false hope in her.

"You must be patient," Micheline interjected. "These things take time."

"Time?" Hannah spun to her angrily. "Time is not something my cousin has. I risked everything for you, including Lily's life. And now because of this, she is in a prison camp, taken from her family. And you won't help." Hannah started from the room. "If you won't help her, then I will."

"Hannah, wait," Micheline implored. What did Hannah possibly think she could do?

But she was already gone.

19

Lily

After breakfast one morning, Lily spied Sofia talking to an older prisoner she didn't recognize, a broad-shouldered man who towered over her. "Who was that?" she asked, when Sofia finished her conversation and walked over with Dorin in tow.

"His name is François. He worked with my husband Felix in the resistance, and they were together when they were caught smuggling explosives. Felix was deported east, but François was sent here. He looks out for me and Dorin and checks in on us from time to time."

The women started back to the barracks to get ready for work. "A group of arrivals," Sofia observed, nodding her head in the direction of the *Appellplatz* where there were new prisoners who had been brought from the nearby station by truck. Lily was curious about who these people were and what they had done to warrant arrest. She wanted to know, too, where they were going to stay. The barracks were filled beyond capacity, with some people sleeping two and three to a berth. There simply wasn't room.

Lily's thoughts were interrupted by a yelp from Dorin. Sofia turned toward her son, who was pointing in the direction of the new prisoners. "Mama, look! A boy my own age!"

Lily turned in the direction he was pointing, and her heart filled with dread. The boy whom Dorin was pointing at was her very own son. Nik and Georgi had been brought to the prison.

Lily stood motionless. At first, she was certain that seeing Nik and Georgi was a bad dream or a mirage. She closed her eyes, praying that when she opened them again her husband and son would be gone, safe at home. She yearned to run to them and devour her son, swallow him whole, not only to hold him close to her once more but also to protect him from this place. But she did not want to do anything to draw attention and risk harm to him or Nik.

"Mama!" Georgi cried as he spotted her. He ran heedlessly toward her and crashed into her with a cry, nearly knocking her over. Touching her child once more, Lily was flooded with joy. She wrapped her arms around him and inhaled him, sweet-smelling and real. Then, as she took him in, worry eclipsed her happiness. He looked like a different child. His head was shaved, and there was a cut in his pale scalp from the razor. Her heart broke at seeing the oversize uniform he now wore, so large that it seemed to swallow his tiny body. His cheeks were already dirty and stained with dried tears that she had not been there to wipe away. "They took us, Mama." His excitement at seeing her subsided as he took in the strange and terrible sight of the prison camp.

Over the top of Georgi's head, her eyes met Nik's. She felt a surge of warmth and terror at seeing him. How on earth had he and Georgi come to be here?

Nik held her gaze for several seconds, as if unable to look away. She wanted to run to him and throw her arms around him. But the line shuffled forward, and he turned from her reluctantly and continued in line toward the registration desk.

Once finished, he made his way through the crowd to meet her and set down the small suitcase he had been carrying. He gently took her in his arms and he kissed her. She pressed herself against him, soaking in the chance to be close and together once more. When she looked up, she saw him taking in the horrors of the camp. How, his expression seemed to ask, could they possibly be expected to live here?

"What happened?" she asked.

"The police took us from the house," Nik said in a low voice. "No warning. I didn't dare resist and bring danger to Georgi." She understood. Fighting back would have meant certain death for both of them. "There was no time to make arrangements or hide." She tried to imagine how confusing and upsetting it had been for Georgi. After the initial excitement of seeing her, he stood dazed and glassy-eyed, as though awakened suddenly from a bad dream.

"This is all Hannah's fault." Lily's own voice sounded harsh, unfamiliar. "If she hadn't stolen my identification card, none of this would have happened."

Nik's face registered surprise. "I had no idea. I'm sure that your cousin feels terrible." It was not in Nik's nature to get angry or to blame, and she was sure he was right that Hannah regretted what she had done. Still, she could not help but be furious about her cousin's carelessness.

They stood together, alone despite the workers and activity that swirled around them. "Darling." Nik raised his hand to her cheek, caressing it. She could feel the dirt on her face, no matter how much she tried to wash. Her lips were cracked and bleeding, and her hair had begun to gray at the roots prematurely from the hardship and stress. She was a ghost of what she had been just a few weeks ago. But she could tell that Nik did not see that. To him, she was still beautiful.

Then she remembered her secret meetings with Matteo. It had been nothing more than coffee and a stroll on a few occasions, but being here with her husband, she felt now the magnitude of her betrayal. Nik really was the sweetest man, and he had always loved her unconditionally. She loved him too, which made her betrayal all the worse. She leaned against him and closed her eyes, allowing him to wrap his arms around her, wanting to forget all that had happened since the war had started, how drastically their lives had changed and all that had been stolen from them.

A sharp whistle blew, pulling them apart. "Come," she said, gesturing for Nik and Georgi to follow her. "We mustn't loiter, or else." She tried to silently convey the dangers of the camp to Nik without alarming Georgi. Thankfully, they were assigned to her barracks. She took one of their hands in each of her own and led them across the camp. "After we get you settled in the barracks, you'll have to report for a work assignment," she told Nik. "I'm in the garment shop."

They passed a wall where there was a prisoner in a squatting position holding a cinderblock over his head as a punishment for some sort of infraction. A German guard hovered over him, screaming orders. Lily put her arm around Georgi to shield his view. "Look!" she said, pointing upward to some geese that flew overhead to distract him from seeing. A pained look crossed Nik's face. Though this was not the first time Lily had seen a prisoner punished, she felt the horror anew in witnessing it with her family. It could all too easily happen to one of them if they were not careful.

As they neared the barracks, they met up with Sofia and her son. "Nik, this is Sofia."

Nik smiled. "A pleasure to meet you."

"We're off to get Nik's work assignment," Lily explained to Sofia.

"What do we do with Georgi while we are at work?" Nik asked. Lily hesitated, considering the question for the first time.

"There's a woman, Tante Sarah, whose job it is to mind the

children while we are at work." Sofia pointed across the field to an elderly woman, holding a baby carelessly with one hand and smoking some sort of hand-rolled cigarette with the other. Prisoners scarcely had access to food, much less cigarettes, and Lily thought perhaps she had gotten it as a special privilege or made it from something she'd found. "She used to be a midwife," Sofia added, as if that detail rendered the woman qualified to watch children. Lily was flooded with doubt. How could she possibly entrust him to this stranger?

"I'll take him over and get him settled," Lily said. "You report to the main administrative office for your assignment. You don't want to be late." There was so much she needed to tell Nik about the camp, how to keep your head low and stay out of trouble. She could not bear it if anything happened to him.

"Very well," he said, touching her cheek. "I hate to leave you again so soon."

"I know. Me too." They had only just been reunited and did not want to part again, even for a while. "But you have to go. I'll see you later."

When Nik had gone, Lily approached the elderly woman. "I'm Lily, and this is my son, Georgi. He just arrived and he needs minding while I'm at work." She hated letting Georgi out of her sight again so soon, but there was no other choice. "Can you do it?"

"I suppose," Tante Sarah said slowly, as though watching children was a choice and not her assigned camp job. Lily thought perhaps the woman wanted something extra in exchange for watching her son, but she had nothing to give. Tante Sarah took a long drag from her cigarette, then exhaled, sending a sour plume into the air. Lily fought the urge to swat it away. Tobacco was not available in the camp, and Lily couldn't imagine what ersatz substance she was burning instead. "He won't be any trouble, will he?" Tante Sarah asked, eyeing Georgi critically.

"No, none whatsoever," Lily answered quickly, giving his hand a squeeze. "He's never any trouble." She bent down to talk to her son. "Georgi, stay here and be good."

"But Mama," he said, too loudly, "she looks like a witch!"

"Shh! Mind your manners," she scolded, hoping Tante Sarah had not heard.

"I want to stay with you," Georgi protested.

"I do too. But Mama has to work." Georgi looked puzzled at the notion. "I can't take you with me. You must stay here. I will be back as soon as I can, and then we will play." Before he could argue further, Lily kissed his cheek and hurried away.

The day stretched long as Lily worked in the tailoring shop, ripping apart old uniforms so the fabric could be repurposed. She wished that she could slip away to check on Georgi. But the workers were not given a lunch break; instead, they were expected to eat whatever they had saved from breakfast. Georgi, who had arrived after breakfast, did not have anything to eat, Lily realized with alarm. If only she had some way to get the small piece of bread she'd saved in her pocket to him. She did not eat it but kept it for him for later. Her stomach gnawed painfully for the rest of the day.

When the whistle sounded, signaling the end of the workday, Lily hurried back toward the barracks. Tante Sarah and the children in her charge were nowhere to be found. Lily hurried into the barracks, but neither Nik nor Georgi were there. Where had they gone? She raced outside once more. Around the corner she saw Sofia, who raised a finger to her lips and then pointed across the field to where Georgi and her son Dorin played.

Lily walked to her. "They found each other so quickly." Sofia nodded. Lily was relieved to have found him safe. Making friends had not been easy for Georgi, even before the war, and Lily could see how happy he was. The boys played, overjoyed at having found one another under such harsh circumstances.

"And Nik?" Lily asked. "Have you seen him?"

"Not since this morning."

The two women watched in silence as the boys played. They tossed an old shoe back and forth, using it as a ball. For a moment, it seemed that they might have been anywhere, without barbed wire or fences. Sofia had a calming presence, and Lily felt a warm connection with the woman. It was odd to think that, if not for the camp, they would never have met.

Nik appeared then across the field, and Lily started toward him with relief. "Are you all right?" she asked, putting her arm around him. He leaned in close, and they walked arm in arm over to where Sofia stood.

He nodded, but she could see that he was drained. "I've been given a job in the *Revier*. There was a complex case." He had been here less than a day and was already being called upon to tend to the most gravely ill patients in the sick bay. Lily was grateful her husband had been given an inside position; she doubted he could have withstood heavy labor. Still, she worried about all of the viruses he might be exposed to there.

"Were you able to help?" Sofia asked.

Nik shook his head. "I'm afraid it's starvation edema. Very dangerous, and nothing to be done about it." She felt his frustration. Nik had always been good at fixing people; it was what he loved to do. But some illnesses just couldn't be healed, and pain was sometimes inevitable.

They gathered the boys and walked to the mess hall and joined the queue of prisoners shuffling forward with bowls in hand. Lily watched as Nik took in the vat of gray liquid that passed as dinner every single night. "Is that all there is?" he whispered.

"I'm afraid so." This was their life now, and there was nothing she could do to ease the blow. When it was their turn, Lily held up her metal bowl and the newly issued one for Georgi for a ladle of watery potato soup. She led them to a table and found a tiny spot for them to sit among the hordes of others. Georgi stared at the bowl of gray liquid warily. Potatoes were one of the many things he did not eat. He pushed the bowl away.

"Georgi, please. That's all there is. If you don't eat it, there will be nothing else today." Lily watched as he processed the concept of not having food, when he had always had enough. Even after Nik had lost his job and the food shortages had taken hold in Brussels, they had always had the basic foodstuffs to keep their stomachs filled. Now, for the first time, she could not shield her son from the hard reality of deprivation.

"Eat," she urged again, her voice rising with frustration. He shook his head, unwilling to try.

Nik put his hand on her forearm. "This isn't easy for him either," he reminded her gently. Of course. Their entire world had been taken in an instant, which must feel even more horrific from the perspective of a child.

Lily remembered then the piece of bread she had kept from breakfast and had not had the chance to give her son earlier. She pulled it from her pocket and handed it to him, exhaling silently when he ate the single mouthful without complaint. How would she possibly protect a sensitive child in a world where sensitivities no longer mattered?

That night Lily, Nik and Georgi started for the barracks. "Do you need the toilet?" she asked Georgi. He shook his head. Worried that he might have to go during the night, she considered insisting. But why make him go to the dreadful latrine any more often than he needed? "Please take him inside for bed," she said to Nik. "I will be there in just a moment."

She walked to the latrine, breathing as shallowly as she could to avoid inhaling the stench that invariably made her gag. When she finished, she started back. The horn had blared, signaling that everyone was to be in their barracks, and the area outside was deserted. No one wanted to be caught out after curfew and risk the swift and severe punishment.

As she neared the barracks, there came a shuffling sound from around the side. Out of the corner of her eye, she recognized Boden, the very guard Sofia had warned her about. The hair on the back of her neck stood on end. Had he been waiting for her?

She tried to run quickly into the barracks, but it was too late. Boden moved closer, blocking her path and leering at her with yellow tobacco-stained teeth. "Frau Abels," he said with mock civility. He took a step toward her, moving too close. A rock formed in Lily's throat. She wanted to step back, but there was simply nowhere to go. Instead, she slid sideways. He followed, and his hands reached for her low around the waist. She stifled the urge to scream. Causing a scene would only bring danger to her family. She looked around, questioning how far he would carry the assault in the open, lit space.

Boden began to pull her from the barracks toward a gardening shed a few meters away. She dug her feet into the ground, resisting. "Sir, I have dysentery." Claiming illness to ward him off was a calculated risk. Sick people were sent to the *Revier*, which was meant to be a medical clinic, but so few people ever recovered and returned, it was considered more of a death sentence.

Boden paused, and she hoped he would be deterred by the prospect of catching a stomach virus himself. But he lunged at her once more. Lily braced for the inevitable. Just then she saw a pile of bricks leaning against the wall of the barracks. She considered reaching for one. They would execute her for assaulting an overseer, but at least she would die with honor. Then she remembered her husband and son. Surely there would be reprisals against them as well. She had no choice but to give in.

A noise came from the doorway of the barracks then. "Mama!" Georgi had come looking for her. At the sound of the child's voice, Boden hesitated.

"Go back," she said sternly. She prayed her son would not come out and risk the guard's wrath.

But Georgi lingered there. "Mama, what are you doing?"

"I'll see you again," Boden said menacingly through clenched teeth. He held her just a second longer, then released her and slunk off into the darkness.

Lily breathed with relief. She wanted to run to the showers and wash the filth of the guard's touch off her. But that was impossible. She walked to the doorway and took Georgi's hand. "You are not to come outside at night," she admonished, leading him inside.

"But when I didn't see you, I was scared."

"I was just going to the bathroom. You must stay. I will always come for you," she reassured, as they climbed onto the hard wooden bunk. Lily and Nik settled into the narrow berth with Georgi pressed protectively between them, their fingers laced to form a kind of protective shield. For a second, as she slipped into the safety of Nik's arms once more, it was as if the incident with Boden had never happened.

But, of course, it had. She trembled, suddenly ice-cold, pressing closer to her husband and son for warmth. The dangers of the camp were more real to her than ever now, the risks greater with every passing day.

Unable to sleep, Lily peered over Georgi in the semidarkness at her husband. Nik, exhausted from the ordeal of his first day, had fallen asleep quickly. Lily took comfort in his familiar shallow breaths; she had missed him. She thought of poor Sofia, whose husband was gone, possibly forever. Lily hated that her own family had to live like this, but at least the three of them were together.

Georgi tossed in his sleep, and Lily wrapped herself around his thin frame to soothe him. His body was sweaty now, clothes damp. She reached for Georgi's forehead, checking him instinctively for a fever and was relieved to find him cool. He had been born weeks early, and his lungs had always been weak and susceptible to infection. She shuddered to think what the conditions here would do to him.

Lily clung to her family tightly. She would do what she must to somehow get them out.

20

Micheline

Micheline walked into the darkened movie theater. A mottled black-and-white film played across the screen as she carefully chose a seat. The theater was empty except for a few German soldiers on leave and a young couple looking for privacy in the last row. The smell of stale popcorn and beer took her back to the trips to the cinema she had made with Matteo as a child. How she wished now she might linger in the cool, dark space and forget for a while, but there was no time. A man she did not recognize came down the aisle to her row. He used a crutch and moved with a slow, awkward gait. He slid into the row and sat down next to her, reeking of alcohol. He pressed a piece of paper into her hand. Just as quickly and without a word, he left again, leaving her alone.

She exited the cinema and stepped onto the Frère-Orban Square. Making sure that there was no one standing close, she uncurled the slip of paper and read it under a pool of yellow light cast by the streetlamp. *13 Bonderstraat, Dienstag*, the message said, signaling the location closest to the barn in Lafelt where the airman was meant to be hiding, and that she was to retrieve him on Tuesday, tomorrow.

Micheline was more apprehensive than usual, now that the convoy of other airmen had been arrested. Whoever had betrayed them might have revealed the whereabouts of the wounded man as well. Part of her considered not going. But she couldn't refuse. She had made a promise to rescue the airman in exchange for Hannah's exit. Though the first part of that plan had fallen apart, there was still a downed flier out there, and she couldn't renege now and leave him stranded. She would take her own precautions, however, by going a day earlier than expected. She would leave tonight.

Micheline lingered on the street corner, waiting now for lights to go out in the tower of Saint Joseph's Church, a signal that it was late and dark enough to depart safety. Nightfall—and the cover it provided—was essential. When the church lights went dark, Micheline started from the square toward the alley where her motorbike was parked, walking it with the engine off until she was far enough away from the crowded neighborhood where the sound might attract attention.

Micheline reached the outskirts of the city, taking the side roads to avoid the police checkpoints. She drove faster now, the icy wind sharp across her cheeks. Lafelt was just under forty kilometers from the city, and she wished that she could make the whole trip by motorbike, but it was not ideal for transporting the airman. Instead, she drove to the rail station in Kortenberg, a suburb east of the city, and parked her bike behind it. There was an old Citroën in the station lot, which the network kept for errands such as this one. She found the key in the tire well and started the engine.

Nearly an hour later, she reached Lafelt, a town not far from the German border. She stopped the car in a wooded clearing several hundred meters from the rescue site. She stepped from the vehicle and looked around to get her bearings. The address she had been given was a farmhouse on the far side of the road, across an open field. She peered in both directions to make sure she was alone. Then she started across the field, which was too brightly lit in the moonlight. At the far end, the farmhouse was nestled in a bowl-like valley, a gentle plume of smoke curling from its chimney. A square, two-story barn stood behind it. Micheline debated whether the farmer was working with the resistance and had given permission for the airman to be hidden in his barn or whether he knew the fugitive was there at all.

Micheline neared the barn and crept around the back. She gave three low whistles, the known signal, and waited for the sound to come back, indicating that all was clear. Silence. Micheline considered whistling a second time and decided against it. Instead, she crept closer to the barn and pushed against the door. It opened with a loud creak.

The barn was empty. The airman was not there.

Micheline's spine tingled. Something was not right. Had Pascal's contact, Monsieur Labeau, been mistaken about the rescue site? Perhaps something had changed. Unnerved, she moved swiftly away from the barn. She paused in the barren, exposed field, uncertain where to go. Nearby there was an irrigation ditch running parallel to the side of the road. Crouching low, she moved toward it for shelter. Then, as she neared the ditch, she stopped short. Something lay protruding from the edge of it. It was a man's arm, she realized.

Moving closer, she saw the man lying facedown. He had a cropped military haircut and was clad only in long underwear. Micheline's concern grew. Pascal had said the airman was convalescing and that he would be well enough to travel by now. What had happened?

Micheline moved closer and touched the man's shoulder to rouse him. When he did not move, she rolled him over with effort and let out a gasp as his eyes stared blankly at the sky. Blood pooled beneath his head, seeping into the earth.

Micheline froze. The airman whom she was supposed to rescue had been shot execution-style, in the head.

Micheline did a cursory search of the area surrounding the ditch, but there was no sign of anyone else or of any sort of struggle. She looked back toward the barn, seeing for the first time two sets of footprints in the mud, one made by large military boots and the other smaller but still clearly a man's. The footsteps were straight and orderly, giving no indication of a fight. The airman had voluntarily left the barn, most likely lured by the person who had killed him. Perhaps, she realized, they had impersonated someone from the network and promised to take him to safety.

Micheline reached down and touched the airman's cheek. His body was still partly warm. The killing had taken place within the hour. Which meant that whoever had done it might still be nearby. She leaped up and studied the ground. A lone set of footprints, the smaller of the two sets of boots she had seen, led toward the forest that lay on the far side of the farmhouse.

Micheline sprinted toward the woods, determined to catch the killer. Inside the cover of the trees, the footprints grew muddy, and she strained to see which way the killer had gone. Her foot caught on a tree root and twisted. She lunged forward, hitting the ground.

She tried to get up but could not. Her ankle throbbed. She heard something in the distance then. Footsteps, growing closer.

The killer was searching for her.

She rolled into the brush as far as she could to stay out of sight. Then she ran her hand silently over the ground, feeling for a rock or anything else that she might use as a weapon but finding none. The killer drew closer in the darkness. She lay trapped like a defenseless animal. Her trail was unmistakable. Any second she would be found.

The footsteps were crisper now as they neared, purposeful. He (Why, she wondered, did she assume a man?) knew exactly where she was, and in another minute he would be upon her. She held her breath. She would fight for her life if she must.

Micheline looked around desperately. In the city or a rail station with other people around, she might have been able to fake a distraction. But here she was isolated and completely alone. In her haste, she had not heeded the warning signs about this mission or her gut instinct when she'd met with Pascal and his contact that something was wrong. It was a trap, and now it was too late.

As Micheline lay motionless, her heart thudded. She thought of the dead airman in the ditch just meters away. Her eyes burned with a mix of grief and shock and rage. He was not the first flier she had lost. One had drowned trying to cross the river, another had simply been too weak from his injuries to survive the journey. And the one she'd helped in Paris had not made it either. But this was different: this one had not been killed by chance or fate. This was the first one who had lost his life because of her failure to see the betrayal before it was too late.

But it was not just the murdered airman by the border that shook her. The line had been taken down at two different places, three, if she counted Lily's arrest. A coordinated attack by the Germans and whoever was working with them, since they were actively seeking to destroy the line. They could not have managed it without inside help, a betrayal. Most people in the network had access to only the information necessary for them to do their job. The traitor had to be close to the top.

And close by. She could sense someone above her in the forest above, listening for her, searching. She could not hide forever. Another step or two closer, and the killer would see her for sure.

In the distance, a dog barked. *"Hallo!"* someone called from beyond the woods. Was it the killer, trying to lure her out? But the greeting had come from the other direction. Through the brush, she saw a farmer, standing by the edge of the trees with a large German shepherd at his side and aiming a flashlight in the

direction of the trees. "Wer ist?" *Who is it?* She did not respond
but lay motionless. The footsteps of whoever had been following her retreated quickly, like a rat scurrying away.

When she was certain that her pursuer was gone, Micheline
straightened. There was something caught in the branches of
a nearby bush. Strands of fabric, she realized, pulling at them.
The maroon color was familiar, but she could not place it, so
she tucked the fabric in her pocket. Then she emerged from the
brush, wiping the sticks and dirt from her clothes as she walked
to the edge of the woods. *"Guten Abend,"* she offered, as there
was nothing at all unusual about her being there.

The farmer eyed her warily. "What are you doing here?"

Micheline considered how much to say. He might be sympathetic to the Germans or even helping them. "I'm looking
for a man. Have you seen anyone who isn't from these parts?"

The farmer pointed to the sky. "White angel," he said, making a falling gesture. She saw then how an airman cascading to
earth with his parachute might conjure such an image. Then
he frowned and held up his fingers like a gun and gestured toward the ditch. "I saw him fall, but I had to wait until nighttime until it was safe to go help him when no one would see.
But by the time I got to him, he was dead."

"Did you see who killed him?" she asked.

He shook his head. Micheline did not know whether to believe him. *"Patrioten,"* he added, placing one hand flat against
his chest and reassuring her they were not collaborators. He
tilted his head in the direction of the main house, inviting her.

Micheline hesitated; she needed to get back to the city and
warn the others. But waiting a few minutes would put some
distance between her and the man in the woods and make sure
he was gone. The farmer led her inside, where his stout wife
cooked at a stove in a corner. Micheline wondered if she minded
the intrusion. The woman, at least a decade younger than her
husband, served Micheline a hearty meal of potatoes flecked

with sausage and watched her with sympathetic eyes. Micheline, her stomach leaden, felt too numb to eat. She accepted the meal gratefully, though, and took a few bites, washing it down with a dark beer the farmer set on the table.

The farmer gestured toward the barn, and she could tell he was extending an offer to sleep there for the night. She would have welcomed the chance to rest, instead of facing the dark nighttime journey back to the city and threats that lay within it. But she could not stay. *"Nein, danke,"* she said regretfully, heading for the door.

Micheline peered outside, then turned back. "The airman, you'll give him a proper burial?" He deserved, really, to go home to his final rest. The farmer nodded solemnly.

Micheline started back across the field in the direction of the car. As she reached the roadside ditch where the dead man lay, she paused remorsefully. She knelt beside him, hoping to find some sort of identification so word of his death could be sent to his family. His body was stiffening now. She did not see any injury other than the gunshot wound, and she debated whether he had been hurt at all, or if that had been a lie and part of the plan to lure her here in the first place. She searched around him, but whoever had removed his uniform had taken his dog tags as well.

Micheline began to straighten. She noticed then something lying on the ground beside the body. A piece of paper, she realized. She reached over and picked it up gingerly.

Unfolding the paper, she gasped. It was a hand-drawn map of the region: Belgium, Holland, Luxembourg and the north of France. Marked on it was the entire network, their safe houses, drop sites and routes. It was shockingly comprehensive. Whoever had created it had been studying their operations, watching for months. This was not an isolated strike. Someone was trying to take down the whole network.

She refolded the map carefully. Then clutching it tightly in her hand, she ran in the direction of the car.

21

Lily

The first transport left at night.

The previous day, there had been an unexpected midday roll call. They stood in the stifling heat as the guards selected people and took them out of line, seemingly at random. At first, Lily had assumed it had been for labor detail or interrogation. She exhaled silently when neither she nor Nik were called.

When those chosen were told to collect their belongings from the barracks and report to the administration building, Lily fleetingly wondered if they were being sent home. Perhaps she should make inquiries whether her family could go as well. But she had learned too much in her short time here to believe that or to ever volunteer for anything. And the looks on the faces of those selected told her they were not being released. *Deportations*, Sofia gravely confirmed later that day. The places in the barracks vacated by those who were taken remained empty for just a few days before new prisoners arrived to fill them.

Georgi noticed the development. "Ooh, a train!" he exclaimed one morning after breakfast, pointing. The rail line ran just behind the camp, the makeshift station several hundred meters from the fence. A large engine, pulling a dozen third-class rail cars, stood on the track in front of it. Georgi pointed to the queue of people who shuffled forward with their few possessions in small torn sacks. "Where are they taking the people, Mama?" he asked, puzzled.

Lily faltered, trying to explain to a child what she did not quite understand herself. "East to work in labor camps to make things for the war." That was the best she could come up with. The explanation, *Arbeitseinsatz*, labor deployment, was what they had all been told.

"But, Mama, if they need workers, then why are they taking such old people?" Georgi's face was childlike, but his logic was beyond his years. Among the people shuffling toward the trucks were many elderly and the infirm who could not possibly work. Lily saw in her son's question the fullness of the lie. Why go to all of the trouble of shipping these poor souls across Europe for labor? It was not for work, she felt certain, but for something much worse.

"I'm hungry, Mama," Georgi whined, changing topics abruptly. For Lily, the pain in her stomach had grown so omnipresent that she scarcely acknowledged it anymore. But for a child, the emptiness was unbearable, and Georgi spoke of it often.

Hearing Georgi's complaint now, Lily's heart ached. They had just finished their meager breakfast, and it would be nearly the whole day before there was anything to eat again. She looked around helplessly. Georgi was not as fussy an eater now as he had been when he first arrived. He took whatever he could get. She had seen him more than once trying to shove blades of grass in his mouth or forage around the rabbit hutch when he thought she was not looking.

"When we get out of here," she whispered, "we are going to have those crepes you loved at Maison Reneau."

"With extra whipped cream?" he asked, seeming to brighten a bit. She considered whether such promises were cruel, and if talking about the foods he could not have might somehow make it worse. But this was hope, and it was all she had to give him, to fill his heart because she could not fill his stomach. He did not complain or ask further but ran across the yard to play with Dorin under the unwatchful eye of Tante Sarah.

That afternoon, Lily returned from her job to collect Georgi. Tante Sarah looked cross, and Lily feared it was because she was late. "That gypsy woman," Tante Sarah said, and Lily cringed at the derisive term. "She hasn't come for her brat yet." Sofia was even later than Lily was.

"I'll mind him," Lily said. Two boys were in some ways less work than one because they kept each other busy. Still, she fretted: it was not like Sofia to be late.

At last Sofia arrived, her face ashen. "We've been called," she said.

"No!" Lily raised her hand to her mouth. "What will you do?"

"Go. There's no other choice." The question had been a foolish one. She could not simply disappear or evade detection. In Breendonk, there was nowhere to hide.

"What about your husband's friend, François? Can he help?"

"I reached out to him. He's devastated, of course. But he's a prisoner, just like us. There's nothing he can do." Sofia paused. "Maybe now that we are being sent, we will find my husband." There was no hope in Sofia's voice.

"When do you leave?"

"Tomorrow morning before dawn."

"So soon." The Germans knew that catching people off guard gave them no time to plan or protest. Lily tried to think of the right words to comfort her friend but found nothing that would not be a lie.

"We'll be fine," Sofia replied, lifting her chin. "Our people have always moved about, adapted to new places. It's what we do."

She could not hide the doubt in her voice. "And I am a strong worker. In the camps, those who are able to work are saved."

"And those who are not?"

Sofia shrugged, unwilling to answer. Dorin would not be old enough to work, and although his mother would fight like a tiger to protect him, Lily could not help but be afraid. She swallowed down her dread. "Of course you will be fine. You're one of the strongest people I've known." Still, the trains and their ominous destination made her deeply afraid for them.

Sofia nodded gravely. "I only hope that will be enough."

Lily wished that she had something to give Sofia, a gift or even just something to help with the trip. But she had nothing. Instead, she wrapped her arms around her tightly. "I'll miss you. I'm glad that we met and that we became friends and our boys did too, even for so short a time."

Sofia hugged her back. "As am I. I shall pray for you and your family and that we will meet again one day." Then she gathered Dorin and started in the direction of their own barracks to prepare for the trip.

That night Lily lay awake in the barracks beside Georgi and Nik. As daylight neared, she imagined Sofia, just a few rooms away in the fortress, rousing a sleepy Dorin and preparing for their journey to points unknown. She was fearful for them and sad, too, at losing the only friend she had known since coming here.

The next morning after breakfast, Lily and Georgi walked out into the courtyard. Nik had been called to his job in the sick bay early. Georgi started expectantly for the field, looking for his friend to play. "Where's Dorin?" he asked when the time for their usual playdate came and went and he did not appear.

Lily's stomach twisted. How was she ever going to break the news to him? She had not told Georgi the previous day that he was seeing his friend for the last time. That had been a mistake, she realized now. She should have shared the truth and let him have his goodbye. Delaying the inevitable had only made things worse.

Lily put her arm around Georgi. "He's gone, darling. Remember that train we saw? Dorin went on a train ride."

"Where?"

"He went home," she lied.

"Lucky! I want to go too," Georgi pouted.

"We can't, darling. We must stay here for now."

Lily prayed her answers would be enough. But Georgi's face crumbled with a mix of frustration and sadness. Suddenly it was all too much. The hunger and hardship he had endured for all of those weeks seemed to build up in that very minute. Georgi's face reddened, and he let out a wail.

"Georgi, please," Lily pled, desperate to stop him from attracting attention. But he sobbed inconsolably.

A horn blared, signaling the start of work. Lily hated leaving Georgi in such a state, but she didn't dare arrive late to work. "Come." She took Georgi to Tante Sarah. "He's a little out of sorts today because of Dorin leaving," she added in a voice too low for Georgi to hear. Then she went to Georgi and kissed his head. "Darling, stay here and out of trouble. I will be back as quickly as I can." Before he could protest or ask to go with her, she turned and raced for the garment shop.

Lily entered the shop and started for the job she'd been working on the previous day, ripping apart the old uniforms. But the overseer, a Jewish woman named Helga who was reviled for wielding power over her own people, stopped her.

"You!" she snarled, and Lily worried that, despite her effort to get to the garment shop quickly, she was in trouble for being late. "You are to take the laundry."

The officers' uniforms were not washed in the camp, Lily knew, but taken to a laundress down the road. Taking the laundry was a privileged job, one that meant going beyond the camp gates for a few hours. It was usually reserved for the more senior workers, prisoners who had been there the longest. Lily had not expected to be chosen so soon.

But leaving the camp to take the laundry meant leaving Georgi, something Lily hated to do when he had been so distraught. She didn't know how long the job would take or how soon she could get back. Lily looked in the direction of the barracks, wishing there was time to at least tell Tante Sarah that she was going. "Now!" Helga ordered, seeming to sense her hesitation.

A few minutes later, Lily found herself trudging down the dirt road outside the camp, pulling a large bin filled with dirty clothes. Helga followed. Lily was surprised: she knew she would not be sent outside of the camp alone, but she had not expected the overseer to go as the guard herself. It felt strange, almost pleasant, to be outside. The bin was heavy, however, and the task made harder by the ruts in the mud that caused the wheels to get stuck. Lily's skin grew moist and her breathing labored. Helga watched her struggle, not offering to help.

As she walked and pulled the cumbersome bin, Lily thought of Sofia and Dorin. The journey east had to be at least three or four days, and she had no idea how one would keep a child calm and still on such a long ride. What fate had awaited them at the end?

At last, they reached the laundress's house, a lone one-story cottage by the edge of the road. There was a small shed out back with steam that curled upward from a chimney. A woman appeared from the shed and gestured for Lily to bring the bin inside. Lily expected Helga to follow her into the house, but she did not. Taking in the house, anger rose in Lily. Surely the woman knew what was happening at the camp. How could she stand by day after day and do nothing?

"Come," the laundress said. "You have to wait while I package last week's laundry for you to take back." Lily was surprised when the woman led her into the main house and offered her a seat in the parlor, a small room with high windows and just

a sofa and two matching chairs for furnishing. The room was
drab, with flowered curtains and faded maroon-and-blue up-
holstery that looked decades old and possibly secondhand. The
rug on the floor was frayed and stained. Lily sank into a chair
with gratitude. After weeks in the camp, though, she could not
help but marvel at the civility of a chair with actual cushions.
It simply felt like heaven.

The laundress set a cup of tea on the table. "I'm not allowed
to give you anything," she said apologetically. "But I'm not
drinking this, and I would hate for it to go to waste." Her voice
was nervous and pinched. Lily understood then that while the
woman was powerless to do anything to help those in the camp,
she could only offer this gesture of defiance as a show of soli-
darity with them.

Lily looked at the cup uncertainly. "Won't I get in trouble for
taking it?" she asked, gesturing toward the window.

But Helga was nowhere to be found. "She always walks down
the road to the next farm while the laundry is being prepared, to
enjoy a bit of schnapps and some company with the old widow,
Herr von Schurmer." The laundress gave Lily a knowing look.
"You have a good hour before she returns."

The laundress left the room. Despite the laundress's reassur-
ances, Lily did not drink the tea straightaway. She felt guilty
drinking the warm, delicious beverage while Nik and Georgi
were back at the camp, doing without. But if she took nourishment here, she could save more of her rations for her family.
She drank the tea in a single gulp and took a coarse sugar cube
to give to Georgi later.

Lily wondered if there was a washroom she might be permitted to use. She stood and walked to the door to the kitchen
through which the laundress had gone. She started to push it
open, then stopped again. The laundress was folding the clothing that Lily was to take back with her into a neat stack. As she
watched, she saw the woman slip a piece of paper into the collar

of one of the shirts. Lily backed quietly from the doorway and returned to her seat, hoping that the woman had not seen her.

The laundress returned to the sitting room a few minutes later. It was clear from her calm expression that she had not noticed Lily come into the room. "You will make sure this laundry goes only to Anhel, the head tailor." Lily wanted to ask what the paper was. Was the woman sending a message to someone in the camp, possibly helping?

When the folded and packaged laundry was ready, Lily stepped outside. Helga had returned, hair a bit askew and gait unsteady. Lily sped back to the barracks as quickly as she could with the cart, Helga following more slowly but still watching.

She delivered the laundry to the garment shop. "This will be your job from now on, once a week," Helga pronounced. Lily's uneasiness grew. Though she had not minded the break from the garment shop, the journey with Helga had been nerve-racking, and she hated being away from Georgi. Now it seemed she would have to do it again and again.

When the final whistle sounded, signaling the end of the work day, Lily hurried to the barracks. She was relieved to see that Nik had returned from work and was watching Georgi. Her son showed no sign of sadness from earlier that morning. He was trying to engage him in a game of tag, but Nik was leaning against the side of the barracks wearily waving him off.

Nik had never been a playful father. He was older and staid, the type of parent who read books and talked about ideas. The kind, she always thought, who would make a good father when Georgi was older. Often when Nik showed Georgi things in nature, he tried to listen and ask thoughtful questions. Georgi shared his father's beautiful mind. But he was also a child, and sometimes, like now, he just wanted to play.

"Papa," Georgi cajoled as Lily neared. He was longing for a playmate now that Dorin had gone.

"Enough!" Nik snapped at the child. Lily stopped, taken aback by the sudden outburst. Nik was normally quiet; this was not like him. But they were all growing frayed around the edges by the strain of the situation.

"Georgi, come," Lily said softly, wanting to ease the tension. She reached in her pocket for the sugar cube she had taken for him, but it was gone, crumbled to dust like some magical object in a storybook that could not cross over into this awful realm. "Let's go wash our hands before supper."

"I'm sorry," Nik said to her in a low voice when she and Georgi had returned from the sinks. His face was wracked with guilt. Even when he failed with Georgi, it was never from lack of trying.

"I know," Lily said soothingly, caressing his cheek. She understood how hard it was to meet their son's needs amid all of the stress and exhaustion of the camp. Their situation was so tenuous. Who knew how long they all might be permitted to remain intact as a family? She did not want Georgi's last memory of their days together to be this. "You must do better. We both must. We may not have forever." Nik nodded in acknowledgment and walked over to Georgi to try to play with him.

Leaving them, Lily went the barracks to collect their food bowls to bring to supper. As she entered the building, the odor of human filth washed over her. She would never get used to that smell, and her stomach roiled.

She stepped toward her bed, then stopped.

Lying on her mattress, crisp and out of place, was a slip of paper. Moving closer, she could see that it was a yellow deportation card.

She did not pick it up at first. She closed her eyes, fighting the urge to turn and run outside. If she stood perfectly in place and did not go forward, she would not read and know the awful news. If she did not see the notice, perhaps when she returned it might be gone. But pretending would not make time stand still or undo what had already happened. When she looked again, it remained there, undeniable and real.

Reluctantly, she walked over and picked it up. The notice bore all three of their names. They had been called together. Whatever fate awaited them they would not be torn apart as so many families had—at least not yet. The date was August 23, less than two weeks' time.

Her mind reeled. Once she had believed that they would be allowed to go back to Brussels, to the life and freedom they had once known. Even after she knew that to be untrue, she still clung to the hope that their Belgian citizenship would somehow keep them from being deported. Now the realization slammed into her like a rock. The road out of here went one way only. The Germans meant to rid Belgium of all its Jews, including the native Jews, forever.

If they were sent to a labor camp in the east, she might be spared and kept for work. But a child as young as Georgi had no hope whatsoever. Her panic rose.

Nik appeared in the doorway then, holding Georgi's hand. The two of them joked easily, Nik's earlier terseness gone. Then his eyes fell on the yellow card she held, and his smile evaporated.

She gestured Nik over, away from their son. "What are we going to do?" she asked quietly so Georgi could not hear. "We have to do something." Unlike when Sofia had been called and sent immediately, they had almost two weeks before they were to go.

Nik shook his head sadly. "There is nothing to be done." His voice was resigned and certain. He put his arms around her and rested his chin on her head.

"But we can't go. We are native Belgians."

"That doesn't protect us now. Nothing will. At least we will go together."

"What about that British soldier," she pressed, "the one who offered you help?" As she spoke, she knew it would do no good.

"Even if we could get a letter to him, by the time he received it, it would be too late." The offer of sanctuary the officer had made a few months ago faded like a distant dream. "Still, I will send word," he added. "You never know."

"And I shall get a message to Hannah. She has so many contacts from the resistance and the network that helps transport people. Maybe she can do something."

"But how will you reach her?"

"I will find a way. There has to be one." Though Lily was still furious with Hannah for causing their arrest, her cousin seemed like the key to their survival.

After Nik left her to go to the washroom, Lily looked out the window and across the camp, thinking. She had to get word to Hannah or Matteo. Lily had told Matteo not to come again, and while she doubted he would give up on her, his next visit might be too late. There had to be a way to reach them, rather than simply waiting.

Lily remembered the laundress, whom she'd seen smuggling a paper into the collar of a shirt. It seemed as though she had been sending a message to someone in the camp. Was it possible that she might send a message from the camp as well? If only Lily had known about the call-up a few hours earlier, she might have tried to persuade the laundress to send word to Hannah. But the laundry was outside the camp, unreachable now.

But the man to whom the laundress had sent the message was not. *Anhel*, she recalled. Reputed to have been one of the finest men's tailors in Brussels before the war, he was now relegated to a workbench in the corner of the shop where he reattached loose buttons and darned socks.

Nik returned from the washroom. "Can you take Georgi to dinner?" she asked. "I need to go back to the garment shop for a minute. There's someone who might be able to help."

Before Nik could ask any questions, Lily hurried from the barracks. The work day had ended, and she worried that Anhel might have gone for the day. But he sat hunched over, sewing, as she approached him. "Hello. I'm Lily. I work in the garment shop."

He glanced up. "I know. I've seen you. What do you want?"

Lily was nonplussed by his gruff tone. She considered turning around and leaving. But the situation was desperate. "I need you to have a message delivered to someone on the outside." She held out the small scrap of paper on which she had hurriedly scrawled a note to Hannah asking her to come quickly. She had written to her cousin instead of Matteo, thinking that a note addressed to the canteen might arouse too much suspicion.

"I'm sure I don't know what you are talking about," he replied evenly.

"Except that you do. I saw when I picked up the laundry earlier that someone sent a message to you. I know." He stared at her evenly, not responding. But he blinked once, an acknowledgment. "Don't worry, I'm not going to tell anyone. But you have to help me. Please, I must get word to my cousin."

He scanned the message, and his eyes widened. "I can't possibly. I have a daughter on the outside. There will be reprisals to her if I get caught." It was not for his own safety he feared, but for his child's.

"Of course I could not ask you to endanger your family." Lily paused, thinking about what to say next. She could not walk away and give up their only hope either. "You see, I have a child also. A son." She gestured across the field where Georgi and a few other children played quietly.

Anhel's eyes followed her gesture, and seeing Georgi something seemed to shift. "I won't deliver your paper," he said. "It's too direct, and it is going to get you and your cousin in trouble."

"I'm being deported. What worse trouble is there?" Lily's hopes fell; her plea had failed.

"I will deliver the message, but I will use a drawing instead of words, so that it cannot be understood if someone intercepts it." He brought his finger to his lips. He would get word to Hannah. "Tell me something, a symbol known only to you and your cousin, that has meaning."

Lily searched her memory. "A sparrow," she said finally. "We rescued one when we were girls." Just as Lily herself needed rescuing now.

"That is all I need to know."

"But…" Doubts circled her mind. "If you aren't sending a paper message through the laundress, then how?" Anhel was a prisoner like herself with no other access to the outside.

"I will deliver your message," he said in a firm voice, warding off further argument. "Now, what is the address?"

As she gave Anhel her address, her doubts redoubled. Would the message reach her? What if she didn't understand? It didn't matter now. The tailor was her best and only hope, and she had no other choice but to trust him.

22

Hannah

Hannah returned to Lily's house late one afternoon. As she entered the foyer, she paused, imagining that life was normal and that she might hear Lily's gentle voice, cajoling Georgi into eating his vegetables. But there was only stillness. Though Hannah still stayed in the house to care for it, she spent almost all of her time elsewhere. It had been terrible after Lily was arrested, but after they took Nik and Georgi as well, she could hardly bear to remain there.

She had not seen them arrest Nik and Georgi. She had simply come home one day and found them gone. They had been taken suddenly. Nik's pipe sat still warm in the ashtray, and Georgi's bowl of cereal remained half-eaten, milk staining the tablecloth where it had splashed over the edge. Horror ricocheted through her. It was bad enough that her dangerous actions had resulted in her cousin's arrest. But now the Germans had taken Lily's family, her innocent son. Hannah's guilt over what she had done to cause all of this redoubled, threatening to overwhelm her.

Hannah had tried to find them and had made the same desperate inquiries she had when Lily was arrested. The answer that came through Micheline was immediate and unsurprising: they had been taken to Breendonk, presumably reunited in the camp with Lily.

Just then she noticed something lying on the ground by the front door. It was a folded piece of paper that had been pushed through the mail slot. It was not stamped post, but the letter carrier might have delivered it anyway; so many mail carriers (at least those who had not been arrested in the dragnet months earlier) were helping to resist the Germans by delaying call-up notices and transporting covert messages.

The handwriting on the outside was not familiar to Hannah. Inside, there was a slip of paper bearing no words, just a hand-drawn picture of a sparrow in a tree. Her heartbeat quickened. The sparrow had always been her and Lily's symbol of their friendship, ever since they had rescued one by the sea. Lily had reached out; perhaps, despite all that had happened, she had begun to forgive Hannah. But Lily would not have sent this cryptic message for no reason. She was trying to reach Hannah and signal something to her. There was a date, August 11 and a time, midnight, written as well. *Today*. Lily, who had told her not to come, was calling her back now, asking for her help.

That night just after nine, Hannah closed the door to the house and started for the rail station. She boarded a train out of Brussels toward the camp. When she reached Mechelen, it was after curfew, and the station was nearly deserted. She found the stationmaster and asked directions, hoping he would not question why she was headed to the camp at such an hour. He eyed her warily before pointing in the direction of Breendonk. She started out of town by foot.

As she walked along the darkened, uneven roadway, her doubts increased. She was out past curfew and walking toward a prison camp. She might be apprehended at any moment. And though Lily had summoned her, she didn't know if or how she could reach Lily inside the camp. Micheline had, without saying as much, warned her not to come here. If she was arrested, she would be in no position to help Lily at all. But Lily had called her, and she could not stay away.

Soon, Hannah saw the massive Breendonk camp rise out of the rolling hills in the distance. As she neared, her heart sank. She had not been prepared for the enormity of it all. The former military fort was surrounded by a moat, and on the other side, barbed-wire fencing stretched endlessly in both directions. *Besucher Verboten*, the sign warned. *Visitors Forbidden*. Hannah might be arrested or shot on sight.

She studied the fortress, which seemed unapproachable, trying to figure out what to do. The grounds were barren and exposed, except for a few clusters of trees in the distance behind it. Bright lights shone down from the guard tower, illuminating the gate and making it impossible to approach without being detected. Hannah walked as quickly and silently as she could around the side of the camp, giving it a wide berth and staying on the far side of the hill in order to remain out of sight.

When she neared the back of the camp, she crept closer to the moat, a thin, creeklike strip of water that separated the camp from the outside. The prisoners were all in their barracks sleeping. How was she ever to find Lily?

She saw something move then inside the camp. A lone prisoner in a striped uniform, making his way from the barracks to what she assumed was the latrine. Hannah inched closer to the moat. "Pardon me," she whispered from the far side.

The man looked over, alarmed. Then he looked down again, and she thought he might ignore her and continue on his way. "Please, a moment," she called softly.

Checking to make sure no one else could see him, he moved toward the fence. "You cannot be here. If the Germans see you here, you will be arrested or shot."

"I'm looking for Lily Abels." Hannah wished she had thought to bring a photograph of her cousin.

"I don't know her. Is she a Jew?"

Hannah nodded. "Belgian."

The man pointed. "You want to go farther around the back side of the camp." He gestured past the stone fort. "The east wing is where the Jews are kept, in a smaller area, separate from political prisoners. There's a low spot in the moat where you can cross, and a place by the fence where you can hide in the trees. Now go, before you get us both killed!"

Hannah started to thank the man, but he had already gone. She crept farther along the fence until she saw the spot, thick with brush, that the man had mentioned. She crouched low as she crossed the moat, water seeping cold into her boots and through her stockings.

Hannah peered through the fence with more urgency now. Where was Lily? Hannah had come at the time she'd asked, but she was not there, and Hannah worried something had happened to detain her.

Just then, she glimpsed two familiar figures walking between two buildings. "Lily!" she cried, instantly regretting how loud her voice was. She leaped back behind a tree as a guard's head snapped in her direction.

The guard looked around but saw nothing out of the ordinary. When it seemed like he was gone and it was safe for her to come out from behind the tree, she moved closer to the fence once more. Lily was starting in her direction now. As she saw Hannah, her eyes widened. Hannah willed Lily not to repeat her own mistake and cry out. Lily put her hand to her mouth to stifle a yelp. Then she checked over her shoulder. Lily's expression was guarded, like prey being hunted.

As Lily cautiously approached the fence, Hannah's stomach twisted at the sight of her. Usually impeccably dressed, Lily wore a filthy striped uniform, and her face was smudged with dirt. Hannah imagined that Lily must find being in such a state humiliating to bear. She had tried, Hannah could see, to pull her hair back neatly in order to maintain some pretense of her usual decorum. But it was simply impossible. The old Lily was gone. Lily had always been thin and was even more so now with the weight she had swiftly lost. She couldn't go on like this, Hannah fretted. Lily was not as strong as she. Surely the hardship of the camp would be too much. Seeing her from outside the camp, Hannah was seized with guilt. It should have been the other way around, herself imprisoned and Lily free.

Lily had summoned Hannah, and Hannah hoped she would be glad to see her. But this was the first time they had met since Lily's arrest and since the full scope of Hannah's betrayal became clear.

"Georgi and Nik?" she asked.

"They're here with me."

"How are you all holding up?"

"How do you think?" Lily's eyes burned with anger. She needed Hannah, but that didn't mean she was ready to forgive her.

"Lily, I'm so sorry." The inadequacy of the words threatened to swallow her.

Her cousin eyed her coldly. "That hardly matters now, does it? It's done." She saw Lily wrestling with a torrent of emotion. Her cousin had never been one to show anger, but the rage that burned inside her was obvious. "I told you!" Lily said, her voice laced with disdain. "I warned you not to associate with that lot, that getting involved would only bring us trouble. But you had to be so stubborn." Lily was nearly yelling now, and Hannah looked over her shoulder, fearful that she would attract the attention of one of the guards. "How could you steal my identification? It was selfish and stupid, and look what you caused."

"I know," Hannah said meekly. She searched for the words that would make what she had done all right. "Here," Hannah said, passing Lily the small parcel of food she had hastily assembled before leaving, a bit of bread and cheese.

Once Lily would have turned up her nose at the scraps but now she took them quickly. She tucked the parcel of food under her arm. "Thank you." Angry or not, it was food, and she could not afford to refuse it.

"You should eat that now, while you can."

"I will save it for Georgi," she said decisively. "There isn't much to eat some days."

Thinking of her cousin and her family in such deplorable conditions, Hannah's guilt surged. "I am working every possible angle to get you out of here. Matteo is, too, of course."

"Matteo..." Lily repeated, an unmistakable catch in her voice. "I'm grateful that your friend is trying to help," she added.

"Lily, I know about you and Matteo."

"I have no idea what you are talking about." Just minutes after berating Hannah for not being forthright, Lily's very instinct was to lie to cover her secret relationship with Matteo.

"I saw you both on the square right before you were arrested. I walked away before the police came," she added quickly, not wanting Lily to mistakenly think that she had abandoned her in her moment of greatest need. "I know about your past together and that, well, it isn't in the past. Matteo told me everything." This last part was not entirely true, but Hannah knew that if she did not say it, Lily would continue to deny everything.

Lily's shoulders softened. "It's true that Matteo and I were lovers when we were young. But I had not been in contact with him for many years. I didn't even realize he was in Brussels until the night I saw you at the canteen."

That was months ago, Hannah marveled. All of this time, she had not known. "When did you first start seeing him again?"

"Only recently, after you brought the wounded fighter to our house. But even then, it was only a few walks. Nothing happened between us. You must believe me, Hannah."

"I do." Hannah could see that her cousin was telling the truth.

"I was going to tell him we couldn't see one another anymore when I was arrested. Not that it matters anymore." Lily looked over her shoulder, an uncharacteristic note of bitterness in her voice. "We've been called up for deportation."

"Oh, Lily!" Hannah understood then why Lily had summoned her. It was the worst news she could have imagined. Hannah had heard deportations were coming. Still, she had hoped that Lily, a native Belgian, would be spared. She had not thought that it would come to this so soon. "When?"

"August 23."

"Just under two weeks' time," Hannah said, processing the news.

"Yes. You must do something."

Hannah looked at her cousin helplessly. "I don't know if I can." Disappointment crossed Lily's face. Lily had always looked up to Hannah, and Lily's admiration had always been a source of pride for her. It pained her to admit to Lily now that she could not help.

"Matteo will help," Lily said with certainty.

Hannah shook her head. "I already asked him and Micheline to help get you out, but she said it's impossible. She won't risk it at the expense of the line." Hannah felt the sting of disappointment and betrayal at Micheline's unwillingness to help.

"Matteo will convince his sister now that we are to be deported. He'll do it for me," Lily insisted. "He must. It's our very last chance."

"But I tried every appeal for your release. And we can't break you out of the camp. It's impossible."

"Then, break us out of the train!" Lily cried, her voice breaking with frustration. Hannah started, taken aback by the boldness of her proposal. What Lily was suggesting was absurd. It was impossible.

But as Hannah turned it over in her mind, an idea began to take shape. "Try to stay calm," Hannah said. "I will be back. Meet me here in two days' time, and I will figure out something."

23

Micheline

When Micheline left the farmhouse, she headed for Brussels. She did not return immediately to her apartment or the canteen, though, fearing that those places might have been compromised as well, known to whoever had killed the airman. Instead, she tried to reach one of her contacts, a florist in the Etterbeek neighborhood, whose shop had sometimes served as a drop box for messages, to send word to Matteo. But the shopkeeper had put up his Closed sign and drawn the shutter when he saw her coming. Micheline did not know whether word had reached Brussels about the murdered airman or whether something more had happened to the network here as well.

Micheline started for an apartment on Rue Jacobs-Fontaine in the northern part of the city, the safe house that they only used for the strictest of emergencies. There she might be able to send a message to others in the network, to warn them of the breach and see if other operations had been compromised as well. She looked for the plant the landlady would put in the window to signal when the Germans had been there, but the sill was empty. That meant it was safe.

Micheline walked through the alleyway on the side of the building and crept in the rear entrance and up the stairs. She unlocked the apartment and opened the door slightly, listening to make sure no one was there. Silence.

Inside, the studio apartment was deserted. But at the kitchenette in the corner was a pot on the stove filled with half-cooked rice, which was beginning to grow moldy. Whoever had last used the apartment, an airman in hiding or a volunteer for the network, had left unexpectedly, their departure unplanned. That person, Micheline suspected, had either been apprehended or fled. And the person or people who had come for them might return. She dared not linger here long.

Hurriedly, Micheline dyed her hair to a nondescript brown with the kit that she had left at the safe house months earlier for just such a purpose and pulled it back into a bun. She changed into an extra outfit, a nondescript blouse and trousers, which she found in the closet. Then she moved to leave. Hearing a sound in the corridor, she froze. She crept toward the door and peered through the crack. It was only the landlady, Micheline realized with relief. She opened the door a bit more. The landlady pointed downward toward the front door, signaling that someone had been there. Though she had not dared to leave the plant on the window sill, she was nevertheless trying to warn Micheline of danger. It was as near as she dared get to tipping Micheline off that the Germans had been—or still were—in the building.

Micheline raised her hand slightly in acknowledgment and then stepped backward into the apartment and closed the door softly. She walked across the room and opened the window, then looked out before climbing onto the fire escape as swiftly and silently as a cat. She took a last look back at the apartment. It had been a good safe house, and she hated to lose it. But it was burned now, useless. She scampered up the ladder to the roof, carefully crossing two more buildings before finding another ladder down to the street.

She paused, considering where to go. The canteen, she decided. Although she was still worried it might have been compromised, she had to warn the others.

When she reached the canteen, it was dark inside. Nevertheless, she went around the back and in through the cellar doors. Inside, she blinked to adjust her vision to the dim lighting. As she started for the stairs to the main floor, she heard a shuffling sound from above. Someone was there. The footsteps grew louder as whoever was in the canteen moved closer to the basement stairs. She looked around, searching for a weapon. There was a cracked porcelain vase in the nearest corner. She picked it up and moved toward the stairwell. The intruder started down the stairs, each step groaning more loudly beneath his feet.

She raised the vase up over her head and stood behind the doorway, waiting. Just as she was about to bring it down, she recognized the familiar set of shoes. It was Matteo.

He stepped into the room, his face registering surprise. "I thought I heard someone. What are you doing down here? And your hair…"

Micheline lowered the vase, then turned the light on low to cast a faint gleam. "The airman…"

"Arrested?"

"Murdered." She let the word sink in.

"By whom?" he asked, bewildered.

"I don't know," she confessed. "A traitor. Someone who knew about the rescue and got there before I could."

"There's even worse news, I'm afraid. The encampment… it's gone."

"Senzeilles?" The news hit her like a blow. "How is that possible?"

"The Germans attacked without warning." Matteo's face was ashen. "They were overrun."

"And the airmen?"

"Many died fighting. Others were taken." She thought of Tomas, wounded and helpless. The Germans would not have bothered to transport a man who could not walk. Surely he would have been shot and killed on-site.

Just then there was a clattering from above. "Stay here," Matteo said softly, then bounded up the stairs before she could protest. Micheline heard the door open, then voices.

Moments later, Matteo reappeared, followed by Hannah. "My cousin and her family have been slated for deportation." Her voice was desperate. "We have to do something." Matteo shot Micheline an uneasy glance.

"What is it?" Hannah demanded. Neither answered. "Tell me."

"The trains...they are headed to Auschwitz."

"The Polish labor camp?"

Matteo shook his head. "It's not just a labor camp. People are killed there, thousands each day. They use gas, either in closed-off trucks or actual bunkers. And afterward they dispose of the bodies."

"All of the people?"

"Not all. The strongest are kept for hard labor. But the elderly, the weak, the children, are all taken straightaway."

"Like Georgi." There were several seconds of silence as the truth lay between them. "This is all my fault," Hannah lamented. "We have to get them out. They must not be on the train when it leaves Belgium."

"How soon?" Micheline interjected.

"Just under two weeks."

"Then, there's nothing we can do. I'm working all of my contacts trying to secure a release for your cousin and her family at the highest levels. But so far, no luck. I can't possibly manage it that soon."

"And escape from the camp is impossible," Matteo added.

"What if we break them out from the train? It will be less guarded than the camp."

"Break them out?" Micheline repeated with disbelief. "From a locked train?"

"There were rumors of a previous break. When the train stopped, a few people were able to jump off," Hannah offered.

"But it was not successful," Matteo said. "One person died trying to jump from the train, and the others were recaptured and killed." What made her think they would have any more luck?

"And that was just some people slipping off the train through a window of their own accord," Micheline added. "You are talking about something far bigger—a planned break. And if we do get them off the train, what then?"

"You can get them out of the country," Hannah ventured.

"You want me to take a woman with a young child across the line?" Micheline asked with disbelief. "Do you know what you are asking?"

"I know exactly what I am asking you to do," Hannah replied, meeting her eyes evenly.

Micheline brought her hand to her brow as she tried to process what Hannah was proposing. "They have no cover story. They will be marked, hunted. There will be nowhere for them to hide."

"If we leave them on the train, they will surely die." The truth of Hannah's statement was undeniable. With deportation to a death camp looming, they simply had nothing left to lose. "You have to help me."

"Help you?" Micheline's frustration bubbled over. "We've been through all of this before. There is nothing we can do, especially now, with the network in tatters."

"But you must. My cousin was arrested because of us. I have to help her."

"This isn't our kind of work."

"It is now. It has to be." Hannah's voice was pleading now.

"The train attack would be a blow to the Germans," Hannah continued, appealing to Micheline's combative instinct. Micheline could not deny that to free the prisoners would strike at the very heart of what the Nazis were trying to do. It would undermine the morale of the German soldiers who were already battle weary and bolster ordinary Belgians who were just trying to hang on. It was not merely the attack: the ripples from it would be felt throughout the country—if they succeeded. If not, the repercussions would be all the more severe.

Micheline struggled with her request. This was bigger and more difficult than anything they had ever done, the very hardest thing at the worst time. Micheline wanted to say no.

Matteo pulled Micheline aside. "Please. If they are sent to Auschwitz, they will die."

As Matteo and Hannah looked at her pleadingly, Micheline wrestled with their request. She didn't want to help. Lily represented everything Micheline hated, a kind of complacency and desire to protect only her own. "Your cousin…" Micheline said to Hannah. There was a hint of accusation in her tone. "She didn't stop her life or choose to help the cause when our country was taken or when all of the foreign Jews were arrested. Now the wheel has turned, and she is the one to be deported. Why should we be expected to risk everything to save her?"

"Because she took me in and sheltered me, and now her own family is paying the price." Hannah squared her shoulders. "It is only right that we should help. And because I am asking you to help me. I'm going to do it either way."

Micheline stared, taken aback by Hannah's defiance. "On your own?"

Matteo stepped forward. "No," he said. "Not alone. I will help you."

"Matteo, you cannot possibly!" Micheline protested.

"Then, don't join us." Matteo's voice was cold. He moved closer to Hannah.

"I forbid it."

"Either way, we will save them. With or without you."

Still, Micheline looked skeptical. "Do you think I am holding back for my own safety?" she flared. "I've never cared about that. No, I'm thinking of what will happen to others. To the people who will pay in reprisal in the camps and on the streets. For the people on the train. For the network. If we fail, they may all die."

"We aren't going to be able to keep this up much longer," Matteo said gently. "They are coming for us, as surely as they did the encampment and the Jews in Brussels and Antwerp. Let's make this count now while we can."

He was right, Micheline admitted inwardly. "This is folly, and we are all going to die, including your cousin and her family. The blood of those people will be on your hands. But I won't leave you to die alone."

Hannah's eyes widened. "Really? You'll help?"

"Yes. If you and my foolish brother insist on trying, then I won't let you do it alone and get yourselves killed. If by some chance this works, we can save many innocent people and deliver a stinging blow to the Germans."

"Many innocent people?" Matteo repeated.

"Yes, of course." Now that she had agreed to the mission, Micheline saw it as a chance to do something larger. "We can't break into the railcar and then only rescue three people. We will free as many as we can, including Lily and her family."

"Oh, thank you! But what's our best strategy? A moving train with locked doors…" Hannah's voice conveyed her uncertainty.

"We need to stop it somehow. We will have to break into

the wagon and free the people in it quickly. Your cousin will need to help us from the inside. We need help prepositioning tools on the train so the prisoners can help break out. And we must identify the strongest people who will be on that train and concentrate them in that car so they have the best possible chance of escaping."

"She can do it." Hannah asserted. "But what will all of these people do once we break them out?"

"Most will have to scatter and try to flee or find places to hide. We can't possibly get them all to safety, but at least they will have the chance."

A chance was all they had to offer. "And Lily?"

"There's an abandoned chateau outside of Haacht that we used to use as a safe house," Matteo said. "It's just east of the town, and if you follow the antitank canal from there to the valley, you can't miss it. We can take Lily and her family there to hide until we can get them out of the country."

Micheline turned to Matteo. "Go to your friends from Group G who work in operations and ask for assistance." The *maquisards* who worked in combat were a separate entity from the escape lines, and Matteo knew them better than she. "We can't do this alone. We need fighters and weapons."

"I thought you said no guns," Hannah interjected.

"For this, there will be." Micheline turned back to her brother. "You must persuade them to help us. Do you understand?" She hated asking favors from the other network, but she had no choice. They had to get done with this and back to the business of saving airmen.

"Yes," Matteo replied solemnly. "I let Lily down once. I can't fail her again."

"And you won't. This is your operation." Micheline faced her brother squarely and placed both hands on his shoulders. "I'm needed elsewhere. Plan this. Find the resources. And don't lose any of our people." She turned and walked from the office into the front of the canteen.

Through the doorway, Micheline could still see her brother and Hannah. "I will go now to get help and be back by dawn," he told her.

"Thank you!" Hannah reached out and touched his arm with a mix of gratitude and affection.

He stiffened slightly but did not pull away. "Of course. I will do whatever I can to help you—and your cousin." He turned on his heel and was gone through the back door. Micheline watched sadly, wishing that her brother could let go of his past hurt and find happiness once more.

Hannah joined Micheline in the front room. "My brother left?" Hannah nodded. "Do you have feelings for him?" Micheline asked bluntly.

Hannah flushed. "Is it that obvious?"

"Yes, but it doesn't matter. He's in love with Lily."

"He is."

Micheline did not bother to deny it. "She's bad for him. Was then. Is now. I know she is your cousin, but that's the truth. She almost destroyed him. When she abandoned him, he wanted to die. She almost killed him once. I won't let her break his heart again."

"Lily isn't like that," Hannah replied defensively. She loved her cousin, and she wouldn't have anyone speak poorly about her. "Not if you really know her."

"Anyway, I'm sorry," Micheline said "that I didn't agree to help earlier. It's just that the network means life to so many. The work has to be about the greater good."

"I understand. So what changed?"

"Freeing these people *is* the greater good. Sometimes I get so caught up in the work of the line that I forget what we are fighting for. I understand that now." Micheline stood up and checked her bag, then hoisted it over her shoulder.

"Where are you going?" Hannah asked.

"Out."

"You're leaving again, now?" Hannah was incredulous. "But we need your help planning the train break."

"I know, but there's a traitor to the network. I went to rescue a wounded airman and when I did, I found him dead. Someone got to him first and killed him. They were searching for me as well, but I got away. I have to find that person and stop them."

"Why? You got away. Isn't that enough?"

Micheline shook her head. "Not when that person is still out there somewhere. There is no telling how much he knows. Whoever he is, he is onto us. He poses a great threat if he isn't caught—especially to the train break." There was a note of urgency in Micheline's voice. "We have to find him." The operation could not possibly proceed if there was someone who might betray it.

"Do you have any idea who it might be?"

Micheline paused, thinking. "When I went to arrange your departure and I agreed to rescue the airman, there was a stranger with my contact, Pascal. He could be the one who sold us out."

"What does he look like?"

"Sandy thinning hair. Gold teeth in the front."

"I don't think it could be him. I saw him arrested at the station along with the airmen. Could it be Pascal himself?"

Micheline considered the question. It seemed so unlikely. Pascal was loyal to the cause—or at least he seemed to be, until now. "Anything is possible at this point." Pascal could be the traitor. He had set up the rescue that was not vetted. Only, he could not have acted alone. He did not have the information about picking up the wounded airman, the fact that Micheline had gone early. The killer had known and had gotten there first. That information would have come from someone else, even higher and deeper in the organization. "Pascal did not know enough to compromise the entire mission. There has to be another traitor."

Hannah shifted uneasily. "Who?"

"That's what I'm going to find out."

"Do you know where to look?"

"No, but there's this..." Micheline pulled out a map and unfolded and spread it on the desk. "This was near the body of the dead airman. It shows all of our safe houses and other locations." Hannah's eyes widened as she realized how serious the breach actually was. "I figure the traitor will be headed to one of these locations next to try to capture more airmen." *Or kill them*, she added silently.

As Micheline smoothed the map, a small scrap of paper fell out of it and fluttered to the floor. Hannah retrieved it. It was a torn matchbook cover, and though the logo was faded, she could just make out the name of the café in Brussels: *La Fleur en Papier Doré.*

"Are you familiar with this place?" Hannah asked.

"Yes. I've been there many times to meet contacts and exchange information. It's a place we considered safe." Micheline's expression was pinched. She held the matchbook cover up to the light. Written on it faintly was a date and time. "August 13 at 3:00 p.m. That's tomorrow."

"What about my cousin?" Hannah asked. "Should I go to her to tell her about the plan so she can prepare?"

Micheline shook her head. "It's too dangerous to return to the camp again. It was a fool's errand to go in the first place. I need you to stay here. Matteo may return, or he may send word about whether the resistance will help us. Someone needs to be here to receive it." The explanation was only partially true. Micheline didn't want Hannah to say too much to Lily or to overpromise.

"But Lily needs to know what the plan is."

"I will try to go to see her on my way to the café and tell her what she must do." By going herself, she could control exactly what Lily and the others on the inside knew.

"You just said it's too dangerous."

"And you just said we have to tell her. You agreed to meet up again in two days' time, correct?"

"Yes, that was yesterday, so she is expecting me tomorrow just before midnight."

"So I'll go in your place."

Hannah stared at her doubtfully. "But you hate my cousin." Micheline had made no secret of her contempt for Lily. Yet she was willing to risk everything to save her.

"True. But if I say I'll help her, I'll help her."

"Very well. But be careful. Getting close to the camp is dangerous. It's heavily guarded, and there is no good way to sneak around without being seen. You must go around the very back to the place where there is shelter from trees and cross the moat there."

Micheline bristled at Hannah telling her what to do. But Hannah was just looking out for her well-being. "I understand. Stay here and await further instructions from Matteo."

"I won't let you down," Hannah said. She looked at Micheline expectantly, seeming to hope for similar assurances. But Micheline would not make promises she could not keep.

24

Lily

Lily waited by the camp fence just before midnight. She had snuck from the barracks and crept low to the shaded camp perimeter at the date and time they had agreed, but Hannah was not here. Five minutes passed, then ten. It would not be safe to wait much longer. By being out in the darkness, she was breaking curfew. Georgi might awaken and call for her, his loud cries alerting the others to her absence. Every second she stood by the fence risked detection and reprisal for her and her family.

Just as she was about to give up and start back, a cloaked female figure appeared through the darkness, head bowed low. Though she moved swiftly, the frost-covered ground broke too loudly under her footsteps as she neared, betraying her secret arrival. "I didn't know if you were going to make it," Lily remarked. Her voice carried an unintended note of recrimination.

"I'm sorry," an unexpected voice said, breathing heavily. "I came as soon as I could." The woman lowered her hood and to Lily's surprise, it was not Hannah who stood before her.

It was Micheline.

Lily stared at her. "I was expecting Hannah."

"Hannah was called away on another mission." Lily was not sure if she believed the explanation. "I'm here to help," Micheline added.

Lily's doubts grew. She knew that Micheline did not like her and would never agree to help. There must be a reason she was here, if not out of the goodness of her heart. But what was it? "Have you been able to arrange our release from the camp?"

"Not exactly."

Lily's spirits sank. Another dead end. "Then, what?"

"We have a plan to get you out."

What did she mean, *a plan*? Hannah had said Micheline was not able to help. Why was Micheline dangling this hope before her now? "But you said getting us out of this camp is impossible."

"It is." Micheline lowered her voice, though there was no one within a hundred meters. "We can't get you out of the camp, so we are going to try and break you out of the train."

"Break us out?" She had suggested that very idea to Hannah out of frustration. But she had not imagined they would actually try it. "That's impossible. The trains are sealed. There will be guards."

"We have men," Micheline spoke confidently.

Remembering the gathering of young people she had witnessed at the canteen months earlier, Lily was dubious. "But the train will be moving. How will we ever get off?"

"We will stop the train and break into the railcar before the guards realize what has happened."

As Micheline outlined the audacious plan, Lily's mind reeled. "This is not doable."

Micheline brushed the hair from her face, impatient now. "You asked for out. This is out," she snapped. "We can't free you from the camp. The train is our last—and only—hope. We have to do this." She paused, her expression growing more solemn. "Auschwitz, the camp that is at the other end, it's bad."

"How bad? Tell me," Lily demanded, but Micheline did not respond. "I'm not a child. Keeping things from me is what landed us here in the first place," Lily added bluntly. "Not telling me doesn't keep me safe. It puts me in more danger."

Micheline nodded, silently acknowledging the truth of Lily's words. They both knew that if Hannah had been more honest about helping the Sapphire Line in Brussels, they might not be standing here, talking through a prison fence. But still Micheline did not tell her.

"You've never liked me," Lily snapped. Micheline did not deny it. "Is it because of Matteo?"

"I despised you for hurting my brother," she replied bluntly. Lily noticed that Micheline used the past tense, though she seemed to hate her still. "And for what you stand for."

"What do I stand for?" Lily demanded.

"Complacency. You did nothing to help others, didn't want Hannah to help. Until you were the one who needed aid."

"I want to live to raise my son. Is that so wrong?" Micheline did not answer. "You drew my cousin into your work and brought danger to our whole family. You are the reason we are here!"

"I'm sorry," Micheline said earnestly. "I certainly never meant for you to be arrested."

"I'm sorry, too, for hurting your brother and for not doing more when I could. But, please, you must help us. Things are very bad in here."

"Not as bad as where you are going," Micheline replied bluntly. She cleared her throat. "Auschwitz is much, much worse than here." Lily tried to imagine a place worse than Breendonk. "Trust me," Micheline said. "You and your family must never reach the train's destination. That is all you need to know."

Lily brought her hand to her mouth. "Sofia," she said. "My friend was sent already." Had she already faced this terrible fate?

"You see now why we must prepare and try to rescue you from the train. If you go east, you will surely be killed."

In that moment, Lily knew Micheline was right. This was their only chance, no matter how slim or terrifying it might seem. Lily did not like Micheline. But she had to trust her. "Tell me," she said. "Tell me what it is that you need me to do."

"We need you to work as a liaison, help us get things ready inside the camp."

"Ready how?"

"There are a few resistance fighters in the camp. They will help you gather tools for the train to help with the breakout from the inside. And they may be able to help you in other ways as well. You must make contact with the resistance fighters who are inside. Can you do that?"

Lily hesitated. Until now, she had survived by keeping her head low and following the rules. But now Micheline was asking her to do the very opposite of that. It was complicated, involved others. Nothing else would keep them safe, though. This might be their only chance. "Yes. Do you know who these people are?" Micheline shook her head. "Then, how am I to find them?"

"You will have to figure that out. You will need to make inquiries among the other prisoners. Carefully. If you talk to the wrong person, you could be caught. Of course, if you can't manage it—" Micheline looked as if she was unsure whether Lily was up to the task.

"I can," Lily interrupted. Still her doubts welled up and threatened to overwhelm her.

"Also, you need to find out which train car you will be in, so that we know where to break in."

"How can I possibly do that?"

"You must find a way. Then, when you have the information, pass it to me. You've been to the laundress, haven't you?"

Lily nodded. "The laundress is sympathetic to our cause, and she can be trusted with messages."

"But the laundry will not need to be taken again for almost a week."

"You must find a way to go sooner."

When Micheline had gone, Lily lingered at the fence. She had been caught off guard by the appearance of Micheline instead of Hannah, as well as by the magnitude of what they were proposing.

Lily returned to the barracks, but was unable to sleep as she considered how to make contact as Micheline had asked. Where to begin? There were hundreds of people in the camp.

François, she remembered suddenly. Before leaving, Sofia had mentioned the man who had been part of the resistance and a good friend of Sofia's husband. He had looked out for Sofia, and she had trusted him. Lily felt certain that even if he was not the right person to help her, at least she could trust him not to say anything.

The next morning after breakfast, she left Georgi with Tante Sarah a few minutes earlier than usual and walked across the courtyard toward the other side of the camp, hoping she might try to make contact before she was expected at the garment shop. There were more guards here, including the one with a German shepherd that lunged at the prisoners as they passed on their way to their jobs. Lily did not belong here and stood out. She had no excuse for being here if stopped and questioned.

She ducked behind a work shed, too afraid to go any farther. "Excuse me," she said in a low voice to one of the prisoners as he passed. "I am looking for François."

The man gestured with his head toward another building behind the fortress. "He works in the machine shop."

Lily walked quietly along the side of the fortress, keeping her head low and not making eye contact with anyone. She neared the machine shop. François, whom she recognized from the time she had seen him with Sofia, had come from a different direction and was about to go inside. "François?" she called to him. Closer, she could see that was fiftyish, tall and hulking, with an unkempt gray beard that he had somehow been permitted to keep.

He turned toward her. "Yes. Who are you?"

"I'm Lily Abels. I was sent by my friend Sofia," Lily fibbed.

There was a glint of recognition in his eyes. "You've had word from her?" he asked eagerly.

"No, but she told me that you were someone who could be trusted. Someone who could help."

"What do you want? I've got trouble enough of my own."

"Not here." She gestured him around the side of the shed. "My family and I are scheduled for the next transport," she explained when they were away from the other prisoners.

"I'm sorry to hear that, but so are many others. What does this have to do with me?"

"Some people on the outside, fighters from one of the networks, are planning to try and free us from the train."

The man's eyes widened with disbelief. "They are coming to help?"

"Yes, they are going to break into the railcar to free us and anyone else they can. But they said they need help from the inside. They told me to find resistance fighters in the camp to ask for support."

"You understand that this will be nearly impossible without a small army?" François said, his expression grim. "How many men do they have? Will they bring guns? What is the plan?"

Lily stood helpless, unable to answer his many questions. "I—I don't know," she stammered, overwhelmed. "They just asked me to make contact with you and the others within the camp so we can get ready."

"What is it that you need?"

"We need to gather as many things that we can use as possible. Tools, whatever we can find to break out of the train when the time comes."

The man paused, seeming to consider the request. Lily fretted that he would refuse. He was not scheduled to be on the train. Why should he risk so much for people he did not know? "I can try to help with that."

"There's one other thing…" She was reluctant to ask for more. "I was told to find out which railcar we will be in. Do you know anyone who might be able to help?"

"I'm not sure. I will make inquiries. Come find me tomorrow, and I will let you know."

Just then she noticed Nik across the field, watching her from the far side of the fortress. "I have to go." She hurried away.

"Darling, who were you talking with?" Nik asked as she neared.

As he wrapped his arms around her, Lily hesitated. She had wanted to tell Nik about the plan at breakfast after she had seen Micheline, but she hadn't dared talk about it in the crowded dining hall. She needed to tell him now. The plan was so absurd she hardly knew where to begin. But Nik had to know. "Remember when we received the call-up notice, and I reached out to Hannah?" He nodded. She lowered her voice. "She and her resistance friends are working on a plan to free us from the train."

"The train?" he interrupted skeptically, pulling away. Her own doubts about the plan echoed in his voice.

"Yes. We have to get ready, and I am finding people in the camp that can help with the breakout."

The lines in his face deepened with concern. "Lily, that's so dangerous. If you are caught, they'll kill you. They'll kill *us*." He tilted his head in Georgi's direction. "You must not get involved. Do you understand?" He cupped her chin, looking deep into her eyes. She did not answer. Nik, taking her silence for acquiescence, kissed her once on the forehead, then walked off.

But as she left for work, guilt enveloped her. She wished she could have told Nik more about the work she was doing and what was going to happen. She would have expected that much honesty from him, demanded it. She had tried to tell him. He didn't understand, though, and pushing the point further would just make him upset. The argument would be more of a distraction than she could afford right now.

The next morning, she went looking for François at the machine shop. But he wasn't there. "He's been ordered to the quarry to haul rocks," another man said. Alarm rose in Lily. Was he being punished for having spoken to her or for some other offense? The heavy manual labor would be too much for someone his age.

Lily could not get to François as easily at the quarry either. It was on the edge of the camp, across a field and well-guarded. She considered waiting until that evening and finding him when he had returned to the center of the camp. But there was no time.

Steeling herself, Lily set out across the field in the direction of the quarry. She kept her head low but walked purposefully, trying to look as if she belonged. She was supposed to be headed to work at the garment shop now. The penalty for being late would be severe, and for being in a part of the camp where she did not belong even more so. If she was stopped, she would say she was delivering a message from one of the foremen, she decided. The lie was hastily concocted, and anyone who checked would quickly see that it wasn't true.

She reached the edge of the quarry, trying to catch François's eye without drawing the attention of the guards. Finally he noticed her and snuck over, motioning her behind a shed. His face was chalky with dirt.

"Why were you sent here?" she asked.

He shrugged. "Why anything? They needed more bodies for the work detail. Anyway, I can't be gone long. I was able to reach out to a contact of mine in the camp office. You and your family are assigned to railcar twelve."

"And the tools?"

"I can have them for you by tomorrow. It won't be much, a file, a crowbar, perhaps a hammer. But it's something."

"Thank you." Lily started away from François in the direction of the garment shop. She had to get the railcar information to Hannah through the laundress, but how? The laundry was not due to go for another week, and that would be too late. Her eyes traveled to Anhel's bench where a bottle of black dye sat. Impulsively she walked toward it. If the uniforms were dirty, she would have to go to the laundress again sooner.

She picked up the dye, then stopped again. Soiling the uniforms would surely result in punishment. She waited until the others were engaged in their work and then quietly tilted the bottle, watching with a mix of horror and fascination as the dye seeped into the crisp uniforms.

Lily returned to her own workstation and began folding garments, keeping her head low. How long before someone noticed the garments?

A few minutes later she heard a loud wail from one of the workers. Helga rushed over to the bin and began to curse. "Who did this?" No one answered. "You will all be beaten and starved until the guilty one comes forward." Lily then saw her mistake: by secretly spilling the dye, she had subjected them all to retribution and punishment.

"I saw a mouse earlier," she offered. "It could have knocked the jar off the shelf." She waited for Helga to see through the lie. Any rodents in the camp would have been captured and eaten by the starving prisoners.

Helga stormed over to her and grabbed her by the collar. "You come with me. We must take these uniforms back to the laundress to try to remove the stains before we are all shot." Lily saw fear in the overseer's eyes then. Though she wielded power, she was a prisoner too and as afraid for her own life as they were.

Ten minutes later, Lily set out with the laundry bin once

again. Helga, in a foul mood, carried a switch, and she would whip at Lily's ankles if she moved too slowly. "Hurry, hurry."

They reached the laundress, and Helga explained their predicament. "I will see what I can do. But the laundry will need to soak for at least an hour." Helga set off down the road.

When she was out of sight, Lily turned to the laundress and pulled out the paper with the names of the resistance workers. "I need to get this message to a woman called Micheline at the canteen on the Rue du Champ de Mars in Brussels." The laundress looked startled. "Can you do it?" she asked. The laundress nodded gravely before disappearing from the room.

Helga returned much sooner than she had on their previous visit to the laundry. She looked angrier than before, and Lily thought that perhaps the man she liked to meet had been unavailable for her surprise visit. "The laundry?" she demanded.

"I'm working on it. But some of the stains are deeply set and will take work. I will need you to come back for it tomorrow."

"Tomorrow?" Helga spluttered. "But we cannot possibly wait."

"I'm afraid there's no other choice." Lily and Helga left the laundry and started back. They had left the cart, and Lily's steps were lighter than they had been on the way there. But Helga trudged behind her, swearing occasionally but otherwise silent.

The next morning, Lily started back toward the laundress to retrieve the uniforms with Helga in tow. She reached the house and started for the door. For a moment, Helga lingered, not walking away as she usually did, and Lily wondered if she would be dissuaded from going to see the widow at the neighboring farm by her seemingly unsuccessful trip there the previous day.

Lily knocked, and the laundress let her in. "The uniforms are ready, except one that I couldn't save. But I still need to pack them up for you." She looked over Lily's shoulder where Helga had thankfully started down the road. "I delivered your message," she said in a low voice once Helga was out of sight.

"I was told that they would send more information as soon as they have it."

"Thank you."

The laundress left Lily another cup of tea before disappearing into the other room. Lily sat down and took a grateful sip. Coming to the laundry was stressful and exhausting, even without the strain of sending messages, and she wished she could be done with it entirely.

A second later, the door to the living room opened again. Lily jumped, startled that the laundress had returned so soon. "Can you come with me?" the woman asked. "I need to show you something on one of the uniforms."

Lily followed her, fretting that the laundress had not been able to get the dye out, dreading Helga's wrath if that was true. But she led Lily through the kitchen, past the pile of folded uniforms and out the back door of the house. She gestured toward a small shed.

"I don't understand."

Then looking across the yard, she let out a small gasp. Standing in the brush close to the shed was Matteo.

"Shh..." he whispered, his voice barely audible from a distance. She opened her mouth to speak, but he brought a hand to his lips, signaling silence. He motioned her over. She turned behind her, but the laundress had disappeared. Looking both ways to make sure no one was looking, she hurried over to him.

"Lily," he said, his voice choked with emotion. "Are you all right?" he asked.

She did not know how to answer the question. Nothing was all right now. He studied her, seeming to search for signs of injury or harm. She was embarrassed by her torn uniform, matted hair and her skin, which was caked with dirt. Her mouth was sour from having not brushed her teeth. He drank her in, not seeming to notice. He took her hand, and she allowed herself to fall into his embrace, seeking a moment's shelter and comfort in the warmth of his arms. "I've been so worried about you," he said, pressing his hands to her cheeks, as if checking to make sure she was real and whole.

She looked at him expectantly. "How did you find me?"

"I heard you had been chosen for the errand. I wish you hadn't been. I didn't know if I would manage to find you. I would have come sooner, but I had to figure out where you were and then how to get to you safely."

"It isn't safe. If Helga, the overseer, returns and sees you…"

"I needed to know if you were safe. If only there was more I could do to help."

"You are working to free me. What more could I ask?"

"Are you hurt at all?"

She looked away, ashamed of how far she had fallen in the weeks since she had seen him last. "I'm fine. But this plan… how can it ever work?"

"It has to." There was a desperation in voice, mirroring her own. "Micheline agreed to help and is summoning every possible resource."

Lily might have stood there forever with Matteo, but the clock was ticking, her two hours winding down. "I have to go."

"Lily, wait. You're out now. We can help you into hiding and then rescue your family."

She considered it fleetingly. Was he really suggesting that she simply leave? "Matteo, that's impossible. If I didn't return, many would pay with their lives, starting with my Nik and Georgi. I have to go back."

"You're going to just go?" *Again*, he finished silently.

She needed to turn and walk away. But like so many times before she could not. "Matteo, please don't."

"At least wait a few more minutes. Please."

She hesitated, torn between her desire to stop time and be with Matteo for what might be the last time and the reminder that every minute she was gone risked the peril of her husband

and son. "Only a moment," she relented. She allowed herself to lean in to his chest, and he rested his head atop hers. She breathed him in, wanting time to stand still, yet knowing every moment they lingered risked discovery.

"I will be there the night of the break," Matteo said.

She could not bear to think of him embarking on what could well be a suicide mission. "Hannah too?" He nodded. "No, she mustn't. She should leave that to the fighters."

"Don't you see? She is a fighter. She's extraordinary."

"She is. Sometimes I wish, though, that she hadn't come to Belgium," Lily confessed. She tried to imagine what life would have been like. She and her family would not have been arrested. "Is that awful?"

"It's understandable. But she deeply regrets what happened. And she cares about you very much."

"And I, her." Lily met his eyes directly. "You have feelings for her, don't you?"

"I do." He looked away. Lily did not want to care. She was married and hardly had the right. But a pang of jealousy stabbed at her, nonetheless. Matteo continued. "That is, I did. But that was before I saw you again. How could I possibly be with anyone else?"

Lily took his hand and squeezed it. "Go," she said. "Love my cousin. What we shared is nothing more than a memory. With Hannah you have a chance at happiness. With me, none." She waited for him to argue, but he did not. "You have to go. Helga will be back at any moment."

"I know. But I don't want to leave you again."

Lily turned to him one last time. "If something happens to me, you must find my son and save him." She wanted to say more, but there wasn't time.

"I swear it." His voice was resolute. "And if something should happen to me, just remember. Remember our night in the *jardin*."

Matteo was referring to the one night they had had together

in their youth, when they had made plans to run away and she had given herself over to him. It was just a few stolen hours before fate tore them apart. Being together now seemed like a refrain, the closest they would ever get to finding one another again. She wanted to stay in that place, before the warmth died and she returned to the cold forever. But she had people counting on her. A husband and son. She could not linger.

"I won't forget," she promised, and then she turned resolutely back to the laundress's house.

When she and Helga returned to the fortress, Lily delivered the laundry, then returned to her workstation. She needed to go see François again, but there was no way to do so in the middle of the day without attracting attention.

At last, when the final horn of the workday blared and the others started toward their barracks, Lily slipped out the back of the garment shed. She looked in the direction of the machine shop where François worked, then stopped. Fifty or so meters away, she glimpsed Boden. Her body tensed as she remembered his attempted assault. Was he trying to approach her again, or was he simply on patrol? Not meeting his eyes, she retreated into the garment shop and pressed herself against the wall, watching until he disappeared.

When she was certain that he had gone, she snuck out the back of the shed once more. She started in the direction of the machine shop, hoping that the delay had not made her too late to see François.

She peeked into the shop and, finding him alone, walked inside. "I thought you weren't going to show," he grumbled.

She considered telling him about her near encounter with Boden, then decided against it. "Do you have the tools?"

François turned to a cabinet behind the workbench and produced a small key from his pocket. He unlocked the cabinet and lifted the bottom to reveal a compartment. Then he hid the items that had been secured in the pipes in the compartment.

Over his shoulder, she could see that there was already handful of items amassed, screwdrivers and hammers and a small saw.

Seeing the weapons, she was suddenly afraid, not just for herself but for François, who was risking everything to help her when he could not escape himself. "Why?" she could not help but ask. Surely a fight this hard and dangerous was better left to younger men.

"You mean, why do I fight at my age?" His eyes had a faraway look, as if remembering. "When the Germans came to our village, they locked all of the women and children in the synagogue and set fire to it. My wife, daughter and grandchildren were all killed." His voice trembled.

Lily's stomach twisted. "I'm so sorry." The words felt inadequate. What had happened to his family was her worst nightmare, and the very thing she was trying to prevent for her own.

"I fight for them. So when I reach the end of my days and see them again, I can tell them that I stood up. If I give up now, all I lost would have been for naught. Or maybe it is simply that I have nothing left to live for." He did not speak for several seconds.

Lily looked at the tools dubiously. "I don't think I should take them all now," she said. "There's a guard who has followed me before, and he saw me coming here."

"Better not to chance it," he agreed. "Go to the garment shop a few minutes early tomorrow morning, and I will sneak them over to you." Lily hurried from the shed, eager to get back to her family.

The next morning Lily asked Nik to take Georgi to Tante Sarah and arrived at work a few minutes early. She looked out the window across the field in the direction from which François should have been coming. But the field was empty, François nowhere to be seen. She waited anxiously. A few minutes more and the other workers would arrive, and she would not be able to take the tools from him undetected. She walked out the back door of the shed. Still he did not appear. She did not know if she had gotten the time wrong or if he had been somehow waylaid. He would not miss a meeting like this without a reason.

She heard noise from the other side of the fortress, close to the main courtyard. At first Lily thought that it was just the prisoners assembling for the roll call. But normally they were quiet and subdued at the early-morning gathering. Today the voices were louder and agitated. She hurried from the garment shop toward the yard.

As she neared the edge of the space, Tante Sarah appeared around the corner of the fortress. She looked as though she wanted to shout but did not dare. She gestured frantically for Lily to come, and Lily started toward her. Terror welled up in her. Had something happened to Nik or Georgi? Lily tried to go faster now, but the distance in front of her seemed to grow, like an awful dream she had once had of running in place, powerless to move. She stumbled on an uneven patch of ground before righting herself and continuing on.

"Your family is fine," Tante Sarah said before she could ask. Lily's body went slack with relief. "Only, François..." she said and led Lily to the square.

Looking up, Lily stifled a scream.

François's body hung lifelessly from the gallows.

25

Micheline

Micheline stepped off the tram near the square and started down the Rue des Alexiens, drawing up the hood of her cloak against a drizzle that had just begun to fall. She walked toward the café, La Fleur en Papier Doré, then froze. Close to the entrance stood an officer of the *Garde Civile*, one of the Belgian police units most complicit with the Germans. Micheline wondered if he was looking for her. Her doubts loomed. She was a wanted woman. The last thing she should be doing was be seen on the streets of Brussels. But the train break could not proceed as long as someone was out there betraying the network. She started toward the café, feeling a sense of relief when the officer did not follow her inside.

Micheline entered the café. It was a historic Brussels institution, which had been frequented by the surrealists of the 1920s. The walls, yellowed and pockmarked with age, were covered with their framed sketches and photographs done in sepia. Candles flickered on each table, casting long shadows. Micheline could see the other patrons (regulars, most likely) taking her in, wondering what this unfamiliar young woman was doing here alone. Normally she would not have cared. But she needed to blend in now.

She took a seat at a high table by the bar and ordered an aperitif. *Arrive early*: that was a lesson she had learned in the early days of the war. That way you could pre-position yourself and not attract attention walking in. She took a sip of the cocktail when the server brought it, savoring the bitter sweetness. She looked across the café. The gathering seemed to be what passed for ordinary these days, a few German officers with their dates and some local officials who had collaborated as well.

In the back of the place, a German officer caught her eye. He was seated alone and seemed to be waiting for someone. That did not mean he had anything to do with the person she was looking for. She looked away. The side door to the café opened then, and a familiar figure walked in. Pascal. Had he come looking for her, perhaps to deliver a message from Matteo? She rose to get his attention, but he was looking away from her and toward the officer. *"Guten Abend, Gruppenführer Helm."* As he shifted, his lightweight jacket gaped at the neck to reveal a maroon silk scarf, unmistakably frayed at the corner.

Recalling the strands of fabric she had found in the bushes near the farmhouse, Micheline's blood chilled. Pascal was the man in the woods, the one who had killed the airman. He was working with the Germans.

Micheline's anger flared, followed quickly by alarm. Pascal must not, could not, see her here. She stood abruptly, and as she did, her purse clattered to the floor. The German's head snapped in her direction. He said something to Pascal, who began to turn. Micheline rushed to pick up her purse, thankful that the contents had not spilled. Still, it felt as though every eye was on her as she started toward the door.

"Wait!" she heard the German call behind her, standing up.

Pascal must have seen her and told him who she was. She should have played it cool, acted as if she was there for social purposes, but it was too late.

Micheline ducked around the corner and started to run. Behind her she could hear the men's footsteps, growing louder. There was a taxi stand at the corner where a single cab sat idling. Desperately, she sprinted toward it. But before she reached the stand, someone else got in and slammed the door, and it sped away.

She ran faster now, crossing the street heedlessly. Brakes screeched as a delivery truck nearly missed hitting her. Its horn blared. She ran for the bus stop at the corner, where a bus was just pulling in. The footsteps behind her were growing louder. In a few seconds, Pascal and the German would be upon her. She reached the stop just before the bus closed its doors. As it started off, the men turned and began to chase it.

They did not see Micheline, crouched behind the bus-stop bench.

Two hours later she arrived at the canteen, where Hannah and Matteo were in the back office. Her breath was strained from running and nerves.

"What happened?" Matteo asked.

"I saw," she gasped. "It was Pascal."

"The priest?" Hannah asked with disbelief.

"Former priest, or at least that is what he said." Micheline was no longer sure that was true.

"Was he with anyone?" Matteo asked.

"A German officer. High-ranking. I heard Pascal refer to him as Helm." Hearing this, Hannah's eyes widened. The implications were unmistakable. "There's no telling how much damage he has done. We have to go dark until this passes," Micheline said, her tone ominous. "Freeze everyone in place." Hiding servicemen from Paris to the foothills of the Pyrenees, the wounded and those in peril would need to shelter in place and hide until new, safer arrangements could be made. They would be trapped in places where they were not meant to stay more than a few hours, stuck for days or even weeks. The entire underground network had effectively ground to a halt, their every resource compromised.

"But what about my cousin?" Hannah asked. "We have to free her still."

"Everything we built is in the rubble," Micheline countered. "How can we possibly move forward with such a dangerous mission?"

"Because there is simply nothing to lose now that everything has been taken." Hannah took her by the shoulders, her voice calm and commanding. "We will rise from the ashes, rebuild anew and come back stronger. But we can't do that by hiding and running. We have to take the fight to the enemy."

"Hannah's right," Matteo interjected firmly. "The raid must go on as planned. No one knows about it but the three of us. Our plans are secure." An uneasy silence passed among them.

"Very well," Micheline said, regaining her composure. She studied a diagram of the camp intently, trying to recalibrate and figure out how they could keep going, in spite of all that had happened. But the equations did not compute, no answer came. Finally, she turned to Hannah. "You will need to take the weapons, both the ones they've collected in the camp and the ones we have here, and hide them on the train."

Micheline pulled a matchbook out of a desk drawer and struck a match. She set the flame to the edge of the map and held the match over the waste bin, watching the paper burn to embers and smoke until it was gone. Then she picked up her satchel and started for the door.

"I will be back in time for the raid."

"But where are you going?"

Micheline paused, not certain how much to say. The raid had to go on, but first the threat Pascal posed had to be neutralized.

"I'm off to catch a killer."

26

Lily

Lily stood motionless, staring at François's lifeless body as it swung from the gallows. Sickened, she tried to look away but found that she could not. The man whom she had enlisted to help, with whom she had spoken just hours earlier, was hanging with his eyes open and mouth agape. His face was swollen with fresh cuts and bruises, and one of his arms hung at an odd angle.

"He came looking for you a short while ago," Tante Sarah said. They were supposed to meet at the garment shop, Lily thought. But perhaps he had caught wind that it was dangerous to do so and was trying to warn her. "Told me his name and asked for you. I looked for you, but you were already gone, and when I told him that, he left. The guard stopped him on his way back to the other side of the camp and took him away. And a few minutes later, this." Though the elderly woman had seen much in her lifetime, she was clearly shaken by the barbarity of it all, and her voice was heavy with grief.

Lily realized with a mix of remorse and dread that François's death was her fault. She had gotten him involved, and it was because of helping her that he was dead. She would probably already be dead too, if things had played out differently.

Lily looked around anxiously, wondering why he had come to see her at her barracks ahead of their scheduled meeting. Had he been trying to warn her about something? If the Germans had found out what François was doing with the tools or where he had gotten them, they might know her role in it as well. Lily did not know if he had talked, how much he had said and whether he had given her up.

"I took the children into the barracks so they would not see," the woman said.

"Thank you." But Lily had no idea when the Germans might cut down François's body. Surely Georgi would see the horrific sight when he returned.

"We should not linger," Tante Sarah prodded. Without speaking further, she hurried away. Lily looked up at the resistance fighter one last time and whispered a word of silent thanks. He had died a hero and honored his family members who had also been brutally murdered. Lily did not know what she believed about an afterlife, but she hoped he had been reunited with them.

Lily returned to the barracks, fearful that the Germans might come for her as well. Despite the atrocity of François's body hanging for all to see, life continued in the camp as if nothing had happened. But the other prisoners, who were getting ready to go to their jobs for the day, seemed more anxious. They moved quickly, heads low, as if afraid they might be killed next.

After checking on Georgi and finding him happily playing, Lily set out for the garment shop. What now? Without François, they could not possibly continue to prepare for the train break. But to do otherwise meant giving up and resigning themselves to deportation to Auschwitz.

As she neared the garment shop, a man passed whom she recognized as another one of the resistance workers. But he shook his head, indicating that they dare not speak. She proceeded into the shop. A few minutes later, he came into the shop and sat down beside her. The other workers averted their eyes, pretending not to notice. Fortunately, Helga was nowhere to be found.

"I'm Joshua, a friend of François's." He said the dead man's name in an almost reverent way, and his eyes were red, as if he had been crying. Joshua, with his youthful, clean-shaven face, had to be thirty years younger than François. Yet it was clear from his sadness that they had been close.

"About François…" She could not find the words.

"It's horrible, I know. He knew the risk of what we were doing, though. He accepted it." The price of fighting for freedom meant acknowledging they might be killed at any moment.

"But what happened? I mean, why?"

"One of the guards stopped him. I think it was because he was on the other side of the camp and had no reason to be there." A lump formed in Lily's throat. "They found the tools he was secretly carrying."

"They're gone?"

Joshua nodded. "All of them."

"No!" Lily's spirits sank with disappointment. *All gone.* Everything they had worked so hard to collect, the very things that were meant to help them with the nearly impossible break, were gone. And surely now the guards must suspect that the prisoners were planning something.

Joshua stood. "I will check in with the others and figure out how to proceed."

"Proceed?" Lily repeated, not quite understanding. With François dead and the tools confiscated, how could they possibly go on?

"Of course," Joshua said impatiently. To him, carrying on had never been in doubt. "We must gather more tools and begin preparing for your transport. However, we may need to work on replacing the tools from the outside."

Lily stared blankly off into space, scarcely hearing his words. "Are you all right?" Joshua asked.

"They killed him!" Lily burst out, the full force of what she had witnessed overwhelming her. "It just as easily could have been me. How can we possibly go on?" she asked, the desperation in her voice building. "They killed François for having those tools. Surely they will kill us all too. We can't do this. If we do, we may all die."

"You must get off the train if there is any chance at all. What other choice is there?"

"Perhaps if we go, the resistance can work for our release from the other end," she offered lamely.

"Lily, no!" Joshua hesitated. "Transport east is a death sentence. We've heard that thousands of people, the elderly and the unfit and even the children, are being killed with gas just after they arrive. Some others are being allowed to live for a time. But it seems as if they mean to kill all of us." Though Lily had known as much, hearing Joshua say it aloud made the peril all the more real. "You see now why you must never reach Auschwitz, why we have to get you off the train. If you don't, you will all die for sure." She did not respond. "This is still the best plan. You have to trust me."

Lily swallowed. She was terrified, and she wanted to abandon the whole plan. But it was still their best and only hope of surviving. She had to keep going for her family. "Okay. What do we need to do?"

"We need to send word to your contacts that our tools were taken and see if they can somehow get us more."

"There isn't another trip to the laundry for nearly a week. How are we to manage that?" Lily's eyes traveled in the direction of the tailor's bench where Anhel usually worked. He was not there today, and she wondered if he was sick or worse. Even if he had been there, she dared not endanger him by asking him to send another message for her, not after what had just happened to François.

"I will try to send word through one of our contacts," Joshua offered.

"But even if you manage that, how will they possibly get tools inside to us?" Lily's mind whirled with all of the impossibilities.

"I don't know, but we have to try," Joshua said grimly, then set off across the camp.

At the end of the work day, Lily hurried to the barracks. Nik was there, having claimed Georgi, and she could see from his expression that he knew about François.

Georgi ran to her and flung himself around her knees as he had done every time they had been reunited in the camp, as though he thought she might again disappear. "Georgi, what is it?"

"I don't want you to go away again," he said simply.

Lily drew him close. "I won't. I promise." But how could she say that? She would die, she vowed then, before she would let him be taken from her again.

Nik gestured her over to the corner so Georgi would not hear. Disentangling from Georgi, she walked over. "You heard the news?" he asked.

"About François?"

Something changed in Nik's expression then. "You knew him?"

Lily realized her mistake too late. Though Nik was aware of Hannah's plan to free them from the train, he knew little of Lily's role as a liaison with the resistance, or how very dangerous her work had quickly become. She dreaded telling Nik that she had been collaborating with François on the very thing that got him killed. Nik was not a child, though, and the time to protect him like one had long passed. She could not keep it from him any longer. "Yes. Hannah has devised a plan to free us once we are on the train, and I was working with him and some others from the resistance to collect tools for the train break. That's why he was killed."

Nik cleared his throat. "But why must you be involved?" He coughed once, then a second time, his face reddening a bit.

"Are you all right?" she asked, concerned.

He waved his hand. "I'm fine. But this plan and your role in it… Surely now after what happened to that man, you see now why you must stop. Let the others plan it."

"No, this is exactly why I must do more. Someone has to step up and take his place, or we have no hope."

"Why must it be you?"

"Because I can." None of them had chosen this war or the positions which they now found themselves in. But each had a duty to play his or her role. This was about more than just survival; she understood that now. Each of them had to make a difference.

Nik coughed again and seemed to struggle to catch his breath. "Are you sure you're well?"

"Fine, it's just the dampness here." He waved his hand dismissively. "I won't lose you," he continued, and she considered whether he was talking about something more than the war. The feelings that he usually kept subdued, buried beneath the surface, burst forth, and she felt then the depth of his love, which she had always known was there under the surface but had seldom outwardly seen.

However, that did not steer her from her cause. "Doing this is the only chance we have of not losing one another."

"If something should happen to you, Georgi could not bear to lose you again." She saw then that his concern came from a place of deep love.

"It is exactly for Georgi that I am doing this," she countered. "I don't want to be away from him or you, even for a second. But if we don't do something, I shall hold his hand as we walk straight into the gas chambers." It was the first time either one of them had spoken the awful truth of those words aloud.

"I'm sorry if I've tried to shelter you too much," he offered.

"You are your own person, and I respect your decision to do this. And if there is something I can do to help, I will."

"Thank you." She moved closer, grateful for his support and the moment to be close to one another.

She sped across the barracks to find Georgi playing with something. "What have you got there, Georgi?" There were no toys in the camp, so the children made their own and played with whatever objects they could get their hands on. "Can I see?" She held out her hand.

He held it up to her, and she was surprised to discover it was a small key. François's key, she realized, recognizing the odd shape. The one from the machine shop. "Where did you get that?"

"It was here on the bed when I came in," Georgi replied. "Can I have it back?"

"Just for a minute," she said. "And then please give it to me. Mama needs it for something." Watching Georgi play with the key, Lily was puzzled. How had the key gotten here? Tante Sarah had said that François had come looking for her that morning. He might have dropped it. But Georgi had found the key on their bed, not the floor. François must have left the key for her on purpose. Perhaps he had been trying to tell her something.

Lily took the key from Georgi. "Stay here," she said, then walked outside. Lily passed Nik, who was conferring with another man about some sort of medical malady. "I'll be right back," she mouthed. She could see the questioning expression in his eyes and was glad she did not have to stop and explain where she was going.

The sun was setting low to the horizon beyond the gate as Lily started across the camp. The grounds were nearly deserted except for a few prisoners making their way back to their barracks. When she reached the edge of the fortress, she peered around it, suddenly immobilized with fear. This was how François had been apprehended, by going where he did not belong. But she needed to know why he had left her the key. She looked out once more to make sure no one was watching and then darted hurriedly across the space.

She walked swiftly into the shed, which was empty after the workday had ended. The now-familiar smell of metal and oil was a sad reminder of François. She crossed the shop to his bench and knelt to unlock the cabinet behind it. The key turned in the lock but didn't seem to work. Her heart sank. Had she been wrong about him leaving it for her?

Lily tried again, exhaling as it finally caught. She pulled at the handle, and the cabinet opened with a creak. Taped to the door inside was a picture of a woman and child. François's family. Trying to ignore the stinging in her eyes, she concentrated on the inside of the cabinet, which was empty. Why had he sent her here on a pointless errand? She ran her hand along the bottom of a cabinet, feeling a hard ridge beneath the felt that covered the bottom. She lifted the fabric to reveal a hidden compartment. She pried it open and felt around inside. There were a few bolts and a piece of frayed wire. Nothing that would be useful to their cause. François had been carrying nearly all of the tools, and there was nothing left.

Lily swiped her hand through the compartment one last time, reaching farther back. Her hand closed around something hard and cold. A gun, she realized with shock. She had never held or even seen one up close in her entire life. She pulled it out. It was old, to be sure, the handle rusted. She did not know if it would even work. Something told her, though, that it would. Lily held the gun tentatively. She did not know how to fire it, didn't know if she could. And being caught with it would mean punishment, perhaps death.

Still, François had left it for her for a reason. She straightened and put the gun in her pocket and left hurriedly, racing back to her family.

27

Hannah

Hannah walked into the canteen and found Matteo sitting behind the desk, his expression grim. "What is it?" Hannah asked, fearing the worst. "Is it Lily?"

Matteo stood up and walked around the desk to her. "No, but it's bad news, I'm afraid. One of the resistance workers in the camp who was helping Lily gather tools was caught and executed."

Hannah gasped. "That could have just as easily been Lily."

"Yes." His voice was grim. "Fortunately she was not with him. But all of the tools they had gathered are gone."

"Gone," she repeated numbly. After all of the struggles, this latest setback seemed too much. Then she straightened. "We will get more tools, and I will smuggle them in to Lily."

"But Hannah," he protested, "after what happened, surely the camp is more guarded than ever."

"I'll manage it somehow," she replied stubbornly. "Get the tools and send word back that I will deliver them tomorrow night. Giving the people on the inside tools to help with the break will give them the very best chance of escaping. You know that, don't you?" He did not answer. "I thought you would never give up on Lily."

"And I never will. I'm still as committed as ever. I will do whatever I need to do to save her life," he added, his voice unwavering. "We have to be smart about this, though. If we all get killed, who will help your cousin then? I'm not saying no, Hannah. I'm saying we must think carefully about how to do this. Your life matters too, you know." He put his hand on her shoulder, and she glimpsed warmth in his eyes, an ember of what they had shared that one night, still burning.

But what had happened between the two of them did not matter at all now. "Not without Lily, it doesn't." She had lost so much in her life: her parents, her fiancé, her child. She could not lose Lily and her family.

"Then, we should prepare to save her." Matteo gestured to the map on the desk. "The question is, where should we attack?"

They huddled closely over the map. "Here." Hannah pointed to a long, deserted stretch of railway track, far from any town. "The track curves, so we can wait out of view. And there's a forest nearby for hiding after."

"But that's so close to the German border," Matteo remarked.

"It's the best option. But it means that we will only have that one opportunity to stop the train before it enters Germany." After that, Hannah thought, Lily and her family would be lost forever. "But how can we stop the train?"

"The railway workers, some of them are sympathetic," Matteo said. "If we can get word to them, they may slow down the train deliberately."

"But it would take weeks to figure out which ones and make sure they are scheduled to work that particular train. There's not enough time."

"I have an idea!" Matteo raced from the room and down the

steps to the basement of the canteen, leaving Hannah alone. Through the floorboards, Hannah could hear him rummaging.

A moment later, Matteo reappeared. "This." He held up a lantern like one might have used for camping. "We wrap it in red paper and place it on the track. The driver will stop the train."

"Really?" Hannah eyed the lamp dubiously. "It's so small."

"Yes, but a red lamp is the signal that workers use to indicate to the engine drivers that something is wrong ahead. They will stop because they have to."

"And then?"

"Then we strike."

"Just the three of us."

"Yes," Matteo replied. "In some ways it will be better than a larger attack. No big explosion or fight. We pry the train door open and free Lily and her family and as many of the others as possible before the train starts moving again or the Germans figure out what has happened." Hannah listened with disbelief. It sounded outrageous, even to her. It was simply impossible. And yet it was their last hope of saving Lily.

"Go to Lily tomorrow and ensure that they are ready. But don't tell her or the others in the camp that it is only us. We don't want them panicking."

"Of course. Then, it's settled."

The next night Hannah went to meet Lily as planned. She had several tools concealed under her clothing, items that might help the prisoners in their break. She would have brought more but did not dare carrying a satchel that would risk drawing attention.

Hannah crept around the back of the camp as she had on her earlier visit. But when she neared the spot where she had met Lily previously, she discovered that the brush where she had hidden had been cleared away. Her uneasiness rose. Had the Germans just cleared the brush as part of routine maintenance, or had they realized people might hide there?

Hannah could not readily approach the camp at the same spot

now without being detected. She studied the fence, trying to figure out another way. The moat, she realized. The ditch sloped low to where it had filled with fresh rainwater. She would have to hide there. Reluctantly, Hannah dropped to her knees and crawled low into the moat. The filthy water seeped through her clothes and wet her skin. She waded through the moat on her knees until she reached the other side. Then she kept low to the ground, nearly lying down to remain out of sight.

A few minutes later, she heard the quiet rustle of Lily's footsteps. She lifted her head from the moat to see Lily, searching for her by the fence. "Here," she whispered.

Lily looked down. "Oh!" she exclaimed softly. They looked at one another from a distance. Lily was perplexed that Hannah was hiding in the moat but then saw she could not reach Lily without being completely exposed. "There's a spot about fifty meters farther along the fence where I can hide behind a shed," Lily offered. "Meet me there."

Hannah crept along in the water until she saw a low structure. It would have been better described as a chicken coop than a shed—if there had been any livestock. She crawled up the bank to the spot near it where Lily crouched in hiding.

"Here, we don't have long." Hannah reached into her dress and pulled out a long file and a crowbar. She slid them through the fence to Lily.

Just then there came a noise from around the other side of the fence. A patrol was coming toward them, inspecting the train. The beam of a flashlight licked the ground. "Hide!" Hannah whispered to Lily, then slithered away from the fence and rolled down the short embankment back into the water. Alongside the lone set of footsteps, Hannah heard the panting of an animal. Her heart sank. The guard had a dog, intended to sniff out people in circumstances such as this. Surely they would both be discovered now.

As the guard neared, she sank lower. Water covered her head

now, filling her nose and ears. She held her breath, willing herself to release only a tiny bit of air at a time. Trapped in the dark, cold moat, Hannah was suddenly hurled back to that night in Berlin. Hiding behind the counter, feeling the shards of glass cut into her skin and watching helplessly as the life drained from Isaac a meter away. She had failed that night, lying frozen and unable to act. She would not fail again but would jump out and let herself be caught so that Lily could remain in hiding.

A few moments later, the guard moved on, and the beam of his flashlight disappeared. Hannah pushed herself up onto the sloped bank of the moat. She could see Lily again, disentangling herself from the coop. But Hannah became motionless, curled in a ball, unable to move farther.

"Hannah, what's wrong?" Lily whispered, noticing her distress. "Are you hurt?"

Hannah was embarrassed to have been caught in a moment of weakness. She moved closer to the spot along the fence where Lily was hiding. "I'm not comfortable hiding because of that night in Berlin."

"I remember you told me how Isaac was killed and how you lost the baby. I'm sorry for what happened. And I'm sorry for not being there for you when it did. I should never have lost touch over the years. When things were bad for you in Germany, I should have helped."

"You had no way of knowing what was happening."

"Maybe not, but I could have tried harder to find out. And then when you came to Belgium…" Lily faltered. "I gave you a place to live. But I should have given you a home. I was jealous," Lily admitted. "Of your friends and that whole world you found. Of you. I had just gotten you back, and then I lost you all over again." Hannah was surprised. She had not imagined that Lily had noticed or cared at all. "I could have done more," she finished lamely.

"Let's not waste any more time on apologies or regrets," Hannah said. These grim few moments might be the last they would have together.

Lily attempted a smile. "When we are out of here and the war is over, we will make up for lost time." Hannah tried to imagine an after, a place free of all danger and pain. It had been so long since she had felt peace that it had simply ceased to exist.

Hannah knew that she should hurry away. Every minute they lingered here risked death. But this was the last time she would see her cousin before the train break, or maybe ever if it did not work. She was not ready to say goodbye.

"Matteo was asking for you."

Warmth flickered in Lily's eyes. "He's well?"

"Yes. Taking too many chances."

"As always." There was a note of familiarity in her voice.

Hannah stared evenly at her. "The way the two of you talk about each other, you would almost think there was still something between you." It was the closest she had come to confronting Lily directly.

"Oh, Hannah, we've been through this before. I've told you Matteo and I shared a past. Not even a past, really. It was just a brief time, many years ago. I agreed to meet him again, and I wish I hadn't. If I hadn't met him that last time, then none of this would have happened, not to me or Nik or Georgi."

"Lily, it wasn't your fault that you were arrested. It was mine. But about Matteo…" The words stuck in her throat. "Do you still love him?"

"I love Nik," Lily said firmly. "But there's always been such a strong connection between Matteo and me. And it's not just that." Lily paused, taking a breath, as though there was something she was afraid to say. "Hannah… Nik is not Georgi's father. Matteo is."

"Oh!" Hannah was startled by Lily's confession, though it did make sense, the timing of when Lily and Matteo had been together all of those years ago. The fact that Georgi looked nothing like Nik. Still, the fact that Matteo, for whom Hannah herself also had feelings, was Georgi's father, set her back on her heels.

"I've never told anyone before."

Lily seemed to cower, as if waiting for Hannah's judgment or wrath. Instead, Hannah put her arm around Lily. "I understand. Matteo doesn't know, does he?"

"No. I have often considered whether I should tell him."

Hannah debated the question. A man should know he has a child. A child should know his father. But so much in this world had been laid bare, shredded by the war. Survival was the thing that mattered now. Not stirring up the past. "Not now," Hannah replied firmly.

Lily nodded in agreement. "No one else can know either."

"And they never will. I won't say a word, I swear it." Lily's face relaxed slightly, and she seemed satisfied. Lily had kept secrets from her, just as she had from Lily, but they were closer now for having shared them.

"Sometimes I'm glad the *Brittany* did not make it to America," Hannah admitted.

"But that chance of getting to America was everything. And if you had made it, you wouldn't be here."

"Exactly. It brought me back to you again. Mind you, a fair part of me would not mind being at the Carnegie Deli and taking in a Broadway show." They chuckled softly at the image, which seemed like something from a dream. Hannah slipped her hand into her cousin's.

"Well, we can go to America together, if this works." There was a quiver in Lily's voice.

"It will work," Hannah vowed. "I won't let you down."

Lily's doubts redoubled, and the crease in her forehead deepened. "An artist and a nurse... Who are we to do this, to execute such a dangerous plan? Just a few women with no training or real equipment." Hannah silently acknowledged the truth of Lily's statement. But who were she and Micheline, really, to undertake the work of the Sapphire Line? No one bestowed courage or freedom or self-determination—one simply decided to take it.

Hannah could see that Lily wanted to back out. The break was even more impossible than it had been, the chance of their succeeding infinitesimally small. But it was too late now. "Even if you are successful, what then?" Lily demanded. "What are we to do once we get off the train? Where are we to go?"

Hannah's mind whirled at the questions. "I will be there, and we will go to an abandoned chateau in a valley just east of Haacht until we can get you out of the country. If something goes wrong and we are separated, make your way there to hide. Follow the antitank canal out of the town until you see it."

They stood by the fence in the shadow of the brush, lingering though they should not. It was to be their last meeting before the train left, and neither was ready to say goodbye. Hannah took a long look at Lily. "No matter what happens," Lily said, "thank you." She squeezed her cousin's fingers tightly through the fence.

"Hannah," she continued, "there's one thing. I know not everyone will make it." Hannah nodded, a tacit admission that in trying to save all, they would surely lose some. "If you have to save just one of us, make it Georgi." The idea of Lily's child going on without her was unfathomable. But if one of them was to live, it had to be him.

"I shall," Hannah vowed. She would save Lily's child, as she had not been able to save her own. "And I will save you too."

28

Lily

The train was to leave in just two days. Lily prepared, checking the one small bag they were permitted to bring, the suitcase with which Nik and Georgi had arrived. They did not have much. No extra food for the trip, except a lone can of condensed milk that she had stashed away. No clothes to swap for their prisoner garb if the train break was successful. She had hidden the few tools Hannah had given her in the lining of the suitcase to distribute to the other prisoners once they were on the train. But even if they did manage to escape, well, Lily had no idea how to prepare for that either since she did not know where they would go. What would happen when they got off the train?

Standing in the barracks before breakfast trying to figure it all out, Lily watched through the open window as Georgi played. He played alone, as he had since Dorin had left. Georgi was playing with a large crate that was lying on the ground, jumping on and off. She estimated that the crate was as high as the railcar might be from the ground, and she felt a surge of both anticipation and fear as she imagined him jumping to freedom.

She walked outside to him. "Can you do that again?" she asked. Georgi looked puzzled. Clearly, he had expected her to scold him for playing on it. "Why?"

"Just for fun." She could not, of course, tell him the real reason: to help him practice for the train break. Georgi complied, climbing on the crate again. He leaped off a bit higher to impress her, then looked up for her reaction. "How was that?"

"Good." There were a half-dozen things the crate could not replicate, like the rough ground below, the fact that the train might even be moving. But seeing him land, upright with his knees bent, gave her a bit of hope.

A man she did not recognize, thirtysomething and wearing the placard of a political prisoner, walked up behind her. "You have to fall backward," he said in a low voice. Did he know what they were planning? Suddenly the operation seemed to have a thousand cracks in it. "Tuck your head and roll. I was a paratrooper before." He winked and kept walking. But Lily's nervousness grew. So many things they could not possibly account for. How would they ever manage it?

Lily walked back into the barracks. Nik appeared to be sleeping unusually late. With his shaved head and gray whiskers, he suddenly seemed an old man. "Darling, you need to get up for the roll call." She noticed then his pallor, and a feeling of dread seized her. She put her hand to his brow and was relieved to find him still warm. He was alive. But, in fact, he was burning with fever. He had not seemed ill the previous night, so it must have come on suddenly. She shook him. "Nik?" He half opened his eyes and mumbled something.

Georgi came in the barracks just then. "What's wrong with Papa?"

Lily managed to keep her voice calm. "He's just sleeping." She shooed Georgi away, partly to prevent him from seeing and also to make sure he did not catch whatever Nik had, praying he did not have it already. Lily looked around the ward helplessly. Then, remembering Nik's medical kit, she pulled it out from under the bed and rummaged through it. She needed aspirin, but he had dispensed it all, and the bottle was empty.

Lily took a cloth from the kit and walked to the latrine to dampen it, then returned and placed it on his head. There was nothing else that could be done. That Nik, who had aided so many others, himself could not be helped seemed a cruel trick. How long had he been ill? She searched her memory of the past few days. Nik had been quiet. She had thought him distracted, perhaps even depressed, but she had attributed it to their situation and his normal melancholy and had thought no more about it. He had developed a worsening cough, she recalled. Why hadn't she paid more attention, insisted that he take care of himself as he did so many others? Guilt surged through her. She had been so busy preparing for the train break that she had not even noticed. She berated herself for not realizing sooner how sick he really was. But even if she had, what could she have done about it?

They were supposed to depart by train the very next morning. Nik could not even walk, so how would he manage to board the train and make the long journey? If the Germans saw how ill he was, they would force him to ride in the sick car and not the car that was to be liberated.

Of course, Nik could not be in that railcar. The realization hit Lily like a rock. He would not be able to flee the train. Hannah had planned the very train escape for Lily and her family, only now Nik could not go. Lily would be forced, unthinkably, to choose between abandoning Nik and saving Georgi, or staying with Nik and forgoing Georgi's one chance to survive. Of course there was no choice: if she could save her son, she had to do it. Nik would want her to do exactly that.

The day of their departure, Lily expected they would leave before dawn, as Sofia and her son had. Instead, they waited around uneasily as the morning passed and the summer sun climbed high in the sky. Lily hoped fleetingly that their journey might be canceled and they might be permitted to stay at Breendonk.

But finally, late in the day, they were summoned to the *Appellplatz*. Lily roused Nik to his feet and helped him from the barracks with the assistance of one of the other prisoners. Once the Germans had accounted for everyone, they ordered those who were to be deported to line up two by two and march to the station. Lily carried their small suitcase carefully, hoping that the tools in the lining would not make noise. She felt the cold metal of the gun François had left her tucked into her undergarments beneath her uniform. She had not wanted to part with it or risk putting it in her suitcase, and she prayed that the guards would not search her and find it.

As they reached the arched entrance to the camp, Lily looked back over her shoulder at the place which she had lived for the past several months. She had dreamed of leaving, only not like this. Now, she would have given anything to stay.

The prisoners began the half-kilometer march to the makeshift depot. As Lily started walking, Nik collapsed to the ground beside her with a thud, his weight nearly pulling Lily with him. "Papa!" Georgi cried with alarm.

"Get up," she pled, willing him to be strong enough. She'd heard stories of the Germans shooting those who did not move when ordered.

Nik remained on the ground, unable to move. A moment later, two prisoners bearing a tattered stretcher came over and put Nik on it. They looked barely strong enough to walk themselves, Lily fretted, much less carry the weight of a grown man. They continued slowly toward the station.

The train appeared larger and more ominous than it had seemed just a few nights earlier when she had met with Hannah. Georgi stared with wonder at the large plume of steam that billowed from the engine. "It's so big," he breathed. But his expression was fearful.

Lily squeezed his hand. "Come, it will be an adventure. And I will be here with you the whole way." Lily forced brightness into her voice, but as they reached the line of cattle cars, her throat tightened. How were they ever to make it?

"Put him in the third car" said the guard as they approached, gesturing at the stretcher.

Lily's dread rose. "But we were assigned to twelve." They had to be in the very last car, the one that Hannah and the others would break into.

The guard looked up coldly. "The sick will all travel together. You will go to car three as well."

Lily's heart stopped. She and Georgi had to be in car twelve when it was liberated. "But my son and I are supposed to go in car twelve. Surely you cannot expect us to travel with the sick."

"Families are to remain intact for when they are resettled in the east." He was lying, she knew. People would be separated at Auschwitz, the weak killed. Resettlement was a myth, told over and over again to keep people from resisting. Keeping families together on the train was part of the fiction. "Car three," the guard said, his voice harder now. Lily knew that arguing would not change the guard's mind and might in fact make him angry.

With silent anguish, she followed the men carrying Nik's stretcher toward the sick car. Their chance at escape was gone. Whatever happened, they would face it as a family. She closed the door on the possibility of escape and steeled herself for whatever fate awaited them.

As they shuffled down the platform, Lily looked at the setting sun. The train, which had been baking all day, would surely be sweltering. She carried a container where she might siphon water if it rained and trickled through the roof of the leaky carriage. Once such survival skills would have been foreign to her, but the months in the camp had trained her to know their most basic needs and find ways to meet them.

As they approached the third car, Lily recoiled at the idea of climbing into the dingy and stifling enclosure. Resisters were being urged forward with whips, and those who refused to go were pulled out of line and beaten. Each railcar was guarded by *Schutzpolizei*, special units brought in to accompany the train. They brandished machine guns, ready to make good on their promise to shoot anyone who resisted.

Lily stayed close to the stretcher that carried Nik. They reached the third railcar. Georgi looked at her uncertainly. "Come," she urged. "It will be just like riding those trains you love to play with, only for real." But as the hot, foul-smelling air met them like a wall, Georgi blanched, unconvinced.

Lily lifted Georgi into the railcar, hoping he would not protest. Then she climbed in herself, heaving the suitcase after her. The tools, she realized. They were meant for the people in the car that Hannah and the others were to liberate. Only she had them here with her and no way to get them to anyone else.

A half-dozen people lay on the floor of the train, looking even worse off than Nik. What was the point, really, of moving these poor souls east? In a humane world, the sick would be deemed too weak to make the journey. But here they were quarantined together and left to die. There were a few other healthy people as well, family members who suffered the same sorry fate as their sick loved ones. She hoped that the sick car might be spared some of the insufferable crowding of the other ones, but more and more people limped into the wagon or were brought by stretcher, pushing Lily and her family to the rear.

The railcar door slid shut and locked with an ominous click. The space was airtight except for a hole in one lower corner where the wood boards had ripped apart and a thin slat near the top of the car above her. Through it, she could see the ground outside. The air was warm and thick, each breath an effort. A layer of sweat began to form instantly on her skin.

Three days and nights to their destination, or at least that was what someone had said. Who knew if that was true? She could not imagine surviving in the dank airless boxcar for ten minutes, much less three days. But with Nik too ill for liberation, the full journey east lay before them, inevitable. Across the railcar, a woman, delirious with fever, wailed endlessly.

"I'm hungry, Mama," Georgi said as the train began to move. Lily, nauseated from the vile conditions, could not imagine eating. She reached inside her tattered uniform for the bit of food she had been able to conceal. The Germans had promised rations for the journey, bread and sardines and meat, just enough to get them through. But those had not materialized. Thankfully, Lily had not trusted in such things and had stowed away her own bits of meals for days. She fed them to Georgi who took them gratefully. She tried to coax a few morsels into Nik's mouth, but he waved it away, too sick to eat. She turned and gave them to Georgi instead, her heart breaking at the way he brightened at a few extra pitiful crumbs.

After Georgi had eaten the morsels, Lily pulled him onto her lap and rocked him as she had when he was an infant, willing him to sleep as much as possible and pass the hours. But he shifted uncomfortably in her arms, tormented by his lingering hunger and thirst and fear. When he did sleep, he tossed endlessly in nightmares. She was struck by how light he had become, almost toddlerlike again. He had always been a slight child, and it seemed that every last bit of fat and cushion had been sheared from his frame. She could feel each of his bones beneath his skin.

Georgi's face was upturned to her, as it had been when she nursed him in infancy. Seeing it, a wave of nostalgia washed over her. She questioned for the hundredth time her decision to bring him into the sick car, increasing his risk of illness or being counted among those marked for death at the end, and taking him from his only chance at survival.

Lily looked out of the narrow slat at the darkened sky. The time stretched endlessly. Yet as the trip waxed on, it seemed like a ticking time bomb, a countdown to certain doom. Though she herself would not be able to escape, she desperately prayed for those in the other car to be rescued before it was too late. Their hope was somehow hope for her as well.

The train moved slowly through the night. By dim moonlight she could make out in a field the remnants of a Great War battle frozen in time, deep cuts in the earth marking where the trenches once had been, great hulking heaps of metal left behind to rot in the elements. In another time, others like herself had struggled and died here. Some had made it, some had not. She saw then that this moment, which meant everything for her survival and that of her family, was in fact just a blink in time, to be passed and forgotten.

The train slowed at a station, and there was a clattering outside. Lily tensed. Thinking that it might be Hannah and Matteo coming to free the passengers, she started to stand up. But she could see through the narrow slat that they were just picking up an extra guard from the platform.

Though it was night and the small station was nearly deserted, a few well-intentioned locals walked along the platform and passed water through the slats to as many people as they could while the train had stopped. It was such a kind gesture, people risking their own safety to provide some aid. Still, Lily grew nervous. It could not be that much farther to the border and then it would be too late for Hannah and the others to free them before they reached Germany.

Lily looked toward the narrow slats, hoping a few drops of water might fall their way. But the sick wagon was marked *Nicht Berühren! Kontaminationsrisiko! Do Not Touch! Contamination Risk!* The people bearing water passed by them quickly, unwilling to chance infection.

Still holding Georgi, Lily stood and strained to see through the narrow slat above. Where along the way would they intercept? Hannah had said they would attack just before the train crossed over the river and they were nearing the bridge. Lily looked out at the barren horizon, praying for some sign that

Hannah and the others were there. The train had left so much later than she'd expected, and she wondered how Hannah and the others would know when to be there to intercept it. As they continued past the planned spot and nothing happened, Lily felt a sinking in her chest. Even though she could not go, she wanted the others to be saved. Something was wrong, though. The rescue had not taken place.

The train lurched unexpectedly, and Lily held Georgi tightly just in time to keep him from falling from her arms. She felt the train screech to a stop. Was this it? She listened down the train carefully for the sound of attack but heard nothing. Of course. This would not be a loud explosion but a quiet, covert attempt. Through the narrow slat, she could make out a distinctive arc of pine trees but nothing more. She imagined the others being freed quickly, swiftly.

"What is it, Mama?" Georgi asked sleepily.

"Shh, nothing, darling." But a pang of longing shot through her. They should have been among the escapees. Hannah and Matteo were risking everything to save her, only she would not be there to save.

Lily turned to see Nik lying helplessly on the floor of the railcar. If she went, there would be no one to protect him. He would never leave her. She knew in that instant she had made the right decision and she could not abandon him.

But what about Georgi? If he could somehow escape, he might be spared the inevitable horror of Auschwitz. Leaving her boy was unfathomable. Without her, he would be defenseless. The point was a moot one, since the railcar which was being liberated was nine wagons away, out of reach. She held her son even more tightly, wishing for the salvation that would not be theirs.

29

Hannah

Hannah awoke early the morning of the raid, ready to go before dawn as they had discussed. But after she had washed, Matteo sent word that their errand was delayed and not to come until seven that evening. So Hannah had paced the house restlessly for hours, not wanting to go too far in case something changed again and they needed to leave earlier.

Finally, at six, she'd set out for the canteen. Matteo was waiting there for her, double-checking and packing the supplies they would need. "Is everything all right?" she asked anxiously. "When I received your word about the delay, I worried that something had happened."

"A contact inside the camp learned that the train was delayed," he replied. "Everything is still set to proceed."

"And Micheline?" Hannah asked, hoping that she had returned or at least sent word.

He shook his head. "Nothing." Her face appeared in Hannah's mind. Hannah wondered again where she was and whether she would make it in time to help with the raid.

They set out, Matteo carrying the few tools they would need for the job. "That's it?" She marveled at the small backpack.

"We don't want to have too much with us."

They set out in the old Citroën, Matteo navigating the back roads out of the city until he reached the motorway. Remembering the night she had driven to the camp with Micheline, Hannah surveyed the road ahead, hoping they would not encounter a security checkpoint.

"I wish you weren't here," Matteo said abruptly.

"Excuse me?" Hannah said, stung by his words.

"I'm sorry, that came out wrong. I mean, I wish you didn't have to do this with me. It's too dangerous."

His words sounded patronizing, and Hannah started to get angry. Then she realized he was speaking from a place of concern. "I feel the same way about you. But I'm the one who caused this whole mess by taking Lily's card. I *should* be doing this."

"No, it's my fault. If I hadn't introduced you to Micheline and gotten you into this work, none of it would have happened. Anyway, here we both are," he said, with a half chuckle. The knots of their past choices and where they had led were too tangled to unfurl. "If only it could be simpler."

"It *was* simple, that night at the cabin."

"Yes." He smiled at the memory, and she knew then that he did not regret what had happened between them. She wanted to say that perhaps it could be that way again someday. But speaking of the future now, with the mission of the train break before them and their lives hanging in the balance, seemed altogether too much.

At last they stopped at an abandoned depot an hour and a half east of the city where Matteo produced two bikes. How he had gotten them, whether they were stolen or borrowed or something else, Hannah did not ask. They pedaled as quickly as they could through the still countryside. The sun was sinking below the hills. Fields lush with late-summer crops of barley and wheat flanked them on either side. Though the expanses of road were largely flat, her legs ached from the fierce pace of trying to keep up.

After a while, the landscape grew hillier, signaling that they were drawing close to the German border. The back of Hannah's neck grew tense. Yet at the same time, she could not help but feel a tug of nostalgia for her homeland. Germany before the war, and Berlin specifically, had been the height of the artistic scene and a safe and even prosperous place for Jews. For everything Hannah had lost there, she could not hate it. It was the place that had made her into the woman she was.

Ahead of her, Matteo slowed his bike without warning so quickly that she almost crashed into him. She braked to a halt, the screeching of her tires cutting too loudly through the air. Matteo dragged his bike hurriedly into the trees for cover, and she swiftly followed. Ahead something was blocking the road. German soldiers. Hannah's breath caught. Had their plans been revealed and the Germans were there waiting for them? No, she realized as they crept closer. The soldiers were working on constructing some sort of fortification or embankment.

But her comfort was short-lived. She and Matteo and Micheline would not be able to intercept the train at the planned spot or anywhere near here because the soldiers might hear the commotion.

"Come," Matteo mouthed silently, moving farther out of sight. He led her through the woods past where the soldiers were working. They pressed forward on a path that ran parallel to the road, unseen but risking detection at any moment.

When they were well clear of the soldiers, Matteo paused biking once more. "That was the rendezvous spot," Hannah said. "What are we to do now?"

"We must find a new stretch of track," he whispered. He stared hard at the ground, thinking. "We need to move the attack spot farther up."

She followed the direction that he was pointing. Everything was wrong about it. It was too close to the German border, far away from anywhere the escapees could find refuge. "We can't go back and risk detection," he said, seemingly reading her mind. "Forward is our only hope."

He was right, of course. But the plan seemed so futile now. The enormity of what they were trying to do sank in, and Hannah felt utterly defeated, ready to give up. "We must keep going if we are to stay ahead of the train," Matteo urged.

"But Micheline will never find us."

"She knows the direction in which we are going. When she sees the blockade, she will know we have moved forward. My sister has the best instincts, and we have worked together so long we are often like one mind. She will find us. Now, hurry."

Hannah was still not convinced. But Matteo was right: this was their last chance, and if they didn't take it, all would be lost. She hopped on her bike and pedaled.

Nearly another kilometer down the road, Matteo stopped his bike. "Here," he said. Hannah surveyed the spot dubiously. Their other location had been on a curve in the track, enabling them to stay out of sight until the last possible moment. But this location was on a straightaway. They would be visible for some distance to anyone who looked. "I know, it isn't nearly as discreet as the original spot," Matteo conceded as he stowed his bike in the brush. "But any farther and we will be in Germany. It's here or nowhere."

Hannah hid her bike as well. As she did, she had a foreboding sense that she would not return for it. She pictured freeing dozens from the train and instructing them on how to flee. But she had not considered until this very moment where she herself would go once the break was over.

"What now?" she asked, looking around uncertainly.

"Now we wait." Hannah was surprised. She had imagined some work to do, to prepare the site. But what was there, really, to do? Matteo carried the lamp, wrapped in red paper, that they would set on the tracks to stop the train. Between them, they had a crowbar and a hammer and a gun. There had been a second, but the other had stuck as Matteo tried to load it before they left the canteen.

"You take this one," Matteo had offered, holding out the gun. "If you know how to use it."

She took the weapon. "I do, actually." In the early days of the resistance, she had insisted Isaac teach her and he had, taking her to a field outside the city to practice. "But what about you?"

He smiled gamely. "I'll manage. If we do this correctly, we shouldn't need to fight. We can break into the train and get away before the Germans notice. The rear of the railcar should be about here when the train stops," Matteo said, marking a spot in the dirt parallel to the track. "I will work at the door, and you try one of the slats and hopefully between the two of us we can get inside."

"The three of us," she corrected. "Micheline will be here."

"She should have been here by now."

"She will be."

"Yes, of course." His voice was uncertain. Did he think his sister was not coming? The time of the train break was drawing close, and Micheline had not appeared. Micheline was not one to break a promise, though, and Hannah believed she would keep her word. Still, Hannah could not help but question whether she would make it on time. What could possibly keep her from joining them?

Matteo leaned against a tree, and Hannah joined him. "The train should be here soon," he said.

The time the train was supposed to arrive neared and they gathered their few things, preparing for the attack. But the horizon remained dark. Ten minutes passed, then fifteen. "It should have been here by now," Hannah fretted. She racked her brain, trying to figure out why the train had not come. The transport might have been canceled or the engine broken down midtrip. Or perhaps the Germans had rerouted the train to another track, headed for Auschwitz out of reach.

"What if—" Hannah began, unable to voice the awful possibilities of failure.

"Look," he said, before she could finish her thought. She turned west to see a light which had appeared in the darkness, so faint she might have imagined it. She prayed that it might be Micheline, but it was too large, too fast, to be a bike or car light. The dot grew into a beacon, and as the train neared, the ground began to shake.

Hannah picked up the lamp, which she was supposed to put on the track. It might have been a child's toy, and yet it was the very crux of their plan. Hannah froze. Were they really going to do this?

And Micheline—where was she? They were going to have to do this without her.

Matteo, sensing her hesitation, leaped forward and lit the lantern, then placed it on the track to warn the driver of the need to stop. "Come," he urged her as the train neared. His eyes were focused. He grabbed her arm, and together they crawled along the track, needing to stay low and out of sight but close enough that they could move quickly when the train stopped.

If it stopped. The train barreled toward them at full speed, and it seemed that the driver had not seen the lantern and would keep going. The engine roared, and she thought for a moment they might be crushed.

Then suddenly there came a deafening screech as the driver applied the brakes, and at last the train groaned to a halt.

Hannah moved by instinct, racing to the last car of the train. She pried at one of the slats with the crowbar, but it was useless. Matteo tried to break the lock on the railcar door with the hammer, but it was stronger than it appeared and he struggled with it, spending moments they did not have. She had hoped that the prisoners inside might have been able to use the tools she had given Lily to start prying open the door or window slats. But the railcar appeared untouched. "Hurry!" Hannah urged. At any moment, the Germans would realize they were there.

Hearing the commotion, the prisoners on the other side surged toward the door. Hannah imagined Lily and Georgi among them, praying they would not be crushed. "Get back!" she whispered, not wanting anyone to get hurt as Matteo hammered at the lock.

Finally, the lock gave way, and the door opened. Inside, the prisoners did not move but stood like scared animals, their skeletal faces ghostly pale. Hannah scanned the group for Lily and her family but did not see them. They must be farther back, she decided. "Come," she urged the people in the front.

They began to slowly shuffle toward the front of the wagon, hesitating at the door, as though there was some invisible barrier that they could not cross. "Jump!" Matteo cried, first in French, then in German. The people stood motionless.

Hannah leaped into the wagon. The stench of human excrement and filth in the warm, close space was revolting. She gave one of the men by the front of the railcar a gentle shove, and he half jumped, half fell to the ground. She hoped he hadn't been injured in the fall. But it worked: people started leaping from the train. A few backed up, cowering, too afraid to make the leap. But others surged quickly forward.

Matteo began to move among them handing out money, giving instructions in a low but commanding voice. "To the woods, quickly."

"And then where should we go?" a man holding a small child asked.

Matteo faltered, exchanging uneasy glances with Hannah. They were glad to have been able to free so many people, but there was nowhere for them to hide. "Deeper into the woods," she said finally. "Go in small groups, no more than three or four, unless part of a single family. Find shelter in barns or sheds. The churches may be willing to hide people, or you can use the money to bribe farmers or villagers."

"Should we go home?" the same man asked.

Home. Hannah considered the word. Most of these people didn't have homes anymore. The Jewish neighborhoods had been decimated, the residences burned and shops shuttered. Any decent homes they once owned had surely been given to non-Jews. "Only return to your town or village if there is someone there you can trust to hide you," she said finally.

As the wagon emptied, Hannah scanned the group. There was a child. *Georgi*, she thought, but he was too slight, his hair more red than dark. She looked hurriedly through the remaining people in the car as they pressed toward the door.

Lily was not among them.

Hannah froze with shock. Where was Lily? What had gone wrong?

When the wagon was empty, Hannah leaped to the ground, then closed the door behind her. "Lily?" Matteo asked.

Hannah shook her head. "She wasn't there." His face fell. "Come, we must go." The guards would discover what had happened and be upon them in seconds. She started for the woods, but he stood motionless, and for a moment it seemed he would refuse to leave. She grabbed his arm and began dragging him toward the cover of the trees.

"She wasn't there," he repeated numbly.

"No."

"But that's impossible. She was assigned to that car, and the Germans are so precise with their rolls." He paused a beat, thinking. "Unless they were assigned somewhere else at the last minute."

"Do you think there was a sick car?" Hannah asked. "Perhaps since her husband is a doctor, he was made to travel there." It made sense. Lily of course would not have left Nik.

"There was. I saw a car, close to the front, marked as contaminated." The most heavily guarded part of the train, Hannah thought with dread.

And the least likely guarded because they knew no one could escape. She started toward it. Matteo grabbed her shoulder. "Wait."

"I have to go for Lily."

"You can't. There's no time." Matteo gestured with his head toward the train. Several guards were running down the length of the track now, nearing the boxcar. If they inspected the inside and saw the prisoners gone, they would surely search the woods. "It's too dangerous. I won't let you. That is, I couldn't bear it."

Hannah saw then that he loved her, every bit as much as she loved him. She knew it then. He wanted to save Lily, but he wasn't willing to forfeit Hannah's life to do it.

"Lily needs me," she insisted. She would not, could not, give up and let her cousin and her family be deported because of what she had done.

"I'll go," Matteo said. "You lead the others through the woods. I will find Lily and meet you." If she was there. But how would Matteo get Lily and her family off the train? And even if he did, how would they escape and find one another again? She had a dozen questions. She knew right then that if she walked away from the train, any chance of finding her cousin was gone. But many of the people they had freed still lingered nearby, uncertain where to go, needing help finding their way. They could not stand here, and if they did, the people whom they risked everything to free and who had trusted them and jumped would surely all die.

"Please find her," she begged. She knew Matteo cared about saving Lily as much as she did, and nothing short of death would stop him. He was perhaps the only other person she could trust to find her cousin.

Matteo nodded and sprinted toward the train once more.

30

Micheline

Pascal was the traitor.

As Micheline made her way from the city center, she struggled to process this information. She had suspected Monsieur Labeau, the Frenchman who had facilitated the rescue, but never gentle, faithful Pascal. He had always been so mild-mannered, and she had always felt a fondness toward him. The realization that she could not trust him, one who had been so close to their operations and knew so much, rocked her.

When she left the canteen, her first instinct was to go to Pascal's apartment to confront him. But that was emotional, she quickly realized. Instead, she headed for the grocery store in the eastern town of Tervuren that doubled as a drop box. There she would be able to leave a message for a contact to have Pascal neutralized. His contact, a German officer, was so high up in the government that he was untouchable. Taking out Pascal was the only option.

She would not kill him herself. She wanted to, but she had other matters to attend to. Instead, she would deliver the information to the resistance who would take him out before he could be a further threat to their operations. More than a dozen airmen were stuck in Paris, unable to proceed. Meanwhile, more were falling from the sky every day, needing places to go. The Sapphire Line was a pipe under too much pressure, about to explode.

Micheline had to go deliver the message, but the timing could not be worse. She had sent word ahead to the shopkeeper that she would be coming so that he could make sure the way was clear. Of course she did not say in the message why she was coming.

She would have to get to the village where the shop was located and back quickly to help Matteo and Hannah execute the train sabotage.

As she neared the grocery store, Micheline's thoughts turned to Matteo. He had been so beaten down by losing Lily years earlier that he had chosen to remain in Micheline's shadow. Only now, if he wanted to help Hannah rescue her cousin, he had to step up and lead. She did not know if he was up to the task. But the spark of the old Matteo she had seen poking through gave her hope. Her brother had been broken for so long and she had done him a disservice by coddling him. The mission was a chance to make him whole again, if only he would take it.

Micheline entered the grocery store. The shopkeeper, an older man with a rim of silvery hair around his balding head, appeared behind the counter, wiping his hands on his apron. An uneasy expression crossed his face. "I need you to deliver a message." The man did not respond. "Are you still willing to help?"

"Of course. It's only that I'm surprised to see you here, especially after the drop location was changed," the shopkeeper remarked mildly.

Micheline's head snapped in his direction. "Changed? Whatever do you mean?"

"The written order I received a few weeks ago told me not to accept any more packages, to redirect them to the bookshop in Haacht."

"Who sent the order?"

"The order came from you."

Micheline stared at him. "I never sent an order."

"But…" The shopkeeper faltered. "It had your code name, your watermark. It was coded with your cipher. I destroyed it, of course."

There was no evidence to corroborate the shopkeeper's story, but his tone was earnest. He had no reason to lie. The picture began to come into focus. Pascal and his accomplices had been running a parallel network, intercepting messages. The scope of the operation was audacious and stunning.

Micheline let the implication sink in. Pascal had access to her desk and her seal. He had been impersonating her, giving orders under her name. Which meant that every betrayal came with her authority. Some might even think she herself had betrayed the network.

"That wasn't me," Micheline told the shopkeeper. "Someone impersonated me. The network has been compromised."

His eyebrows raised. "A breach?"

"I'm afraid so. You've heard nothing unusual?" she asked.

"Nothing."

"Pascal is the traitor," she said. The other cells, the ones who depended upon him needed to know. "You haven't seen him?"

"No." Micheline was not surprised. Pascal surely would have gone dark after she saw him at the café. "Tell me what I can do to help," the shopkeeper said.

"I need to get orders to the resistance to have the threat neutralized. Can you put the message through?"

The shopkeeper nodded. "I will help however you need."

"I need to send word to Group G." These were Matteo's contacts, and under other circumstances she would have asked him to deliver the message. "Tell them that Pascal is Brutus." The reference to the traitor who had betrayed Caesar was a familiar one among the networks. "They will know what to do." Micheline turned to go.

"Wait," he called, and she turned back. "And me? What am I to do?" He was not offering help now but asking for it. Though the shopkeeper had to be close to sixty, he looked at her like a helpless child. Micheline knew he was thinking of his family. That was the thing about the line and its brave volunteers. The partisans acted alone and could disappear into the woods at a moment's notice. The poor souls who helped them, though, had families and businesses and could not easily flee. They were trapped in place. She wanted to tell him to get away. But it was impossible.

She started from the shop. "Wait!" the innkeeper called after her again, as if he still had more to tell her.

Before she reached the exit, the door swung open to reveal two men in German uniforms, blocking her way. Their guns were pointed directly at her.

"You are arrested in the name of the Reich."

31

Lily

There was a noise at the door to the railcar. Lily jumped, shoving Georgi behind her to protect him. Nik and the other patients all lay motionless, too sick to move, and the few other people who had accompanied them into the car did not react. Lily reached under her dress and tore the taped gun from her skin, holding it low to her leg. She had never fired a gun before, but she was prepared to use it if she had to.

There was a cracking sound as someone broke off the bolt that locked the door. Lily reared back as the door slid open. Then, seeing a familiar figure, she was overcome with relief. "Matteo!" she cried as he climbed inside the car. Matteo gestured her over to the entrance hurriedly and she led Georgi carefully around the others who lay on the carriage floor, staying close behind him.

"We broke into the other car," he said. "You weren't there. I thought something had happened to you."

"They assigned Nik here and forced us to come with him."

The train began to rock as the engine prepared to go once

more. They only had a few moments to get off the train before it would be moving again. Matteo peered over her shoulder at Nik, a concerned look spreading across his face. "We can't take him with us. In his condition, he would never survive."

Lily looked at Nik, the undeniable truth sinking in. Nik would never live through the rail journey or what lay at the other end. "You and Georgi need to come with me now, while you can."

"But there's no way I can leave my husband," Lily protested, tears of desperation filling her eyes.

Matteo looked as if he wanted to argue with her about going. But he knew her well enough to recognize that she would not budge. "Let me take Georgi." Matteo gestured toward the child.

"But..." A thousand protests rose inside her. She couldn't possibly be separated from her son again. She wouldn't be abandoning him, though: she would be giving him to Matteo and offering him his only chance at freedom, while not deserting Nik. Matteo would protect Georgi like his own. Even if he did not know the truth, he would lay down his life for the boy.

"Take him." She thrust Georgi at Matteo, knowing if she didn't do it quickly she would lose her nerve and never let go. Matteo wrapped the boy in his coat.

Georgi stared at Matteo wide-eyed, apprehensive of the stranger. "The man who came to our house that night," he said, remembering.

"Yes, the man from the house," Lily repeated, aching that she could not tell him how much more Matteo really was to him. Lily pressed her hands to Georgi's cheeks and kissed his forehead, wanting to hold him in that moment forever. She pulled away from him with effort. "You have to go now," she said to Matteo.

Matteo stood, his eyes pleading. "Are you sure you won't come with us? I think Nik would want you to."

It was true. Nik would insist that she save her own life and live to take care of Georgi. But it was also true that he would never leave her. Lily shook her head. "I can't. Go now," she said firmly, then took a step back into the rail car toward Nik. The train lurched forward.

Matteo took Georgi's hand and started to climb from the railcar. "Matteo, wait. There's something else." She needed to tell him while there was still time that he was Georgi's father. But as she opened her mouth to speak, the words stuck in her throat. Suddenly a shot rang out behind them. A German guard had hopped down from the train and was racing along the track toward their wagon, his pistol pointed in their direction. Matteo pushed her and Georgi down to the floor of the railcar. Lily realized then that he was weaponless except for the crowbar he had used to break into the railcar. "Here!" she cried, tossing him her gun.

Matteo faced the guard and returned fire. The guard crumpled to the ground. Just then, the train began to move.

Matteo picked Georgi up again and started to climb down from the wagon. But as he did, another shot rang out. Matteo fell backward from the railcar, his grip on the child releasing. "No!" Lily let out a shriek, then grabbed Georgi as he wobbled near the edge. His foot slipped from the railcar and dangled midair as he hung precariously, caught between one world and the next as the train picked up speed.

Lily started to pull him back into the railcar. But doing so was consigning him to a horrific end. Behind him, the open sky and fresh air beckoned, representing a chance. Lily did then the only thing she could do for her child.

She let him go.

She released Georgi's hand, and he sailed backward. "Mama!" he cried. Lily was seized with regret. What kind of mother threw her own child from a train? But it was too late now, the decision made, their fate sealed. The train sped forward, and Georgi disappeared into the darkness behind them.

The door to the railcar banged shut, eclipsing Georgi from sight.

Lily sank to the floor of the car amid the sick and dying,

wracked with despair. Georgi was gone. Had he fallen beneath the moving train? She prayed that he had landed safely and that Matteo would be able to find him. She had sworn not to be separated again from her child. And then in the name of saving him, she had broken that promise. Everything that she lived for was gone, and there was no way she could go on without him. She selfishly wished they had both died instead, together.

Hearing a noise behind her, she turned. Nik made a raspy noise, struggling to speak. "Nik." Lily crawled toward him, praying in his delirium that he did not realize what had happened or know that Georgi was gone.

She leaned close to hear him, his words not more than breath. He uttered just a single syllable. "Go." Then he fell back, unable to say more.

Lily paused, not sure that she had heard him right. But the word hung in the air between them.

Nik would not make it. Lily knew that, as surely as she knew her own name. But still she could not leave him. She studied him, memorizing each line in his face, like a map of the life they had shared together. She felt a pang of remorse for all that she had not been able to give him. He was a good man, and he deserved unconditional love, without any encumbrances from her past.

"Go," he breathed again.

Lily wanted to argue, but he was right. To stay here was to watch him die, but to go after Georgi was to give her child— and herself—a chance to live. He was setting her free.

In that instant, she knew she had made a mistake by not going with Matteo and Georgi. The possibility of life was so much better than suffering and inevitable death. She wrapped her arms around Nik, cradling his head like a child. "I will always love you," she said, kissing him a final time softly on the lips.

Then she walked to the door of the railcar and tugged at it, but it was sealed shut once more. She was trapped.

Something caught her eye. The corner of the railcar where

the slats had ripped apart, forming a hole no bigger than a shoe-box. Lily could make out the smoke and darkness on the other side. She stepped toward it hesitantly. Through the tiny space, she could see glimpses of the outside world passing. *Hope.*

Lily pulled at the edge of the hole, but the boards around it remained firmly in place. Shards of metal and wood ripped at her already cracked fingers, causing them to bleed. She hurried to the suitcase and opened it, pulling out the crowbar Hannah had given her and used it to pry at the wood around the hole. She tore at the wagon with all her might. The boards around the hole gave way, creating an opening just big enough for her to squeeze through.

Lily looked back at Nik with a heavy heart. He had sacrificed everything for her. She had failed him and their marriage vows in his time of greatest need, and it seemed that every decision she had made, selfish and wrong, had brought them to this mo-ment. But his eyes were closed, as if already gone.

She pushed through the opening and stood on the narrow ledge of the railcar, staring at the ground in disbelief as it raced by. How had she gotten to this place? One minute she was shop-ping and taking her child for walks in the park, and the next she was dropping from a moving train to try and find him. Life had changed, the whole world she had known and everything she held dear gone in an instant.

Lily looked from the ground to the starry sky, which seemed to beckon her. She wanted to freeze time so she would not be faced with the unthinkable need to jump. She didn't even know if she could do it. But each second she waited drew her farther away from Georgi and her chance of finding him again.

She took a deep breath and leaped.

32

Hannah

Hannah watched from a distance with helpless disbelief as Matteo raced back to the train and boarded the sick car. She held her breath, waiting for him to appear with Lily and Georgi. But the train started moving, taking all of them with it.

Hannah stifled a scream. She wanted to run after it and save them all. But there were more than three dozen people they had freed from the train, who had valiantly jumped in hopes of freedom. Some had run off into the woods, but others stood uncertainly, waiting for her to tell them what to do. "Go quickly," she instructed. She distributed among them the rest of the money Micheline had gotten from the resistance, not sure what good it would do for the escapees. "Spread out and find shelter in the forest or villages," she reminded them.

"Come with me," a tall, strong prisoner said to those who remained. Hannah assumed he was one of the Dutch resistance workers Micheline had mentioned, who had helped Lily plan the escape from the inside.

"Can you manage them all?" Hannah asked.

He nodded. "I can try."

When they had gone, Hannah started back toward the tracks where the train had stood moments earlier. Matteo was gone, as was Lily and her family. She retrieved her bike from where she and Matteo had stowed them before the break and rode it along the tracks, following the train for more nearly two kilometers, her breath growing ragged as the route went up a hill. At the crest, she stopped, peering into the valley on the other side. The railway continued for as far as her eyes could see. She considered going farther after the train. But it would be nearing the German border now, and Hannah had no chance of rescuing anyone alone.

They might not be on the train anymore, Hannah rationalized. Matteo might have persuaded Lily to jump farther up the tracks. But even if that was true, Hannah did not know which way they would have gone.

She looked at the tracks ahead once more, then turned to look behind her. There was no sign that anyone had been here. If she had not seen the train break with her own eyes, she might not believe it had actually happened. But neither Lily, Georgi or Matteo were anywhere to be found, and there was nothing more to be done by staying here. Her search options exhausted, Hannah decided to return to the city and the canteen to see if there was any word about what had happened to Matteo or the others.

Hannah made her way back to Brussels under cover of darkness, finding the nearest station and leaving her bike there to catch a train back to the city. The city streets were thick with police, as if the reverberations of the train break had been felt even this far away. Hannah crept swiftly through the back alleyways. She prayed that Micheline had returned, with an explanation as to why she had never appeared to help with the train break.

But when she reached the canteen, it was dark and shuttered. One of the front windows was broken and red tape placed across the front door. *Zutritt Verboten!* a sign read in German. *No Entry!* The police had been here as well.

Hannah hesitated. It was not safe to be here. But she had to know if Micheline had returned. She slipped around the back and inside. Micheline's desk sat untouched. She had not returned.

Hannah stood alone in the canteen, still shaken. Lily was missing, and Georgi too. Matteo had not returned since going back to the train. Whether he had found Lily or whether she and her family were still on the train headed to Auschwitz she did not know. Micheline had never materialized for the rescue, which could only mean that something terrible had befallen her as well. Everyone Hannah loved was gone. And it was all her fault.

Hannah heard a noise from the basement. Someone was here. Tensing, she looked around for something she could use as a weapon. Matteo appeared in the doorway then, looking pale and shaky. She threw herself into his arms, overwhelmed with relief. "Thank God you're okay."

He blanched as she touched him, and when they pulled apart, she could see that his shirt was wet with blood. "You're shot!" she cried.

"It's superficial," he said dismissively, but that did not quell her worries. She knelt and pulled back his shirt, revealing a gunshot wound. The bullet had thankfully just grazed him. He had lost a fair amount of blood, though. She pressed on the wound, trying to slow the bleed, but it did not stop completely.

"There's a medic kit in the desk," he said, and she rushed to get it. When she returned, he opened it and poured alcohol on the wound. She helped him crudely affix a bandage.

"That's going to go septic," she fretted. "We have to get you help." If only Nik was still here to treat him. Matteo waved her away, and she saw pain in his eyes that she knew was deeper than his wound. "What happened? Did you find Lily on the train?"

"Yes," he said. Hannah's hope rose. Matteo continued. "She was in the sick car with Nik and Georgi. But she wouldn't come with me. I persuaded her to give me the child, but when she went to hand him to me, I was shot and…" He could not finish.

"Georgi's dead?" she asked, dreading the answer.

"I don't know. I fell from the train. He was on the edge with me. Lily could have pulled him back inside. Or he might have fallen as well, but he wasn't there when I looked for him."

"No!" His words slammed into her like a rock. Georgi was gone. "And Lily?"

"I would assume she's still on the train." His face bore a haunted expression. The plan had not worked at all.

Matteo buried his head in his hands, seemingly overwhelmed by all that had happened. Without thinking, she leaned in to offer comfort. Quickly realizing her mistake, she braced for rejection, expecting him to pull away. Instead he remained still, allowing her to draw him close. She put her arms around him, and this time he did not resist but embraced her in return. He buried his nose in her hair where her neck met her shoulder as if trying to lose himself there.

The depth of her feelings washed over her then, threatening to knock her off her feet. Despite everything, she still loved him. She felt vulnerable and exposed. She had sworn never to open herself up again to risk of that kind of pain. Yet here she was, powerless to stop it.

None of this mattered at all now. Her cousin, the very person for whom Hannah had engineered the break, was still on the train, headed to Auschwitz. But her son perhaps was not. Hannah stood. "I have to go find Georgi."

"Hannah, he might still be on the train as well. And even if he got off somehow, surely a child so young…" The awful truth lay unspoken between them. Even if he had survived the fall, he could not possibly have survived being all alone in the woods.

"It doesn't matter," Hannah insisted. "He could be out there. Hurt. Scared. I have to try."

"Hannah, the countryside is swarming with Germans, searching for the people who escaped the train—and us. It's too dangerous."

"He's my nephew, for God's sake! I owe it to Lily to find him."

"At least let me go for you."

"You can't go now. You need medical help." The bandage she had applied just minutes earlier was already seeped in blood.

Matteo looked as though he wanted to argue further. But he sat back, too weak. "There is a convent of Dominican Sisters in Lubbeek to the east. Do you know it?"

"No, but I can find it. Why?"

"They've acted as a clearinghouse for us since before the war, relaying information about people's whereabouts and even sheltering refugee children for short periods of time. I don't know that they would have information about Georgi, but they aren't far from where we intercepted the train, so if anyone would know about a lost child, they might."

"Stay here," she said. "I'll go." He nodded. Even if he had been strong enough to leave, he would attract too much attention being obviously wounded.

"Hannah, wait. There's something else. My sister. She didn't come." The distress in Matteo's voice was palpable.

"I know. Maybe something delayed her," Hannah offered, trying to comfort him. But she knew it was wishful thinking. Nothing would have stopped Micheline from being there at the train break. More than likely, something had gone wrong.

"Not Micheline. My sister has never failed to turn up when she said she would. Not once in her entire life. Something awful happened. I can feel it." The words hung ominously in the air between them. "I have to go find her."

"You can't possibly now."

But Matteo would not be dissuaded. "My sister is out there. She needs me. She would not leave me if the situation was reversed."

"I will go," Hannah promised. "After I search for Georgi, I will go look for Micheline."

"But how?" Matteo asked. "We don't know where she's gone."

"That's true," Hannah admitted. "All she said was that she was off to catch a killer. Do you have any idea where she would have gone?"

Matteo seemed to think for a moment. "She wouldn't go to kill someone herself, but she would send word through the network. She has a contact in Tervuren, a grocer, who sometimes sends messages for her. She might have gone there to send a message to the resistance about the traitor, but I'm not entirely certain."

"That's our only lead," Hannah replied decisively. "I'll start there."

"Take the car," he said, passing her a set of keys. "And be careful."

"I shall. But what about you? You can't stay here." She paused for a moment, thinking. "The chateau outside Haacht. Micheline said it was vacant. Do you think it's still safe?"

"It's worth a try. There's nowhere else to go."

"You go there and wait for me. I'll meet you there as soon as I am able." She looked at his wound, fretting. "I hate leaving you alone like this. You need medical care."

"I'll be fine. The best thing you can do is go find Georgi and my sister." Hannah nodded and hurried from the canteen.

An hour later, Hannah stopped the car on the gravel driveway outside the convent in Lubbeek. The medieval church set among rolling hills was like something out of a storybook. Closer though, she could see that the stained-glass windows were cracked and the stone facade crumbling. The steps were wet, giving off a damp, ancient smell.

Hannah rang the bell and heard it echo through the halls inside. The arched wooden door swung open, and a nun appeared. Her face turned guarded, and Hannah realized then how she must look in her filthy, tattered clothing. "Can I help you?"

Hannah paused, unsure how much she could safely say. "I'm looking for a lost child."

Something flickered in the woman's eyes. "Lost?"

Hannah decided to take a chance and say more. "From one of the trains."

The nun's expression hardened. "I don't know anything about the trains," she said defensively.

"But you know about a child? He's eight." The nun stared at her unyieldingly. "Please, he's my nephew."

"There is a little boy." Hannah's breath caught. "He came here alone at night, saying that he became separated from his mother."

The nun disappeared back inside to fetch the boy. Could it possibly be Georgi? She imagined reuniting him with Lily. Surely if the child could be found, his mother could be too. Her hope rose at the thought of making things right.

The nun returned with a little boy in tow. Hannah's heart sank like a stone. The child was not Georgi.

She stared hard at him, wanting to be wrong. But his hair was red, not black, and his face was freckled where Georgi's skin was alabaster. She was seized with the impulse to take this child, any child, to fill the void.

The child looked lost and confused. Had he thought he was being reunited with his mother as well? Hannah knelt before him. "Where did you last see your mother?"

"We jumped together." The boy spoke matter-of-factly about things a child should never have to know.

"You were on the wagon that was freed?" Hannah felt certain she would have remembered if there had been another child about Georgi's age.

"No, but when we heard the others getting out, we decided to take a chance. Papa was able to get the door open." It had not occurred to her that the sabotage of the train might have given others the courage to try to flee as well. "Our father was killed right away. But I rolled too far, and when I woke up my mother was gone." Hannah tried not to imagine what might have happened to Georgi.

Hannah turned to the nun. "Can you keep him here?"

The nun pressed her lips together. "For now." The convent would only be a safe hiding place for so long.

"You haven't heard about any other lost children?"

"I'm sorry, I haven't." They had been fortunate enough to find one child. What were the odds of them finding two?

Hannah set out from the convent, feeling dejected and hopeless. She wanted to keep searching for Lily and her son, but she had already scoured the countryside around the site of the train break. He could be anywhere or, worse, he could be gone.

With her only lead exhausted, her thoughts turned to Micheline. Matteo had said that she might have gone to the grocer in Liège. She had not returned. Hannah harbored little hope that Micheline would still be there. But perhaps the grocer would have some idea where she had gone.

She drove the car to the village, a half hour north. When she reached the main thoroughfare of the town, she pulled the car to the side of the road. She saw a postman delivering the mail. "Pardon me," she said. "Can you direct me to the grocery store?" She prayed that the small village would have only one.

He pointed her in the direction of the shop. Though it was the middle of the day, it was shuttered and dark, the door locked, which seemed an ominous sign. Had Micheline made it here?

Perhaps the grocery had gone out of business because of the war and Micheline had not known. But through the window, Hannah could see sparse but fresh goods on the shelf. The shop had closed only recently, seemingly without notice. Perhaps the owner had been called away on a personal errand or emergency.

Hannah looked up. There was an apartment above the shop, and one of the windows was ajar. She walked to the door and rang the buzzer beside it. No one answered.

More determined than ever to find out if someone was there,

Hannah walked along the building to the alley beside the shop, searching for another entrance. A fire-escape ladder ran along the side of the building, and Hannah contemplated climbing it.

Then something at the back of the alley caught her eye. It was a tire protruding from behind the building. She hurried closer.

Seeing something familiar, she let out a yelp.

Behind the shop sat the twisted wreckage of Micheline's motorbike. Hannah's stomach hardened with dread. Micheline would never abandon her bike voluntarily. She knew then that something was very, very wrong.

33

Lily

Lily awoke in complete darkness, unsure if she was alive or dead and buried. Knives seemed to shoot through her, reminding her that she was very much still here. She rolled over, stifling a cry as pain shot through her ankle. Had she broken it? She spat out dirt which had somehow gotten into her mouth when she had hit the ground. Her head throbbed.

Lily adjusted her eyes, trying to get her bearings. She could not remember the actual moment she had jumped, just a blinding light before she lost consciousness. *Georgi*. The image of her son flying from the train into the darkness seared itself into her memory. She had to find him.

She reached down and examined her ankle, deciding with relief that it wasn't broken. She had to keep moving. She had no idea where she was or how long she had been unconscious, whether the Germans might still be near. And she did not know where the others were. The place where she had jumped was nowhere near the location where Hannah and the others had ambushed the train, but far east of there, away from anyone. She worried that she had waited so long that she might be in Germany.

Lily tried to stand, her leg nearly buckling from the pain. One of her shoes was missing. She felt around the ground, but did not find it. With one foot clad only in a sock and the other severely injured, she began to limp. She looked desperately for woods or other shelter. She had to stay out of sight. In her prison uniform, she would stand out, be apprehended immediately. But the strip of track where she had landed was in the middle of an open field with no shelter as far as the eye could see.

Lily started west, her progress on her injured leg painstakingly slow. She had to find some sort of shelter. But she followed the tracks, in spite of the risk, retracing the route the train had taken in hopes of finding the place where Georgi had fallen. She did not dare to imagine that she might find him but perhaps a clue as to what had happened to him and which way he had gone or been taken. But she found nothing, and when she reached the location, marked by the distinctive arc of pine trees, where the initial train break had taken place before Matteo boarded and they had kept moving east, she was forced to admit there was no sign of him.

There did not seem to be any point in following the tracks farther. She needed to find a place to hide so that she could decide what to do next. To the north of the tracks beyond the trees, she spied a plume of smoke and sniffed an acrid odor suggesting someone was burning brush. She started in that direction, cutting through the woods.

Forty-five minutes later, Lily reached the edge of the woods where it ended near a road. She saw two farmers talking between their predawn chores by a fence, and she leaped back into hiding behind a tree. They looked like simple peasants in brown and gray work clothes, unlikely to cause her harm. She leaned in closer, realizing with unease that they were speaking German. Still crouching, she tried to listen. She could make out the words *train* and *escape*. Word had gotten out. People would be on the alert for Jews who had fled.

Lily tried to slink away, but she caught her bad ankle and tripped, falling forward into the ditch along the road. She stifled a yelp. The farmers stopped talking, and although Lily could not see them, she imagined their heads snapping in the direction of the ditch. *"Wer ist?"* one of the farmers called. Lily lay motionless in the ditch, bracing for him to discover her. She had no hope of escaping quickly. But a moment later, she heard a door slam as one farmer went back inside and a lone set of footsteps grew fainter as the second walked away.

Lily peered out of the ditch, and when she was certain the road was deserted, she climbed out once more. But it was daylight now and unsafe to continue along the open roadway, especially in her striped uniform. She could not go much farther on her wounded ankle anyway.

She paused, leaning against a tree, and looked around desperately. There was a barn a bit farther down the road, several hundred meters from the farmhouse. She hobbled toward it, certain that at any moment someone would emerge from the farmhouse or come down the road and ask what she was doing there.

Finally, she reached the barn. Inside it was empty except for a cow and some chickens. A ladder led to a loft, and Lily thought she might be able to hide there if she could manage the climb.

She started for the ladder. Just then, a girl of about fifteen with white-blond hair walked into the barn. Seeing Lily among the livestock, she froze.

"Wait!" Lily cried, too loudly. The girl opened her mouth to scream, but no sound came out. Then she turned and bolted for the door.

Lily gathered herself and prepared to flee. But before she could get out of the barn, the girl returned with an older woman carrying a tin cup. She eyed Lily for several seconds without speaking.

"Guten Morgen," Lily offered, trying to think of something to say to explain her presence in their barn. But before she could speak further, the woman held the cup out to her. Lily drank the still-warm milk greedily, savoring the richness. It was the most nourishment she had since her arrest, and she could soon feel the strength returning to her limbs.

"Wait here," the woman said gruffly. Then she left the barn with her daughter in tow. Lily debated whether she should flee now, while she had the chance. What if the woman had gone to tell someone she was there? But Lily knew she would not make it far on her ankle.

A few minutes later, the woman returned alone, carrying a dress and worn boots. "Here, put these on," she said. She knew Lily was one of the escapees and was helping her anyway. Lily stepped behind the stall for privacy and put it on, then buried her stained uniform in the hay. The dress was a bit too large, gaping at the neck with an extra fold of material. But it was better than the prison uniform, and Lily welcomed the feel of the soft fabric. The boots were too big as well, so she laced them as tightly as she could without further hurting her ankle.

"You haven't seen anyone else like me?" she asked, hoping against hope for some word about Georgi. "Perhaps a child?"

The woman shook her head. "I'm sorry, no."

No, of course not. Though she had not expected her to have news of her son, Lily felt a crush of disappointment.

The woman motioned Lily from the barn. Was she kicking her out? "It isn't safe to stay around here. Some of the people in this village help the Germans—including my husband."

"But where am I to go?"

She pressed some coins into Lily's hand and pointed in the other direction. "There's a small train depot just over two kilometers west of here. Stay off the road." Lily was dumbfounded. Surely she could not get on the train with other passengers. And even if she did, where could she possibly go? The woman was right, though. She needed to get as far from here as possible.

Brussels, she thought. She knew, or hoped anyway, that Matteo and Hannah would be there as well and could help in her search for Georgi. Of course, she could not return to her home there or even to the city. The Germans might be looking for people who had escaped from the train, including her. But she could not hide in the countryside alone forever.

She remembered then the chateau Hannah had mentioned outside the city where they were supposed to meet if they got separated. There was no reason to think that Hannah would go looking for her there, since she didn't even know that Lily had jumped from the train. But the chateau was closer to the city, and perhaps if she made it there, she could get word to Hannah that she was alive and hiding and in need of help.

"Thank you," she said, starting slowly away.

An hour later, Lily reached the station, a low-roofed building on the edge of the nearest town. She stood alone on the platform, wishing there were more travelers in the early morning to help her blend in. A train came, and she boarded with a few laborers clad in blue overalls. She marveled at the second-class car, such a contrast to the boxcar she and her family had traveled in just days earlier. She thought again of Georgi, seeing him once more in her mind's eye. Her heart cried out for her son as she relived the last moment she had seen him. She had not meant to drop him from the train alone into the darkness. But letting him go was the only way to give him a chance at survival. Only, what chance did he have now? Surely he could not have survived such a fall. And if he had, he was out there somewhere, lost and alone. Lily thought, too, of Nik, alone on the train near the end of his terrible journey, sick if not already gone. She pressed her head against the glass, hoping no one would see her holding back tears.

Lily got off the train in Haacht, a market town just east of the city. Outside the station, she paused to get her bearings. *Fol-*

low the antitank canal out of town, Hannah had said. Lily found the canal, which had been built before the war in futile hope of staving off the Germans. She followed it east out of town as Hannah had instructed and across a patchwork of rolling fields in the direction of the chateau.

The canal ended, and Lily climbed a hill to get a better view. It was a warm August day, and though she was cautious not to be seen, Lily marveled at walking freely, as she had not done in months. But for her despair over her family, she might have found the stroll pleasant. She spied the chateau on the far side of a sloping valley and started toward it.

Lily approached the stately home, sprawling and elegant like a castle. It was hard to believe that such a place was deserted when so many undoubtedly needed shelter. But when she got closer she saw why: it had clearly been hit in an air raid, one of the high walls half caved-in, part of the roof gone.

There was an undetonated bomb lodged in the front walkway, and she gingerly made her way around it. Near the front entrance she paused, peering through a shattered window to make sure no one was inside. She pushed on the front door, which was un-locked and opened with a creak. She listened to make sure no one was there. Then she stepped into the massive foyer. The marble floor was cracked, great chunks of stone protruding jaggedly. A chandelier lay in the middle of the floor, its glass shattered to bits that crunched under her boots as she walked. Through the crumbled ceiling, she could see a patch of cloudy sky.

Lily doubted it was safe to be in there, but she had no other choice. She stepped carefully through the foyer into a grand living room with elegant oak furniture. Everything was covered in a thin coat of plaster dust. There were hooks on the walls where paint-ings had once hung and a smashed china cabinet that someone had looted. Lily looked uneasily through the gaping hole where the front window had once been. This part of the chateau was visible from the road, and anyone who passed by might see her.

Given the state of the house, Lily worried that the upper floor might not be stable. She decided to go down to the basement to hide. She found a doorway with stone steps leading down. It was nearly dark in the windowless cellar. She felt for a light switch on the wall, but when she flicked it, nothing happened. She hurried back upstairs, ignoring her ankle, which ached painfully, with each step. She found the kitchen, then located a stub of a candle and some matches in a cupboard.

Lily lit the candle, then used it to illuminate her way back down into the cellar. The faint light licked at the walls. There had once been a wine cellar, she could see, but it had been ransacked. She could only hope that whoever had looted it knew they had already gotten everything and would see no reason to return. The ancient stone gave off a damp smell.

She sat in a corner of the cellar and tucked her legs under the dress, her ankle aching worse now. She was suddenly aware of how very alone she was. Georgi was gone. Nik was on the train or at the camp, if he was even still alive. She had seen Matteo shot right before her eyes, and she had no idea what had become of Hannah. She did not know where a single soul she loved was at this very moment. The tears, which she had held back since she'd awakened by the railway tracks, burst forth now. She shook with grief, her sobs echoing in the cavernous space until she could cry no more. Exhaustion overtook her then, and she tilted her head back and slept.

Lily dreamed fitfully of Georgi, chasing and finding him, only to lose him over and over again. She awakened sometime later. She reached for the child in her sleep, an instinct honed from years of motherhood and the nights sleeping with him in her bed at Breendonk. Her arms closed around emptiness. The full realization of where she was and all that had happened slammed into her.

Lily sat up, uncertain if it was day or night or how long she had been asleep. The candle stub had gone out, leaving her in darkness. She couldn't stay here without food or water. She would have to keep moving. She stood, her ankle throbbing anew.

Just then, she heard a noise. She tensed, hoping it was mice rustling in the walls. But the sound was overhead and heavy. Footsteps.

Lily jumped back, away from the stairs. Hannah had said the chateau was abandoned and safe, but now someone was here. Were they looking for her? Or perhaps they were hiding too and didn't know she was there at all.

Lily looked desperately around the cellar for an alternate exit, but the stairs were the only way out. Resigned to face whoever was coming in, she started for the stairs.

As the door swung open, she stopped with surprise.

There, in the abandoned chateau, was Hannah.

34

Micheline

At the very minute Hannah and Matteo had needed Micheline most, she was trapped far away in a German prison, powerless to do anything.

When Micheline had been arrested, she had considered fighting. But both policemen had pistols trained on her. Her own words to Hannah reverberated: *If you reach the point where you need a gun, you've already lost.*

Micheline had turned back to look for the shopkeeper, but he had disappeared. Traitorous bastard. She raised her hands and let the men lead her outside to a police car that was waiting. *Don't let them take you in a car.* That was one of the earliest lessons she had learned in her training. There were only two men: if she caught them off guard, she could take one down and slip away from the other. But she looked down the street at the row of unfamiliar houses with windows shuttered. There was no safe house here, no kind soul who might give her sanctuary even if she could get away. She had no choice but to let them take her.

In the back of the police car, her mind raced. The rescue mission had been a trap. The shopkeeper who relayed the message to her, once an ally, had betrayed her. Was it for money or another motive? Perhaps he had simply been a pawn, unaware that the message he'd relayed was, in fact, a trap. Micheline berated herself silently. She had let down her guard. And it was going to cost her everything.

The police took her to the Saint-Gilles prison, a massive, castlelike structure in the southern part of the city. They threw her into a windowless cell in the basement of the structure that smelled of cabbage and urine, and they left her bound and gagged in the darkness without food or water for more than a day.

Then finally, they came for her.

They led her to a large interrogation room with bare walls. The stone floor was unmistakably stained with old blood, too much to ever be properly washed away. Micheline tried not to think about how it had gotten there. But after the guard chained her to a chair and left the room, she had nothing to do but imagine what had happened to those who had come before her—and whether she would suffer the same fate. Some of the network operatives carried a cyanide capsule for moments just like this, choosing to die rather than suffer interrogation, but she did not.

At last the door opened. Through her gag, Micheline stifled a gasp. Standing before her was the very traitor she had hunted. He was beyond her reach now, untouchable.

"Pascal," she breathed after he reached over and removed her gag. "But why? Why would you turn on us?"

"I didn't turn," he snapped. "I was loyal to the Reich all along. My father was in the German army, and he was killed in the trenches during the Great War. When I was old enough, I joined the Nazi Party to honor his memory and embraced its ideals. Quietly, of course, so that I could gather information for the cause."

"So you were never a priest?"

"I joined the seminary. It made an excellent cover. After the *Führer* came to power, it allowed me to infiltrate some of the very monasteries and religious organizations which were trying to save Jews. And then when we occupied Belgium and you began the wretched business of rescuing airmen, it let me get close to you."

It had worked, Micheline admitted begrudgingly. She had not questioned his story as she had others who came to the network. "You did this to us," she said. "Destroyed our operations."

Pascal sneered, his once-gentle face hardened with anger. "You give me too much credit. Think about it. I never could have pulled this off on my own. No one man could. Besides, you didn't trust me, and you never gave me enough inside information." The full extent of his resentment was laid bare now. "No, I needed help from someone else. Someone high up and close to you."

"But who?" Micheline racked her brain. Who would do something this heartless to her, to the Sapphire Line?

"That is the question. It had to be someone high up. Was it one of your lieutenants? Or perhaps even someone closer to you?" he taunted. "I'll never tell. And you'll go to your grave not knowing."

"But if you have an informant, then why do you need me?" There was something they wanted from her. Otherwise they surely would have killed her straightaway.

"Because you are the lynchpin, the one we wanted in the first place. Getting you meant taking down the whole network for good."

Micheline smiled faintly through her pain. "Fool! Don't you know that no one person is the sun?" They were a constellation of stars, basking in the collective glow. Micheline was, to be sure, a bright one. But a single star nevertheless.

"Informants only have so much information," he persisted. "You know everything." This was true. Micheline was at the epicenter of the network. No one, not even Matteo, possessed the full extent of her knowledge. "And now you are going to tell us."

"No." Micheline was also better trained than anyone to withstand interrogation. Of course, preparing for torture was one thing, experiencing it quite another. She only hoped she could hold up.

"Let's start with an easy one." He walked behind her chair and dragged it without warning close to the desk, where there was a blank pad and a pen. Then he unbound her arms. "The names of all of your assets and their whereabouts. Then we'll move on to the safe houses." He was referring to the most closely hidden safe houses, the ones that had not been indicated on the map she'd found. She had never mentioned those in her work with him, and she was unsure how he knew about them. She reached out with a sweeping motion and knocked the paper and pen to the ground.

The guard reentered the room and lifted her from the chair and bound her arms once more. The cuffs were attached to a chain that hung from the ceiling. Pain ripped through her back and shoulders as he raised her arms high behind her until she was lifted up off the ground and dangling from the cuffs in midair. Another few centimeters and her shoulders would dislocate or the bones snap. "Again," Pascal said, picking up the pen and paper. "Your lieutenants."

"I'll never tell," she managed through gritted teeth. "You'll have to kill me first."

They beat her then as she hung, first with fists and later with a pipe against her back and sides. It was the first time in her life she had been struck, and the pain from each blow was more agonizing than the last. When they finally released her, Micheline collapsed in a heap, unable to move.

The guard left and came back again, dousing her with a bucket of icy water to revive her. She was hoisted by her cuffs and the beatings began once more. She forced her mind to leave her body and tried to focus her thoughts on moments of joy from her past. She traveled over the hills to where she and Matteo used to play as children.

They lashed her with a whip, on her back and then her face. Her body went very hot and then cold, and large black spots clouded her vision. But still her thoughts were only of the others. Where were Matteo and Hannah? They had been counting on her, and were surely wondering why she had not come.

Pascal spat the question over and over again. *Who?* But as Micheline lost consciousness, she realized that it was not his question she was hearing, but her own. *Who had betrayed the network and brought them to this?*

Later, Micheline awoke on the cold floor of her cell. "Who was it?" she cried from the floor, her body too broken to sit or stand. "Who was the traitor?"

The echo of her own voice was the only response.

The next day they brought her to the interrogation room again. Pascal was surprisingly civil this time, offering her a cigarette, which she declined, and a cold compress for her face. She was familiar with this game. They would grind you to a pulp and then offer a bit of kindness, hoping that in a moment of grateful weakness you would cave. *Not bloody likely*, as her British counterparts would have said.

Micheline waited expectantly for Pascal to begin his questioning again. Instead, he spread a map before her on the table. It was a duplicate of the one she had found by the dead airman in the woods. "You can see we know everything," he offered. She did not respond.

"Your brother is here," he said quietly, his voice tinged with a hint of smugness.

"Teo." She had so desperately hoped that the train break

had been a success and that he had gotten away. But Pascal was claiming he had been arrested as well. Her heart ached for him. She saw her father then, berating her for failing to protect Matteo, the one thing she had sworn to do. Suddenly she was a girl again, shamed for letting him get hurt. She was the younger of the two, yet somehow the responsibility for their protection had always fallen to her.

"Is he all right?" she asked finally, showing her concern in spite of herself.

"All right?" Pascal laughed contemptuously. "Of course. Your brother was not brought here as a prisoner. He's been working with us all along." Micheline stared at him, too surprised to speak. "Yes, your darling brother," Pascal sneered. "He was the traitor. How could you not see it?"

"No!" she spat. Pascal was lying, trying to break her. But even as she rejected the idea, the truth of it formed undeniably before her. The way Matteo always seemed to have just what they needed when no one else could help, even her. *Don't ask.* Matteo's words reverberated in her head. He had a knack—no, a gift—for making things happen, procuring the impossible. Now she had to ask herself at what price those gifts came, what he'd had to give in order to achieve them.

"He did it all for that whore nurse," Pascal added. Had Matteo really given up the whole organization, including his own sister, for Lily? Seeing the glint in Pascal's eyes, she realized this could just as likely be a cruel trick, designed to make her cave. Because if Matteo had really told them everything, they would not still need to sit here and question her at all.

"I want to see my brother," she demanded as though she was the one in charge. She needed to see his face and know if the accusations were true.

"You'll never see him again."

"No!" she cried out and lunged at him, straining against her bonds. The guard dragged her from the room and threw her into her cell before slamming the door.

Pain ripped through her, and she tore at the cinder blocks, her scream turning to a wail.

35

Hannah

"Hannah!" Lily cried, her voice ringing loudly through the cellar. She threw herself into her cousin's arms.

Hannah stared at Lily as if seeing a ghost. She touched Lily's hair and cheek to make sure she was really there. "But how?" Lily was pale and seemed thinner than she had just a few days ago. She had changed from her camp uniform into a dress that Hannah did not recognize, but her disheveled hair and scraped skin still bore evidence of the trauma she had been through.

"You told me about the chateau and how to get here. I remembered, and I hoped that you would too."

Hannah nodded. "That was a good idea. But I still don't understand what happened. You weren't in the railcar. You were still on the train when it continued to the camp. And you didn't go when Matteo came back for you."

"I was assigned to another car because Nik was ill. I couldn't leave him, so I gave Georgi to Matteo. Or tried." Her face fell as she relived the horror of losing her son. "Later when I realized there was nothing more I could do for Nik, I jumped."

"You jumped from a moving train," Hannah said, marveling at her cousin's strength. "Are you injured?"

"I only twisted my ankle. But before that, Matteo was shot. And Georgi…"

"I know. Matteo told me."

"Matteo's okay?" Lily's voice was full with concern. "When I saw him shot, I thought for certain he would die."

"He's fine. The wound was superficial. There was a lot of bleeding, but it didn't hit any organs. He's already up and around."

"That's so like him."

"Yes." The women shared a strange moment of quiet affection for the man they both loved. "And Georgi?" Lily's voice was pleading, almost desperate.

Hannah shook her head. "No sign of him yet." She emphasized the last word, wanting to give her cousin some hope that would keep her from crumbling. She considered telling Lily about the other boy she had found. If that child had made it, surely there was hope for Georgi as well. But somehow it seemed cruel to share that another boy had been found while Lily's son had not. "We will keep looking," she promised.

Tears streamed down Lily's face. "I never should have let him go."

Hannah shook her head. "You did the right thing. It was the only thing you could do to give him a chance to live. If you and he had stayed on that train, you would both be dead by now."

"Like Nik," Lily said flatly. "He's gone, I know it."

"I'm so, so sorry." She wished that she could offer Lily hope for her husband as well. But a person as sick as Nik would have been taken from the train and gassed immediately—if he had even survived the journey. Lily started impulsively for the stairs. "I have to find Georgi myself."

Hannah grabbed Lily's arm, stopping her. "No, you must stay here. There are SS fanned out across east Belgium all the way to Brussels, looking for people who escaped from the train. What good will it do to find him if you are arrested again?" Lily did not answer. "I will go make further inquiries, but you must wait and hide."

"But how can I possibly just sit here? What am I to do?"

"Rest. I will go find you food."

"I can't bear to sleep," Lily said, "because then I have to wake up and live this all over again."

"I can't begin to imagine how painful this is for you." She wrapped her arm around her cousin's shoulders. "But you should at least try to rest. You are going to need your strength for whatever comes next." She prayed Lily would not ask what that would be, because Hannah simply did not know. Exhaustion won over, however, and Lily sat down, tilted her head back and closed her eyes.

Hannah slipped from the chateau and down the road, relieved that she had found Lily. Matteo was supposed to come there as well, but he had not appeared. She wondered if he had been delayed or, worse yet, detained.

Pushing the worry from her mind, Hannah focused on finding food for her cousin. She did not have time to go into the village, nor could she afford the questions that a stranger appearing might raise.

Hannah paused, considering what to do. She recalled that on the way to the chateau she had seen an abandoned roadside farm stand. They clearly did not have much to sell, but perhaps they could be persuaded to part with something.

She retraced her steps to the farmhouse and knocked. She heard shuffling noises from behind the door, and a few seconds later an older woman appeared, her expression wary at the arrival of an unexpected caller. "I'm sorry to disturb you," Hannah began, "but I saw your farm stand, and I am looking to buy some food."

The woman shook her head sadly. "We have nothing to sell anymore."

"Please, anything," Hannah pressed, not wanting to say more about Lily or why she needed the food. She reached in her pocket and pulled out a few coins.

The woman took the coins and then closed the door, leaving Hannah outside. Hannah worried that she might keep the money and offer nothing in return. A few seconds later, the door opened once more, and the old woman returned carrying two carrots and an apple. Hannah fought the urge to protest. The coins she handed over should have bought five times as much, but she was in no position to argue. "Do you have any bandages?" she asked instead, thinking of Lily's ankle. But the woman shook her head. Hannah took the produce and left.

When Hannah returned to the chateau, she brought the food that she had found to the kitchen where there was a long marble countertop that was surprisingly pristine and perfectly intact. As she placed the items down she heard a sound and froze. It was footsteps below, coming from the cellar. At first she thought that Lily had awakened and was moving about, but the footsteps were too heavy for her slight cousin. Someone else was downstairs. Weaponless and feeling vulnerable, she started down the stairs to confront the intruder. Her panic rose as she saw that there was a man standing over Lily as she slept.

Then, as he turned toward her, she relaxed. It was Matteo. "You're here," she said, flooded with relief. "When I arrived and didn't see you, I was so worried."

"I went a bit slower because of my wound, and I had to hide a few times along the way to avoid the police," he replied. "Plus I stopped to see a contact along the way. He was able to give me some bandages and a fresh shirt." He turned back to Lily. "Thank God she's alive," he whispered. "About Georgi…does she know?"

Hannah nodded. "The child at the abbey was not him."

"I'm so sorry," Matteo said. "I swore to her that I would protect him. And I tried so very hard to hold on to him."

"It's not your fault. She knows that. You were shot."

"Still, I should have managed it. I will find him, I swear it on my life." How could he possibly promise such a thing? "There was another child found, I just heard, staying with a family not far from here."

Hannah felt her heart begin to race. She dared not hope again. "You can't tell Lily."

"Of course not." That would be cruel. Having her hopes dashed once had been hard enough for Hannah. For Lily, it might be too much.

"From what I was told, he looks like Georgi. I wasn't going to say anything to you until I had the chance to see for myself. I was going to check when I stopped here. But right now we have to find a way to get Lily out of Belgium. I will arrange it."

"How?" Surely getting out of the country was even more impossible now.

His eyes were steely. "I will manage it somehow."

"And I will go for the child."

Matteo passed her a crumpled slip of paper bearing an address. "But there's something else. It's Micheline. She's been arrested."

"No." Hannah had suspected that something had happened to Micheline when she did not show for the train break and all but confirmed it when she found the bike. Still, the news felt like a blow. "We have to get her out."

Matteo shook his head. "She's in the military prison at Saint-Gilles. There is nothing to be done."

Just then Lily stirred. She opened her eyes groggily. "Matteo?" Lily sat up, and Matteo knelt beside her.

"Are you all right?" he asked tenderly.

"Yes. Only, Georgi…" Her eyes filled with tears.

"I know," Matteo replied, "and I am going to find him. But right now we have to get you to safety."

Lily tensed. "Where will I go?"

"Out of the country. Across the channel to England."

"But I can't possibly leave Georgi."

Hannah went to her side. "We will keep looking for him and bring him to you straightaway. But Belgium isn't safe for you, and you will be no good to him if you are arrested again or worse."

"No!" Lily shook her head emphatically. "I could never leave without him."

"Listen to me. If you don't go, you are as good as dead. And if you die, you will never see him again. Go to England, and I will find him and bring him to you."

Lily looked at her cousin trustingly. "Fine," she said softly.

"I will go and make arrangements for your departure," Matteo told Lily. He started for the door with Hannah behind him. "You go and check on the child," he whispered to Hannah, too low for Lily to hear.

Hannah could scarcely imagine the heartbreak if the child was not Georgi again. She turned to Lily. "Matteo can take you to the city and put you on the train. You'll go, right?"

Lily nodded. "You aren't coming?"

Hannah took Lily's hand. "I will come see you at the station before you leave. But I need to stay and keep looking for Georgi." Once Hannah was the one meant to leave. Now Lily would be going on without her. The cousins stood holding hands for several moments, neither wanting to part. Though Hannah planned to come to the station that evening and see Lily off, they both knew that meeting again was a gift promised to no one. "I have to go," Hannah said reluctantly.

"Be careful," Lily pled.

"I will. And I will see you soon."

When Matteo and Lily had left, Hannah set out and raced in

the direction of the address in the village Matteo had given her where Georgi possibly was. She stopped before a modest home with well-tended flower boxes in the windows. *Brousseau* read the brass nameplate by the mailbox.

Hannah peered through the window, bracing herself for another disappointment. There was a boy of about eight seated at a piano, plucking at the keys. At the sight of his familiar black curls and dimple, she let out a yelp. "Georgi," she breathed, taking him in. She started toward the door, then stopped. How would these people react to her appearing without notice and claiming the child?

Before she could knock, the door to the house swung open, and a stout, middle-aged woman wearing a white apron appeared. Her hair was swept up in a tight bun. "Can I help you?" she asked briskly, crossing her arms.

"I'm here about the child in your care."

The woman's eyebrows raised. "Albert?" They had given him a new name. It occurred to her not for the first time that they might not want to give him up.

"His name is Georgi. I'm Hannah, his aunt."

"I'm Karolina Brousseau. He wouldn't tell us his name," the woman said, a note of apology in her voice. "He has barely spoken." She understood then. Georgi was, of course, old enough to tell his name, but he had been so terrorized by the Germans and his time at the camp, that he no longer dared. "We lost our own son to the war, and we have no one. We were hoping to keep him."

Georgi appeared in the doorway then. Taking him in, she was at the same time relieved and sad. Under the care of these strangers for just a few days, he had already begun to recover, his cheeks filling out and hair returning in a peachlike fuzz that must have been like when he was a newborn. It was clear that these people had cared for and fed him and treated him like their own.

"Aunt Hannah?"

"It's me, darling."

Georgi hesitated, and she feared they would be like strangers. But he moved closer and his familiar shape filled her arms. "Where are we going?"

Hannah wanted to tell him that she was going to take him to his mother but didn't risk it, in case it was too late and Lily was already gone. "Away." She turned back to Madame Brousseau, who had looked forward to the prospect of raising another child and was surely sad to see him go. "Thank you."

Hannah took Georgi's hand. "Come, we must hurry." She led him as quickly as she could, needing to get him to the rail station to reunite with his mother before it was too late.

36

Lily

It was nearly nightfall when Matteo and Lily set out from the chateau for the rail station in the city. Matteo spoke little on the drive but kept his eyes set on the road, his expression grim. She could feel the weight of it all on him, his sister's arrest and trying to get her out and heaven knew what else. She wanted to reach out and reassure him. She considered taking his hand. But it was all mixed up and wrong somehow.

On the outskirts of the city, he stopped by an unfamiliar warehouse and indicated that she should get out of the car. "We need to get you to Gare du Midi," he said as he led her around the back of the warehouse where a white municipal van was parked. Matteo opened the back door to reveal an unfinished compartment containing tools and sacks and other work equipment. "There are checkpoints in the city. We have to hide you."

Lily hesitated for a moment, then climbed in and lay on the floor, not protesting when Matteo covered her with some filthy burlap sacks. Under other circumstances, she would have felt humiliated at being forced to travel in such a way, and in Brussels no less. But now she was broken and weary and willing to do without complaint whatever would give her the best chance at survival.

The van bounced her up and down uncomfortably as Matteo drove down the uneven road. It screeched to a stop, and Lily prayed it was not a checkpoint. She held her breath, exhaling a few minutes later when they continued onward. As the vehicle moved slowly through the Brussels streets, Lily felt for the familiar twists and turns, trying to imagine where they were, how close they were to her home.

A few minutes later, they stopped again, and the engine quieted. Matteo opened the rear door of the van. "We're here," he said, helping her out into an unfamiliar alley. Her ankle, though a bit better, was still sore when she walked. "Take these transit papers," he said, passing her a folded document. "They aren't real, and not nearly good enough to get you to America or even England." Like the papers, Lily reflected, for which Hannah had been waiting for so long. "But they should be good enough to get you over the border and into free France."

Lily's mind whirled as she processed the journey that lay ahead of her. Pushing down her doubts, she hurriedly tucked the documents into her sleeve. Matteo led her through the side streets toward the station. Lily paused, turning longingly in the direction of her old neighborhood, saying a silent farewell. For all that had happened, it broke her heart to leave Brussels for good. How she wished she might go to their house one more time, if not to take the photographs and things most dear to her, then at least to be in that precious space once more. But Nik was gone and Georgi too, and without them the place she called home had simply ceased to exist.

Matteo led her up the stairs and to the station. At the entrance, Lily stopped short. There were German soldiers and police scattered among the travelers inside, and some of those might be looking for her and the other escapees. "It will be okay," Matteo said, urging her on. They hurried through the station to a secluded bench by a coffee kiosk.

Matteo consulted the departures board. "Platform nine." Lily looked down the empty track. Her nerves jumped. Each moment they loitered in the station risked discovery. She could not withstand being arrested and imprisoned a second time.

A few minutes later, engine lights appeared in the distance beyond the open end of the station. Lily exhaled slightly. Though her escape was by no means certain, seeing the train arrive felt like a promise, a reason to hope. She would feel so much better once she was ensconced in the railcar.

She looked over her shoulder, thinking of Georgi, hoping he was okay, wherever he was. Her heart screamed. Once she went, she would be hundreds of kilometers away, even less able to find or help him. She could not bear the idea of leaving without him.

She turned to tell Matteo that she had changed her mind and would not go. But if she stayed and was arrested, her chance of someday reuniting with Georgi might be lost forever. Hannah was right: this was the only way. But leaving still felt like an unimaginable betrayal. What kind of mother would abandon her child?

The train rolled into the station, stopping at platform nine. "Come, we have to get you on the train," Matteo said.

Lily stood, then hesitated. "But where's Hannah?" Hannah had said she had an errand but promised to come to the station and see Lily one last time. Now Lily would have to go without the chance to say goodbye. "She said she'd be here."

"Lily, she's on her way," Matteo said. "She went to get—" He stopped short, seeming to think better of whatever he was going to say.

"What is it?" she demanded. There was an uneasiness behind his eyes, something he wasn't telling her. "Tell me." She braced for the worst, an instinct honed through the war.

"It's nothing... That is—" He broke off, as if fearing he had already said too much. Instinctively, she pulled the papers from her sleeve and opened them. They were made out for two people, Georgi and herself. She looked up at Matteo questioningly, not daring to ask aloud. "There was a child found and we thought perhaps it might be Georgi. Hannah went to try and get him, only she isn't back yet."

Lily's heart leaped into her throat. "Why didn't you tell me?"

"Because we didn't want to get your hopes up. There's every chance that it isn't him."

"But it might be. I can't go without knowing."

"You must. This is exactly why we didn't tell you. Leaving now is your only chance," he insisted.

A woman passing by eyed them warily. "Lily, Hannah should have been here by now," he continued, lowering his voice. "If she isn't here yet, there's a reason. She couldn't find Georgi, or something happened. Either way, you need to be on that train. I can't protect you any longer. If Georgi is alive, I will find him and bring him to you. I swear it."

Lily yearned once more to tell him the truth about their son. A mix of emotions overwhelmed her then. Hope that Hannah might have found Georgi. Disappointment that she had not managed to bring him here. The desire to leave, and the reluctance to do so without her child. "But now you must go," Matteo pressed. "Save yourself so that if we find your son we can bring him to you."

Matteo was right, she conceded silently. She started down the platform as smoothly as she could on her sore ankle. She marveled at the ordinary passenger train, which again seemed like such a wonder after the boxcar she'd ridden in. Then a train had spelled her family's doom. This time it would be her salvation. If she made it. She walked more quickly now, aware of the number of German soldiers and police in the station, the very real possibility that she might be stopped and questioned at any second. Lily pressed forward resolutely, on the path to her new life, alone.

As they neared the train, she turned back once more. "Matteo…"

"Lily, we've been through all of this. You must go," he said, mistaking her hesitation for reluctance to leave.

"It isn't that." She took a deep breath. "About Georgi…" He should know, in these final moments, the truth about his son. Not because it would make him try harder to find the child—she knew he would already move heaven and earth for her—but because he deserved to know.

Before she could speak further, a train whistle blew low and long. "Come," he urged. This time he went ahead, leading her onto the platform. At first, her legs were leaden. She could not imagine taking another single step away from Georgi. She wanted to turn back and refuse to go. But Matteo was looking warily over her shoulder now. Turning to follow his gaze, she saw a group of German police walking toward her with unmistakable intent. "Quickly," he urged, taking her arm and leading her to the door to the train. She willed her legs not to shake, to hold her up so she might walk normally.

She crossed the threshold of the train, then looked back. The Germans were about a hundred meters away, and the train due to leave in less than a minute. Would the doors close before they reached her? She saw someone else behind them, running toward her. *Hannah!* Lily stifled a cry, fighting the urge to call her cousin's name. Hannah moved awkwardly, slowed down by something.

A child walking behind her. Hannah had found Lily's son.

Lily started to step off the train to get Georgi. Matteo put out his arm. "Stay here," he said firmly. He sprinted past the police in Hannah's direction to Georgi and urged him to move faster before giving up and picking him up. He carried Georgi toward the train. Could he make it in time? Lily's heart yearned to get off. But if it left the station, her and Georgi's only chance for escape would be gone. Lily put her foot in the doorway so it would not close. She would jam it with her entire body if need be. Then she reached her arms from the train, willing Matteo to move faster.

The police had noticed as well and were following Matteo now. Lily wanted to signal to him but sensed that he already knew. He walked purposefully toward her, but he was still twenty meters away as the train lurched and prepared to leave.

Lily held out her arms as if to catch her son. But the distance was too great for them to breach. The police were closing in now, guns drawn. Any second now, they would be upon Matteo and Georgi.

There was a sudden commotion in the station behind, Hannah shouting loudly. She was creating a scene deliberately to draw the Germans away from Matteo and toward herself. It seemed that it might not work, that there might be enough police to apprehend Matteo and Hannah both. But then the officers on the platform turned away and began to pursue Hannah instead.

Matteo lurched forward, nearly throwing Georgi toward her. "Mama!" he cried, unmistakably hers.

Lily caught him, staggered backward as she struggled to hold his weight. "My boy, my boy!" She kissed his cheeks and forehead, feeling to make sure he was whole and really there.

Then she looked up at Matteo. "Come with us," she said. She knew he would not flee but would remain behind to help Hannah. Guilt washed over her. She should stay and aid her cousin who had given everything for her. But her first duty was to save Georgi.

"I'll go for Hannah," Matteo said, reading her thoughts. "I'll make sure she is all right."

"And you?"

"You and Georgi will be safe." He could not promise the same for himself. "That's enough for me."

The train began to roll. This was the last time that she would ever see him, and she had just seconds left. The Germans were getting closer to Matteo now. "Your son!" she called before stepping back and letting the doors close. "He's your son!"

Matteo's eyes widened with recognition, and he reached a hand out for her. But the Germans were upon him then in such number that he disappeared beneath them, and only his outstretched hand remained. The exodus, which they had planned in the camp so many weeks ago, was now happening.

Lily wrapped her arms around Georgi and closed her eyes, screaming silently into his familiar sweetness.

37

Micheline

Micheline prayed that they would kill her first.

She had been brought the previous night by truck from the prison to Tir National, the national shooting range northeast of the city. The Germans had turned the former military training facility into an execution site, and seeing it, Micheline knew that there was to be no return.

And in the end, she had told them the truth—or part of it anyway. "Me," she answered wearily when they asked about the head of the Sapphire Line, for who would believe that a twenty-three-year-old girl had run it all? Her ribs were broken from the beatings, making every breath agony. They had shaved her head, taking the curls she had always prized. There were other indecencies too that she had blocked from her mind, that would haunt her for all of her days—or at least as many days as she had left. But improbably, she had been allowed to keep her blue cape, which she wore now like a kind of armor, shielding her from the pain that was all around her.

She could not tell what time it was from her windowless cell, but several hours later she heard scraping outside, and a guard carried in a tray with shaking hands. It contained a slice of bread that was just a bit moldy and a cup of real tea. She eyed the plate warily. Had the food been poisoned? Then she downed the bread, too hungry to care.

The guard watched Micheline closely. Did he think she would try to escape? "I know you," he whispered. "You're Safir." So the Germans knew her code name. Micheline was not entirely surprised. "My brother was one of the Frenchmen helping you at the border." Micheline lifted her head, scarcely daring to hope. Perhaps the guard was an ally.

"Is there any chance of escape?"

The guard shook his head. "Impossible, I'm afraid. I can try to get a message out, but there is nothing they can do to free you."

The guard stood patiently waiting while she drank the tea, the hot liquid scalding her split lip. When she had finished, the prisoner leaned close to take the tray. "Your brother is here," he whispered. Micheline's heart sank. She knew Pascal was lying when he'd said Matteo had betrayed her. It had been a bluff, intended to get her to speak. But the guard's eyes were wide and guileless, his expression sad.

"When?" she asked. "How?"

"Arrested at the rail station."

She hoped they might bring Matteo to her, that they might be put in the same cell. But the Germans were too cold for that small comfort. She did not sleep at all during that time but listened for any sound of him.

In the end, they brought her brother to her for ten minutes. He was beaten worse than she, bloodied beyond recognition. "They wanted the names of everyone," he managed through a jaw so swollen she was sure it was broken.

"Did you give them?" she asked.

He looked surprised. "No, of course not."

"Pascal said you were the one who betrayed us."

"Never."

Micheline knew then that he could not be the traitor. "You did well. I'm sorry for doubting you."

He seemed to brighten through his pain. "We got Lily and Georgi onto the train." Still through everything, her brother thought of that woman. Micheline cursed her name silently.

"What about Hannah?"

He shook his head. "I think she was arrested at the rail station as well, but I can't say for certain." Micheline pictured Hannah then and asked her forgiveness. Not fulfilling her promise to get Hannah out of Belgium was her second-greatest regret.

"And the others?"

"All gone, even before I was taken. Arrested or fled, the safe houses raided." One week. That was all it had taken for the entire network to fall.

Then a thought started to nag at her, uneasily around the edges. "Teo, the Germans said someone else betrayed us besides Pascal, someone high up. It wasn't you, and it wasn't me, and the only other person—"

"Was Hannah," Matteo finished when she did not. "Hannah would never betray us."

She swallowed her doubt. "I guess we will never really know who did it."

"They are going to kill us."

"Yes." She did not deny it. The Germans thought they had gotten everything out of her that they could and had no further use for either of them. In fact, she would tell them nothing and take any remaining secrets she held about the Sapphire Line to the grave.

"I'm going to try and send word to the line and see if there is anything they can do to help us."

Micheline smiled inwardly. Sweet Matteo still had hope. "The network is gone," she said gently. "There is no one coming to save us. But I will try to send word to Hannah and let her know what has become of us and give her instructions to go on."

"Tell her that I loved her, if you can. I only wish I had known that sooner. And ask her to help Lily care for my son."

"Your son?" she repeated, unsure she had heard him correctly.

"Yes, Georgi is my son," he said, a moment's light coming into his eyes. "With Lily. I didn't know it until just a few days ago."

"Our family will go on." For so long she'd assumed they would be the last. But now she saw it, a faint glimmer in the darkness, like the lights of a train, drawing nearer.

A few minutes later the door opened again, and the guards came in for Matteo.

She searched to find the words for what might be their very last time together. She could see the tears in the corners of his eyes as they led him away.

The next morning, the same guard silently brought her food, his eyes sorrowful. Micheline had always thought prisoners were served a fine last meal, but here it was nothing more than an extra slice of bread. She did not eat it, for what was the point of taking sustenance if one was only going to die? She pushed it away. "Give it to another prisoner." It was the very last thing she had to offer.

"I wish there was something more I could do," the man said in a low voice.

"There is. I need to send a message." The guard hesitated, and for a moment, Micheline thought he would refuse. He shut the cell door and walked away. A few minutes later, he returned with a scrap of paper and a pencil. "You must hurry," he said, his face pale. "They are coming for you now." Micheline scrawled her message quickly and addressed it to Hannah, care of her cousin Lily's address, which seemed the best hope of reaching her.

But before she could hand it to the guard, he raced from the cell, too afraid to be caught helping her. Micheline's hopes fell. She would not be able to get a message to Hannah after all. She tucked the scrap of paper into her blue cape, which lay crumpled in the corner.

Then they came and took her from her cell and led her to a courtyard behind the prison. The stakes stood a meter apart. Halos of red that no one had bothered to scrub away stained the ground below.

And already chained to one of the stakes was Matteo.

"Michou," he said, managing a smile when he saw her. She imagined they were back at the canteen, planning a mission.

There was fear behind his smile, though, and she tried to find the words to offer comfort. "You did well, big brother," she said, her voice cracking. "Mama and Papa would be so proud."

He shook his head. "You, Michou, were always the best of us."

The firing squad was taking its place now. A guard walked up with a blindfold. Matteo raised his hand, refusing. "I want to die watching the sun rise."

Micheline reached out her hand to touch him, but her fingers fell short. "Look at me," she commanded firmly. She stared deep into his eyes, taking him away from here. She hummed *Dodo, l'Enfant, Dors* (Sleep, Baby, Sleep) to take away his sadness and pain. It was the lullaby their mother had sung to them as children.

She reached out once more, and he used his last ounce of energy to lift his hand so their fingers could graze. Then, his arm fell limply to his side. "I think Mama and Papa are waiting for us."

There was a crack of gunfire, and his eyes widened. "No!" she cried out in spite of herself, hating that she gave the Germans that satisfaction. Matteo gave a final gasp, and his hand went slack. He looked removed from his body now, as if someone else. She knew in that moment he was gone. Only then did she allow herself a single sob.

Micheline stood alone on the very firing range where Edith Cavell, the heroic nurse who had rescued so many airmen during the Great War, had been executed. Micheline knew then she had earned her place in history. She only hoped that time would judge her half as well.

Micheline looked up, knowing Matteo had gone before her and was there, calling her home. She saw now the destination of the network across the Pyrenees to the green hills, so close she could touch it.

It had all been worth it. Lily and her son had survived. They had built a network, strong and resilient, that would rise again. There were others who would go on to fight. The real work, she saw now, had been not in the missions she had carried out herself but in training others to carry the torch when she no longer could. Like comets, there would be new ones after these stars faded into darkness. Micheline was not a religious woman, but in her final moments she sensed with undeniable certainty something larger than herself.

As the guns were raised, she lifted her eyes to the dazzling bright sky. She saw all of the soldiers that they had saved then, and the ones they had failed, coming toward her like a giant army to take her home.

38

Hannah

Hannah stood alone on the Southampton dock, watching the reunions that were not hers. Her bones felt brittle; everything ached. Normal life was too garish, too brightly lit. Even among other survivors, she felt different and alone. Would she ever fit in anywhere again?

It had been almost six months since she had last seen her cousin. The last thing she remembered at the station was the Germans closing in on Matteo as he carried the child. Without thinking about it, she had screamed to distract them and draw them away from the train. It worked. The Germans had pounced on her, and the train pulled from the station with Lily and Georgi on it. She could not see beyond the officers' tall shoulders whether Matteo was arrested. Though she did not resist, one of the police raised a billy club. There was a deafening thud against her temple, and everything went dark.

She had woken up in Breendonk, the very prison where Lily had been held. The irony that they had somehow switched places, that she was now here and Lily freed, was not lost on her. But there was no one left to save her. Word had come by another prisoner that Micheline and Matteo had been killed, put before the firing squad. Lily and Georgi had escaped Belgium, or at least that was what she hoped. Hannah was completely alone. She was resigned to dying in the camp. She deserved no better after all that she had done.

Then just as improbably, after five months of imprisonment, she was called to the camp office, and she went fearing the worst. "You've been released," the camp *Kommandantur* said through gritted teeth, clearly angry to lose a prisoner.

The camp *Kommandantur* gave her some used street clothes and put her in a car. The car drove to Antwerp and deposited her at the dock to leave at the very same place where she had disembarked and met Lily when she'd first come to Belgium. It was almost as if her life had been reset, and none of it had ever happened.

Of course, it had happened. Hannah had lost almost a third of her body weight in the camp, and her once-straight posture was stooped. Some scars from the camp would never heal. But she was here now. Free.

"Hannah!" Her cousin drew close now on the dock in London with Georgi in tow. For a second, Hannah feared that Lily might still bear any resentment or ill will. But Lily threw herself into Hannah's arms, any vestige of what had happened in the past long gone.

Hannah pulled back to look at Georgi, who stood by his mother's side. It had been so long she worried she might be a stranger in Georgi's young eyes. But he raised arms to her. "Tante Hannah!"

She bent down to hug him. "You've grown so much!"

Then she straightened to embrace Lily once more. "How did you get out?"

"I was able to get out of Belgium and into free France on the fake papers Matteo gave me. There was a British airman Nik had treated before we were arrested," Lily said, a catch in her voice as she said her husband's name. "I contacted the airman through the British consulate in Marseilles, and he helped us. I asked him to help you as well, but there was nothing he could do." Hannah held her breath, waiting for Lily to ask more about the circumstances leading to her own release and was relieved when she did not.

"It's all right. We're here now, and that's what matters. But Micheline…" Tears formed as she thought of her lost friend.

Lily's eyes widened with realization. "She's gone, isn't she?"

"Yes."

"I'm sorry. I know she was a good friend."

"She was more than that. She saved us all." Lily nodded. "I know she was an extraordinary woman. And how very much she meant to you. We owe her our lives, all of us."

"Matteo is gone too."

Lily pressed her handkerchief to her lips, as tears welled up in her eyes. But she did not seem surprised; some part of her already knew. "So many losses. Did they ever find out the truth about who betrayed the network?"

Hannah hesitated. *Lie to her*, a voice screamed. She had only just reconciled with her cousin, and she did not want to tear things apart once more. But lying had caused them so much pain. She could not do it again. So many people had been denied the gift of the truth.

She had to do it now if they were to start a new life, free from the encumbrances of the past. "It was me."

Hannah could still feel the stinging in her eyes as she left the canteen that day, Micheline's refusal to help her imprisoned cousin painful and raw. Hannah had joined their cause, sacrificed everything for Micheline and her precious network. But in the end, she had not mattered enough to Micheline to merit help.

Hannah could not let Lily and her family be deported. She had to do something. So Hannah would find a way to help Lily herself. But how? She knew no one in Brussels outside of Lily's family and the network.

Then as she had left her meeting with Micheline, she encountered Pascal on the street. "It's a pity about your cousin," he said, and she was unsure if he was talking about her arrest or something more. "Of course, I could help you."

Hannah eyed him skeptically. She had only met the resistance worker, a former priest, a few times at the canteen. He must have overheard their conversation. But why was he offering assistance now? "Thank you, that's very kind. But Micheline will help."

"Micheline, bah! She cares only about the network, not your cousin." Pascal had always seemed so loyal to Micheline. But now his contempt peeked through. "In fact," he added, his voice conspiratorial, "she despises her." This was true, Hannah was forced to admit, though only to herself. Micheline hated Lily for hurting her brother. Not only did she not want to help Lily, she would be just as happy to see her gone.

Still, Hannah resented hearing it from Pascal. "This is none of your affair."

Seeming to recognize that he had gone too far, Pascal raised his hands and took a step back. "Micheline has taken on too much. She's a danger to herself and to others. But if you wanted to share just a bit of information, perhaps I could find you a contact at the prison camp who could help your cousin."

"Information?"

"Things that Micheline has told you. She trusts you, gives you more access than most. Such information could be valuable to the Germans."

"Betray Micheline? No, never."

"No, of course not. But you have to look out for your own interests. Yours—and your cousin's." Hannah knew better than to confide in Pascal. But as he walked away, his words echoed in her ears.

After she left Pascal and returned to Lily's house, his words ran in her head: *just a bit of information…help your cousin*. Micheline would not, or could not, help. Lily and her family were days away from deportation, and after they were gone, there would be nothing at all Hannah could do to help. She was quite literally out of options.

She turned the idea over in her head as she walked up the stairs to her room. She did not know Pascal well, and the duplicitous way he spoke about Micheline made Hannah loath to trust him. If only there were someone else…

Her eyes traveled to the painting on the easel, which she had never delivered, and she thought then of Gruppenführer Helm. *Abwehr*, his card said. Intelligence. He would be interested, she felt certain, in hearing what she knew.

Hannah picked up the painting and raced from the house. When she neared the German's stately home, she stopped short. She was betraying Micheline and the Sapphire Line, and she hated herself for it. But she was the one who had gotten Lily arrested, and her first obligation was to her cousin. By not helping Lily, the network had failed her.

She knocked on the door and was surprised when Helm, not a maid or other servant, opened it himself.

"Frau Abels," he said. He did not seem to be aware that her cousin, whose name Hannah had used last time they met, had been arrested. "What a pleasant surprise."

"I'm sorry to call unannounced."

"Not at all. I thought you had forgotten about me." He gestured to the painting. "It's finished?"

"Yes," she handed it over reluctantly.

"Do you have any more to sell?"

"I'm afraid not. But I could accept a commission for one. I was hoping to speak with you about another matter as well, though."

"What is it?" He looked puzzled.

"My cousin is in Breendonk."

"The life of a single Jew is hardly my concern," he scoffed.

"I have information," she said. "Information about resistance and evacuation activities that could be of use." Of course, she had not meant to betray the network. She would give just a piece, some outdated or useless trivial information to make the man think he was getting something so he would free Lily. "I can give you this much now, as a show of good faith. And after my cousin is out, everything," she lied.

He laughed. "Do you think I am stupid? I could have you arrested for this, tortured and interrogated to find out what you know." *Do it*, Hannah thought, daring him. After all that had happened, her freedom meant so little. If she was arrested, though, she would not be able to help Lily at all. Whereas if she talked, even just a little, she might be able to free Lily and her family.

She wished she could ask Micheline before acting. But Micheline was not here. And she did not know the answers to everything. She had her own interests.

Hannah turned to the German and began to talk, hoping she had not made the worst mistake of her life. "There's a network of agents," she began carefully.

"This much we already know," he snapped impatiently. "And we know of this woman who runs it, Micheline. Where is she now?" the German asked, rubbing his hands together gleefully like a greedy witch.

"She went on an errand to rescue a wounded airman."

"Did she leave already?" There was an unnerving glint in the officer's eye. She noticed that he did not ask where she was going. She feared somehow he already knew.

"I don't know."

"That's all you have to tell me?" he asked, a note of anger creeping into his voice. "Surely you don't expect me to help your cousin for just that."

"I think she left. She might have stopped at the camp—" Hannah realized she had said too much.

"This camp, where is it?"

Hannah faltered. She could not give up everything. But the German would not help her cousin unless she said more. She took a deep breath. "In the Senzeilles forest. That's all I know. Will you help my cousin now?"

"Yes, yes, of course," the German said, though his tone suggested anything but. He closed the door, and Hannah hurried off.

She had given the German just a few pieces of information. She had not known that they already had Pascal as an informant and that her information would lock with what the Germans already had in a single perfect puzzle to bring down the entire network, including Micheline herself.

Only later, when Micheline told her about Pascal being a traitor and seeing him with a German officer at the café, did she realize they were connected.

And in the end, the German had not helped Lily at all. Instead, Hannah's request had brought attention to Lily in the camp and caused her to be listed for deportation even sooner than expected.

Lily stared at her in stunned silence. "I don't understand."

"Micheline wouldn't help me, so I went to find help for you myself." All of the time they had been looking for the betrayal, it had been right here, Hannah herself. She had been so desperate to help Lily at any cost. The enemy had needed an opening and when she offered it, they readily exploited her weakness. "I made a deal with a German officer to give him some information to free you, before Micheline agreed to help. I was desperate. But it backfired, and it caused everything to fall apart. I'm so sorry. I never meant for any of this to happen."

"You saved us. It worked."

"How can you say that? First I caused your arrest. And now because of me, Micheline and Matteo are dead."

"We're standing here, aren't we?" It was true that they had made it. But had the cost been too great?

In fact, it was Hannah's betrayal that had saved her own life as well. When the camp *Kommandantur* granted her clemency and she saw the signature at the top, she'd been shocked. It was Gruppenführer Helm's. *For cooperation with the Reich* read the reason for her release. Hannah was revulsed. Accepting his help would mean she was forever branded as a traitor. Part of her would sooner die in the camp than accept it. But it was her only chance at freedom, and in fact, she was not given a choice.

Hannah's mind reeled back to the last time she had seen Micheline before she was arrested. She should have told Micheline the truth then and there. But she could not bear to admit how she had betrayed the network.

"A package came for you," Lily said suddenly, pulling a parcel from her bag. Hannah was incredulous. How had anyone known she was coming to England, much less where to find her? She studied the label. It had been addressed to Hannah at Lily's house in Brussels, but forwarded to Lily in care of the Belgian embassy in London. "The attaché who helped me arrange for your freedom received this and sent it on to me."

Hannah tore open the package. "Oh!" she cried. Inside was Micheline's sapphire cloak, the one she almost always wore. She raised it to her nose, inhaling the familiar scent. There was a bit of crusted blood around the collar that spoke volumes about what Micheline must have suffered.

A small envelope fell from the cloak and fluttered to the ground. Hannah knelt to pick it up, recognizing the familiar handwriting. The envelope was still sealed, the postmark months old. Hannah tore it open. Inside was a scrap of paper with a note shakily written in crude pencil.

Hannah,
Matteo and I are to face the firing squad tomorrow at dawn. Continue the work of the escape line. Make them pay, every last one.
Also, my brother wanted you to know that it was you he loved. Help Lily care for his son.
Safir

Tears fell down Hannah's cheeks, staining her papers and threatening to smudge them. "What is it?" Lily asked with alarm. Unable to speak, Hannah passed the paper to her. Lily's eyes filled with tears as well.

The cousins stood motionless, sharing the magnitude of their loss. Then there was a nudging between them, Georgi growing restless. "Mama, I'm hungry," Georgi said. They shared a laugh at the familiar refrain. Though the losses of the past were great, the needs of the present left no time to mourn.

"Are you ready?" Lily asked. "I have a flat here where we can stay until we can make plans to go to America. We can have the life there you always wanted."

Hannah hesitated. She had every reason to move forward now. She spoke finally. "No." Micheline's last words to her ricocheted in her head: *Make them pay, every last one.* She considered staying for just awhile to rest. But the longer she remained here, the harder it would be to leave, and if she lingered, she might not go at all. No, she had to leave now. The past it seemed, would always keep its grip, like an indelible fingerprint left in wet concrete.

"Micheline wanted me to find everyone who betrayed the network and bring them to justice. I have to go back." At first Hannah thought the mission was about exacting vengeance on those who had betrayed them. Now she understood it meant something else. Hannah would make good on her charge, returning to Belgium and running the escape line until every last airman was sent home.

"But you can't simply go back, after you risked everything to get out. It would all be for nothing."

"I can, and I must. It wasn't for nothing. You and Georgi are safe. I'll come back too, as soon as I've finished the mission."

Lily looked dubious. She had seen too many people not return as promised. She looked momentarily as though she would argue. "I understand. But surely you don't have to go right away?"

Hannah considered the question. She couldn't simply turn and hop back on the ship. She would need to book passage and perhaps make contact with the Belgian government-in-exile to plan before returning to Europe. "I suppose I have a few days," she conceded.

"Then, come." Lily held out her hand. "Let's make the most of the time we have."

Wrapping Micheline's sapphire cape snugly around her shoulders, Hannah took Lily's hand, and together the two women started for home once more.

★ ★ ★ ★ ★

AUTHOR'S NOTE

When I first discovered the true story of the mission to liberate prisoners from a train headed for Auschwitz, I was stunned. And I had so many questions! On one hand, I wondered: How could people be so brave as to undertake such an unthinkable and dangerous attempt? At the same time, I wanted to know why more people had not tried to do the same thing to some of the countless trains that carried victims across Europe to the concentration camps. I decided that I wanted to write a story about both the saboteurs and the people they sought to rescue.

In writing *Code Name Sapphire*, I created a fictitious family who were imprisoned on the train: Lily and Nik and their son, Georgi. But I wanted to embody in them the spirit of the real prisoners, parents and children, medical professionals and intellectuals. And although in real life, the three principal rescuers were men from the Jewish Defense Committee, I decided in my story to make one of them, Hannah, a Jewish woman, working in collaboration with other arms of the Belgian resistance. So many stories of women have been lost to a history that ignored them. Who is to say what women did behind the scenes without receiving credit? I also sought to recognize in Sofia the plight of the Roma community during the Holocaust, which has so often gone unnoticed.

I decided, also, to interweave the story of the train rescue with another remarkable aspect of the war: the escape lines throughout Belgium, Holland and France, and the heroes who bravely spirited downed Allied airmen safely out of Europe. Many of the leaders and volunteers of these well-organized lines were courageous women. The line I write about, the Sapphire Line, is fictitious, but it was inspired by real lines, including the Comet Line.

If you would like to learn more about the true history that inspired this book, I recommend that you read *The Twentieth Train: The True Story of The Ambush of the Death Train to Auschwitz* by Marion Schreiber, *The Freedom Line: The Brave Men and Women Who Rescued Allied Airmen from the Nazis During World War II* by Peter Eisner, *Little Cyclone* by Airey Neave and *The Prisoners Of Breendonk: Personal Histories from a World War II Concentration Camp* by James M. Deem.

The demands of storytelling often force authors to make difficult decisions about which aspects of history to keep and which to bend. Here, the ship on which Hannah attempts to travel to America was modeled after the *St. Louis*, but I have changed the name because my dates are different. In fact, the ship would have more likely departed several months earlier in the fall of 1941 before the German ban on Jewish emigration went into effect. There are questions, too, regarding whether upon returning to Europe, Hannah would have been admitted to Belgium and called up, or whether she would have been forcibly deported to Germany instead.

Also diverging from true history, I have put Lily and her family on a much earlier transport train than the actual train which was rescued. Lily and her family are sent east in late summer 1942 on one of the first transports when in fact the real train that was liberated was the twentieth train in April 1943. The Germans did not begin deporting Belgian Jews in actual history until 1943.

I have Lily and her family interned at the Breendonk camp, where they might have been at nearby Mechelen. The canteen where the network has its headquarters in Brussels was in fact the former building of the Theosophical Society. And as previously noted, I have altered the identities and demographics of those who actually undertook the heroic train break in my story.

One final historical note: in this book, Matteo describes the Association des Juifs en Belgique, also known as the Judenrat, a council of Jewish leaders during the war as collaborators. Although this is how some historians have characterized them, there are also accounts that they saved Jewish orphans. So it is a very complex picture and worth remembering that the perspective of one character should not be taken as an assertion of truth.

I endeavor as always to note where I have made a conscious decision to deviate from history in a significant way, both for accuracy's sake and to avoid the perception of error, but there may be other instances, as well.

What remains unchanged is the heroism of the volunteers who rescued airmen and those who attempted to liberate the train, as well as the bravery of the people whom they tried to save and the countless other victims.

Pam Jenoff

ACKNOWLEDGMENTS

Unlike my previous book, which was written during the darkest hours of the pandemic, *Code Name Sapphire* was born in a time of hope, when we began to see the light at the end of the tunnel. I am appreciative to return to a world where we can gather at book events while still thankful for the technology that lets us connect from all over the world.

There are so many people in the book world to thank and I'm afraid if I mention some, I will miss others. To my author, book influencer, book blogger, librarian and bookseller friends, thank you for all you do. And eternal gratitude to the readers for showing up year after year and reminding me why I do this—you give me the strength to wake up early every single day.

I've been blessed to work with the greatest people in publishing for more than fifteen years. I am so very grateful to my dream team: my fierce agent and faithful friend, Susan Ginsburg, and her assistant and junior agent, Catherine Bradshaw, and to my gifted editor and collaborator extraordinaire, Erika Imranyi, and her editorial assistant, Nicole Luongo. I would like to thank my patient, talented and hardworking publicist, Emer Flounders (who knows how to make any book tour stop across the country into a day trip for me), as well as my beloved publishing geniuses, Heather Foy, Amy Jones, Randy Chan and Rachel Haller. To everyone at Park Row, Harlequin, Harper-Collins and HarperCollins Canada, especially Craig Swinwood, Loriana Sacilotto, Margaret Marbury and Brent Lewis, I owe my career to you.

Warmest thanks to my wonderful publicist, Kathleen Carter, (overjoyed to finally have the chance to work with you!), and to my social media assistant, Amara Borst, for teaching me so much and keeping me in line. Gratitude to my book counselor-in-chief, Andrea Peskind Katz. Thanks also to meticulous copy editor, Vanessa Wells, and historical fact-checker, Jennifer Young. And a special shout-out to my college friend Adrian Cox for his expertise on Brussels. My deepest appreciation to Monique and Linda Mendel, who reached out just as I was nearing completion of this book to share the remarkable experience of their parents on The Twentieth Train (the train which served in part as inspiration for this book.) As usual, the mistakes are all mine.

My world does not run or exist without my village. Love and thanks to my husband, Phillip, who among his many gifts can juggle children and has cooked every dinner since the first Obama administration; my mom, who helps us eight days a week; my brother, Jay; my in-laws, Ann and Wayne; and my friends Steph, Anzi, Mindy and Sarah. I'm grateful to my colleagues at Rutgers and to doggie day care (seriously), and to our amazing public school system and to my shtetl at the JCC. And my heart and soul go to my three not-so-little-anymore muses, who make the whole journey worthwhile.

QUESTIONS FOR DISCUSSION

1. Which of the women did you identify with most closely: Micheline, Hannah or Lily?

2. How do you think Hannah and Lily's relationship changed over the course of the story?

3. Where do you think Hannah and Lily wind up in five years? Ten?

4. What was the most difficult choice each woman faced in the book? Did you agree with her choice?

5. Lily and Hannah were both shaken from their lives from the war and thrust into new experiences that changed and challenged them. Can you describe a similar time in your own life?

6. Can you see any parallels between the themes in the book and our lives today?

7. How did Lily's role as a parent influence her decisions?

8. How was Hannah affected by her past?

9. What do you think drove Micheline's determination?

10. Did you find the ending of the book surprising? Satisfying?

11. Is there anything else about story that you would have liked to learn?

12. Did you learn any history from the book that you had not previously known?